I0565000

The Pyramids
of
London

Andrea K Höst

All characters in this publication
are fictitious and any resemblance
to real persons, living or dead,
is purely coincidental.

The Pyramids of London
© 2015 Andrea K Höst. All rights reserved.
ISBN: 978-0-9872651-9-7
EBook ISBN: 978-1-925188-02-8
www.andreakhost.com
Cover art and map: Julie Dillon

ACKNOWLEDGEMENTS

With deep thanks to Sherwood Smith,
Antoine, and KA, for making this book better.

AUTHOR'S NOTE

This book is in Australian English. A character
list and glossary are included at the back.

Map of Albion and Danuin, showing
the Prytennian Dragonates

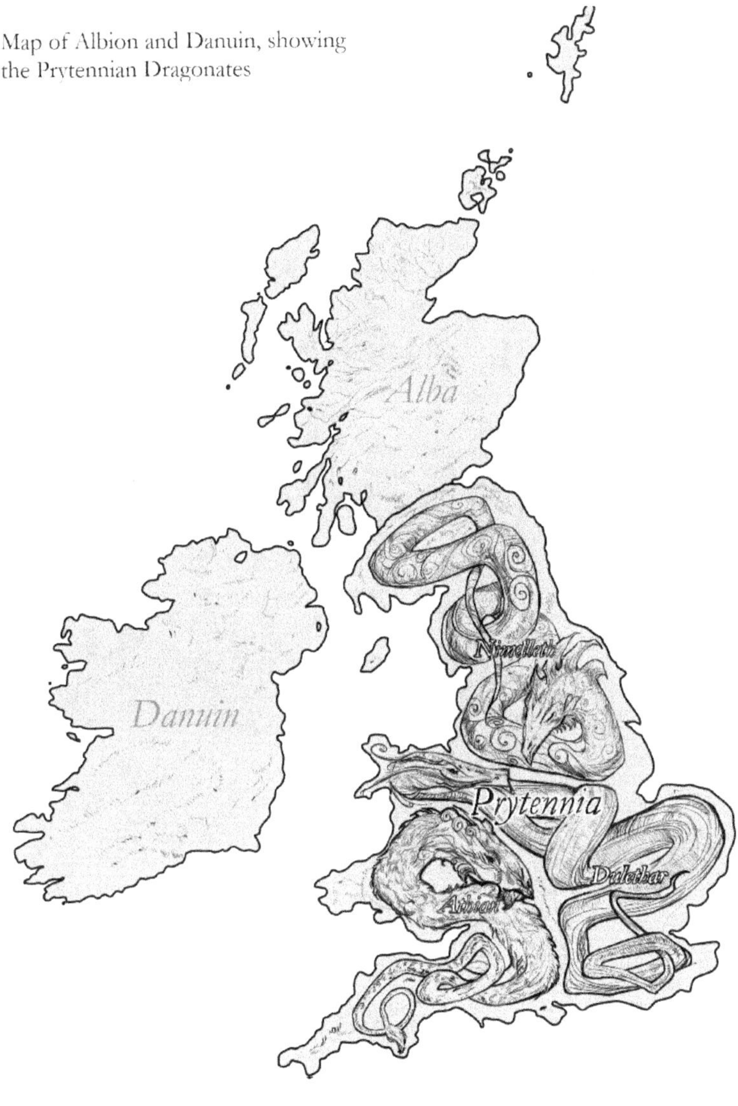

Alba

Danuin

Nimdletta

Prytennia

Dilethar

Albion

ONE

Sunlight picked out motes of dust, and burnished mellow wood to match Arianne Seaforth's hair as she strolled through the Southern Nomarch's library. Heavy bookcases jutted from the inner wall, stopping short of the many-paned windows, and Rian walked along a corridor formed by the gap, watching a drama of wind.

A rope had snapped. The First Minister's airship canted to one side, and then the ballonet bounced, threatening to smash the gondola onto Sheerside House's sweeping back lawn. The very problem First Minister Aquila had come to discuss was likely to strand her in Prytennia's battered south.

Rian had travelled to Sheerside by train, not airship, and even heavy iron had shuddered beneath the morning windstorm. The journey had shown her a landscape scoured: trees and crops stripped by weeks of gusting onslaught, animals all either hiding or huddled in protective masses. Occasionally a roofless house displayed its innards.

It was unusual for the second windstorm of the day to be prolonged, and Rian would in other circumstances be uneasy, but today she felt little more than academic interest, for she had come to a vampire's house to hunt a murderer.

Lyndsey. One overheard name, and a location discovered from a discarded envelope, with no guarantee that either of them were connected to sudden death. Scant basis for the ten year sacrifice coming to Sheerside entailed, but in the months since Aedric and Eiliff's deaths, gaining a position to follow that name was the only real progress Rian had made.

Movement drew her attention away from the airship. She had reached an area clear of shelving—one of the library entrances—dominated by a long reading table, the near end of which sat in the direct fall of sunlight. The reflection off the polished wood dazzled, so she had failed to see a young man sprawled at the far end of the table until he'd lifted one hand, thumb canted to form a partial frame for the scene outside. Blinking to help her eyes adjust, Rian moved away from the window, and the youth's hand dropped to rest flat. Otherwise he barely moved, head remaining pillowed on one arm as he studied her.

"And what are you?" A soft, dreaming voice, cut with a note of derision.

Having no idea where he stood in the hierarchy of the House, Rian replied neutrally: "Newly arrived."

"A non-answer." He still didn't move, but swept his gaze up and down, taking in travel clothes that were well kept and nicely cut, but far from new. "Another governess for the brats? No, I have it." His nose wrinkled. "You're the new Wednesday."

"Wed—" She realised what he meant, and held back instinctive rejection. She didn't like what being here would entail, but there was no point pretending it was not going to happen. "That's certainly one way to term it."

"Come down in the world?" It wasn't a sympathetic question. "Let me guess—someone died and left you without sufficient fortune. You wanted to be kept in style?"

"That's a very Roman attitude," Rian said, unbothered by such a wide shot. She considered him: a slight young man, not wearing a coat, and the laces missing from his shirtsleeves. His dark brown hair was several inches long, tousled and not quite curling. He didn't match his surroundings any better than she did. "What are you, the resident starving artist?"

His eyes narrowed. "What makes you say that?"

Rian lifted one hand, thumb canted at a right angle, and used it to partly frame the scene through the window. The gesture was something her father had often used. Out in the wind, a basket barrelled across the lawn, but the airship's attendants were winning their battle with its tethers.

"I have some interest in photography," the young man said, sounding less than amused. Annoyed she'd seen that. "Could you be one of the Pyrial? No, you don't seem nearly lack witted enough to mistake which appetite's involved."

"You obviously feel strongly about blood service."

He made a low, disgusted noise. "It's the most pathetic of ideas. That kind of bond—it's not meant to be a business transaction." He'd finally found the energy to sit up, all the better to glower at her.

"Meant to be? What is it meant to be, then?"

He shifted one shoulder, a sketch of a shrug. "Raw. Revolting. Profound. Anything but watered-down, antiseptic domestication."

Perhaps he was the resident poet. Rian would have left him to his opinions, but since the primary reason she had accepted the chance to become the 'Wednesday' at Sheerside was to investigate its occupants, she couldn't pass up any opportunity. And for all she knew, this was the 'Lyndsey' she was searching for. After so long failing to make any progress, she wasn't going to turn away on account of a little annoyance, and so refocused the calm centre that had taken her through far more difficult conversations.

A voice with a hint of a northern accent forestalled any attempt at subtle interrogation. "Dama Seaforth?"

Rian turned. A man had opened the library's door. Tall and impeccably dressed in light tunic and a long pleated shendy in summery shades of blue and cream, he had his eyelids blackened in the Egyptian manner, the kohl only a few shades darker than his skin.

"I'm Evelyn Carstairs," he went on. "Are you ready for your tour of the building?"

"Yes, indeed."

As Rian headed for the door the poet-photographer switched his glower to the new arrival, who simply nodded and said: "I beg your pardon for interrupting, Dem," and moved so Rian could precede him.

Rian heard the poet murmur as she left the room, and thought he said, "Dairy orientation," but paid no further attention, looking with interest at her guide. What day would he be to her 'Wednesday'?

"I knew Sheerside House was large," she said, "but I underestimated the tangle. I thought I'd followed the directions on how to find you, but—"

"But if ever there was a *mot juste* for Sheerside's design, it would be 'labyrinthine'," Carstairs said. "Start by thinking of it in three sections. The tower, which is the oldest, holds the offices. The centre block surrounds the tower and is where you'll find the kitchens, most of the dining and function rooms, and the entrances to the Underhouse. The residences, the newest and largest section, brackets the centre block. There's also the Underhouse, of course, but you won't need to concern yourself with that yet. It's not barred to you, but the lighting in most areas is kept low, and there are some dangers."

Not least the vampire she had come to serve: Msrah, Nomarch of the Southern Dragonate. "I think I'll concentrate on finding my way to my room, to start with," Rian said, and he smiled and obligingly took her upstairs, then taught her how to reach the nearest bathroom, the breakfast room, the main and garage entrances, and finally a day room with an elegant arrangement of chairs and lounges, and even a piano. Glass-panelled patio doors rattled in the gale.

"This particular room is given over to us—Lord Msrah's Bound," Carstairs said. "It's quiet most days, and more active in the evenings."

"Will my nephew and nieces be permitted here?"

"Of course." Carstairs paused at the doors, looking right, and Rian followed his gaze to see the region's greater pyramid, much taller than the Nomal House's tower. The main portion was slate grey, while the upper third was capped with a green-tinged stone.

"There are fifteen children currently part of the household," Carstairs continued. "Including the Lord's son Kafele. Most, like your charges, will be away at school until the end of the summer term. When they are here they will be given some supervised activities and of course are forbidden the Underhouse, but are otherwise free to explore. It's a glorious place for a child. So long as the chaos is limited, play is encouraged. I had endless adventures learning its corridors."

"You grew up here?" Rian asked.

"My parents are also of the Nomarch's Bound," Carstairs said. "After I had my fill of travelling, I returned." He smiled, perhaps in response to her expression. "It's the politics that drew me back. Lord Msrah has a finger on the world's pulse, and I missed knowing so much about what was going on."

The patio doors rattled violently, and he turned to pull a chased bronze lever. With a subdued whir, metal wings descended. Rian had seen the blue and silver expanses above the windows when she arrived. Ma'at's Wings: protective blessings in the Egyptian style. She had not realised that they functioned as shutters.

"Are there levers outside?" she asked, picturing herself locked out after some midnight snooping.

"Yes, though they will sound an alert if used," he said, directing her toward a collection of chairs by the fireplace. "And if the House is under attack the shutters can only be released from inside, either at the central control, or with an override."

"Does that happen often?"

"Actual attacks, no. More than a few false alarms. See over there—" He indicated a series of labelled bellpulls. "The red is the alarm. That will lock down the entire House. The last time there was any real reason to use it was nearly twenty years ago, during the Automaton Riots. If it's something less than an invading force, use the Security pull."

He went on to describe routines of the household: meals, mail, laundry, cleaning. The location of the Nomal House's Circle, and also arrangements to accommodate visitors who did not bow to the Trifold. And then, at last, the part of Rian's future that was the price of her investigation.

"You must begin to prepare yourself at least two days before you are due to serve the Lord," Carstairs said. "Conserve your energy so your ka is at its peak. Avoid alcohol, and foods that affect the potency of your blood— strawberries, peppermint, cinnamon, aniseed—the list is quite long. You'll find a copy in your room, but we simplify the issue by placing 'safe' meals in green serving dishes. It's no disaster if there is some slip, but of course we aim to be as efficacious as possible. Do not use tobacco or opium at all.

"The Lord usually rises in the early afternoon. On the day you are to serve, be ready any time from midday. You should not leave the house on the day of your service, and no further than the grounds during the two days before. Ensure that your clothing does not prevent access to your wrists."

Watered-down, antiseptic domestication. Rian shook the thought away as Carstairs rose and pulled back one sleeve to expose walnut-toned flesh. There were no marks, no scarring.

"Avoid perfumes during the preparation days, and of course wash well. The Lord will send for you soon after rising, and we usually wait here or in our rooms as a matter of convenience. He will lick your wrist, which will numb the physical sensation somewhat, but not enough for your skin to not know it has been pierced. Unless circumstances are unusual, he will take little blood—between a spoonful and half a cup. Only if he has been injured will he need more. The amount of ka he draws from you will vary considerably, particularly if he has weather work to do. Life force recovers more quickly than blood, so there will be times when he draws heavily, and when he does so, the wound will be shallow, merely an access to your ka, rather than your blood. Only on the rarest of occasions will he deeply drink both. You've gone very pink."

Startled, Rian laughed. "It's...odd to apply to myself," she said, and saw comprehension in Carstairs' eyes. It did not help that he was a more than attractive man. Habitually correct, but saved from pomposity by an equal measure of charm.

"There is an inevitable amount of embarrassment," he said. "But the Lord is very good, and sees no need to underline certain aspects. It's not the drawing of blood, but the ka that is the challenge to face. First because it hurts—it always hurts, a sensation almost as if your breath is being stolen away, or as if you are being threaded through a needle. During the bonding, the Lord will draw only lightly on your ka, to limit your distress, but he will drink deeply of your blood. Then he will cut his finger and mingle his blood with that at your wrist, before allowing you to drink from him. Not a great deal, and after the first time only a few drops, to keep you at a balance. You will feel his ka transferring to you, and when you have drunk you will stay in the Underhouse while the Lord's blood reproduces in you. As you were warned, there are risks—there can be very individual physical reactions to colonisation—so you are monitored during the transition. For the first week or so after the bonding you will be sensitive to light, but you will stabilise as the colony matures. You will likely begin to be aware of the presence of living creatures near to you, and notice an increase in physical strength. And, since the Lord is of the Shu line, you will become quite sensitive to changes in the weather."

Because she would have gone part of the way toward becoming a weather vampire. Not a small change. "That must make days like this—"

"Gales can try the nerves, yes. Though it is useful for avoiding being caught out in the rain. Once the growth of the Lord's blood has stabilised it will be considerably more beneficial for him to drink from you, and your ka will have become aligned with his so that, while it still hurts when he draws it, it is—" He paused, full lips quirking. "It is a sweet pain."

Many centuries of literature had dwelled on that 'sweet pain', so this was certainly not news, but it was rare to discuss it with someone who had experienced it.

"What are unusual circumstances?"

"Outside of injury? If something has prevented him from feeding for a period. Difficult manipulations of the weather. Or if he journeys somewhere we cannot go, when he may store against future need. It is rare that we wouldn't travel with him, however."

"Evie, the Lord wants you."

The speaker was a freckle-spattered young woman in a blue tea gown of the Continental style. Carstairs stood immediately, with a murmur of apology for Rian, and resumed his coat.

"This is Dama Hackett. Delia, Arianne Seaforth. Dama Hackett will look after you, Dama Seaforth."

"Been having the speech?" Dama Hackett asked, as Carstairs strode briskly off. "Are you thoroughly mortified?"

"Just squirming." Rian smiled at the red-headed woman, and added her to her list of possible suspects. "Are you—?"

"One of the Lord's Bound? Yes and no—I'm technically still bound, but the Lord has begun the process of releasing the bond. Though they say it never leaves you fully. You're my replacement."

For some reason this made Rian feel awkward, but the woman patted her arm companionably.

"And *so* looking forward to it. I'm off to kick up my heels, disport on sun-kissed beaches, dance in the snow and racket about, mad and wild. To...to live a disorderly life."

"Is it so very structured here?" Rian asked, as they headed back toward her bedroom.

"Your time will be structured. Sheerside itself can be very variable, since so many dignitaries visit to consult Lord Msrah, and new staff are always coming and going. Today everything's been a hidden hive thanks to the First Minister arriving—or, more to the point, not leaving, and bringing extras. But—" The woman shrugged. "Two weeks from now will be my hundredth birthday, and I've seen the world change and change again, but I don't feel like I'm living in it. And..." Her lips curved. "And, to be frank, Evie was starting to look a little too tempting. After dallying with *both* his parents over the years, *and* having wiped his bottom for him when he was a tot, I can't quite reconcile myself to temptation."

"That sounds very..."

"Incestuous? Or—that's not the word for it, but let's say the idea gave me pause. If you'll take my advice, fill your time: whether it's a side position with Lord Msrah's administration or writing books or proving some extreme scholarly point, or competitive gardening. Something that can take you out of the role of Bound. Being paid well to present your wrist once a week throws all sorts of perspectives out of balance. Especially when those couple of minutes with the Lord are so impossibly intense."

"There wasn't any difficulty about leaving?"

"No. Don't fret about that. After the initial ten years, you can give notice at any time."

"Is turnover high?"

"Not really. People seem to fall into two groups—those who serve ten years and then leave, and those who stay for decades, until they grow restless. I don't know of anyone who has broken contract with Lord Msrah, though of course it happens elsewhere. I'm second oldest of the Lord's current Bound, and Evie is the youngest, having served two years. We do make a nodding acknowledgement to seniority, though those of us who work with the Lord's administration complicate any attempt to keep a real hierarchy. Oh, good, they've brought up your trunk."

And unpacked it, which was an aspect of a large household that Rian would need to keep in mind. There was nothing written down, but she could risk no hint of her true purpose. Could her target be among the servants? A place this large would have dozens.

"The house was partially wired last year, which is a luxury I most definitely will miss. I'll leave you to dress for dinner. The Lord doesn't always expect us to dine with State guests, but we do make useful table fillers—"

Sccrrrttt. Trrckttt.

Delia Hackett's warm smile dropped away, and she backed toward the door, staring at a large box sitting on the dressing table. "What—?"

The thin, secretive sound came again, and Rian stared blankly at the box, square-tied with coarse twine. But then she remembered a sleek blond head, eyes determinedly lowered, and a box thrust at her during the last moments of the previous day's school visit.

"It's a gift from Eleri, one of my nieces. She's following her parents' profession." Rian unpicked the knot, and lifted the box lid to reveal a layer of tissue paper shifting fitfully.

A wooden arm rose, dragging down the concealing paper, and Rian caught her breath—not so much at the sight of an automaton, but the particular form it took. There was even the faintest scent of turpentine, to conjure memories of sunny afternoons in the studio. Old paint had been refreshed, and posable wooden joints replaced by delicately-worked bronze-gold metal, but this was definitely a former friend, not seen for years.

"My father's mannequin. He brought it back from Lutèce when I was ten," Rian said, pulling away the last of the tissue. "I called him Monsieur Doré, and painted the monocle and moustache on him. I thought he'd been lost years ago. So Aedric had him."

She hesitated, then lifted the now-still automaton out of the box and sat him on the dressing table. Over two feet tall, the mannequin was even heavier than she remembered, but the joints repositioned smoothly and silently, and the wood and metal figure could be sat upright without sliding.

"But it was trying to get out?" Dama Hackett took a step closer.

"Eleri probably added a movement," Rian said. "I suppose it was meant to be a gift for my brother's birthday, and the charge has run down."

"And now I feel a fool," Dama Hackett said. "And have opened wounds. I'm so sorry, child."

With a charmingly inconsequential grace the woman brushed over awkwardness and moved on to instructions on how to reach the dining hall, before leaving Rian to freshen and dress for dinner. Rian closed the door firmly, then looked back at the dressing table.

The automaton now sat leaning forward, the head turned toward the door. The face was merely flat planes marked by the curling moustache and the thin gold circle of the monocle, lacking any eyes at all. Yet Rian felt quite certain it was looking at her.

"Well, Monsieur Doré," she said. "You are a most unexpected development."

The automaton shifted, attempting to stand, but then slumped, tilted, and remained unmoving as Rian returned to the dressing table.

Gingerly, she cleared the box away and then touched a wooden arm, not quite certain whether she should be afraid. There had been stories all through spring and summer of automatons spontaneously activating, running wild. But then, there'd been such stories since the first automatons.

When her cautious prodding produced no response, Rian laid the mannequin face down, and puzzled out a way to unfasten the back. The mechanism she exposed, intricate and cramped, centred around a globe of faded purple crystal.

Her eyebrows rose. "Now this is beyond excessive."

Lifting the globe out of its casing, she held it toward the window. Fulgite had transformed Rome's lightning into a workable force they called fulquus—the lightning horse— capable of hauling the world into a new age of machines powered by crystals. Which it had then promptly stranded, as supplies of fulgite ran painfully short.

An automaton the size of Monsieur Doré could be comfortably powered for weeks with a crystal a quarter the size of Rian's smallest fingernail. This globe, as large as a pigeon's egg, was tantamount to pulling a wheelbarrow with an Iron Dragon's steam-forced engines. It represented a considerable amount of money, especially since the theft of Prytennia's last fulgite shipment had led to a tripling of already intolerable prices. The shape was unusual: smooth and rounded instead of faceted, and it offered a puzzle, and a new layer of complexity to her investigation.

"You might have mentioned this, Eleri," Rian murmured, and suspected her greatest challenge was not murderers or vampires, but three children who considered her a stranger and an interference. Perfectly true, of course, but they at least shared the same goal. Now did the gift represent a last-minute decision to trust—or a challenge?

"First step, a portable dynamo," Rian said, since she could hardly send such an unusual piece to be charged with the rest of the household crystal. But a dynamo should be a simple enough request in an establishment the size of Sheerside House.

That decided, Rian fastened Monsieur Doré's back, buried the fulgite in her tin of bath salts, and turned her thoughts to suitable dress for a dinner with the First Minister.

Two

With over thirty people at table there was little chance to get to know the rest of Lord Msrah's Bound during dinner, but Rian found nothing to object to in her position between Evelyn Carstairs and an Alban man with cut-glass cheekbones that Evelyn introduced as Lyle Blair, an attaché to Alba's Lord Protector, Prince Gustav. Prince Gustav provided a looming presence at the far end of the table, sitting to the left of the Queen's sister, Princess Leodhild herself. First Minister Aquila was a muted presence beside two such vivid personalities, and Lord Msrah absent altogether.

"I knew Sheerside House's reputation," Rian said, "but this is exceeding my expectations by an order of magnitude. I didn't realise one of the Suleviae was here."

Her tone was light, but ghosts from Rian's childhood stirred, conjuring the shadow of seemingly-insurmountable walls, that sense of standing at the bottom of a well, ankles sunk into mud. Here she was at the same table as royalty, including one of the three living avatars of the goddess Sulis, and no-one considered her out of place. So why could she not keep herself from remembering an impossibly embarrassing conversation? Why did her mind dredge up that terrible realisation of inadequacy?

Perhaps it was because she was back in Prytennia, where strangers would not first and foremost position her as 'foreigner', and could instead reduce her to an ignorant village girl with a notable mother and no worth of her own. The imposter at the table.

"Not quite an ordinary day," Evelyn was saying. "And unsurprising that Princess Leodhild would be particularly concerned with these events." He shot a quick smile past Rian to Lyle. "And Prince Gustav, of course, is always ready to find himself necessary."

The Alban's professional aplomb was unshaken. "Alba is suffering along with the south, so naturally His Highness is anxious for a solution to be discovered."

"Invited himself along," Evelyn translated. "How are you enjoying being run ragged, Lyle?"

"It's fulfilling." The blond man's voice deepened on a note of sincerity.

"I didn't expect you to enjoy all that Swedish energy."

"Neither did I, truly. But—" Lyle glanced toward the end of the table as a golden prince threw back his head in a gust of laughter. "Don't be fooled by the bluff and bluster. There's a mind there worth following. And if I can steer the Swedish ship in Alba's favour, all the better." He added a hint of a smile to Rian: "Though, of course, I didn't say that, Dama Seaforth."

"Please, call me Arianne. And steer away. I take it you two know each other well."

"I went to school in Alba," Evelyn explained. "Lyle was my nemesis."

"We competed endlessly for various honours," Lyle said. "All the traditional Alban-Prytennian rivalry, but eventually I began to appreciate the spur to excel."

"More to the point, one of our tutors stepped in and assigned us an unwieldy shared project," Evelyn said. "We had to make peace or fail."

"And almost ran into disaster trying to find a third option. Long story."

"Involves a donkey," Evelyn said.

"An ass." Lyle's utterly correct expression slipped, and he laughed, then shook his head. "Enough. I'd far rather talk about you, Arianne. What would you call the colour of your hair? Caramel?"

"In this light, that's not a bad description."

"Evelyn told me you're here in order to support your brother's children?"

"That's right. Eiliff and Aedric's estate...well, I managed to settle it without leaving any outstanding debt, but nothing remained beyond a handful of keepsakes. The children are all at Retwold—the youngest, Griff, had just started there before the accident—and even one set of that school's fees was enough to make me blink, let alone three. The twins are nearly sixteen, and all three are..." She paused, thinking of the automaton upstairs, the workings delicate and exact. "It would have been shameful, to not give them every opportunity."

"To do this, for your brother's children." Lyle's gaze swept briefly past her, before he added: "You are remarkable to make such a sacrifice."

"Lyle..." A note of reproach shaded Evelyn's voice.

"Whatever one thinks of blood service," Lyle added.

"My brother meant a great deal to me," Rian said neutrally. "So I don't think of it as a sacrifice. Though the routine here will certainly be an adjustment."

"Arianne comes to us from a most distinguished family," Evelyn said, firmly shifting the topic. "You've probably seen at least one of Henri Bordonne's paintings, and Prytennia might never produce another sculptor to equal Charlotte Seaforth."

"I should have recognised the name!" Lyle said. "I only yesterday was studying your mother's statue of the Suleviae at the palace. Incomparable."

"I've never seen that one," Rian said. "Or, at least, not all of it at once. I remember her working on the individual parts, for years, but they were all shipped off as soon as they were done."

"Are you an artist yourself?"

"No. I was thoroughly trained, of course, was given every opportunity to follow in my parents' footsteps, but I had neither the talent nor the passion. Aedric was the creative child, and I the phlegmatic one. I organised my father for several years, then travelled."

"Organised? Was he in such disarray?"

"When my brother was preparing for college we found that my father had allowed the family finances to descend into chaos. It didn't help that his agent was shamelessly cheating him out of most of the profit for his work. Father—he was much older than my Mother—had begun to decline, and even at his best he never could interest himself in anything but art."

Rian briefly reflected on those last years, when her father had displayed increasingly childlike behaviour but had produced some of his most innovative work, then shrugged and passed on to entertaining the two men with descriptions of her travels, of grape-picking in Aquitania, and untangling the Dacian Proconsul's archive.

"You travelled alone so freely?" Lyle said, with faint surprise, then added quickly: "I mean—" He flushed.

"Oh, I had friends and relatives to keep me company," Rian said lightly. "And fortunately I'd returned to Lutèce and sent a note of my new address before the accident happened. My family is scattered across the Continent, but on Eiliff's side there's only a thoroughly cantankerous great-uncle up in the Lake District."

One of the servants leaned in at this point, to place a concoction of strawberries and cream in front of Lyle and Rian, and a sugared pear before Evelyn.

"The clean menu for Dama Seaforth, Tessa," Evelyn said, and the girl murmured an apology and removed the strawberry dish, returning a few moments later with a second sugared pear.

"To never eat strawberries again," Lyle murmured.

"Well, not for ten years," Rian said philosophically, and picked up her spoon.

ooOoo

An evening enjoying the mildly competitive flirtation of two attractive men left Rian reflecting on Delia Hackett's reasons for leaving. Both her dinner companions were perhaps ten years Rian's junior, and in other circumstances Rian would merely be deciding whether and which. But even when she had cleared away the small matter of suspecting everyone of murder, Rian would not be able to ignore the complications of the workplace, or taking lovers who aged when she did not.

It was a not insignificant problem, and reoccurred to Rian after the meal had broken for an early night in consideration of London visitors who had risen before dawn to beat the morning gale. Pausing in the hallway, Rian was caught by a scene on the stair leading to the next floor.

In her early forties, Princess Leodhild cut a magnificent figure. Her curling black hair cascaded over shoulders left bare by a daring modern inversion of traditional Prytennian evening dress, the criss-crossing gold laces displaying her warm brown skin and full figure to great advantage. Prince Gustav had spent the evening mesmerised by her generous décolletage, and was now apparently determined to fall into it.

For one of the Suleviae, a mortal aspect of the Trifold Goddess, no lover could take primacy over duty, and every affair must be weighed for political consequence. Was this straightforward attraction, or did Prince Gustav think to gain some advantage? What cost to Prytennia in a night's pleasure with the Lord Protector of the realm's nearest neighbour? Should rumours that the Prince was close to an engagement with France's Princess Heloise be taken into account?

A lifetime of questions like that made ten years of remembering not to eat strawberries seem...not trivial, but manageable.

Whatever the case, Princess Leodhild seemed to at least be listening as the pair disappeared around the curve of the stair. Rian looked away, and caught Lyle in the same motion. The Alban offered her a conspiratorial grin.

"My professional duties fortunately have limits."

"Corralling a tom cat would be quite an accomplishment, besides," Rian murmured.

"He's usually a little more circumspect," Lyle said. "But, ah—" Colour touched the Alban's cheeks, his professional poise lost for an instant.

"But it's Prytennia?" Unperturbed, Rian shrugged. "Foreign notions of propriety are unlikely to diminish Princess Leodhild."

"Of course not." Lyle looked around the clearing crowd, and Rian realised he was checking on Evelyn Carstairs, caught up with First Minister Aquila. "Arianne...Dama Seaforth, could I speak to you privately for a moment?"

Curious, since the man's serious tone didn't seem to suggest an imminent proposition, Rian led him to the Bound's day room, testing her ability to find it. The gale beat against the still-closed shutters. No-one at dinner had discussed the persistence and increasing strength of this latest windstorm, but Rian doubted it had been far from anyone's mind.

"I am not—" Lyle began, then shook his head, tugging at the high collar of his shirt. "I mean no disrespect to Lord Msrah, who is an exemplary man, but, ah, there must be something I can do to help. Will you allow me to speak to the Prince on your behalf?"

At a loss as to what business she might have with a Swedish Prince, Rian tilted her head, studying the young Alban. He was wonderful to look at, the cheekbones matched by a fine physique. And a picture of earnest solemnity.

"I see." Rian smiled. "You're wanting to rescue me."

"To offer at least some possibility of an alternative. We have wonderful schools in Alba. And Prince Gustav would almost certainly take great delight in scoring a point against vampirism in circumstances that don't impact Sweden's current overtures to Prytennia. I'm sure you've thought about this deeply already, but—ah, I can't not say something, can't not offer. Blood service is...is...even if it's possible to reconcile people agreeing to be treated as cattle, there's so much more to it than a business exchange. The fact that the Lord Nomarch chooses not to exercise the control the bond gives him doesn't make it any less real."

"You're the second person to say something of the sort to me since I came to Sheerside." Though the young man from the library hadn't been offering alternatives. "You tried to talk Evelyn out of this as well, didn't you?"

"I almost destroyed our friendship trying to change his mind." Lyle sighed, and sat down at the piano, absently tracing the curved wood hiding the keys. "To give his parents credit, they sent him to Alba deliberately, to allow him to experience a life that didn't revolve entirely around a vampire. But how could a few years erase all the time spent learning this place was normal? You understand that beyond Msrah—that a thing that is far more than a polite and urbane...that it's a human shape with—and it will be literally living inside you—!" He shuddered.

Rian found herself a seat. "I don't find that aspect particularly horrifying," she said. "Medicine has been teaching us that a great many things live inside us, after all. Evelyn certainly seems to have taken no harm from it."

"Even so, I'm right to believe you would not choose this life for yourself, am I not?"

"I wouldn't be here if not for my brother's death, no. And there's some parts I expect to find challenging. But this is a measured choice, not one of desperation." Rian paused, then added: "My mother shared some of your discomfort. She didn't visit a Thoth-den her entire life, because the idea of vampire blood inside her—even if it was healing her—turned her stomach. We always went to the nearest Daughter of Lakshmi if we were ill. That advantages me now, because I'm one of the increasingly small number of Prytennians harbouring no trace of any of the symbiont lines, but mother died before she was forty, of something a Thoth-den could easily have corrected.

"I've never been sick enough to need blood treatment, but I wouldn't hesitate if it meant my life, so the symbiont itself isn't enough to turn me away from blood service. The danger, the Bond, and the...accompanying sensations are larger hurdles, but I'm satisfied with Lord Msrah's reputation. I think the hardest thing for me will be staying in the one place, and the length of the contract. I'm used to a lot more freedom. Though, pragmatically speaking, three children have already changed that."

"They'll be everywhere soon," Lyle murmured. "Rome is considering officially allowing vampires within the New Republic's borders, instead of simply turning a blind eye to those already there. Sweden allows their phials and potions. Even Alba!"

Rian glanced at Lyle's left wrist. He wasn't wearing long, cross-laced Prytennian cuffs, but instead sported thistle-stamped cufflinks. He grimaced in response and shifted his hand so she could see the image of a bird's wing hovering below the surface of the skin.

"Yes, how two-faced can I be, to eat at a vampire's table, use the vampires' protections, but want to rescue you and Evelyn?"

The wing was a visual indication that Lyle had taken a Dose, temporarily preventing himself from fathering children. Like Rome, Sweden still did not allow vampires within its borders, but vampiric medical knowledge and, lately, their vaccinations, cures, and particularly the Dose, had been permitted and widely taken up. Many months of hot debate had been spent on the fine hypocrisy of forbidding vampires, but using a derivative of their blood.

"In a hundred years there won't be a village on this planet that doesn't have its own parasite," Lyle continued miserably. "Keeping the herd healthy."

"And all of us carrying a tiny trace of monster?" Rian contemplated the possibility that she could live to see that future, if she chose to stay in Msrah's service. "Given I can name at least three countries where vampires literally cannot set foot, you can be sure some of the herd will remain, ah, undomesticated. And while I appreciate the gesture, Lyle, I'm not looking to be rescued."

He shook his head, then summoned a smile. "Of course not. Forgive my departure into melodrama. My sister tells me it's my greatest weakness: always seeing the worst in the things that make me uncomfortable."

"Listening to your instincts isn't such a bad thing," Rian said, standing. "Goodnight, Lyle."

Leaving him with a nod, Rian traced her way back to her room. It did not matter that the Alban had apparently detected a level of reluctance in her. It was true enough that she wouldn't choose this life, but she needed to be pragmatic about housing and schooling three children.

And it was a small price to pay for Aedric.

THREE

Something was wrong.

Rian shifted in her new bed. The room was stuffy, but she didn't think the summer heat had woken her. Had it perhaps been the absence of noise? The muted rush and roar of wind no longer rattled winged shutters. Or could it be—? Rian fumbled for the switch of the bedside lamp, and looked quickly at the dresser. But the automaton hadn't moved.

A distant thump and crash brought her to her feet. While she expected some noise at night in a vampire's house, that had had the distinct air of large things breaking. Reaching for a light robe to cover her nightgown, Rian surveyed the room for a suitable weapon. Not even a fire iron.

More noise followed, an enormous scrabbling as if a rat the size of an auroch had found its way into the roof cavity. It approached so rapidly Rian had no chance to do more than jump backward as the ceiling collapsed, depositing a veritable monster into the room.

It had a distinctly human face mounted on a catlike body apparently fashioned from pale marble. A dozen whip like limbs tipped with blades of blue enamel were attached to its back, arranged to form tentacular wings. Perhaps most disconcerting of all were a pair of fine breasts, bare and gleaming with a high polish that had not been lavished upon the rest of the creature's body.

It shook itself, made a low, rumbling sound, then noticed Rian trapped in the corner between the bed and the shuttered windows. The wings stirred, and the floor groaned as the thing shifted its weight, but Rian was already scrambling across the bed to the dressing table.

This simply trapped her in a different corner, but it gave her a larger selection of inadequate weapons, ranging from a spindly chair to a collection of toiletries and cosmetics.

Cursing her decision to put her pistols into storage, Rian opted for a bottle of scent, hoping to at least confuse and distract long enough for a dash for the door. The locked door.

A turn of a key represented only seconds of delay, but nothing in the way the creature prowled forward made delay sound like a good idea. Whatever the thing wanted, she had its attention, and the head-lowering, ready-to-pounce stance didn't suggest a midnight conversation.

With few other options Rian tossed the scent. As the bottle left her hand, a figure dropped from the gaping hole in the ceiling, landing by the creature's chest in time to receive a shower of crystal shards.

The newcomer swore, a hand going to his eyes, and, as Rian recognised the young man from the library, two of the whip like limbs slashed down at him. One of the enamelled tips ploughed deep into his shoulder and chest, while the other severed his raised hand at the wrist, sending it arcing through the air to land, palm up, in the centre of the bed.

It was not quite true to say vampires were blood. Vampires were a conjunction of a god-touched creature too small for the eye to see, and a larger, living vessel. The symbiont permeated all the flesh and tissues, even the bones of its vessel, but it was doubtless true that blood was the focus and central factor of vampiric existence. Rian recognised the library photographer as a vampire when the spurt of blood trailing the severed hand stopped mid-air, and then returned to its source. The wrist of the severed hand lay without even oozing, keeping its blood safely contained.

He'd been knocked to the floor by the force of the creature's blow, and his other arm hung useless from the wreckage of his shoulder, flopping like a newly-landed trout as he tried to shift it. Distant shouting intruded on the scene, but Rian had no hope of outside help, and hurled her heavy silver hairbrush before snatching for another missile, hoping to buy the wounded vampire a few seconds for recovery.

The winged creature ignored the object bouncing off its face, and again the dagger tips arced down. In response, the vampire raised his head, the whole of his damaged body straining as if lifting some enormous weight. And the monster halted.

The freeze wasn't total. Bladed wings still crept down, at a glacial pace that the vampire had no difficulty avoiding as he staggered to his feet. Rian let her breath out, then headed for the door. Time to retreat, before the thing broke loose.

The vampire turned, the movement sharp, barely restrained, and she hadn't even enough time to recognise her danger before he slammed her into the wall and opened her throat.

A great gash, torn rather than neatly punctured, blood spurting extravagantly into his mouth. Rian barely felt the pain of it, drowned as it was by a sudden sense of being torn in two. Vampires fed on the blood of others to maintain their bodies, but they sustained their beyond-human existence with ka, life-force, and this vampire was draining hers.

Carefully-researched expectations were rent, shredded, with nothing of a measured business transaction in the experience, but instead an agony beyond anything she'd ever encountered.

Flailing for any weapon within reach, Rian found nothing, so boxed his ears, but even with one arm useless and the other truncated, the vampire still effortlessly kept her pinned, ignoring her attempts to beat him off. Already it was too hard to move, her legs sagging and her vision fading. She became overwhelmingly aware of cinnamon. Citrus. Sandalwood. The bottle of scent she had thrown.

He had been thoroughly doused, and if Rian had had the strength she would have laughed, because the wretched stuff was called *Egypt*.

Into the rising grey blur came a sensation as sharp as lemon on a cut. Collapsing onto the floor, her own hand clasped weakly over a wound grown fire-hot, Rian could feel the flesh knitting together beneath her fingers. Vampires sealed their bites with a lick of saliva or a few drops of blood. He must have used more than that, but the heat of healing only made the rest of her colder, all but a fraction of her life, the essence of her taken away. He wouldn't even pay for killing her. The Exsanguincy Act, forever controversial, would excuse her death. An unlucky circumstance, practically an accident. Like Aedric's.

Rian could not accept that, not with a shadow still on Eiliff and Aedric's names. It meant too much to their children. And, damn it all, her own pride should not allow her to die so uselessly.

An enormous crash brought a brisk, reviving breeze in its wake. The windows and shielding shutter wings were gone, and bright moonlight outlined the vampire, looking down. His shoulder showed no trace of injury as he turned from the gaping hole to cross to the bed, collecting his severed hand and tucking it by the fingers into his belt.

"...right...about revolting..."

He considered her dispassionately. "I haven't bound you. A binding from me would probably kill you, though that looks to be rapidly becoming a moot point. Before you go over the edge, care to explain why that sphinx was after you?"

It didn't seem wise to admit she had no idea. "What...makes...you think...was?"

"It came in a set of two, apparently trying to reach Leodhild, but this one abruptly diverted directly here."

Rian felt too tired to be surprised. Too weary to answer, and not at all inclined to explain brothers and envelopes and investigations ended before they were begun. Every breath had become a production, an achievement with a distinct beginning and end. Pride never was enough to live on.

"Did its work for it," she observed, as detached as the vampire watching her die.

Her eyes must have closed, because now he was crouched before her, prying one lid open. She realised someone was banging away at the door, but her attention was focused by a renewed wave of scent.

"...reek."

"And whose fault is that?" the vampire said. "Consider it an achievement. Few have ever come so close to getting me killed. *Attend me.*"

Two words become cliché thanks to their appearance in countless plays and stories: the classic words of a vampire imposing his will. Rian could feel it—a sudden muffling, as if a blanket had settled over her mind and contracted—but she slipped beneath, not by any exercise of strength, but thanks to a sucking weariness that stole all her attention. Inhalation. A slow release, and then a pause. The breath after that a distinct and separate thing, a new mountain to consider climbing.

"Tch. Useless." Irritably, he pressed his truncated wrist against her mouth. Warm, wet flesh met her lips, punctuated by a sharp scrape of bone. Blood...*crawled.*

Rian flinched from the thick liquid moving of its own accord across her tongue. A separate flood of strength accompanied the sharp taste of iron. Ka, expanding her chest as if she was a balloon, the vampire's exasperation and annoyance a distinct presence, hot and sharp and briefly as much a part of her as his blood.

"We'll continue this if you live."

Her mouth filled with bees. Pinpricks of fire as the blood began to work its way into soft tissue rather than flow down her throat. A hive, setting up house. That image fit, suggesting a thing of many parts driven by a common purpose. But the will, the direction, lay outside, standing on the far side of the room.

Her last sight of him was a silhouette gazing out into the night, holding the amputated hand to his wrist. That inevitably brought thoughts of Eluned, though of course her niece could not simply reattach severed flesh. While Rian was becoming a part of this man. Bound, joined by blood and ka, a separate kind of limb.

Belonging to the wrong vampire.

FOUR

A drum. A smith's hammer. A river that jolted and surged and pounded. The flow of it was so clear, from the tip of her nose to the smallest toe. Each inhalation made it flare, and Rian was light, a glorious blaze, a pillar of strength and power, exultant.

A white-gold flicker stabbed at her eyes and she winced, turning her head to an embracing blue haze. Her awareness shifted from the river inside to more familiar senses. Warmth. A thick stillness. A hint of sun-dried linen. Dull hunger. No pain. Legs and arms and the normal weight of self, comfortably supported by a well-stuffed mattress.

Behind her, a separate river pounded and surged. Something more than hearing told Rian it was there: a torrent of life separate and distinct from her own. Slowly, she turned back, lifting a hand to block any chance of looking directly at the dagger-point of incandescence. A man sitting next to the piercing light turned to place something over it: a ceramic shade that muted the brilliance to almost comfortable levels, except for a vivid rim around a smoke vent. With the glare cut away he became more than a shape.

"Lord Msrah."

"The extreme sensitivity to light will fade in a few hours," he said, voice soft and measured. "But you will struggle with the sun for some days to come."

"That...is that a candle?"

"It is. Dama Seaforth. I owe you my deepest apologies for the inadequate protection of my House."

Everything was blue-tinted, but she could see him quite clearly: a round-cheeked youth of middle height, hair held in a queue, dark skin highlighted by violet notes. The gentle irony he'd displayed during their initial interview in London was entirely absent.

"What was that...sphinx?"

He knew. She could see it, sense it, even as he shook his head.

"An attack aimed at Princess Leodhild, it seems, which fortunately failed to harm her. It does not pay to underestimate any of the Suleviae, even if the Sulevia Leoth is now more associated with Prytennia's industry than her defences."

Wondering why he lied, Rian slid a hand up to explore her throat, searching for damage. Questing fingers found only unbroken skin, but the memory of teeth, of pain and a sharp note of terror, made her shudder. And then start to think through how strange that encounter had been.

"That vampire—I met him in your library," she said. "Not directly in the sun, but it was so bright in there."

"Yes. A behaviour that develops as we age. All of us can tolerate a certain level of exposure to strong light. I could go upstairs now and walk in the garden if I wished. It would feel like death—I would, indeed, be slowly turning to stone, and would not recover fully until I drank. But there is also a...piquancy involved, should one be willing to risk misjudging one's tolerance."

Rian puzzled through this, and concluded that the library vampire had been hurting himself for the fun of it.

"He bound me," she said, the words not quite a question. She knew what had happened, but wanted confirmation, to have disaster put into words.

"His only means of retrieving an exsanguincy," Lord Msrah said. "Though I admit it surprises me that he made the attempt, since the danger of creating a ghul is high. And he is not fond of blood service."

"I had that impression too."

Trying not to picture herself as a ghul—a corpse brought to unlife by the vampiric symbiont—Rian worked herself gingerly into an upright position and was relieved to discover herself clothed, if only in a light sleeping gown.

"I suppose it's an achievement to be bound to someone whose name I don't know. Not even the line—is he Shu?"

"Amon-Re." Lord Msrah pronounced the name as a distinct sentence, as if even speaking it was an event. "And it is an achievement to survive a bonding to that line in any circumstance. As for his identity, he has been calling himself Comfrey Makepeace, which I imagine is an example of his humour. He is better known as Heriath."

It was not often Rian was reduced to gaping, but this was the last thing she had expected.

"The Wind's Dog? That—?"

She almost finished with 'brat', and stopped herself with a deep breath. There was no-one in Prytennia who did not know the name Heriath, even though he hadn't been publicly sighted since the disaster of the Three Sisters' War, and was thought gone to stone. He predated the Suleviae, and had been bound to serve their rule when Brangwen the First had been crowned. For the vast part of the Trifold Age he had been a moving force: assassin, spy, and agent of the Crown as Prytennia had expanded from one to three dragonates. It had been the Suleviae who had beaten back the waves of invasion that so frequently threatened Sulis' domain, but until the Three Sisters, Heriath, the Wind's Dog, had been a shadowy partner in every success.

The vampire she had met bore no resemblance to the Heriath of legend, but Lord Msrah seemed quite certain.

"I...am surprised to be alive," Rian managed. Not only because the Amon-Re line—that of Egypt's rulers—was said to kill almost all who hoped to be raised to it, but the potency of a vampire's blood increased with age. Lord Msrah was entering the ranks of Shu seniority at four hundred years, but the Amon-Re line was altogether a different order of strength. Heriath...at minimum he would have to be twelve centuries.

"Your will to live is clearly far from trivial," Lord Msrah said. "I regret that I can no longer accept your service."

He took an envelope from the table, handing it to her. Heavy with some object, it was addressed in a loose, looping scrawl. It took Rian several blinks to decipher the word 'Wednesday'.

Tugging the flap open, she tipped out a key: heavy, tarnished, and as large as her hand. A faded paper tag was tied to it with fine cotton thread, the writing tiny and exact. An address in London. There was nothing else in the envelope, no note or explanation.

"I don't feel any particular compulsion," she remarked. "I could simply not go to this place, couldn't I?"

"I do not recommend that course. Although it is common for a colony to decline and the bond to fade if it is not maintained, there is always some slight chance of a neglected symbiont spontaneously separating from the original colony's will. In your case, because both your blood and ka had been drained so heavily, the Amon-Re symbiont was able to completely dominate your system. If Heriath does not affirm his control of it—and soon—your colony will achieve independence and finish raising you."

She would become a vampire. There would be no going back from that after ten years. No strawberries forever.

"And he—I take it he's no longer here?"

"The attack was two days ago, and the party from London returned the morning after. The key was forwarded when I sent word to the palace that you appeared likely to survive."

A little cough of laughter escaped Rian. "He's not going to make this easy for me, is he?"

Her reaction brought an answering smile to Lord Msrah's boyish face. "Very likely not. But I have a suspicion you are equal to the challenge. You are at least alive to face it, and for that I am very grateful. There is a variety of etiquette involved in dealing with another's

Bound, but do not hesitate to apply to me if you are in need. I will not forget—"

A quiet tap interrupted the Nomarch, and the room's blue haze brightened by several degrees as the door opened. Evelyn looked in, and Rian realised that she'd felt the approach of another living river before he'd even knocked.

"My Lord? Mayor Desh-aht has arrived."

Lord Msrah rose. "Thank you, Evelyn. Please assist Dama Seaforth with anything she requires." The vampire bowed to Rian, repeated his apologies and regrets, and left.

"How are your eyes?" Evelyn asked, as the door closed. He crossed to grip Rian's hands. "And the rest of you, of course. I am so sorry, Arianne. What a mess this has become."

"It's certainly not what I was expecting," Rian managed to say, struggling with a sudden rush of sensation. Concern mixed with a deep note of grief, and then cutting through it a spike of straightforward desire, reminding her of the thin cloth of her gown and making her almost sorry when he released her. "I feel...unexpectedly good, actually. The candle was a challenge, but I can't remember the last time I felt so physically *well*." She touched her throat again.

"One step toward godhood," Evelyn murmured, sitting in the chair Lord Msrah had vacated.

Rian gave him a startled glance for his tone. "Don't tell me you're a Marculist?" The argument that those who Answered were not gods, merely 'powers' feeding on souls, enjoyed an increasing popularity, but Rian hadn't expected to find a proponent at Sheerside House.

"No. Gods are gods. That our understanding of them is limited and contradictory is far from surprising. Still, I've met dozens of vampires, and many more Bound, and though they—we—are certainly god-touched, thanks to whatever strain is living in our blood, there's no sign that even Hatshepsu was able to use rept as a stepping stone to transcendence. Like all other mortal-born souls in the Egyptian field of influence, vampires become ba, and then ready themselves for the journey to their Otherworld. Vampirism doesn't even require allegiance."

He leaned forward then, and brushed fingers to the back of her hand, making Rian realise she'd raised it once again to explore her throat. Notes of sympathy and concern showed her that that first flood of outside emotion had not been imagination—and that a conversation about Marculism did little to ease certain memories.

"I knew another Bound who had come to the role through a near-exsanguincy," Evelyn told her. "He found much to be pleased about in his position, but it took him years before he did not need to brace himself, just a little, before his Master fed. To train his mind not to expect pain and terror and death come far too early. I truly am sorry, Arianne."

"Were...were they at least able to kill those sphinx things?" Rian asked, because the idea of being bitten again did seem to be something she was not ready to think about.

"No. Both of them were successfully driven out of the building, where Princess Leodhild could call upon larger triskelion to defend her. A sight not usually seen outside the solstices, and cause enough for any attacker to retreat." Evelyn chuckled. "Or it could have been the vision of Prince Gustav bounding about naked and waving an axe of prodigious proportions. No-one's venturing a guess as to where he produced that from."

Rian shook her head, trying to fit these events into her own personal puzzle. "So it was definitely an attack against the Sulevia Leoth? The sphinx I saw didn't look like an automaton. Some kind of living statue."

"Yes. You can imagine how all this is being received. Egypt was already a favoured suspect for the windstorm problem—weather vampires, after all—and while Egypt and her client nations aren't unique in producing statues resembling our night visitors, the probable link is hard to overlook. The reactions have been—" A grimace competed with a bubble of laughter. "Wrong of me to react with fascinated interest, I know, but the whole world is shifting in response to the possibilities. Is Egypt attempting to annex Prytennia? Will it move on other client nations? Are local vampires to be trusted, or do their pilgrimages, and the jot they're required to send to Thebes, make them automatically suspect? It's a tremendous mess right now, and so exhilarating. All of which is beside the point. Are you hungry?"

"A little. Less than I'd expect if it really has been two days."

"We poured enough diluted honey down your throat to make the difference, I expect," Evelyn said. "I'll fetch you a tray. There's a water closet through that door."

Honey for the hive, Rian thought, as he departed. Binding her to the line of the pharaoh, and to the Wind's Dog: someone considered amoral and deadly, and who had sat in a library hurting himself and thinking about photography.

Her infiltration of Sheerside House had lasted less than twelve hours, and she was left not only with the ongoing problem of the children's maintenance, and the prospect of travelling urgently to London while avoiding light, but a state of thraldom to someone she suspected she would find very annoying. Every plan undone, the destruction neat for its completeness. Lips curving in sour appreciation, Rian shook her head to clear it, then began putting the situation in order.

Lord Msrah had not told her what he knew about the sphinxes, and she had not told him that the Wind's Dog had made a last-ditch effort to save her life because one sphinx had appeared specifically interested in her. There were few enough reasons such a creature would be determined to kill Arianne Seaforth. She had annoyed the occasional person, but owned little intrinsic significance, and no reputation beyond notable parents. Only her presence at Sheerside House, combined with a connection to a double murder, seemed likely to produce an attempt to remove her from play.

The vampire Heriath had saved Rian so he could question her, because the sphinxes had also targeted Princess Leodhild. If they had—somehow!—been sent by Aedric and Eiliff's murderers, then she would be able to put the Wind's Dog to good use. He, presumably, would be less eager to accept the easiest solution than the Caerlleon authorities, who'd shown no interest in looking beyond the surface of the deaths. And, after centuries spent as the Suleviae's personal agent, Heriath would have both experience and the resources of the Crown at his disposal. So, the wrong vampire might not be such a disaster after all.

By the time Evelyn returned, Rian had settled a rough course of action, and was ready to be interested in food. She looked over the well-appointed tray with rising anticipation, then paused to pick up two thin blue envelopes. Telegrams. She would not put it past her three enterprising charges to be demanding updates.

"Lyle asked me to pass on his considerable distress and to request the honour of taking you to lunch," Evelyn said. "Since this Makepeace fellow apparently resides in London, and Prince Gustav is in residence at Alba Place, Lyle will at least be on hand if you find yourself in need of assistance."

"What do you know of Makepeace?" Rian asked, slitting an envelope to distract from her surprise at what he plainly didn't know. Then she frowned at her first telegram, attention stolen almost completely from Evelyn's response.

HEARD GOOD NEWS STOP, it read. TEMPORARILY RETURNING ALBA BUT INSIST LUNCH SOONEST STOP

HAVE EVELYN PASS ON ADDRESS STOP UNTIL RETURN
LYNSEY LOVE TO HELP STOP LYLE

"...been down several times before," Evelyn was saying.
"My mother remembers him showing up early in her
service, so he's at least a century-passed vampire. A sun-
seeker too, from what I've seen of him, which tends to
suggest age, though it apparently can come on quite early
in some of the strains."

"All vampires do that then?" Rian asked, handing him
the telegram in order to stop herself from reacting to a
sought-after name. "Lord Msrah was telling me a little
about it."

"Relatively rare behaviour, from what I understand.
While the rept state is several steps up from mortal decay,
most stone-blood don't seek it prematurely." He smiled
down at the telegram. "Prince Gustav must have whirled
himself back to Din Eidyn and dragged poor Lyle in his
wake. But Lynsey will definitely be glad to do anything
she can for you. She lives for rescues and grand causes."

"I have no idea who Lynsey is," Rian said, quite as if
she hadn't come to Sheerside House specifically to find a
'Lyndsey' somehow connected to the place.

"Lyle's little sister. Very active in the United Albion
League, and thoroughly redoubtable. I'll give you her
London address, and pass on yours. And, if you permit,
come to visit myself, when I'm free to do so. Currently our
usual schedules are completely disarranged."

"Of course," Rian said, the warmth of her response not
simply because she had found a breadcrumb to lead her
through the maze around Aedric's death. "I'll have to
apologise to Dama Hackett. I suppose this will delay all
her plans until another replacement is found."

He looked away. "Delia...her room was opposite
Princess Leodhild's. The sphinx crashed right through it."

"She—? I didn't know. How awful." For a moment
Rian felt a distress disproportionate to the death of a kind
stranger, a jolt to make the room swim. Realising she'd

put her hand to her throat yet again, she forced it down and added: "I'm sorry Evelyn."

"I was teasing her only a week ago, about her long list of frivolous things to do. And now the most I can do is rationalise death, tell myself Delia had lived a long and comfortable life, that it was quick, and she wouldn't have known or suffered. She is seeing Annwn now, and is surely a strong enough soul to travel on a grand tour of the Twilight Islands. But that is what my head says, while my heart shouts 'unfair' and tells me I failed her."

"Dance in the snow." In response to his startled glanced Rian went on: "It's what Dama Hackett told me she planned to do. You can't undo what happened, but you can dance in the snow for her."

Evelyn shook his head, but then his lips shifted to a reluctant curve. "That sounds like Delia. And she would enjoy the idea, very much. She always made fun of my attempts at dignity. Will you dance for her with me? Some time after Midwinter?"

Rian agreed readily to this, and watched a part of Evelyn ease as he told several fond anecdotes of a woman who had been part of the extended family he'd known growing up, and who had obviously been an early crush, words never spoken making her loss doubly regretted.

Sampling breakfast, she tried a segment of peach, then opened her second telegram and read it in silence.

"It's Wednesday at the moment, yes?" she asked.

"Thursday morning."

Rian read the telegram over, and said: "Then I need to check some train schedules. A late afternoon express to London would be ideal, to minimise the amount of sunlight I have to deal with, and also to leave after meeting a train arriving at four."

"And you need to do that—?"

"To collect an express delivery from Retwold School. My nephew and both nieces have managed to get themselves expelled."

FIVE

Nine hours. A thousand stations. A window that opened a bare few inches, and only let in Saharan gusts and an excess of smuts. Long before the final approach to Sheerside Station, Eluned, Eleri and Griff Tenning had been reduced to puddles on the seats.

"Nothing Aunt Arianne can do to us will match the trip here," Eluned said, easing a finger beneath the sweaty itch of straps holding on her right arm.

"Could stand us in the sun another hour," Eleri replied, tilting her head back as she considered the possibilities. "Give us more liver paste sandwiches."

"Don't talk about those sandwiches." Eluned swallowed a bubble of oily gas, and checked on Griff, lying on the opposite seat. He never travelled well.

"She should be glad," Griff said. "And she doesn't get to punish us."

He'd said the same thing, hours earlier, but the defiance had been worn down by the long day, and he sounded half his thirteen years.

Aunt Arianne didn't seem the type to hand out strict punishments, but it was hard to be sure. They knew so little about her, and Eluned hadn't been in a state to pay much attention in the first days after their Aunt had brought the news, or during the funeral. Since then, one of the few things Eluned had been able to remember from before had been her mother's reaction to one of Aunt Arianne's rare letters: pure exasperation. "Your sister flits around the Continent as if the world was arranged for her entertainment. Never doing anything of value, or caring to take a true interest."

And Aunt Arianne hadn't seemed to care, not deeply and properly. She hadn't cried at all, or even hugged them more than once—not that they would have welcomed it if she'd pretended they were close, like real family.

Her endless calm was infuriating, but finding the truth too important for Eluned to jeopardise by giving in to anger. And at least Aunt Arianne had believed them when they'd insisted it couldn't be an accident, had become an ally, and not drawn back on finding a way to get into Sheerside.

"Suppose they have monster attacks very often?" Eleri asked, fanning Griff with the newspaper they'd spent their last hoarded coin on that morning. "Only make a fuss about them if Princess Leodhild is involved?"

Griff didn't even respond.

"I can see the Nomal House pyramid." Eluned pressed her face to the compartment window to improve the angle of her view. Vampires used pyramids to intensify their powers, and since Shu vampires controlled the weather, the home of the Southern Nomarch was sure to need one as large as this.

Eleri paused in fanning. "The Aquae Sulis one in the distance again?"

"The capping stone is a different colour. It's very close. We must be right on the station."

As if in response, the train commenced the series of clanks that signalled a halt, and Eleri joined Eluned at the window. Griff put his arms over his face and breathed deeply. Not a good sign. Griff, for all the enormous energy he could expend, was not robust or resilient, and the past few months had strained his nerves to a high pitch. Too much upset produced fevers, and Eluned couldn't guess how the hot day and uncertainty would mix with the more ordinary travel sickness.

"It will be something to stay at a house that has its own station," she said, dividing her attention between her brother and the first glimpse of platform. "I wonder how far it is from the station to the main building?"

"A mile and a quarter," Griff said immediately. "There's a service village around the station. Twenty-two structures. The village is on a hill, and there's a view of Sheerside House from the station."

He'd told them so at the beginning of the journey, and the reminder of the architectural treat waiting for him was enough to make him sit up and study again the rough map he'd already drawn up of the locale.

"Look at that peculiar woman with the umbrella and veil," Eluned said. "In this heat! She...oh."

"It's the Aunt. Recognise the dress."

Eleri's flat pronouncement brought Griff to the window, but the slowing train had already juddered past.

"Check you haven't left anything under the seats," Eluned said, moving briskly on from this oddity. "And straighten your shendy, Griff."

Griff tugged his knee-length red and blue skirt so the blue panels once again faced front and back, then swiped a foot under the seats in search of dropped valuables, collecting the pencil and rubber band the action produced. There was little else—they'd been ready since Aquae Sulis, failing to anticipate how long the last few stations would take in an unexpectedly strong afternoon wind storm. At least the final leg had lacked the couple who had shared their compartment most of the way from Caerlleon, all surreptitious stares and whispers.

"Tennings Together," Eluned muttered, and unlatched the compartment door as the train jerked to a halt. The remaining traces of the afternoon's hot wind whisked around them, not exactly pleasant, but an improvement by several degrees on the heat of the compartment.

A rambling pink-and-white rose smothered the stone fence immediately in front of them, most of the petals missing or scorched brown by the winds. Eluned contemplated it for a moment of disappointment and fellow feeling, then turned to face the aunt who—for the next few years at least—had far too much say in their choices. Shaded by a sturdy black umbrella, a wide-brimmed summer hat, and a draping of opaque veil that hung past her shoulders, she presented a bizarre picture, especially compared to the tall, beautifully dressed man leading her toward them.

"I see," Eleri said. "Newly bound. Sensitive to light."

"This is certainly not a fashion statement," their aunt said. "You three look thoroughly cooked, and well past done. We'd best fix that first. Evelyn will make sure your luggage has arrived. Anything other than the three school trunks?"

The lightly amused, untroubled voice bothered Eluned enormously. Impossible not to think of all the times they'd arrived home from school before, to be enveloped in warm hugs and excited chatter from people who loved them, instead of this vaguely entertained stranger.

At their nods, their aunt continued. "Past the end of the platform there's a picnic set out beneath a very large tree. Go wait there. Hold off eating."

The last thing Eluned thought she wanted to do was eat, but the shade cast by the towering beech had a revivifying effect, enough for her to at least cast a speculative eye over a positively sumptuous collection of dishes.

"I could be sick *all* over her," Griff began appreciatively, but then his attention was caught by the view. The station stood at the lip of a small valley, and across a vividly green gap an enormous building crowned the horizon. It was too distant to make out details, but more than enough to distract.

Eluned ran fingers through her short blond hair, then glanced up as her twin reached out to shift the right sleeve of Eluned's tunic, exposing her upper arm. The skin around the liner and padded socket was red and chafed.

"Should have had the new arm by now," Eleri said.

"It's the heat, not the fit." Eluned pulled her tunic's neck to one side, and craned to see the harness straps without triggering any of the arm's functions. They weren't so tight as to cut into her, but they'd definitely rubbed.

The question of strapping was postponed by their aunt's return, lugging a full bucket and accompanied by a uniformed man carrying another two.

"Griff, do you have anything in your pockets you'd rather not get wet?"

"No," Griff said, eyeing the buckets with interest as he patted the sides of his shendy to make sure.

"Excellent. Stand over here, where the water will drain."

After a nod of thanks to the station master, Aunt Arianne upended her entire bucket over Griff, who gasped and then wriggled all over, sending water droplets in every direction. Not reacting to the secondary shower, Aunt Arianne picked up another bucket.

"Eleri next. Eluned, there's a convenience in the station if you would prefer not to wet your arm."

Eluned hesitated only a moment, then headed into the billow of steam from the departing train, seeking out the room. She had long carried a glass shield of pride to help her to never flinch from stares, but after a hot and weary day that shield's weight was almost beyond bearing. Still she unfastened her dress, removed the dark wood and pale metal arm, and did not let herself think of the station master, and the rather handsome man called Evelyn, and a house full of strangers.

When Eluned returned, and had handed the arm to Eleri, their aunt hoisted the third bucket. The water felt icy, shocking away any lingering queasiness, and then there were enamel mugs full of the same cool water, and stone bottles of ginger beer to pour.

"We have an hour before we're due to leave," Aunt Arianne said. "Plenty of time to dry off and recover. We'll be on our way before it starts to rain."

Griff looked up at the unspoiled blue of the sky, and then at their veiled aunt. "You can tell? That it's going to rain?"

"According to Evelyn, Lord Msrah has decided it will rain, since the large holes in Sheerside House have been sufficiently patched. Evelyn—Dem Carstairs—is one of Lord Msrah's Bound, and will be taking a tactfully long time over your luggage, to allow us a chance to talk."

Griff scowled and grabbed a sticky bun before turning to face across the valley. "The whole thing was silly. All that fuss about a window."

"It's complicated—" Eluned began. She did not want to talk about the false sympathy, the way certain people had acted as if Eluned particularly was a danger to herself: someone whose parents were so inept they'd dropped an automaton on their own heads.

"Looking for an excuse to get rid of us," Eleri said. "Decided we lowered the tone. Doesn't matter. Important thing is here."

"Our goal is our first concern, that's true enough," Aunt Arianne said, to Eluned's surprise.

"You're not mad?"

Eluned could read nothing from the slight sway of the veil, and wished their aunt would take it off. She had trouble enough reading this near-stranger as it was.

"If you make a habit of throwing away your tuition, I'll respond by sending you to cheaper schools, but in the short term there are other matters to focus on. To which point, I may have made some progress, but have also suffered a significant set-back. I am Bound, but not to Lord Msrah."

Eleri dropped her mug, and Griff choked on the remains of his bun.

"How?" Eluned managed, and listened to a story about a monster falling through the ceiling, and a vampire so badly injured he had turned on the nearest source of blood and ka and taken without limit. The law called attacks like that exsanguincies and—unless someone truly important had been killed—only fined the vampire. But it would still mean an awkward fuss, and so Aunt Arianne's vampire had used a bonding to try to keep her alive.

"Messy," Eleri commented, managing in her usual abbreviated way to encompass all and nothing of what Eluned burned to say. "What's the progress?"

"A Lyndsey. Or a Lynsey, rather. The connection is tenuous—Lynsey is the sister of a friend of Dem Carstairs—but a few pointed questions have produced no others. She is going to call on us in London."

"We're going to London? Now?"

Eluned struggled to keep her dismay out of her voice, while Griff said: "There was something worse," and glared openly.

"When the Express arrives," their aunt replied, her cool voice never wavering, even though the swaying veil suggested she'd turned to look directly at Griff. "To a mystery destination, which we will track down tomorrow morning. The vampire involved, who is known as Comfrey Makepeace, has connections that may be useful to us, if he can be brought to exercise them. But before we reach that point, I wanted to ask you about Monsieur Doré, Eleri."

"You found it then." Eleri glanced at Eluned, then back at their aunt. "Thought it better not to show you that until you'd stopped selling everything."

The sale of the house and workshop had been a sore point with Eleri in particular, and one reason for not telling Aunt Arianne the whole story.

"That huge chunk of fulgite was related to the automaton that's missing?"

"Commission came with two pieces of fulgite the same size and shape, possibly artificial. Seemed to take charge, but wouldn't release it consistently, and said to be haunted. Mother was asked to investigate normalising the release, design automaton that self-activates."

"So the second piece—?"

"Gone like the Commissions Book and the automaton."

This was the test moment, far more than any reaction their aunt might have to their expulsion. All along they'd kept the existence of the fulgite from her, telling her only about a mysterious commission for an automaton. Not truly because they were worried she'd sell the fulgite, but because she was a stranger, and their mother had thought her unreliable.

All Aunt Arianne said was: "Why did you send Monsieur Doré with me, Eleri?"

"Ran out of ideas to make it release the charge. And problems at school. No place to keep it safe."

Their aunt's response was cut short by Griff, twisting sharply away from his contemplation of Sheerside House to blurt in a spray of crumbs: "Do we really have to go to London? Now?"

The veil swayed again. "Your father was a bad traveller as well. Yes, we have to go to London. Dem Makepeace...Dem Makepeace was not able to see me through this bonding, and I need to make contact with him before it takes me rather further than I care for." She fished in a pocket of her dress and tossed a labelled key to Griff. "Think of it as a treasure hunt, with that our only clue. The reward for success is not having a vampire for an aunt."

The man who was Lord Msrah's Bound came back before they could properly react to this calm announcement, and Aunt Arianne introduced each of them in turn.

"A pleasure," Dem Carstairs said, drawing his sandal-shod feet together and bowing. In his calf-length pleated shendy and light tunic he looked like he was never anything but completely unruffled, and his gaze didn't linger any longer on Eluned than it did on Eleri and Griff. Of course, Aunt Arianne had probably warned him.

"Would Lord Msrah allow me to return with Griff?" Aunt Arianne asked. "He has a particular interest in architecture, and was looking forward to Sheerside House enormously."

Dem Carstairs immediately volunteered to give Griff a personal tour, and entertained them with problems caused by the Nomal House's convoluted structure, and how often guests 'looking for the bathroom' ended up in Lord Msrah's private office in the Underhouse. He completely diverted Griff, and Eluned was glad to sit in the shade and try not think about sweltering carriages.

"Is that the storm or the train?"

Aunt Arianne's question broke Eluned out of a threatened doze, and she looked over the vivid green valley to discover a bank of black clouds crashing across the sky. But it wasn't distant thunder they could hear.

"It's a Dragon!"

Bad humour entirely forgotten, Griff surged to his feet and raced back to the platform, pelting at full speed to keep pace with the ornate engine steaming to a halt.

There were only three dragon engines in Prytennia—the newest and the best, and beautifully constructed in honour of the three dragons who slept beneath the land. Eluned and Eleri couldn't resist chasing Griff down and joining him in admiring the beautiful flowing lines of the engine, all black and silver in honour of the Sulevia Seolfor, who tended the dragons and could draw on their pale fire.

"Why is it Nimelleth?" Griff shouted, over the hiss of venting steam. "Shouldn't it be the Dragon of the South?"

Despite the heat of the day, they crowded around the heavy engine and Eleri, as usual, somehow communicated a technical interest to the driver and won them a brief invitation into the dragon's head to admire the boiler: fulquus-powered rather than using coal.

"...swapped stokers for a guard," the driver was saying, when Eluned followed Griff and their sister, and the man who had lent a hand to haul them up patted the twin guns at his belt.

"Is it true the new engines won't use steam at all?" Eleri asked. "Or fulgite?"

"The short-haul ones servicing London won't," the driver agreed, swiping a handkerchief across her ruddy face. "The ones they're digging tunnels for will run on special charged tracks. Though if you followed the line back, you'd still find steam and coal behind the power. It's simply the delivery that will be different."

"Less easily stolen," said the guard, with a glance toward the heavily-reinforced hatch that shielded the train's fulgite.

"Have you been raided?" Eluned asked, eyeing the man's weaponry with interest.

"Not yet the Dragons. But the exchange stations where we swap out our spent fulgite are having some fine and exciting nights."

"Best get to your compartment," the driver advised. "This is only a short stop. You'll see London as the sun sets."

Reluctantly they clambered down and peered along the length of the train for any glimpse of Aunt Arianne. No sign.

"Through-way carriages," Eleri said, pleased. "We won't be stuck in the one compartment."

Before they could clamber into the nearest carriage, the tall Dem Carstairs emerged from the farthest and beckoned, and they raced all the way down again. He laughed as they panted up.

"The cooling-down exercise seems to have been wasted. Though the rain should make up the difference. Pile on, pile on, before you're left behind. I shall hope to see you again, for a tour in more pleasant weather."

As Griff and Eleri obeyed, Eluned paused to hold out her hand, because she would not let herself be rude, no matter how daunted she happened to be. "Thank you for the lunch."

"My pleasure." He took her hand and bowed over it, even though it was her left and that usually caused at least a moment's hesitation. Then, lowering his voice, he added: "Your Aunt appears determined not to show it, but she suffered a very violent and painful attack, one that nearly took her life. Look after her."

He handed Eluned up before she could properly react, as the guard came along to close the door.

"Step to your right, dama," the guard said, as Eluned caught an echo of Griff's voice, and headed along the narrow corridor to their compartment.

"First class, Ned!" Griff cried, from his position perched on the curving back of one of the benches lining the walls, so sumptuous they looked like rows of winged-back chairs. "And see this?"

He reached up to not quite touch the waving woven triangle in the upper corner of the wide compartment.

"Simple automation," Eleri commented, pointing out another in the opposite corner. "Electric lighting, too. Whole train's been designed to take advantage of the fulgite."

A shudder and a jolt warned of departure and their Aunt, standing at the window, lifted a hand in farewell. A roll of thunder accompanied the response from Dem Carstairs, and heavy drops struck the glass as the train pulled away.

"That should cool matters down considerably," Aunt Arianne said, not sounding as if she'd been recently attacked by anything more than mild curiosity.

Their mother had once said their aunt lacked any form of sensibility, so perhaps nearly dying was the kind of thing she could simply take in her stride. But whatever the case, Eluned doubted she was immune to heat.

"You must be boiling under all that, Aunt Arianne. If we pull the blinds and turn out the lights, will it be dark enough for you?"

The veil swayed ambiguously, and the subsequent: "It's worth a try," came in the same tone, but even so Eluned was suddenly certain that she'd surprised their aunt. And that was not a nice realisation.

Resolving to do better, she jabbed Griff to get him to come down, and double-checked their belongings were sufficiently stable as the train picked up speed. The guard passed, but merely tipped his hat rather than asking for tickets, and then showed Eluned the trick to blocking the windows and damping the lights. The result was so effective it was clear the compartment had been modified with vampires in mind.

"The Nomarch must use it," Eluned said, finishing her thought aloud as she plumped into one of the seats and contemplated in the half-light the basket containing the remains of their picnic, ensconced on the seat opposite. A carpet bag was tucked beside it, and she could make out the shape of her own wooden fingers curling shyly over the top.

"Griff, please check the compartments to either side of us," Aunt Arianne said, stripping off her gloves, then lifting hat and veil together.

"Right."

Griff banged the door open carelessly, and even though it wasn't bright out in the storm-gloomed corridor, their aunt still flinched and threw up a hand. But then dropped it as the door bounced shut once again, remarking: "Not as bad as before."

"You—" Eluned reached out and pushed the corridor door wider again, so the light fell across their aunt's face.

"This Makepeace person a Thoth-den?" Eleri asked.

"No, one of the rarer lines, but all vampires and Bound enjoy some level of preservation." Aunt Arianne touched her cheek, then her fingers strayed down to her throat before dropping. "I foresee some highly entertaining conversations thanks to this, but probably a few annoying misunderstandings as well."

Aunt Arianne was four years younger than Father, which made her quite old, almost thirty-seven. She shared Griff and Father's honey-brown hair, and wore a certain air of authority and sophistication, but now lacked the faint imperfections of skin, and minute sagging that came along with years. It was already difficult to call this woman 'Aunt', but it would be doubly so now.

"Barely look seventeen," Eleri said.

"Oh, it's not that bad, surely? I was thinking twenty, or at least nineteen. Seventeen, and I'll get lectures when I go out dancing." Aunt Arianne touched her throat again, then shook her head. "Not a development I can justly complain about. What's the situation, Griff?"

Griff, ducking under Eluned's arm, said: "There's a lady in the very end compartment. The other two are empty."

"Good. The noise of the rain should mean even a Bound would have trouble from that distance. Close the door. I want to get back to the subject at hand."

"This Lynsey person?" Eluned asked, sitting down.

"No, Monsieur Doré. You fitted him out to test the haunted automaton stories?"

"Yes. No set routines, merely as wide a range of possible movement as I could manage." Eleri bounced her heel absently. "No response. In other devices, the fulgite releases a charge, but often stops unexpectedly."

"How long did you test the automaton's response?"

"Finished the modifications ten days ago."

"It never did anything." The motion of the train was having its usual effect on Griff's mood.

"Null result, not proof of the negative."

"Not entirely null, either," Aunt Arianne said. "He didn't move a great deal, but Monsieur Doré most certainly gave me a passing acquaintance with a 'haunted' automaton. My response was to remove the fulgite, and now that I've had time to think it over, it brings with it a possible reason for why a large and very dangerous living statue would come bounding through a ceiling into my room."

Eluned had wondered about that, ever since Aunt Arianne had told them she'd been attacked. "That thing was after the fulgite?"

"Perhaps. And if that proves to be the case, then what did the other one want..."

Eluned and Eleri finished her sentence in chorus: "...with Princess Leodhild?"

Six

Eluned had never stayed in a hotel before, and a year ago would have enjoyed the luxurious Ketterley enormously. Everywhere she looked there was a wealth of patterns and decorative touches, and even a few vases of flowers, despite the winds. And yet they woke no response in her. She simply looked, instead of adding them to her sketchbooks.

Like the train compartment, the hotel had been arranged by Lord Msrah's staff, and underlined how rapidly their circumstances had changed. The arrangements that would have given them a home had completely fallen apart, and all Aunt Arianne would say about Dem Makepeace was that she had no idea of his finances, and didn't have a formal bonding agreement with him.

Nor would their aunt speculate further about the fulgite or Princess Leodhild, only adding that not becoming a vampire was at the top of her list of priorities for the moment, and whisking them through a breakfast and departure at an uncomfortably early hour.

"She's a trompe l'oeil."

"A what?" Griff tore his attention from the hotel foyer's ceiling, puzzled, but Eleri nodded.

"Especially now."

Gathered together at the top of the Ketterley's sweeping foyer stairs, they watched a little constellation of hotel staff orbit their aunt. Eluned had noticed before that Aunt Arianne had a knack for getting people to want to help her, but it had become much more marked now that she was deceptively young. And it surely didn't hurt that, despite her tight purse strings, she was dressed in a very elegant and modern version of traditional Prytennian daywear: her white shirt had decorative laces down the arms, the hunter green outer panels of her knee-length doubled skirt flared to reveal the patterned ivory layer beneath, and a day belt of sage cloth hugged and emphasised the curve of her waist. Matching sage undertrousers were cut close to the line of her legs and it was all fashioned from the lightest of cloth: an outfit chosen to cover skin while managing the summer heat.

"It means a trick of the eye, Griff. An object painted to look like it's something else." Eluned, dressed in her uniform of shirt and summer shendy because all her other clothing was too hot or too small, started down the stair. "Aunt Arianne acts very open, but it's all an illusion."

"Like we haven't been keeping stuff back from her? How does that make her an illusion?"

Eluned, who had slept badly thanks to a collection of chafed patches of skin, shrugged and regretted it. Their aunt, finishing arrangements for their baggage to be called for, smiled brightly at their arrival and led them outside, lowering her veil. Only the speed with which she was getting things done betrayed any hint that she might be worried.

"Cab, dama?"

"Please."

"May we have that autocarriage, instead of a hummingbird?" Eleri asked immediately, pointing to the single automaton-drawn carriage standing behind two more modern self-propelled vehicles.

"Good choice," the hotel doorman said. "No-one knows London better than Mama Lu." He made a complicated beckoning gesture, and the autocarriage drew out of line.

Eluned, who preferred hummingbirds both for their speed and relative quiet, hid her sigh and reflected that at least the open carriage was wide and looked comfortably sprung, unlike many of the boxy little hummingbirds. A plump woman wearing a straw hat decorated with flowers was sitting at the controls, and nodded them in cheerfully.

The automaton—for Eleri had explained on past occasions that only a single device was involved, even though it looked like the front half of two horses—was quite detailed: the two proud metal necks could lift and turn, and the ears even swivelled. The legs, hooves shod neatly in vulcanised rubber booties, had a fine stepping movement, and the thing was obviously better at making turns than the last couple of autocarriages Eluned had seen.

Unlike Eluned, Eleri never had the slightest difficulty striking up conversations with strangers, and immediately asked if she could sit up front.

"If you like, duck," the driver replied, obligingly making room on her bench. "Call me Mama Lu. Where can I take you?"

"Do you know Vine Street, Lamhythe?" Aunt Arianne asked, tugging at her veil again even though the sun was still quite low.

"That I do." Mama Lu touched her own hat in response, her round and amiable face lighting with curiosity before she turned to answer Eleri's questions about the controls.

Eluned settled down next to her aunt with a sigh, and inched a finger beneath the strap that crossed her shoulder. No matter how she shifted it, the leather would slide back to wear against the raw spots. And yet she hadn't left it off, despite Eleri and Griff both making pointed remarks. It was true that she was stared at no less when wearing such an obviously artificial arm, but she could do more.

The autocarriage started off, drawn effortlessly by its four front hooves, and Eluned caught at Griff's shirt as he stood to better peer into the great open pit next to Paddington Station, where part of the new underground track was being laid.

"Think of it, Ned," he said, sitting down as they picked up speed. "Miles of it, everywhere underneath us. There's entire brickworks dedicated to the project." Sitting in the rear-facing seat, he slewed around to address the cab driver. "Will you learn to drive a train instead, when people can get anywhere in London by going underground?"

"Won't happen, duck. Even with the clever digging machines, there's years upon years of construction to go, and when there's a station under every part of London, there'll still be gaps in between them. Some folk wouldn't walk to the end of the street, if they could help it."

Eluned tilted her head back to take in the red brick buildings, the spinning blades driving household dynamos, the golden cap of the nearest pyramid, and a minor fleet of airships lifting into the blue vault of sky. "Look, the new Wingbird type!"

"They're getting off ahead of the morning windstorm," the driver said. "Hold on, this turn's a sharp one."

The intersection was frenetically busy, with hummingbirds, a bus, and two big haulers all converging, but Mama Lu took them through it at a smart pace. As they swung sharply onto a main road, Eluned's eyes widened as she spotted a girl with a sharply pointed face raised up on a seat above a single middle-sized wheel in the centre of three tiny wheels on extended legs that flexed and bent as she turned. The curious machine's engine made a sound like a frantically purring kitten.

The girl, alertly watching the traffic, caught Eluned looking and spun effortlessly to match pace with the autocarriage.

"Newspaper, damini?"

"That—what is that called?" Eleri's tone matched Eluned's own excitement.

"Not seen a dragonfly before? Out of Nathaner's Workshop. Sweet, yes?" The girl reached out adroitly to accept the coin Aunt Arianne was holding out to her, and fished into metal panniers built into her seat. *"Daily Yell?"*

"Courant."

Eluned glanced at her aunt, and before the girl could zip off pushed herself to say: "How fast is that thing? Could you go buy something and come back before we get too far?"

"That would depend on what it is," the girl replied, with a wide grin.

"Umbrella. Or parasol."

"Not a problem."

"I'll take them around the Circus, Sun Li Sen," their driver said, as Aunt Arianne silently reopened her purse. "Don't drag your heels."

"No, Grandmother." The girl bowed her head hastily to their driver, took the new coin, and zoomed away.

"She's your granddaughter?" Griff asked, still trying to look in every direction at once as they passed a thousand fascinations.

"One of them." Mama Lu clicked her tongue. "She'll go far, little minx."

Eluned eyed her aunt, who had tucked her purse away and now unfolded the paper, holding it up so it blocked the slanting light of early morning.

"Well spotted," Aunt Arianne murmured.

"At first I thought you were worried about running out of time, but you wanted to get there before the sun was too far up, right?"

"Sunlight seems much harder to deal with than lamplight. As for running out of time, according to Lord Msrah I should have a couple of days before I'm in real danger. Besides, from what I've seen of Dem Makepeace, he's likely to not be home, or be conveniently out of town, purely for the entertainment value of keeping me waiting."

This prompted a rich and unexpected chuckle from their driver. "You four are heading for Forest House?"

"If that's number three Vine Street." Aunt Arianne lowered her paper a little, then hastily raised it back up. "You know the place?"

"The House of the Keeper of the Deep Grove? I should think so."

This sounded promising. Aunt Arianne's description of her new vampire had made it seem like they'd be stuck in a cellar with barely room to turn around.

"So Dem Makepeace is a vampire *and* a dryw?" Griff asked.

"He's no seer." Mama Lu laughed again. "Vampire, yes, and technically the true Keeper of the Deep Grove, but he has nothing to do with the Order of the Oak, and has long appointed someone else to look after Forest House. It's stood empty these past eight years, since Dama Fulbright passed. It's good to learn he's found another Keeper."

Eluned glanced at Aunt Arianne, but the veil made it impossible to read any reaction. Still, she had to be pleased, as Eleri and Griff so obviously were, because 'the House of the Keeper' would maybe have room for a workshop, and perhaps be an interesting building in itself, and surely this Deep Grove would offer a wealth of the shapes and forms that Eluned so liked to work with. A garden, unlikely to be as large as the one at Sheerside House, but more than the postage stamp they'd had back in Caerlleon.

The thought failed to excite her, which was a strangeness she had suffered all summer. Even the prospect of the gardens at Sheerside hadn't moved her, and despite all she'd seen the past few days her sketchbook remained unopened. It wasn't only that the world kept moving with Mother and Father gone on to Annwn. Eluned had accepted that, and the sharp hurt no longer consumed all her waking hours. But a part of Eluned herself had flattened and been lost, and she did not know how to get it back.

The girl on the dragonfly caught up with them as they circled a statue of a laughing Epona standing on the back of two horses, and then Mama Lu took them over the river, cheerfully answering a stream of questions from Griff, and even letting Eleri drive, once they'd turned off the busy roads. Eluned caught a glimpse of a grand curve of green to her right and shifted to try for a better look down the next street.

"Is that the Great Barrows? Is this Deep Grove nearby?"

"It is, though that's Sceadu Barrow and Vine Street is north of Seolfor Barrow. A short walk from its tip."

Eluned exchanged a look with Griff and Eleri. "Would we be able to hear the Song of the Solstice from the house?"

"I should think so. Though, being so close, you should absolutely join the crowds. There's nothing like it."

"Kites," Eleri said, and they gave full attention to bright points of colour rising above rooftops. Eluned's mood remained as high as the dancing scraps of silk until she noticed the area they were moving into, which was full of tidily-kept but very compact houses. This did not bode well for an expansive garden.

"Do you worry about your fulgite getting stolen?" Griff was asking their driver.

"Not from Ha and Mu here. With hummingbirds, all you need do is lift up the driver's seat and do some sharp work with a crowbar, but these old models are a good deal sturdier."

"Is that why you keep it?" Griff had his head thrust between Mama Lu and Eleri's shoulders. "I can't remember the last time we rode in one."

"Not many of them about any more, duck. Too much maintenance. Too noisy. Never did make much sense in the first place, but that's Romans for you—the show's half the point. I keep Ha and Mu for old time's sake. I got my start driving for First Minister Halned, and when he retired he gave me his autocarriage. Gave me a big step up, that did." Mama Lu let out a satisfied sigh, then added: "Turn right up here, duck, and we'll be on Vine Street."

Eleri, always quick to master anything mechanical, turned neatly, and a long stretch of terraces opened before them. Well maintained, but many looking as if they had no garden at all, or only a tiny yard. Down at the end of the street, though, taller buildings loomed on the right, and Eluned eyed them hopefully as they rolled past a public house.

"That's the Lyre and Razor," Mama Lu said. "Run by a pair of sisters. Aquitanian, but none the worse for it. From this cross-street ahead, to our right and one block down, is a grocer and post office. If you need a cab, run down there and if there's not one waiting ask for one to be sent on. It's a good neighbourhood, near but not amongst the playhouses, and quiet most weeks, though lively during the solstices, of course."

She nodded genially toward the green slopes in the near distance, but all Eluned cared about at that moment were the buildings up ahead. Warehouses. Another terraced row facing them, a little less compact than the houses they'd been passing, but lacking more than postage stamp gardens. Despite that inner flatness, she found herself disappointed.

Inevitably, their driver told Eleri to pull up, and Eluned saw her own feelings reflected on Griff's face, but at least he kept his mouth shut as he contemplated their future.

Take the positive and move on, their mother would say, and so Eluned resolutely admired the fresh paint and clean windows.

As their driver said, "Here we are ducks," the door of the house Eluned was studying opened, and a girl dressed in a sari of the medical clan the Daughters of Lakshmi stepped through.

Ducking her head at having been caught looking, Eluned turned away. The doors of the warehouse opposite were papered thickly with posters proclaiming the latest offerings of the playhouses, of the Brass Menagerie, of fine soaps, and silks all the way from the Huaxia kingdoms.

"Would you mind waiting until I'm certain we can open the door?" Aunt Arianne asked, as she handed over coin.

"Not a problem, my pet. Fish under the lad's seat and you'll find a tool or two you can put to clearing some of that paper away."

Blinking, Eluned followed the driver's gesture toward what she had thought a warehouse. Just a blank wall of bricks and an enormous double door, so coated in posters that only the top and bottom were visible. There were no windows until the top third of the building, where squares of glass were protected by stern metal bars.

"Closed up long?" Eleri asked, as Griff fished up a chisel and crowbar from beneath his seat.

"Eight years since Dama Fulbright," Aunt Arianne murmured, stepping down. "There seems to be a service door built into the right half of the larger one. Shall we see if we can find a keyhole?"

Eluned glanced back at the terrace house in fascinated comparison, and again met the eyes of the Daughter of Lakshmi, who pulled her own door shut and marched off down the street as if to deny any staring.

"Why is it disguised as a warehouse?" Eluned asked Mama Lu.

"The Deep Grove has always been a guarded place." The driver laughed. "In more ways than one. Ah, it's a fine thing to have some good news."

Fired with curiosity, Eluned clambered down to help tear away the layered posters, exposing the person-sized door built into the weighty and very solid larger entrance. Griff eagerly fished the key up from inside his shirt, where he'd been wearing it on a bootlace, and turned it with only a little difficulty. The door didn't budge, but Eluned and

Eleri together dug their fingers in and pulled it free of the grip of old poster glue.

"Rather an oversized vestibule," Aunt Arianne remarked of the room beyond. "Breach the inner fastness for me." She gathered up the tools borrowed from Mama Lu and turned back to the autocarriage.

Griff headed to a shadowy second door, and Eluned turned to the one they'd passed through, finding two thick wooden slides.

"Lend me your shoulder, Eleri."

With the accompaniment of much tearing of paper, they pushed open the two great outer doors, exposing a room the same width as the doors, and around six feet deep. There were benches to either side, racks for shoes, places for umbrellas, and dozens of coat hooks. Dust swam in the air.

"What *is* this place?" Eluned could not imagine any family needing such an entrance.

The second set of doors were paned with dark glass and far from warehouse-like, though still on the large side. They unlocked easily and glided open when Griff pushed them inward.

His delighted inhalation—followed by an enormous sneeze—told Eluned that the place at least offered something of interest to their architecture-mad brother, and she and Eleri eagerly stepped around him into a hall that filled the whole three stories of what was most certainly not a warehouse.

Two trees of glass. They rose first as leadlight columns then spread, opening fingers of twig and leaf until the entire upper half of the far wall was lost to transparent foliage. Most of it was frosted white, but pale motes of colour glimmered where translucent branches supported flowers, fruit, and tiny birds.

Between the windows of intertwined trees was a third doubled door, a tall pointed arch of dark wood, severe and plain. Again there were sturdy bars, and Griff was already racing to slide them open.

The rest of the hall was empty but for stairs that began halfway back along the walls to either side, and curved up to join a walkway above the vestibule then climbed again to a second walkway. Discreet doors revealed the place extended to either side of the hall.

"And so the Deep Grove?" Aunt Arianne murmured, coming up behind them. "I was expecting trees, but my imagination seems to have fallen short. Lead on, Griff, lead on."

Griff needed no urging, throwing open the hall's rear doors, pausing to survey the wealth of greenery, and then letting out a yelp and racing forward along a slate path between the trunks of ash trees.

"Got yourself a garden," Eleri said.

"More like a forest," Eluned replied, wondering what about trees had so fired Griff, whose interest in greenery was usually confined to removing any from his plate.

The open doorway was easily wide enough for all three to pause on the heavy stone doorstep. Aunt Arianne lifted her umbrella against the play of sunlight through a canopy of green, and they surveyed a long rectangle bounded on all sides by brick walls over which only the roofs of warehouses rose. The rectangle was divided into two squares by a shorter central wall, and on the near side of the dividing wall the slate path led through comfortably spaced trees and split around a circle of standing stones almost completely buried in a thick spread of purple-crowned thistle.

"A circle?" Eluned said. "Is this place a grove, or does it belong to Sulis?"

"Set up for a lot of visitors. But what's—"

Breaking off, Eleri strode ahead down the path, and Eluned dogged her heels, past the stone circle to where the split path merged back into a single line of stones. To the Gate.

If the whole of the house seemed set up to allow a stream of people to visit the grove and circle of standing stones, this final barrier, rising twice the height of a tall man, clearly made keeping people out its business. Yet it was beautiful, the bars of stern black metal supporting an interlacing of copper gone green with age: verdigris leaves hiding all but a few glimpses of the space beyond the dividing wall. Grapes rested heavily among the green: some silver dark with neglect, others dusky red, a metal that Eluned did not recognise.

And through it all, untarnished, wound two golden amasen, the ram-horned snakes sacred to Cernunnos. They met at the junction of the gate's two halves, at the height of Griff's head as he peered through the hole framed by their open jaws.

"It's only trees," he announced.

"Circle's on this side, so why the gate?" Eleri asked. "Must be something important in there."

"Perhaps this side belongs to Sulis and that side is the Forest Lord's?" Eluned traced the pattern on one of the amasen's curving horns. "This is glorious, a masterwork. Aunt Arianne, I don't think this is a minor grove. Did this Dem Makepeace..."

Glancing back, Eluned realised their aunt hadn't followed them to the gate, but was instead standing back at the joining of the path. Veil and umbrella made it impossible to be sure, but she seemed to be looking up, not at the gate at all.

"Aunt Arianne?"

After a moment their aunt said: "It will indeed be interesting to see what Dem Makepeace has to say for himself. Does the key fit that lock, Griff?"

"No. Something round needs to go here, I think."

"Then shall we explore the rest of the building?" Aunt Arianne said, turning away.

Grimacing, Eluned followed obediently, but lagged behind to study the worn shapes etched on the standing stones, and the delicious shadows made by the serrated leaves and plump thistle heads.

Not reliable, and sadly superficial. Their unfailingly-blunt mother had said that the one time Eluned had asked about their aunt, and Eluned had been puzzled by the description in the months since Arianne Seaforth had come into their lives. But anyone who could walk away from that gate as if it held no more interest than a chain link fence definitely lacked something.

Quickening her step, Eluned chased after Eleri and Griff, and raced with them through receiving rooms, kitchen, a wine cellar, sitting rooms, bath and bedrooms and a long attic punctuated by dormer windows. The rooms were plain compared to that magnificent hall, but nicely put together and with a comfortable selection of aging furniture swathed in dust cloths. Most rooms featured large windows looking south, and every time they pulled back curtains or threw open shutters they were treated to a view of hidden trees, handily sheltered from the summer's scorching breezes by high walls. The dappled light made wonderful patterns across the attic floor.

"I can see part of the Great Barrows," Eluned said, as she examined the fastening of one of the windows. "We'll be able to hear the solstice singing and see the triskelion without going outside at all."

"Maybe two blocks away, or three?" As Eluned opened the window, Griff climbed up on the wide sill and craned not to see the barrows, but over the highest branches of the space below. "The warehouses look old, but the wall looks older. They built a wall around this place, and later added the warehouses to hide it? But there's only trees and the standing stones. I can't see anything else down there."

"Plenty of walled groves about," Eleri said, less interested in the view than poking about the long attic's collection of old furniture, boxes, and trunks. "Pack all this down one end, make an excellent workroom."

"So this is home now?" Griff leaned out to inspect the spread of windows below him critically.

"Maybe?" Eluned rubbed her shoulder, then shrugged despite the burning points of pain. "Let's go find Aunt Arianne and see what she wants to do."

SEVEN

They found their aunt on the first floor, sifting through a pigeonhole desk. Even indoors she wore her hat and veil, and Eluned thought it an appropriate underlining of her status as stranger to the family.

"Feel free to pick bedrooms," Aunt Arianne said, turning toward them. "If we concentrate on getting the dust out of those, and part of the kitchen, that should be enough to go on with until Dem Makepeace deigns to let me know whether this constitutes some form of alternative employment, or is merely his idea of a meeting place."

"Could anyone be that silly?" Griff asked.

"Never underestimate any person's capacity to ignore the convenience of others."

Aunt Arianne stepped toward the open window. Eluned didn't need to see her aunt's face to recognise surprise, and narrowly beat Griff and Eleri in crossing to look out.

The wall dividing the hidden grove in two was not as tall as the outer one, but still rose higher than the first floor. The well-spaced trees allowed Eluned an almost clear view of the top of the wall, and the row of half a dozen glossy black birds.

"They're watching us." Griff, who tolerated very little that was furred or feathered, moved back from the sill, and even Eleri shifted uneasily.

"Crows or ravens?" Aunt Arianne asked.

Unless one took flight, Eluned couldn't be more than half certain. "They're very quiet. Crows hardly ever shut up."

These didn't speak at all. They perched in a close group, their only movement an occasional head bob or settling of feathers. People were forever pointing to passing crows or ravens and spouting rubbish about the Morrigan watching, or Odin's spies. This was the first time Eluned had believed it.

Griff tugged Eluned's sleeve. "But why would any—"

A blur of green struck the row of observers, and five crows launched skyward, a riot of wings and harsh cries. The sixth was gone. Gasping, Eluned craned to see, spotting only a lone feather spiralling down. The body—presuming there was one—had to be on the far side of that dividing wall.

"More than trees, then."

Wondering if Aunt Arianne had maintained that light, amused tone even while a vampire nearly killed her, Eluned said: "Unless it *was* a tree. It looked leafy."

"Perhaps." Aunt Arianne turned abruptly away, crossing to pull the dustcover off a high-backed armchair tucked in the far corner of the office. Sitting down heavily she added: "Another question for Dem Makepeace."

"But why would anyone be spying on us?" Griff asked doggedly, from the position by the door where he'd retreated. "Do you think it's Them?"

'They' were the unknowns behind Mother and Father's deaths. But Eluned, reaching to close the window, shook her head. "If it was Them, we'd surely have noticed birds hanging about before now." She began folding the panels of the interior window shutter back into place.

"Something to do with the grove," Eleri said. "No sign before."

"Maybe." With the room now restored to stuffy gloom, Eluned turned to their aunt. "You're getting worse."

"So it would appear." Aunt Arianne lifted off her hat and veil. "Don't worry: I'll give fair warning if I develop an urge to bite."

Griff giggled, but Eluned was focused on practicalities. "Vampires drink blood if they're hurt by the sun. Do you think eating something would help?"

"That's possible." Aunt Arianne fished in the flat pouch laced to her day belt. "Shall we anticipate lunch? Bring enough food to tide us over until tomorrow, and some soap. See if they have salve for your shoulder, as well."

Eluned took the coin purse without commenting on this, but Eleri spoke up:

"Needs a new arm, not salve."

"Can she not have both? I've budgeted for necessities, so don't hesitate to tell me what's required. It's luxuries that will need to be postponed until I've settled the question of employment."

"Will give you a list," Eleri said promptly, and led the way out of the room, her attention clearly diverted to her design for a replacement arm. But as they opened the door into the vestibule, she returned to less technical matters.

"What did he say to you? That Carstairs? You've been different towards the Aunt since."

Eluned didn't answer immediately, not quite able to explain even to Eleri the anger and frustration she'd struggled with ever since Mother and Father died. She did not like nor want to admit to the roiling at the back of her thoughts, the longing to find and hurt, to *demolish* whoever had taken their parents away. The police's quick dismissal of the idea of murder had left her seething, and the slow steps of their search had been like fingernails down her spine, working her anger into tighter and tighter knots. For a while she'd almost hated Aunt Arianne for not once crying, for being the person they were stuck with instead of Mother and Father.

"Dem Carstairs said Aunt Arianne nearly died," she admitted. "And asked me to look after her."

"She's supposed to be looking after us," Griff pointed out, emerging into the street and frowning at three men gawking from the entrance of the next warehouse down. "She hasn't even asked why we were expelled."

Eluned took care to nod politely before turning in the opposite direction and striding toward the corner. The rising wind tugged at her hair and shendy, and she gazed determinedly ahead.

"It's not all that important why. We're not going back there. Besides, the kind of person Aunt Arianne is doesn't matter to me nearly as much as who I am. What does it say about me that it keeps surprising her when I notice she's in pain?"

"Says you're observant," Eleri replied. "Take your point—no value in being at war—but not going to sit about while the Aunt chases after this Alban woman. Should be working on that mannequin."

"No, I agree with her there." Aunt Arianne had refused to allow Eleri to even unpack their grandfather's mannequin. "If those sphinx statues are hunting the artificial fulgite, then recharging it or trying to release charge from it might draw their attention."

"Do nothing? Stupid."

"She's going to ask her vampire about it," Griff put in.

"Him? Connections to the palace and to a grove? Investigating the wind storms? Could even be one of Them."

"If he is, he'll be able to order Aunt Arianne to Tell Everything anyway," Eluned said. "Besides, he already thinks she's connected to the sphinxes somehow, and if he's involved in the rest, he'll know about the fulgite." A far from satisfactory situation, but there was nothing they could do about it.

They turned the corner into a full gale, roaring down a long row of warehouses on one side, and terraces the other. The morning windstorm.

"What we *can* do is see whether anyone else has been investigating haunted or unresponsive fulgite," Eluned went on, struggling to be heard. "You'll have to visit at least one workshop putting together the new arm. There's a lot we could find out."

"Like how much it would be to buy one of those dragonflies," Griff said, and they discussed this delightful if unlikely prospect for all of the windy walk down the long boundary of their unexpected back garden.

The street that ran behind the Deep Grove was much wider, lined with grander buildings, and busy with a flow of through-traffic. Directly opposite, buildings framed the northernmost entrance to the Great Barrows, while the nearest corner of the crossroads held a cluster of stores centred round a grocer's.

"Cobbler and baker, and a teashop across the road," Griff said. "Not bad. D'you think they'd sell the makings of a kite here, Ned?"

"I think kites probably count as luxuries. And there's so much in that house that we might have enough for a dozen kites and not know it."

"Not ours," Eleri said. "Last Keeper died and all her things were packed up, left there. Why?"

"No heirs, perhaps?" Eluned suggested, then quieted as they turned to climb the double step into the grocers', and discovered a crowd. There was scarcely room in the customers' area of the store for them to slip in at the back out of the gale.

"...to be the new Keeper," an elderly woman was saying authoratively. "The Moonfire Feast is less than a year from now. Dem Comfrey can hardly do that himself, so it only makes sense that he's appointed a replacement for Dama Fulbright."

"But another of the stone blood?" a portly man asked. "That's far from likely. Are you certain, young Nabah?"

"Clothing that covered her completely, a veiled hat and an umbrella. In this heat, what does that mean but vampire?"

The self-assured voice belonged to the Daughter of Lakshmi, her orange and yellow sari barely visible through the small crowd. Eluned exchanged a glance with Eleri, thinking it would be best to step back out, but then a single voice rose clear above the murmur of discussion.

"Aunt Arianne's not a vampire. She's only bound to one."

It was one of Griff's special pleasures to make unexpected pronouncements, and he did not quail as nearly a dozen people turned to stare.

The elderly woman, her daybelt a most impressive piece of tooled leather with many dangling pouches, produced a muted bark of laughter. "Never was curiosity so swiftly rewarded," she said. "My pardon, children." She added a conspiratorial smile. "Not that I won't push for more: do you mean that your aunt is bound to Dem Comfrey?"

"Someone called Makepeace. He sent her a key." Griff, still wearing the key on its knotted shoelace, displayed it proudly.

"Indeed! This is grand news. Welcome to Lamhythe, young damini. I am Reswen Chelwith, Warden of the Borough."

Her gaze, like that of the crowd, had gone from Griff to Eleri and Eluned behind him, and inevitably to Eluned's right arm. This was a progression Eluned was entirely used to, although she could never train herself not to notice it. Instead she hefted her glass shield, and smiled politely as Eleri introduced them all before looking firmly toward the tall girl behind the shop counter.

"What can I get you, dama?" the girl asked obligingly, just as the man behind the opposite counter—one dedicated to postal services—cleared his throat.

"Customers only, please!" he called out, in a surprisingly deep voice for such a stretched and skinny man. "Make room, make room."

In excited good humour the crowd decamped, leaving only the Tennings and the Daughter of Lakshmi, who produced a letter and a coin for a stamp.

Taking a relieved breath, Eluned smiled her thanks at the shop girl, who said: "Not that I'm not madly curious myself, mind you. I'm Melly Ktai. That's my Dad. Welcome to Lamhythe."

"Thanks."

Now that the crowd had cleared out, Eluned's attention had been caught by the rows of gleaming jars on the shelves directly behind Melly. Through the glass she recognised old favourites—sugared almonds, humbugs, marzipan mice—but many more colourful shapes.

"We'll have three of everything over there," Griff said immediately.

"We'll have thruppence worth mixed," Eluned said, equally firmly. "And..." She briefly scanned the selection of things that were not sweets, and listed enough to cover their needs at least for a couple of days, conscious of the weight of her aunt's purse. The windstorms had done terrible things to prices.

Melly's father came around and reached down one or two things from the highest shelves, although Melly was almost tall enough to manage. The pair moved with a dancer's ease around each other, almost identical but for height, and Melly's cloudy hair puffing out in three distinct triangles, while her father's was so short it was barely visible against the rich dark brown of his scalp.

"Ned!" Griff said imperatively. "Get these as well!" He had found a collection of illustrated maps—four sections of London with miniatures of all the buildings beautifully drawn.

"You'll have to ask Aunt Arianne," Eluned said firmly. If he was given his way, Griff would buy a dozen atlases' worth of maps every day.

"Seen any of the folies yet?" Melly asked, as she knotted string around their freshly-wrapped purchases. "I only saw one the once, back when Dama Fulbright was still alive. At least, I'm sure that's what it was."

"Don't know what that is," Eleri replied, as Eluned asked: "Is it something green, and fast?"

"That'd be them," Melly said. "It's good luck to see them. Unless, of course, you're in the Deep Grove without permission."

"In which case, very bad luck indeed," Dem Ktai said. As his daughter turned to make change, he handed Griff a gleaming toffee apple, one eyelid dropping. "A turn of fortune would be most welcome."

Griff promptly hid the apple behind his back, but his clear elation won a puzzled glance when Melly handed over their coin. As Eluned led the way out, swinging parcels by their strings, she heard the girl's voice lift in an exasperated "Da!", but was distracted from more by Dama Chelwith, waiting at the bottom of the steps.

"Do let your aunt know I've mustered the Wings," the woman said. "And that we'll be down directly. After eight years without so much as an airing, I can imagine the state of Forest House. Knowing Dem Comfrey, he won't have put an ounce of effort into preparing the place."

"All dust and cobwebs," Griff said agreeably, pausing in a stout effort to bite into the side of his apple. "What happens at this Moonfire Feast?"

"Why, the Queen and the princesses—Sulis in the form of the Suleviae—come to the Deep Grove," Dama Chelwith said, whisking a smear of dust from his shoulder, and then ruffling his hair. "It's very important there be a Keeper able to let them in."

Beaming, she nodded at Eluned and Eleri, and then turned, waving a hand at someone on the far side of the crossroads. Off to organise the Wings—the county volunteer force—to clean the house of the Keeper of the Deep Grove.

"What happens if this Makepeace person really does only want to meet Aunt Arianne here?" Griff asked.

"Then he'll have a clean house, for when he does appoint a new Keeper." Eluned shrugged, ignoring the throb of skin beneath straps. "We can't change any of that."

She glanced toward Vine Street. Ahead the Daughter of Lakshmi marched, back straight, resolutely not looking in their direction. Only one of the many who seemed to consider their arrival an event. "I think the bigger question is what happens if we stay."

Eleri clicked her tongue, impatient but resigned.

"Better get back, warn the Aunt. In case that urge to bite has come on."

ooOoo

Forest House was large, but the dozens of people who flooded there in response to Dama Chelwith's summons made a short afternoon's work of the cleaning and minor repairs required. The grove itself needed the most attention, and Eluned helped pick up fallen branches and pull up the thistle thicket.

The stones they exposed were thin slabs, uneven in height and shape, and etched with symbols too faded to read. Once the bulk of the crowd had departed, Eluned returned to trace her fingers over the worn faces. She was puzzling out the shape of a triple luck spiral when a group of new arrivals approached with apologetic smiles.

Retreating through the trees, Eluned watched as a woman circled the newly-cleared stones, reaching up to touch the crown of each as she passed, then stepped reverently within. Stopping in the precise centre, she raised her face to the fading sky, tilting her body back, and letting her arms hang loose and relaxed. Eluned wondered what she prayed for. Most prayers to someone as vast as Sulis only reinforced personal or territorial allegiance, but in the stronger circles sometimes a small blessing might come your way, a tiny piece of luck.

The grass and dirt at that centre spot was already distinctly flattened, for the woman was far from the first to pray to the sun in a grove of the Horned King.

"A place where Sulis and Cernunnos meet."

Eluned blinked, then turned to her aunt, who was veiled once more, but had left her umbrella behind now that the sun had dropped below the shielding walls.

"The circle isn't quite in the Deep Grove," Aunt Arianne went on. "That's the area beyond the gate, dedicated to Cernunnos. Every twenty-five years, the Suleviae come to renew the Treaty of the Oak. This is one of the most important groves in Prytennia."

Looking back at the circle as the woman swayed and dropped to one knee, Eluned said: "Did anyone explain what the Keeper's supposed to do, exactly?"

"Let people in. Keep people out. Strictly speaking, it appears that the Keeper's only true duty is to open the gate to the Suleviae every twenty-five years, but some public access to the circle is usually permitted. Dama Fulbright inherited the position from her mother, and did not care for it. She allowed the public in to the circle once a year if the neighbourhood was lucky. According to Dama Chelwith, at any rate. Others have insisted it was every month, every week, every day."

Aunt Arianne followed a narrow path between the trees and the kitchen windows, and stopped to survey the service passage leading to the street. The outer door to this had been concealed by more posters, and it opened only from the inside. A wholly practical space, it featured a freshly restrung clothes line, a collection of stone bottles, two bins, and, currently, many trodden fragments of thistle.

A shrunken, white-haired man was busily sweeping this last away, but stopped when he spotted them, and propped his broom against the passage wall so he could come to greet them.

"Dama Seaforth. You will keep the Grove open a little longer, won't you? So those held up by their professions can visit?"

"While the light holds," Aunt Arianne replied. "After that, it will be up to Dem Makepeace."

As the man retreated, Aunt Arianne tilted her head back, her veil swaying. At first Eluned thought that she, too, was praying, but her stance was wrong, and following what seemed to be the direction of her gaze, Eluned spotted a curious patch on a branch near the top of the garden's dividing wall. Not mistletoe, as she first guessed, but a finer, denser clump of leaves, tucked flat against the branch. Tiny spots of colour caught the eye: flowers or berries among the foliage.

"Why is it interesting?" Eluned asked.

"Because it has a heartbeat."

Two startling revelations in the one serene comment. Eluned responded to the more immediate. "That's a folie?"

"Most likely."

"It's so small! The way they've been talking about these things, I was expecting something more impressive."

"The most dangerous thing I ever met didn't exactly make a strong first impression."

Aunt Arianne dropped her hand from where it had crept beneath her veil, then walked away. The clump of leaves above didn't so much as quiver, but Eluned still found it difficult to turn her back on it. She took a long breath, and—as she sometimes did when particularly nervous—activated her right arm and made the precise movements of her shoulder to bend the artificial arm as if to applaud. Meeting the hand with her left, she pressed skin to metal joints and beautifully-carved wood, and closed her eyes against fear.

Then she returned her arm to resting mode and hurried to catch up with her aunt, who was inspecting the freshly-polished gate blocking entry to the rest of the garden.

"You can hear heartbeats?"

"Blood. I am enormously aware of blood."

"That's not a very reassuring thing to say, Aunt Arianne."

Her aunt laughed, and turned away from the coiling metal snakes. "I am being very grim and portentous, aren't I? I shall balance myself thinking up intricate plans of revenge, should Dem Makepeace leave me to pass some point of no return. How are you feeling?"

"I like the house," Eluned replied, sidestepping the question.

"So do I. Your sister has been rearranging the attic into a workroom, somewhat hampered by Griff's attempts to discover kite-making materials."

The long attic, when they reached it, had been dusted and then divided into two distinct halves. Anything resembling a bench had been cleared and placed down the right end, and all the other furniture crammed into the left half. This done, Eleri had joined Griff in unearthing the attic's hidden treasures, ably assisted by Melly Ktai, the Daughter of Lakshmi called Nabah, and a handful of others closer to Griff's age. Eluned was always impressed by how her brother and sister could start chatting away to people.

"No," Griff was saying. "Dem Makepeace was chasing the monster when it fell through the ceiling. And when the monster nearly killed him, he killed Aunt, nearly. And bound her to keep her from dying, which meant that she couldn't be bound to Lord Msrah. Then he didn't even stay to finish the binding properly, just sent her that key. Is he always like that?"

Melly Ktai shrugged. "Like we'd know? He talked to Dama Chelwith when Dama Fulbright died, asked her to have the house shut up, but otherwise he's like the folies: we all know they're there, but hardly anyone's seen them."

"Still the real Keeper?" Eleri asked. "How long?"

"Grandama says he used to come to Forest House parties, back when there were lots of Fulbrights," offered the youngest of the helpers, a boy around ten.

"And he'd been Keeper before there were Fulbrights there," added a slightly bigger girl. "He's *old* old."

Griff, excavating a chest of old-fashioned clothes, held up a girdle curiously, then said: "What sort of vampire is he, Aunt? You said he wasn't a Thoth-den."

"No, not Thoth," Aunt Arianne said as—to Griff's obvious glee—the other occupants of the attic spun to look at her. "Your trunks have been delivered, and are waiting in your rooms. Re-pack these first, and wash for dinner."

With unusual abruptness Aunt Arianne retreated down the stair, and Eluned supposed that the attic, bathed in a lovely sunset, was still too bright for her. Forest House was definitely not arranged for the convenience of vampires.

"Didn't answer the question," Eleri said.

"I'm not sure she knows." Eluned picked up a red pleated shendy and tossed it into the nearest trunk, well aware that Eleri and Griff wouldn't remember being told to clean up when there were more interesting subjects taking their attention.

"Ma'at," said the girl called Nabah. She also stooped to collect a piece of clothing, and folded it neatly. "My mother checked at Demar House when first we heard of this vampire who is the true Keeper. Dem Makepeace is one of only five Ma'at vampires in Prytennia, and has been on the Register of Blood since twenty-nine fifty-five."

"Over two hundred and fifty years old?" Melly clicked her tongue. "I wonder if Ma'at's a particularly strong line?"

"Or if the Aunt's vampire is close to becoming stone." Eleri ignored the re-packing in favour of examining an old lantern.

"I didn't even know there was a Ma'at line," Eluned said, and poked Griff until he started helping to clean up. "What can they do?"

"Ma'at is Order, isn't she?" Melly said. "And she weighs the spirits of the Egyptian dead. And Ma'at's wings protect, of course. Maybe it's something to do with protection—that would go with being Keeper."

"Ma'at vampires can tell when you're lying."

A boy a few years older than Eluned strolled from the stair to the clear area set aside for Eleri's workroom, and Eluned reflected that Forest House was going to be a difficult place to live if the whole neighbourhood thought themselves free to wander about as much as they pleased. But it was an unusual day, and after all the front doors were wide open.

"Only that?" Griff asked. "How boring."

"Very much so," the boy agreed, ignoring how they all stared at him. He looked out of place, dressed formally in a tunic and ankle-length pleated shendy of pristine white. "An incredibly dull lot. They usually end up as judges. The occasional detective."

He started to say something else, but paused, stepping closer to the line of open windows. Eluned immediately crossed to the nearest.

"They're back?" Griff hurried to join her. "This is the third time. Did you see them after lunch, Ned?"

Eluned shook her head, trying to make out the dividing wall. The south-western sky might be cherry-painted, but during the climb to the attic the grove had been swallowed by shadow. The one clear point below was the path up to the near edge of the circle, where a family were nervously heading toward the light of Forest House.

"I can only sort of see the top of the wall," Griff complained. "How many are there? There were five after lunch, and there should only be four..."

Griff fell silent, gripping Eluned's shirt. No-one spoke. Below was shadow, stillness, and something on the dividing wall. Not crows or ravens, but a great mounded shape. A momentary gleam of gold had led Eluned's eye to it, as if the night had blinked.

Fascinated, and also reluctant to risk drawing the thing's attention, Eluned remained as still as possible. The line of open windows felt like an exposed throat.

"The Aunt."

After a confused moment, Eluned again peered over the lip of the roof. One of the people who had gone inside was leading Aunt Arianne toward the circle. But then Aunt Arianne stopped short, head turning in the direction of that waiting bulk upon the wall, and she said something to send the other person back. Alone, without her hat and veil, she looked tiny and defenceless, and Eluned drew breath for a warning.

"No, don't call out to her." The older boy had moved to the central windows of the attic. "This place has a reputation for a reason."

"People know not to trespass, sure." Melly had caught up an old walking stick and held it at ready. "Still no reason to stand here and watch."

She, too, drew her breath to shout, and then let it out in a gasp as the grove exploded into movement. Branches whipped and snapped, and there was a low rumbling noise, followed by a hard thud. Details were impossible to make out, but the intensity of violent battle was clear. Eluned put her arm around Griff as he pressed into her, and Eleri tucked in protectively on his far side as something bulky clawed upward to the roof and bounded away in a scattering of tile.

Smaller shapes appeared briefly on the very rim of the roof, then dropped back down into the grove, while a distant shout suggested the creature had leapt to the street on the far side of the warehouses.

"Grandama was coming to collect us!" one of the younger children cried, pelting off, and they all streamed after her down Forest House's series of stairs, slowing only when they reached the landing on the first floor.

Dama Chelwith, obviously just arrived, turned to look up at them, and then held out her arms. The younger children rushed down, but Eleri and Eluned stopped with Nabah and Melly, staring. Aunt Arianne was walking back inside, followed by the boy in white.

"He jumped out the window!" Griff gasped, catching them up. "That's Aunt's vampire!"

EIGHT

Rian was too relieved that he'd shown up to be annoyed or frightened when the so-called Comfrey Makepeace dropped without warning from the sky. Two days contemplating vampirism had made stark many things she did not want to give up, sunlight being only the beginning.

"Do you always arrive from above?"

"Do you always have a trail of powerful creatures turning up in your orbit?" he asked, voice as languid and dreaming as it had been in Lord Msrah's library. "What was it that your collection of children were talking about that comes in groups to sit on the wall?"

"Ravens."

"Oh." His tone turned dismissive. "That'll be the Oak lot. They never shut up about who should have the role of Keeper here."

"Lovely." Rian frowned at the scene in the Hall, with excited children pelting down stairs, and a collection of neighbours clustering toward Dama Chelwith.

"Dem Comfrey!" Dama Chelwith, hands on the heads of two of the children, smiled warmly. "A most timely arrival."

"Good to see you again, Reswen. Can you arrange those still here into groups, so they're not alone when returning to their homes? And let the local constabulary know. I doubt this visitor is interested in passers-by, but there's always the possibility of a chance encounter. I'll look to see if it's still in the area."

He walked back into the grove, while Rian turned her attention to Griff, bright-faced from running, and urgently tugging her sleeve.

"He said Ma'at vampires can tell when people are lying!" Griff whispered, then added in a louder voice: "Did you see? What was out there?"

"Something between a bull and a bear," Rian said, adding to Dama Chelwith: "Are attacks on the grove common?"

"I would say 'no'," Dama Chelwith replied, "but I'm afraid I have no real way of knowing whether there are many incidents such as this. The folies ably repel any who would enter by stealth or force."

"Would be no roof tiles left if that happened very often," Eleri said, trotting down the final set of stairs. "Maybe followed the vampire here."

"Perhaps." Rian smiled at the two girls trailing Eleri, ignoring their startled reaction to a close view of her unveiled face. "Thank you for all your help today. Hopefully it won't be so dramatic in the future."

"You didn't run away," said the girl she'd first seen coming out of the house opposite. "Weren't you frightened?"

"A little. But I could see how many folies there were." A dozen or more, for all that she'd been quite sure there'd been only one a short while earlier.

It took some time to clear the house, to send on their way people who wanted to speculate about monsters, and remark on the fact that she could see in the dark, and didn't she look young? The practice with the multiple front doors appeared to be to leave the small outer access door open, with a lantern in the vestibule, and as Dama Chelwith led her grandchildren off, Griff helpfully tested a bellpull that seemed to sound in all parts of the house.

"Go wash up now," Rian said, ushering him inside and closing the house door. "We'll talk over dinner."

"Do you think he'll come back?" Griff asked, so worked up he began spinning around his sisters. "Did he do— what does he have to do to make you not become a vampire?"

"I have no idea. I never knew there was more to it than an exchange of blood and ka."

"Hope he doesn't get eaten by a bear before the next step," Eleri observed.

"That *would* be awkward."

Rian left them to clatter back up one floor, and headed for the kitchen. The benefits of electrical wiring had not yet reached Lamhythe, but Forest House had otherwise been well maintained and fitted with modern conveniences before its closure. Dama Chelwith had even managed to arrange for the gas line to be reconnected and the geyser carefully checked over before it was lit. There was a scattering of fulquus-powered lamps, but the fulgite was missing, a discovery that had caused considerable embarrassment among the crowds of volunteers, and had warned Rian that the house was not necessarily so well-defended as the grove.

All this eager generosity would require some form of reciprocal gesture Rian decided, surveying a kitchen table laden with covered dishes. She totted up the likely cost of afternoon tea for an entire neighbourhood, then turned sharply at a faint sound.

Her reflection scattered among panes of glass, but the gas light was not so bright she couldn't see through to tree trunks. Nothing else. But her new awareness of blood made clear two tiny rivers in the branches above the windows. Having seen what they were capable of, Rian was not certain if she should find the folies' presence comforting, and noted absently that her hands were shaking.

That was not due to the garden battle. Instead it was a third presence, directly above her now, with a heartbeat much slower than any other she had felt. A slight and ancient creature descending the stairs.

Rian was not by nature inclined to nerves, but her hands would not still, so she busied them clearing the table, uncovering such dishes best eaten immediately, and searching out plates and glasses. Pride and simple common sense told her to set fear aside, to overcome the memory of teeth. She had gone to Sheerside House to become a meal for a vampire, and the extreme she had encountered was as much a part of the stone blood's existence as Lord Msrah's scheduled domesticity.

Standing at the head of the table, she met the eyes of her vampire.

A thousand years had produced quite a collection of portraits of the Wind's Dog. Rian had seen Vensium's, and Tylette's, and the mosaic at Salinae. All rather different images, but every one featuring a hollow-cheeked man with streaming black hair, a banner of darkness. Prytennia's infamous assassin and spy.

Rather than hidden death, this short, slender and tousle-haired youth called to mind a dreaming poet. He was far better dressed this time around, but there was still a weary calm about him, lightly mixed with derision.

Entirely without intending to, Rian raised her hands and clapped them together, producing a staccato beat. Astonished, she struggled to stop herself, then realised what was happening.

"Very funny."

"Hilarious." He allowed her hands to still. "And you'd give someone this control over you for a tidy yearly sum."

"For something I wanted, at least. I take it this means you've done whatever was needed to complete the binding?"

He didn't reply, but did *something*. Rian swayed, overwhelmed by a wave of dizziness. It felt like all her blood was running backward. Groping for the nearest chair, she dropped into it

"I've asserted control over the colony," he said, watching with a complete lack of sympathy as she gasped and shuddered. "An interesting sensation. Part of myself, sitting before me."

Refusing to lose her temper, Rian closed her eyes briefly, then managed to say: "You've never bound anyone before?"

"I've no interest in building a herd. Or keeping you as a pet. Forest House should sufficiently cover whatever income I can be said to have cost you."

This was excellent news. "How long before the binding wears?"

"One to two months, usually. We'll see what happens."

There was a note to this answer that she didn't like, and she studied him narrowly. "But?"

He lifted a shoulder. "The colony is at a self-sustaining level, dominant in your system. It's unlikely to diminish naturally."

In the pause that followed Rian could distinctly hear running feet, could sense the bright river that was Griff, racing not to miss out on any excitement. She thought of strawberries, and sex, and hoped the Wind's Dog would do her the favour of not dying in the near future.

"So I will inevitably become...a kind of vampire that can tell when people are lying?"

His expression changed, the smallest alteration, and for the first time Rian truly believed that this boy was Heriath, famous for dealing in death.

Then he tch-ed, and sat down at the opposite end of the table, dropping the air of menace—or perhaps simply hiding it once again behind the guise of something less dangerous. "That tedious prig told you."

"I was curious to see whether you would. And yet, I *can* tell if people are lying, sometimes."

"The heart beats faster. The liar's emotions intensify, are more controlled, or don't match the words. It's not so sure as the Ma'at line, who simply see lies as a colour. But more nuanced."

Aware of Griff's rapid approach, Rian said: "I'll keep that in mind," and philosophically abandoned any thought of giving him half-truths.

The Amon-Re line, that of Egypt's god of air and sun, was rumoured to possess all manner of gifts, but none were confirmed beyond the usual unnatural speed and strength, and the pharaoh's unique ability to command other stone blood. Makepeace—it would be simpler to call him that—had also done something to hold the sphinx in place. As his Bound, Rian would possess only a pale echo of his powers, but they would still be useful for her investigations.

"Did you catch it? Did you kill it?"

All bright enthusiasm, Griff approached her vampire with far less caution than Rian would prefer, but Makepeace didn't seem bothered, merely turning his head to study the boy.

"Should I have killed it? Would you have liked that?"

Griff, who had somehow managed to achieve scrubbed-pink cleanliness in less time than it would take Rian to walk to the bathroom, plucked at the seam of his shendy, but showed no other concern at the question.

"Well, I don't want it to come back," he explained. "*Could* you kill it? If all you can do is tell when people are lying?"

"I also hit quite hard," Makepeace said, as Eluned and Eleri arrived, less obviously excited, but almost as speedy as their brother. "And killing it wouldn't tell me why it was here, or what it wanted." He turned back to Rian. "Though perhaps you can answer that."

"Does that mean you didn't catch it?" Rian asked, and suspected from his lack of response that he had expected to, and was annoyed. "And no, I don't know either. I have at most some wide guesswork." She surveyed her small audience, then said: "Sit down, you three. We can talk while we eat."

Makepeace waited without comment as food was dispensed, but when Rian introduced the Tennings he said: "Is this something you want children involved with?"

"They were involved before I," Rian said. "Eluned, will you tell him the start of it?"

Eluned, however, had other points to cover first. Finely-sketched brows drawn together, she said: "How did you get here? The grove might be in shadow, but most of the streets weren't."

"Perhaps I've been here all along."

"What? Is there a secret room?" Griff stood up, clearly ready to race off to hunt for it. "It would be in the cellar, wouldn't it? Do you live down there?"

"Is he lying?" Eluned asked Rian, but Rian couldn't tell, and said so.

"Could have been nearby," Eleri said, frowning in response to Makepeace's faintly amused expression. "Or took an enclosed car."

"But *is* there a secret room?" Griff repeated.

"There's a safe hidden about somewhere, I know that," Makepeace said. "Though I haven't a clue where. What, then, is the start of it?"

"Fulgite," Eluned said. "Artificial fulgite."

NINE

She'd intended to shock him, but Eluned couldn't spot any reaction from this strange boy who was really an old man.

"What about it?" Dem Makepeace asked, when she didn't go on.

"That's what started it." Eluned had her glass shield well in hand, refusing to act hesitant before this dangerous stranger. "At the beginning of spring term our mother accepted a commission to investigate fulgite that was said to be haunted, and hardly ever released its charge. Mother's early research had been on charge drain, though she'd moved on to advanced automata control mechanisms." Eluned did not look down at the arm that had been the reason for the change. "We don't know who commissioned her, but we do know they gave her two pieces of fulgite, round, about this big."

She held up thumb and forefinger in a not quite closed circle.

"Whoever brought the fulgite to her wanted mother to find a way to make the charge release reliably, and create an automaton that did not rely on physical switches to activate movement."

Dem Makepeace propped his chin on one fist, waiting. Eluned glanced at Eleri, who took up the thread of the story.

"Mid-term break. Mother hadn't made any progress. Father had nearly completed the automaton, said the charge would release when he triggered functions. Never moved on its own. Mother asked me to create a small second automaton, one that could operate on a weaker charge. Gave me one of the round fulgite. Did that over the rest of spring term.   No result.   It never released charge that I could verify.   Then the—then Aunt Arianne came."

They'd been called to the head's office and left with a stranger with hair the same colour as Griff's and their father's. Nothing could be worse than that meeting.

"I was in Lutèce," Aunt Arianne said.   "Aedric and Eiliff's lawyer notified me by telegram. I reached Caerlleon two days after they had died, and by that time the Caerlleon coroner had already decided an inquest wasn't necessary, that it was a clear case of accident. They had been working on an industrial automaton, a top-heavy thing. A rope was not properly fastened, bolts had been loose, the bracing had failed and the thing had simply toppled onto them. There were three other people in the house: Aedric's apprentice, and two day staff, a cook and a housekeeper. It was Monday, and the apprentice had only just arrived for the week, and was having breakfast with the day staff in the kitchen when they heard the noise of the fall."

Aunt Arianne glanced out the window, then back at the vampire. "My brother and sister-by-marriage took safety measures very seriously, and I did not believe they could have been so impossibly careless, but I wasn't certain something was wrong until I brought the children back for the funeral."

"Commissions Book was missing.   And the special automaton."   Eleri's voice flattened in remembered irritation.   "Fulgite was a secret, so Willa—the apprentice—had been told automaton simply a show piece, but she should have noticed the Commissions Book. Said automaton must have been completed and collected, and mother must have put the Commissions Book away somewhere. Stupid."

"All our parents' work was recorded there," Eluned explained.   "They always kept it in the same place, and besides, we searched everywhere for it."

"Someone else had too!" Griff put in. "Searched. They'd been in our rooms."

The vampire didn't even blink. "The world-shaking discovery of a method of creating artificial fulgite is announced on an almost weekly basis. Unless some hoodwinked investors tracked your parents down, it's as likely a motive for murder as a bottle of Dama Wilder's Patented Cure-All."

Eluned stood up. "Our parents weren't cheats," she said. Vampire or not, he had no right to suggest anything of the sort.

"He knows that, Eluned." Aunt Arianne pushed her plate away. "There's a wide difference between finding a way to unlock stored power, and creating an appearance of stored power. I didn't know the exact nature of the commission Eiliff and Aedric had been working on—the children only told me that an automaton was missing. But when I prepared an accounting of the business, there were two large cash deposits that suggested someone had provided funding they didn't want traced. I could find no documentation whatsoever. Aedric had recorded only the fact of the deposits, against the name 'F Project', but there was no contract, no schemata, no correspondence. Every clue to identity was missing."

"When they were first commissioned, Mother and Father were pleased because the payment was good," Eluned said. "They didn't tell us anything until the mid-term break, but I remember the day they came back from the first meeting, and put all this money in the cash box to be banked. That was before we left for the beginning of spring term. When she put the money away, mother said that it would be an interesting challenge, and she'd have to 'thank Lyndsey'. Then there's this."

Pressing two sections of her right arm exposed a storage slot—for Eluned always liked to have a secret space in her arms—and she drew out paper, curled into a tube. The vampire accepted it with lifted eyebrows, and unrolled three sheets: a sketch of the missing automaton as they'd last seen it, and two envelopes that had been flattened out, then decorated on both sides with minutely detailed sketches of rooftops, all chimneys and gabling.

"Mother always gave envelopes to Griff," Eluned said. "Because he uses up so much paper."

"Date on the first sketch is the day they went to that meeting," Eleri added. "Second is the mid-term break. Hold them up to the light."

The vampire silently obeyed, and even sitting a seat down from him Eluned could clearly see the translucent shape of a tower with outstretched wings.

"Took us a while to track down who that belonged to," Eleri said, with the satisfaction of the one who had been successful.

Dem Makepeace lowered the envelopes, looking down the length of the table at Aunt Arianne.

"You sold yourself to Msrah on the strength of a watermark?"

"It was the best lead."

"A watermark." The vampire looked like he was trying—not very hard—to stop himself from laughing. "You realise that whoever commissioned your automaton would have no reason to steal it? That there may be a second party involved?"

"That's a strong possibility. But knowing more about the first could lead us to rivals, saboteurs, or at least reasons. Besides, the desire for secrecy suggests a strong motive to tidy up loose ends, and it's very odd that whoever it is hasn't inquired after Eiliff's progress. Griff is quite certain about when he was given the first envelope, and the second clearly arrived while the children were away at school, during the period a second cash deposit was made. Other than a passing reference to someone called Lyndsey, the only information we have about Them—about whoever commissioned this—is the fact that their payments came in envelopes marked with the crest of Sheerside House."

Dem Makepeace muttered something under his breath, then said: "Where is the second automaton?"

Aunt Arianne left to fetch it, and the vampire propped his head back on his fist, idly turning over Griff's pictures.

"You could ask Willa questions and know whether she was lying," Griff said, getting up to search the covered dishes for sweets. It was typical of Griff that he would chat to the vampire like he was simply an interesting neighbourhood boy. He might back away from a bird, but even what had happened to Aunt Arianne wouldn't faze Griff when it came to a person, unless that person was behaving in a way that made Griff uncomfortable.

Dem Makepeace at least seemed fairly tolerant—or not hungry at the moment. "That's the assistant? Do you think she's lying about something?"

"She was lying about who finished the last of the treacle tart. And she's lying about something that happened after the funeral." Griff triumphantly lifted a wedge of nut-studded cake, and turned to enjoy their expressions.

"What?" Eluned exchanged a glance with Eleri, who clearly shared her surprise. "What do you mean?"

"When we went back at the end of spring term, and Aunt had us pack up the bits she was letting us keep, Willa came around. She wanted to know what Aunt was going to do with all of Mother and Father's things. Said she wanted to buy pieces to add to her tool set."

"More likely wanted schematics," Eleri said. "Not creative."

"Whatever she wanted, what was she going to pay for it with? Willa never had any money, and she got taken on by Theyan's Workshop. They're room and board only for the first year. She said that herself when father took her on."

Griff's prodigious memory could be more than useful, though he also tended to remember tiny grudges, like who had the last slice of a treacle tart made for the New Year's Feasting. And he'd obviously hugged this fragment of news to his chest all through the first half of summer term, waiting for the right moment.

"Tools are a good investment," Eleri said, unimpressed. "Probably borrowed money for them." Eleri certainly would have if she'd been able, and had yet to forgive Aunt Arianne for not keeping their parents' workshop intact.

"She was asking for someone else," Griff said, with complete confidence. "Even I could tell that."

The vampire said: "Tell me more about how these automata were to be constructed."

Eleri did that, producing a flood of technical detail on how their parents had been trying to create an arm for Eluned that was as fully responsive as a normal arm.

"I can currently trigger a few set movements," Eluned added, her glass shield steady. "Position one, position two, hand grip. Nowhere near precise control. Our Thoth-den had told Mother and Father that my upper arm still contained all the...the body's telegraph wires that carried messages to the missing part of my arm. If they could find some way of reading the signal, they could give me greater control."

"Did they succeed?"

"Not yet," Eleri said, as Aunt Arianne returned, carrying a long box with a square tin sitting on top. "Not reading the commands of the body. More progress on the other half of the problem: an array of movements triggered by a flow of fulquus. Used that."

"So the commission, substantively, was for an automaton that treats fulgite as a mind capable of issuing commands?" Dem Makepeace had lost the lazy note to his voice.

Aunt Arianne, lifting the mannequin from its box, said: "Eleri passed this to me when I visited on my way to

Sheerside. I didn't open it until my first night there, when I heard it trying to get out."

The mannequin, familiar for the many weeks Eleri had worked on it, stayed upright when Aunt Arianne propped it in a sitting position against the box, the small head with its painted monocle and moustache tilted quizzically to one side.

Explaining how she'd seen it move, and removed the fulgite, Aunt Arianne opened the tin and fished inside, lifting out a purple sphere. She looked down at it, brows rising, then crossed to Dem Makepeace and held it out to him.

"I don't think these monsters are chasing me about. I think they're chasing that."

She dropped it into his hand, and there was an odd quiet moment as Dem Makepeace simply sat there, the fulgite resting in the palm of his hand. The whole room felt strangely more focused, as if an unexpected light had flickered into life.

Then the stillness passed, and he put the fulgite on the table and said: "You were surprised when you touched this. Why?"

"I could hear a noise. Distant and strange. I thought it was wind at first, but..."

Aunt Arianne shook her head, eyeing the fulgite as if she expected it to move. Dem Makepeace put out one finger and pushed the crystal lightly, so that it rolled a couple of inches before curving to one side around the nub that stopped it from being a perfect sphere.

"Whether this is the target, or you are, the decision to put you here seems to have been a good one," he said, suddenly brisk. "Fit that back into your toy, and we'll see how much of the Keeper role I'm handing over to you."

"So there's more to it than letting people into the Grove?" Aunt Arianne asked, as Eleri moved to obey.

"Not necessarily. But I can't simply give you the key, and Cernunnos often rejects, and has been known to strike down particularly unworthy petitioners." He offered Aunt Arianne a provoking sort of smile. "If you don't consider yourself equal to the risk, you can use the house and the Keeper's income until I find someone to truly act in the role."

Aunt Arianne gave no hint of being daunted. "Do you consider yourself equal to three able assistants?"

He glanced at Eluned, Eleri and Griff. They stared back at him, and though there was no reason whatsoever for him to replace Aunt Arianne as guardian if something happened to her, they all pictured it, and no-one looked pleased.

Then Dem Makepeace shrugged irritably. "The danger's probably only significant if you should be, say, a disguised Roman with a pocket full of curse tablets," he admitted. "There's a good chance of being ignored, though."

"Then by all means let us resolve that question. But first a few of my own."

While they tidied away dinner, Aunt Arianne asked more about being Keeper. Having settled whether she would be able to come and go from Forest House as much as she liked, and who she was obliged to let in, she said:

"Lord Msrah recognised that sphinx. Did you?"

Still busy propping up his chin, Dem Makepeace said: "Any vampire who has made the Century Passage knows those sphinxes."

"Century Passage?" Griff turned from picking at one of the covered dishes. "That's the pilgrimage vampires make to Egypt?"

"Pilgrimage is a very poor word. It's a compulsion. After a century carrying stone blood, Hatshepsu's control asserts itself. You're called to the Djeser-Djeseru, Hatshepsu's temple at Thebes. If you don't go present yourself, there's all sorts of increasingly debilitating consequences."

"Even though she's been stone for centuries?"

"Even though. Patmahset doesn't admit to making the call on his Pharaoh's behalf, but since the jot isn't paid until after the Century Passage, he has a rather large motive for ensuring it happens."

Patmahset was the Nesweth—the king of Egypt—and the oldest known living vampire, raised not long before Hatshepsu went to stone. Technically Hatshepsu was still ruler—called Pharaoh in much the same way Prytennian people talked about "the Crown"—because Egyptians had a second life before they reached their Otherworld. But there was a lot of argument about whether Hatshepsu would have passed through that stage by now, and either become a god or gone to the Field of Rushes. She certainly hadn't Answered.

"Do you think the Nesweth sent the sphinxes?" Eluned asked.

"They're not his to send. The two sphinxes who turned up at Sheerside are the ones that guard the passage to Hatshepsu's receiving chamber. There's plenty of sphinxes at Hatshepsu's temple, but that pair are distinct—both smaller than the ones lining the entry avenue, and with those enamelled wings. And the breasts," he added, dryly. "Being within reach, they've achieved quite a gloss over the last millennia or so."

"Can all Egypt's sphinxes come to life?" Griff was agog. "Are they like the clay guards of Judah?"

"They're not known for it. But that pair were dedicated as shabti. Those are servants given to the soul for use when it reaches the Field of Rushes. Not that I've ever seen any shabti moving before, either, but in theory they carry out physical tasks in the Otherworld on behalf of the Third Life."

"You believe Hatshepsu herself sent those sphinxes— and the windstorms—to Prytennia? To chase pieces of fulgite?" Aunt Arianne sounded outright incredulous.

"I find shabti stirring from the tombs to chase fulgite that might control automatons...a ridiculous muddle. But dangerous in possible consequences. Fortunately very few saw that pair at Sheerside, and the detailed description has been suppressed." He stood up. "I don't suppose a name and dedication are carved on your toy anywhere? No? Well, bring it with us. The safest place for it is the grove."

"Sphinx couldn't be involved in Mother and Father's death," Eleri said, picking up the automaton. "Never get into the workroom without damage."

"Most shabti are smaller than your automaton. And Hatshepsu..." He paused, a purely entertained expression making him look fully awake for the first time. "A thousand shabti were placed in Hatshepsu's chambers at the Djeser-Djeseru when she entered rept. And a thousand shabti have been added every year since. That's why they keep expanding the wretched place."

TEN

Everyone knew that it was the three thousand, two hundred and eleventh year of Maatkare Hatshepsu's reign because most countries had adopted Egypt's count of years as a common reference. Even Yue, whose dragons had Answered as long ago as Egypt's gods, still found it handy when dealing with other realms. Eluned was less certain exactly how long it was since Egypt's Pharaoh had become stone, but could always rely on her brother's memory.

"One million, five hundred and one thousand little sphinxes?" Griff said, as they followed Dem Makepeace back into the Hall.

"Shabti are usually shaped like people," Dem Makepeace said, pausing before the open doors leading into the grove. "Not that I've heard of any recent attacks by miniature stone armies."

"Better as spies," Eleri said, and they all looked out into the grove. The hall felt very large and empty and exposed with the inner doors wide open and the trees full of shadows—and folies. Somehow, Eluned could not find the thought of them reassuring.

"There are advantages to the guardians of this place knowing you three properly," Dem Makepeace said, perhaps catching their hesitation. "Unless you consider yourself an enemy of Cernunnos, there's no particular danger, though you will not stray from my side, nor will you tell anyone what you witness or have discussed this night."

"No," Eluned agreed, echoing Eleri and Griff. Too much was bound up with their investigation to risk blabbing.

"No," Aunt Arianne said, a beat later. She was frowning.

Dem Makepeace stepped beneath the trees, and Eluned didn't allow herself to hang back, trailing him to the gate. It seemed to float at the end of the path, golden coils and silver fruit glimmering in pitch. Could the quick polish it had received that afternoon have made even that dusky red metal so reflective? Could star and distant gas light reach so far?

The key was a metal circle Eluned hadn't even noticed Dem Makepeace carrying. She only caught the movement as he pushed it into the space between the twin amasens' jaws, turning it easily. After a click the gate swung inward, and a cool breeze swept past them, setting all the leaves of the usually sheltered trees whispering, and bringing a crisp hint of pine with a darker note of loam.

Eluned shivered, took a deep breath, and found herself more excited than afraid. It did not make sense, for that breeze to stream from one end of this high walled space. And it was not sensible for her to eagerly follow the vampire who had nearly killed her aunt. Yet she did, impatient when he paused to close the gate behind them.

The trees here crowded close, making it necessary to weave and duck beneath low-hanging branches. Eluned kept a sharp eye on Dem Makepeace's white tunic, vivid through the gloom. Though it no longer stood out so clearly, and the trees...

"How?"

"Different time of day?"

Dem Makepeace glanced up at a sky the bleached and fading blue it had been before dinner. Ahead a trace of a stone path cut through widely-spaced trees and the tumbled remnants of ancient buildings. Birds called, the evening chorus in full throat to emphasise the quiet they'd left.

"Days in the Great Forest run long," Dem Makepeace said. "The nights can last for years, if you've offended."

Aunt Arianne, contemplating a vine-decked coil of stone almost her own height, shifted shielding leaves to reveal the carved head of another amasen, only a few flecks of faded gilding remaining on the horns.

"When you spoke of Cernunnos responding to petitioners for the key, you meant directly, didn't you? Cernunnos. Responding."

"Of course."

"How disconcerting." For once Aunt Arianne sounded as if she meant it. She looked like she was thinking hard.

"What are, what were all these buildings for?" Griff asked, as upright and alert as a pointer hound that had sighted its quarry. Impressive that he did not race off to explore among the tumbled drystone walls, but perhaps the squirrels leaping from pillar to pillar, or the sheer volume of the birdsong held him at bay.

"Hurlstone," the vampire replied. "Village and temple. Before London."

Not fully understanding, knowing only that her throat was full and tight, Eluned took two steps off the remnant path, then managed to stop herself, obedient to her agreement to stay close. But it made her ache to do it.

"Who's that?" Griff asked sharply, looking past Eluned, and she turned, searching.

Beyond a knee-high wall and a stream framed by willow and drooping spruce, a girl stood shoulders back, face raised, arms hanging loose. Twilight was not a good time to pray, but so long as there was light in the sky you could hope to catch Sulis' ear.

Instead of answering, Dem Makepeace changed direction, stepping over the wall and then crossing the stream on a tumble of stones that had once been a pillar.

"He serious?" Eleri murmured, as they followed. "Don't just go meet Cernunnos."

The gods—the grander ones like Cernunnos—rarely came to the living world. Their presence was too great a strain. But humans did not simply go visiting the

Otherworlds either, except of course when their souls went to the gods who held their allegiance.

Eluned, unspeakably excited by something that should make her flinch, couldn't make her voice work, but Griff muttered: "Don't just walk out of London either. I think that must be a statue."

He was right. Even when Dem Makepeace stopped right in front of her, the girl didn't move, and now that Eluned could see her feet it was obvious: she stood held in place by a little pile of stones, grass growing thickly through it.

Aunt Arianne, voice muted, said: "The one who made you?"

"Good guess," Dem Makepeace said, not looking back at them. With great ceremony he knelt, settled down to rest on his heels, and then put both hands to his chest and bowed, so low he was folded down completely.

Caught between shock and fascination, Eluned stared from him to a statue that seemed embarrassingly naked now that she knew that this had been a real person. A vampire in rept. The stone was a waxy pale grey, and the books said it would feel like hard soap beneath the fingers. Despite standing outside exposed, no details were eroded, and Eluned could clearly make out the edges of fingernails, of eyelids. No hair, because that was the one part of a vampire that was not preserved, but if she were taller and had brown frizz to tease into three triangles, she'd look a lot like Melly Ktai.

"Why isn't she wrapped up?" Griff asked, curious. "And underneath a pyramid?"

Dem Makepeace stood, fortunately showing no hint of offence.

"Bindings aren't necessary. They're a carry-over of the preservations performed on those not stone. And she preferred the sight of an eternal sky to whatever assistance her ba might gain using a pyramid to gain strength before moving on."

Egyptians had three lives. The first much the same as everyone else, and then a second where their bodies were maintained like houses, something to rest in after nights outside the world as invisible bird-people called ba. That was the complete opposite of Prytennia, where everything was done to ensure that your body didn't tie you in place. But then, while Prytennians wanted to quickly move on to Annwn to be judged fit for a happy new life among Arawn's islands, Egyptians needed to grow in strength as ba, because the journey to their Otherworld was very dangerous. And some, the strongest among them, might choose to fly not to their Field of Rushes, but outside the worlds altogether, transcending mortality to become stars.

The Egyptian way didn't seem so bad if the house you spent your days in was a statue in a forest.

"Looks young," Eleri murmured.

"She was barely older than you when she was raised." Dem Makepeace smoothed his shendy, glanced at the fading sky, and started down a different path out of the clearing.

Curious to know the girl's name, Eluned followed, and was immediately caught once again by her surroundings. So many plants, both familiar and strange, the scents changing with every touch of breeze. At the top of a small rise stood a stony pavilion lacking only a roof, and commanding a view over the surrounding forest to steal all attention.

Trees were no surprise, but the tower was, a sliver of shining silver far to their right. And white-capped mountains swallowed the opposite horizon, surely higher than any Prytennian peak. Clouds hid the tallest of them, teasing the eye with hints of something regularly shaped and monumental. And below that an ocean of trees, rising and falling with the hidden curves of the landscape, a mosaic of greens endlessly varied.

The Great Forest. An Otherworld. They truly were in an Otherworld.

Noticing she was behind, Eluned hurried to catch Dem Makepeace as he rejoined the path marked by statues of amasen. Words, an unspeakable urgency, blocked her throat, and at a point before the path left the ruins and curved away into thickly-set trees she threw sense to the wind and said: "Wait!"

The vampire who had not quite killed her aunt stopped obediently, and Eluned, who was not shy even if she was not easily social, found herself stammering in the face of limited patience.

"C-could I come back here?" she asked. "Just to...to look at it?"

For a long and painful moment he simply gazed at her blankly, as if she had said she wanted the moon. "You'd have to ask Cernunnos that," he said finally. "Though I would imagine your aunt has a few firm opinions about doing so."

"What consequences?" Aunt Arianne asked, ignoring the barbed smile he offered her. "Beyond allegiance given?"

"For asking? Likely nothing. For coming here?" He left off being provoking to consider the question seriously. "The Great Forest is not the Horned King's alone, and I am far from the only one able to enter it. Hurlstone itself holds no dangers, and if you're accepted by the Deep Grove's guardians you'd have protection against anything that might stray by, short of a god. But this is one of the greatest of the Otherworlds, and to treat it as a plaything would be to invite being played with."

Despite his almost indifferent tone, Eluned felt censured and drew breath to protest, to explain. But the struck-gong feeling overwhelming her seemed impossible to put into words, and she subsided in unfamiliar confusion.

Aunt Arianne said coolly: "If something is so important to a person that they would stand before a god—truly before a god—and ask for it, the reason is unlikely to be trivial." She smiled at Eluned then, both serious and wry. "Not that I wish you to fling yourself into dangerous situations heedlessly. While Dem Makepeace's description did rather make Hurlstone sound safer than London, I trust you to spare my nerves any outright idiocy."

"Stray gods," Eleri added, not discouraging but clearly dubious, and Griff said: "Will you really ask?"

"I don't know," Eluned admitted.

"Any other requests?" Dem Makepeace said, his tone entirely obliging, but not even Griff believed it, and so they silently followed the vampire beneath the trees.

With the sky only visible through breaks in the foliage, it immediately became almost too dark to keep track of the path, and Aunt Arianne moved to stand between them so that she could guide them around occasional hazards. The birdsong dropped away, and the wind rose, uncomfortably cold, stirring up the scent of leaf mold.

Through the velvety pitch, blobs of light provided dim beacons, and as they approached the first Eluned saw that it was another stone amasen, with a soft white light leaking from between its coils. The forest outside that gentle glow seemed even darker, and she could no longer see patches of pale sky above. But the wind had dropped and she could *hear*.

Griff pressed back against Eluned's side, and she squeezed his shoulder and told herself that the *tok tok tok* was likely a bird, and the rustling no doubt a badger or squirrels, and that was most certainly the call of a fox and not someone crying out. It did not help at all to glance at Aunt Arianne's face when they reached the next amasen, and see her gazing out into the forest with wide eyes. Beneath these trees, perhaps it was better not to be able to see in the dark.

Even if she came only in the daylight, and kept to Hurlstone, would she be simply courting danger, and wholly unequal to it? More to the point, could she really ask permission of Cernunnos to come here? The Horned

King might bring bountiful harvests and healthy babies, but it was only through carefully maintained treaties that the lands within his dominion were not swallowed by forest. And to offend against Cernunnos in any woodland was to risk drawing the attention of his hunt.

They had passed the last of the glowing amasen, but Dem Makepeace still walked unhesitatingly toward a bluer patch of darkness up ahead, which became a clearing, a bowl of soughing grass fringed by trees. Beneath a depthless sea of stars stood a tiny hill, crowned by the Oak.

Sprawling boughs embraced forest and sky, reaching so far they hung beyond the slopes of the hill. The trunk was wider than ten men embracing, gnarled but solid. And every bit of it could be clearly seen because countless balls of glass, flickering softly, hung by slender chains from the branches.

"We will kneel at the foot of the hill," Dem Makepeace said, continuing forward without break. "Wednesday will go up alone and kneel on the stone at the crest."

"Who's—?" Griff began, then stopped when Eluned squeezed his shoulder. It was obvious Dem Makepeace meant their aunt, but this wasn't the time to ask why. Griff knew that, of course, but walking through a place where he could hear so many animals and not see them had been far from easy for him. Dem Makepeace had talked about this as if it was such a simple thing, but Eluned had never been so daunted, and Aunt Arianne surely was as well, though she did not falter when they reached the bottom of the hill and Dem Makepeace gestured for her to go past him.

The grass was high and seed heads tickled when Eluned knelt. One of the hanging glass globes was only a little way above them, and as a mote of light detached itself she saw that the light came from glowing white moths clinging to the outside, feeding on tiny flowers within.

There were fewer globes around the trunk, and Eluned could see very little of Aunt Arianne after she knelt past the top of the slope. The breeze had dropped, and the loudest sound was the clothy flutter of wings, and Griff's breathing, growing ever harsher.

Eleri leaned down to Griff's ear, and Eluned couldn't hear her words, but guessed them even before Griff repeated: "Tennings Together." The old reassurance, one they'd turned to more than ever this summer. Alone they each had their vulnerable points, but as their own minor trifold they covered each other's weaknesses.

This, though, was a greater test for Griff than they could have anticipated. Even Eluned, wildly excited, had to fight with uncertainty. Could she do it? Ask Cernunnos himself for leave to visit his forest? For something so simple and selfish as wanting, longing, to look at it properly? Aunt Arianne had been careful to point out that a request like that would mean a tie of allegiance, a permanent bond. That wasn't a small thing, even if Cernunnos wasn't known as a harsh god.

And when should she ask? What if Cernunnos came and went and Eluned had not had a chance to speak? But if Cernunnos came down to them, would Griff be able to stand it?

Dem Makepeace, on the far side of Griff and Eleri, leaned forward so that he could see Griff's whitely set face, then said: "Sleep."

Griff closed his eyes, and his breathing slowed, but there was no other sign that he'd obeyed. He didn't even slump sideways. This was a power all vampires had, to put someone into a trance. They did it so they could feed without causing pain—or protest. Father had once explained that Prytennian traditional dress, with the high collars and cuffs criss-crossed with laces, had originally been designed with the idea of preventing vampires from biting you without you knowing.

It didn't seem that was what Dem Makepeace wanted, though, since he simply straightened again.   Eluned discovered why he'd thought it necessary when a tiny scraping sound behind them was all the warning she had before the amasen arrived.

Enormous snakes.   Enormous snakes with curling golden horns. The first came from Eluned's right, rearing up to look at her. Thicker than a man's leg, and a pale cream in colour, with a very black tongue that flickered an inch from Eluned's nose. She let her breath out in shock, but also in wonder, for its fluted head and dark eyes were beautiful.

But it was an act of will to stay still as another slid between her and Griff, and she felt the weight and warmth of it brushing past. It looped around her brother and nuzzled his hair, and Eluned reminded herself desperately that the amasen were signs of great good fortune, that they brought bountiful harvests and drove away pests, and would shed their golden horns and leave them as gifts for those particularly favoured, and that a dozen of them, in shades of green and brown and cream, surely meant that the Tenning family would be lucky for years to come if only they could get through the next few minutes without screaming.

Dem Makepeace, barely visible among the coils, scratched one between its horns, and it closed its eyes and tilted its head like a dog whose most particular itch had been attended. Greatly daring, Eluned copied the gesture, and found the patch between the horns was soft and velvety. The cream amasen leaned into her touch until a pale green fellow pushed it out of the way, and then she had four of them competing to be petted, and Eleri was cautiously taking on two, and they exchanged a glance that clearly said: "We must never tell Griff about this."

Aunt Arianne was coming down the slope, herded by a particularly large green and tan amasen, and with a much smaller creamy-pale one wrapped around her throat like a too-tight scarf. When she reached the bottom all but that small one slid away, and as they moved the air seemed to pulse.   All the moths sprang into the air, and beat chaotically upward, taking most of the light away.

"Watch," Dem Makepeace said, again leaning to address Griff, though Eluned's eyes had not yet adjusted enough to see Griff's reaction. He did not move, at least, and his breathing remained steady, but under starlight alone, Eluned could only make out broad shadows. The shape of Dem Makepeace as he straightened. The outline of Aunt Arianne as she knelt to Eluned's right. Antlers.

The Horned King could be man or hart, and at first Eluned could not decide which of these followed Aunt Arianne down from beneath the Oak, was only certain of the antlers, wide and many-pointed. Two silver torcs hung glimmering from the tines, swaying with the motion of the god's approach. The air shuddered with every step.

The hart form, a stag at the height of his strength. He walked directly up to Eleri, and dropped his great branched head to examine the automaton sitting on the ground in front of her, snorted like a thunderclap, and then was lowering over Eluned, inside her head.

That was the only way to describe it.   Cernunnos sorted through her thoughts, her feelings, her self, examining the request to visit his kingdom, shaking aside petty words to lay bare the loss, the fury, the sense of being broken, that had weighed on Eluned ever since Aunt Arianne had told them Mother and Father had died. How a part of her she'd thought central had curled up and vanished, and Hurlstone was so full of all the things she usually loved that it filled her with the belief that the missing part would come back.

The Horned King threw back his heavy head, the twin torcs ringing, and shattered the air with his cry—the stag's harsh bellow accompanied by a genuine thunderclap out of a clear sky. The sound pounded the ears, so close to a literal blow that Eluned almost didn't feel a tinier hurt, but she looked down to see the small amasen, a pale rope sliding toward Dem Makepeace. The flesh between Eluned's left thumb and forefinger throbbed.

When she raised her head, Cernunnos was gone, and they were just a line of people kneeling at the base of a hill topped with a tree, and as in a dream Eluned followed along as Dem Makepeace told them it was time to go, and led them silent along the path, pausing only to prop the automaton on a stone pillar, guarded by the small amasen, before they returned to Forest House.

The warmer air brought Eluned back to herself, and she gasped and looked confusedly at a pale sky candy-striped by dawn. Then Aunt Arianne held her right hand next to Eluned's left so they could compare matching snake bites. And, as they raised those hands toward the ornate gate Dem Makepeace had closed, glimmering on the ghostly edge of tangibility, discover keys.

ELEVEN

Rian was magnificently out of sorts.

She knew it for a nonsensical reaction. For the first time in her life she had been showered with good fortune. She had been given back her youth, and would enjoy the benefits of the Bound without the constraints and uncomfortable intimacy of the role. Physically she felt very good indeed, and she had gained both a home and financial stability. More, it promised to be a life of ease, involving a tiny amount of work and bringing with it privilege and respect. Cernunnos himself had appeared before her and accepted her in the role. On her new desk rested a formal letter of appointment, accompanied by a discreet outline of the terms of her position. And an invitation.

Too many mixed feelings. They served no purpose so Rian set them and the letters aside, taking instead a fresh sheet of paper. All this oddity with Forest House was so much distraction. The important development was that Prytennia's deadliest spy had gone to Caerlleon to look over the circumstances of two deaths. Meanwhile, her energetic charges, after a day of recovery, were off asking innocuous questions at the nearest automaton workshops. To decide her own course, Rian needed to put her thoughts in order.

The artificial fulgite was key, she was sure of it, but she had to think beyond whoever had given it to Eiliff and Aedric. Unsealing an old bottle of ink, she tested the liquid, found it serviceable, and made herself a list.

1. Commissioned two automaton and provided round fulgite.

2. Helped arrange the commission. Lyn(d)sey.

3. Provided funding in envelopes from Sheerside House.

4. Sabotaged industrial automaton's safety bindings.

5. Stole/took delivery of special automaton and fulgite.

6. Searched house/removed Commissions Book (when?).

7. Asked Willa to buy items from estate sale?

8. Sent sphinx shabti to Sheerside House. (Hatshepsu???)

9. Targeted by sphinx shabti (for fulgite?). Princess Leodhild?

10. Sent ravens. (Order of the Oak?)

11. Sent bull-bear.

This last entry worried her. As widely-travelled as she was, Rian had never heard of anything like that creature. And if that thing had been after the fulgite, then someone had decided that she or the children had it: a new development since there'd been no approach of that sort since the original search of the Tenning house.

The jangle of bells interrupted, and Rian slid her list beneath the blotter. She was going to have to give serious consideration to day staff, and Dama Chelwith would no doubt have the ideal people, sitting waiting for the request. Rian would then be a person with servants. Another adjustment.

Constantly picturing people as pulsing rivers of blood was perhaps the largest change, and three were waiting on the far side of the door. Expecting another helpful deputation of locals, Rian discovered instead three reasons to be pleased.

"Evelyn! And Lyle! It's good to see you both again." Rian smiled at the two men, and the tall blond woman who could be no-one but the person Rian was most interested in speaking to.

"Arianne!" Evelyn began, but then looked past her, eyes widening. "What in the world?"

"Come in and gape," Rian invited, gesturing with the hat she'd carried down with her. "It's too distracting isn't it?"

"I wasn't at all certain we'd found the right place," Evelyn said, stepping in and staring at the soaring ceiling and spectacular windows. "This is not what I expected from Makepeace. Inside or out."

"Technically, I don't think he's ever lived here," Rian said. "But he has the disposition of it."

"Remarkable," Lyle said, his stares as much for Rian's face as the room before he took himself in hand. "Arianne, I'd like you to meet my sister, Lynsey Blair. Lynsey, this is Arianne Seaforth."

Lynsey, built on Nordic lines, was an inch or so taller than Evelyn, and kept her oat-coloured hair in two thick braids down her back. Her voice was warm, rich with a northern accent as she said: "I've been hearing a great deal about you."

"Welcome to Forest House," Rian said, and very deliberately held out her hand to clasp the taller woman's in greeting.

"I can see where the name comes from," Lynsey said, her grip firm and her dominant emotion a calm curiosity. No hint of recognition or guilt. "Are those real trees on the other side of the glass?"

"Let me show you," Rian said. "Words are a little inadequate."

Since the day was sunny, she settled her hat and veil before pulling back the heavy bar, and stayed in the shade of the doorway as her three visitors, exclaiming, walked beneath the trees. Had it been a false lead? Lynsey at first glance seemed a perfectly amiable person, possessing a poised dignity, and...and Rian had a weakness for tall women, and should not let that lead her into ready trust. Her not-entirely-reliable new senses were merely a starting point, and it would be stupid to rush to frank questions.

Briefly closing her eyes, Rian listened to the shushing of the very top-most leaves. She couldn't ask for a better aid to her self-command than this oasis of calm. During the morning windstorm the grove had been scarcely disturbed, and the single folie present was tucked well back on the far side of the dividing wall. She had not so far unlocked the gate and ventured into the rest of the forest, but knowing it was there was a balm. And yet she had spent the day frowning.

"The Deep Grove," Evelyn said, returning to Rian. "This is the Deep Grove, isn't it?"

"You know of it? Dem Makepeace is the Keeper."

"Truly? That's...not what I expected from him." Evelyn shook his head, smiled at his own astonishment, then tweaked the edge of her veil. "The sensitivity hasn't eased?"

"It is, slowly, after growing somewhat worse. It's manageable so long as I stay out of direct sunlight.

Lyle, hearing this as he returned with his sister, held out both hands, saying: "I was devastated to hear you'd been attacked, and the consequences of it. To be bound is bad enough, but in such circumstances, to a person you had no agreement with?"

"Fortunately Dem Makepeace seems to be even less fond of the idea of blood service than you, Lyle," Rian said, ushering them back indoors away from the bothersome light. "He's willing to let the bond lapse."

Or at least not further it, a point that she clung to given his apparent determination to infuriate her. The lack of warning and explanation had extended not only to the kind of vampire she would apparently inevitably become, but even what petitioning Cernunnos would entail. He'd thrown her into an act of allegiance hoping she would balk or fail.

And yet she had to maintain some kind of link, or give up humanity altogether. Until he went to rept, she was part of him. His blood reproduced in her body, her ka attuned to his.

Rian turned that fact over for the thousandth time as she served tea in the small, well-shuttered parlour off the kitchen, and told her guests a highly edited tale of her new role of delegate Keeper.

"I don't think Dem Makepeace thought I'd be accepted," she said, swirling a few stray leaves around the bottom of her cup. "I suppose I don't give the impression of someone who's spent any time in forests."

"Have you?" Lyle asked.

"Oh, yes. My parents built their studio on the edge of the Cadell Forest. The house was constantly full of guests—artists—and it could get very rowdy. I'd find my peace in the forest, and that's something I've kept up no matter where I've travelled. Still, I had to think very hard about taking on this role, once I began to understand the level of allegiance I would be giving. It's rather more serious than a ten-year contract as a Bound."

A monumental leap, in fact. She did not think this particular permanency the source of her general dissatisfaction, though it discomforted her that she didn't remember all of her encounter with Cernunnos. He had rested a hand on her forehead. There had been something, a wordless conversation that had left her turned inside-out. She could still feel the warmth of his touch, but the details had been rubbed over.

Refocusing with effort, Rian smiled at Lyle and said: "What happened to being whirled off to Alba?"

Evelyn answered. "He was whirled right back again when the Lord Protector heard about the Huntresses. Which is why I'm here as well, since Lord Msrah was called to London to, ah, welcome such prestigious visitors."

"The...really? There are Huntresses in Prytennia?"

"Five hands of them. They arrived last night." Evelyn cast a smiling glance at Lyle. "Prince Gustav's sources are impeccable. He reached London before Lord Msrah."

The elite strike force of Egypt's military was made up entirely of vampires of the Sekhmet, Pakhet, and Bastet lines: the lioness, the caracal and the cat. There were few deadlier in combat anywhere in the known world.

"They're...looking for the two sphinxes?"

"Oh, no, they're here to offer Egypt's assistance in solving Prytennia's weather issues." Evelyn's face was alive with mirth. "Not a Shu among them! The afternoon papers are full of that little fact."

"One day your love of drama will bite you somewhere awkward, Evelyn," Lynsey said. "What would you have done if Lord Msrah hadn't been called to London?"

"Been very restless. But I am most fortunate in my Lord—not least for the chance to check on you, Arianne. I was picturing, well, not this."

"I anticipated a garret," Rian said. "As it is..." She shrugged.

"You're uncomfortable here," Lynsey said, to Rian's surprise.

"Not precisely, but...I've been trying to work out why I'm not straightforwardly overjoyed with a Royal appointment falling into my lap. This house, and a salary far more than a competence, all for opening a gate every twenty-five years? I think the problem is it doesn't feel earned. As if I've cheated my way here. Or perhaps I'm angry that it's sat here empty for so long."

"Wasteful," Lynsey agreed. "Though it seems to me that the role is more than opening a gate."

"True enough. Controlling access, which seems to be a large issue, even within the neighbourhood. I've arranged for a noticeboard to be put up by the outer doors so I can post days the doors will be opened, and I was thinking of putting regular notices in newspapers, if only to stem the flood of letters. I received five yesterday and seven this morning asking whether I would permit joining ceremonies, along with a remarkable lecture from the Wise of Chalk Grove telling me I should *not* let people in, and to expect a deputation of the Wise. This is not at all what I thought to be doing."

"You've the freedom to travel, though?" Evelyn asked. "More so than with Lord Msrah?"

"There doesn't seem to be any bar against it. Though I expect to be relatively settled for the next few years." She smiled at Lynsey with a casual civility that would allow no hint of her deep interest. "You live in London? Evelyn mentioned that you're a member of the United Albion League. You believe there's a Dragon of the North?"

Lynsey lifted a hand dismissively. "The dragons are beside the point. It's Arawn who grants access to Annwn, and his Hunt has repeatedly been witnessed over the border. We do not know what limits his territorial allegiance, or what will happen if we simply choose to join Alba and Prytennia under the name of Albion."

"But the Suleviae are confined to the dragonates. They won't be able to defend the north."

"Prytennia's airships have no such restrictions. Nor do the Nomarches, or, for that matter, the army. It would not be so secure as Prytennia under Sulis, but why not at least try it to see if it gains us territorial allegiance? Under a method less desperately divisive than the requirements of this ridiculous Protectorate."

Evelyn chuckled. "You don't think Prince Gustav will win himself a permanent nest?"

"That vote only passed thanks to certain absences, and much stirring up of fear of Rome. It's already foundering. There's no way enough Albans will make personal sacrifices to the Aesir."

Lynsey glanced apologetically at her brother, who shrugged and said: "I don't recommend underestimating Prince Gustav. Yes, on current numbers the term of the Protectorate won't be extended, but a vote for a united

Albion is even less likely. And Prytennians so associate their borders with the dragonates that they're positively superstitious about reaching beyond them."

"They also started with one dragonate and now have three," Lynsey pointed out.

"The Suleviae won't push for territory they can't defend," Evelyn said. He paused, then added blandly: "Though a few more years of Prince Gustav turning up on their doorstep every five minutes might change that."

Lyle, briefly abandoning correct behaviour, pretended to throw a seedcake at him, and Evelyn ducked and laughed.

Lynsey, watching them with fond tolerance, said: "The position isn't as clear as you might think. But we mustn't bore Arianne rehashing old debates when we came to offer our help."

Rian, who had been trying to fit an effort to unite Albion with a plot revolving around fulgite, seized the convenient opening.

"My goals in the short term revolve around clothes and transportation," she said. "It sounds as if purchasing a hummingbird is a fraught investment, thanks to the fulgite scarcity."

"You'd do better using taxicabs," Evelyn agreed. "Though given the prices this last couple of years, perhaps the best sense is buying a hummingbird and then hiring a well-armed chauffeur. Or two. At this rate, by the end of the year horse-drawn will outnumber fulquus-powered once again—just when the streets were starting to be manageably clean."

During the light debate that followed, ranging from whether Rome was deliberately creating a fulgite scarcity, to the vexed question of where the Republic was mining it in the first place, Rian could discover no glance or intonation or vampirically-sensed emotion that suggested that fulgite held particular significance to any of her guests. She tried a different tack, mentioning how Griff's disappointment at not seeing Sheerside had been suitably mitigated by Forest House, and then asking Lynsey if she'd been to Sheerside.

"Oh yes. It's Evelyn's great joy to haul unsuspecting newcomers about the place, and point out where people were murdered or fought duels, move on to ghost stories, and then lose his victim in one of the oldest sections."

"Only you, Lynsey," Evelyn said. "And it wasn't deliberate. Well, not completely."

"We first visited when I was sixteen and Lynsey twelve," Lyle explained. "We took her into the Underhouse." He grimaced. "She found her way to Lord Msrah's private rooms, of course. Fortunately her blood is not right for him."

"Lynsey is a great favourite of Lord Msrah," Evelyn said, ignoring the note of genuine relief in Lyle's voice. "He taught her to fence."

"My first lessons, at any rate, and I continued learning back home. I still haven't defeated him, but he no longer holds back quite so much."

"Fencing." Rian liked the idea on multiple levels. "Do you have a recommendation for a tutor, Lynsey? I've found myself thinking of self-defence lately."

"I can introduce you to my London class," Lynsey said. "I've taken a position out of the city, but the new instructor is excellent."

Rian asked where Lynsey would be working, only to have Evelyn interrupt.

"You've never agreed to involve yourself in Folly's latest extravagance?" he asked. "I thought you were joking."

"The principle of the idea seems sound to me. Besides, the pay will be very good."

"Folly? Lord Fennington?" Rian suppressed any hint of heightened interest. Dyfed Fennington was perhaps the richest person in Prytennia, infamously eccentric, but with many connections to industry. Just the sort of person who might fund an investigation into haunted fulgite—or perhaps be behind the initial invention. "You're teaching him fencing?"

"He's starting a school," Evelyn said, shaking his head in amused contempt. "Not content with his other toys, he wants some children to play with."

"Lord Fennington is converting the Tangleways Estate," Lynsey explained. "He believes that Prytennia's current system of schooling is limited and arbitrary, and he wishes to chart a better path."

"Fencing and horse riding as part of a national curriculum."

"Physical education." Lynsey was unperturbed by Evelyn's mockery. "Sport, art, music, the sciences, literature, domestic and mechanical crafts. A framework of minimum standards and paths to excellence to be rolled out to all the village schools."

The mention of village schools roused unhappy memories for Rian, but she simply asked: "Would you recommend it, this school-to-be? Or will it be all excess and a waste of time?"

"You're thinking about it for your three? The teachers I've met so far are very good. The workload will be demanding, and I would expect some very annoyed parents when it becomes clear that mere attendance is not a guarantee of success. But if Lord Fennington manages to attract sufficient students for the first few years, they will gain a great deal."

"Charged an exorbitant price to be test subjects in Folly's latest passion."

"I thought you liked Lord Fennington," Lyle said.

"I do," Evelyn replied. "Who doesn't? But he flits from interest to interest like a butterfly. What happens in a year or two when he discovers a new passion?"

"He'll find a suitable Head to take over," Lynsey said. "And depending on that person, and the number of students remaining, the school will founder or prosper." She smiled at Rian. "There's an open day on the twenty-fifth. I'll send you the information and you can make up your mind away from Evelyn's naysaying."

"The way you look now, you'll be mistaken for a student," Lyle added to Rian, with a mix of discomfort and fascination.

"Going to school with them would be an excellent way to appal my nieces. I'll have to give it some thought."

A crash followed by a solid thump brought all three of her visitors to their feet. Rian rose less hastily, focusing her senses to catch the departure of a half-dozen tiny rivers, and noticed Evelyn also looking toward the grove.

"I'd better check what that was," she said. "Would you care for a tour?"

As they climbed she explained folies and watching ravens, and was entirely unsurprised to find black feathers in the attic next to a fallen trunk. The Order of the Oak was certainly taking an interest.

But no raven had opened the chests crowded into one half of the attic, or disturbed the piles of clothing she'd been sorting through that morning. Something had managed to creep in here and start searching, before the folies noticed. And there'd been no river.

TWELVE

"We walk on the faces of the dead."

The South London Orientation and Expeditionary Force blinked up at their navigator, Melly.

"We're walking on grass," Griff corrected. "And there's only skeletons below. No faces."

"Skulls have faces enough," Melly said. She raised her bag-laden arms, a stretching, expansive gesture. "I love this place, but no matter what anyone says, we're walking over people. Rooms of bone and teeth."

Climbing the last few feet to the top of the rise, Eluned turned to gaze back at the city. London was such a flat place that this must be one of the best views of it, unless they could gain permission to scale one of the three major pyramids that rose higher than any other building. One of those was not too terribly far south, but most of the view was a grand sweep of tile and shingle, the spinning blades of roof-mounted dynamos, and the occasional tips of lesser pyramids.

Turning inward, Eluned could remove the city completely from her view, replacing it with rounded green slopes marked by a tinge of brown thanks to the summer of windstorms. London's Great Barrows were shaped like three overlapping almonds—a perfect triquetra to symbolise the coming together of the Suleviae as Sulis. The south-west barrow was almost deserted, only a handful of kite flyers ahead.

But Melly's words made it impossible to see simply a hilly park. Beneath them were halls and pits lined with stone and people: the bones of those who had died, separated by type and neatly stacked. Freed by Arawn's Tears of all the weight of flesh, bones could not anchor spirits in the living world, or hold them from the Grey Shores of Annwn.

A tight bubble had expanded in Eluned's chest, and she gripped the handle of the carpet bag she carried. They had said their goodbyes at Caerlleon's Black Pool, and she no longer felt like she was suffocating every moment of the day, but there were times when the thought that her parents no longer had hands to touch made her want to scream.

"Ar-rrooo!" Griff cried, pretending to be one of Arawn's hounds and chasing Dama Chelwith's two grandchildren, Redick and Falwen, toward the intersection of the three barrows.

"How does he have so much energy after all today's walking?" Melly asked, then added in a lower voice. "Stupid thing for me to say. Sorry."

"Doesn't matter," Eleri said, putting her bags down and wriggling her fingers. "Definitely will come back with kites," she added, critically surveying two girls as they launched a multi-jointed extravagance.

"Not during one of the windstorms." Even in an ordinary breeze Nabah needed a firm grip on the trailing section of her sari as they followed the younger three toward the centre of the barrows. "Or you will be donating your kites to Danuin. Do they always offer to employ you, these workshops?"

"Caerlleon ones never did," Eleri replied. "But they knew Mother and Father were teaching me."

"You did not seem very much interested."

"Neither of those are worth my time," Eleri said. "Maintenance shops. School first, university, then a workshop of my own."

"Why not a workshop now? Or work to put together the money for one?"

"Mother thought a wide view important. And I like lessons."

Nabah gave Melly an oddly significant glance, but the taller girl simply looked over her head.

"We've all of summer break now, before we have to think of school," Eluned put in, thoughts on a gate and a ruin and a forest. "Plus the last bit of term," she added, unrepentant about expulsion.

"There are waiting lists for the better ones," Nabah warned. "Tollesey only has vacancies in the upper forms if someone leaves."

"Is that nearby? Do you both go there?"

"I've already finished," Melly said. "And Nabah—" She hesitated. "Nabah might be leaving a vacancy there soon."

"You're finishing up? Have you decided not to be a doctor?" Eluned knew that children born in the families of the Daughters of Lakshmi didn't have to go into medicine, but she was willing to bet that it would feel like deciding not to belong.

"A doctor, yes, of course." Nabah's voice held no shadow of doubt. "But the Raya...the Raya of Karnata has rescinded the ban on the Daughters."

"I hadn't heard that," Eluned said, sharing a look of surprise with Eleri. When the Karnata Empire's Raya had forbidden women from practicing medicine and ordered arrests, the Daughters of Lakshmi had fled their homeland, eventually asking for asylum from the Queen of Prytennia. That had been nearly two hundred years ago, and the Daughters had become part of everyday life in Prytennia, particularly in surgical matters where Thoth-den vampires could not always help, or with those who objected to vampire 'taint'.

"Are you—are all the Daughters going to leave, then?" Eluned asked.

"It's an individual choice." Nabah shrugged, though there was a tiny crease between her brows. "I at least can speak the home tongue, although I am told my accent is terrible. This is no easy choice, but...Lakshmi is not here. Our practice might not depend on godly assistance, but

Lakshmi is still more than a namesake for the Daughters. In Her name do we offer the riches of health, but our prayers have not brought Her here, so we cannot achieve individual allegiance, and our souls go to Arawn."

Gods were very territorial. Most of them were not so completely bound by borders as Sulis—else Rome could not have conquered half the world with Jupiter's lightning—but often travel led to one-sided devotion. Cernunnos was one of the gods who transcended borders. He protected forests all across Europe, and had even been known to answer petitioners in far-flung points around the world.

The two neat punctures by the base of Eluned's thumb itched, and she tried to think soberly of the consequences of allegiance, but images of Hurlstone took her instead. Yesterday, after sleeping most of the day, she'd had no chance before sunset to do more than check on the mannequin. And she'd looked in again this morning, but only a glance because Eleri was keen to start their tour of workshops, and collect what she needed to create a new arm. It fascinated her how inconsistent the time of day appeared to be in the Otherworld.

Impatient to get back, Eluned stepped up her pace. They had nearly reached the central intersection of the three massive barrows. It made a fourth hill, higher and outlined by a narrow ditch that Griff, Redick and Falwen were currently jumping over in unison, chanting the titles of the Suleviae with every leap.

"The Shadow!"

"The Light!"

"The Song!"

Eluned herded everyone onward, helped along by the arrival of a girl walking a half-dozen dogs of all sizes, sending Griff zooming ahead once again.

"You never stay and listen to the Solstice Singing from your home?" Eluned asked as they passed Melly's store. "You're even closer than we are—it must be so loud."

"It is! But you have to go. There's nothing like it, and they're so happy when you sing back. I can't hardly believe you've never seen one of the triskelion."

"We were too young the last time the Solstice Singing was in Caerlleon. And we never travelled to one." Always bad timing, too busy, or the crowds would be too big—but perhaps really because their father shared Griff's travel sickness. Eluned had never known that.

"What if Aunt sends us away for school?" Griff said, dropping back to join the conversation.

"Then we can come home for the Singing," Eluned said firmly, then paused as a quiver ran up through her feet. "Is the ground...?"

"It's the tunnel digger," Nabah explained, clearly used to the odd vibration.

"For the underground rail?" Griff asked, then shifted from eager interest to suspicion. "I thought they weren't scheduled to go south of the river until next year."

"That's so," Melly said, with a wide grin. "The lines that they're admitting to. But they're digging south of the river all the same. Here, and in Skepsey, and in Twitting. People have felt it all over."

"There are not yet the big cut and cover excavations, like at Paddington," Nabah added. "And if you go where they're using the digging automatons to tunnel under the Tamesas, the vibration is much stronger. These are smaller tunnels."

"For the vampires to get about in the day," Melly added.

"For the Parliament's private escape route," Nabah countered. "Or their secret postal engine. Routes to lay electricity lines. Or a tunnel to the centre of the Earth. Or it's mole people robbing banks, or even the Dragon of the East, restless in her bounds. Officially, there's no digging yet, south of the river."

They enjoyed themselves making up more outlandish reasons, and Eluned could see that Griff thought he now knew how Dem Makepeace had reached their house before sunset, and was eager to confirm that theory. But it had been a long day of walking, and the bags full of parts and equipment felt three times as heavy during the final trudge past warehouse after concealing warehouse. And then there were all those stairs to Eleri's new workroom, though surely they could put that off in favour of a visit to the kitchen, and some quality sitting-about.

Thinking only of putting her bag down, Eluned was not pleased to discover two people in Forest House's vestibule, one tugging the entry bell. The stranger turned as they crowded the outer door, and Eluned saw with faint dismay that it was a member of the Order of the Oak, her distinctive creamy brown surcoat featuring a triple row of dark brown oak leaves woven into the hem.

The woman at least wasn't frowning, and the very large man with her didn't even seem to notice them, staring vaguely at an umbrella hanging from the coat hooks. He and the woman made something of a matched set in their Oak-mark garb, both with glossy brown curling hair and skin tanned almost dark enough to match. On the chest of the man's surcoat a single large oak leaf was woven, showing he was a Wise of the Order of the Oak—a dryw. He would have a grove of his own to look after, and people would come to him for foreseeing.

"There seems naught home, children," the woman said, a border accent softening her words. "The price paid for rudely arriving without writing ahead."

"Aunt's probably upstairs," Griff said, as Eluned put her bag on the nearest bench. "It takes an age to get down, unless you run."

Before the woman could respond, the towering man made a pleased noise—the same sound Griff would make spotting a thick wedge of cake—and caught up Eluned's left hand in both of his.

"What—?" Eluned started to flinch away, but the Wise's hold was careful and she realised that it was the bite mark that had caught his attention.

"The Horned King's blessing," he said, his voice a gentle rumble. "To see His mark fills the day with light."

Eluned supposed it was new to have people stare at her left hand rather than her right, but the man, although a little strange, radiated such genuine delight that it was impossible not to smile back at him.

"What does he mean?" Nabah asked, clearly fascinated.

Difficult. They were not supposed to talk about their visit to the Great Forest. "There was a little amasen in the grove," Eluned began, and was saved from more when the main door of the house opened. Aunt Arianne looked out, along with the man from Sheerside, Dem Carstairs, and a blond man and woman behind them.

"Lost the key?"

The smile dropped from the Wise's face, and he let go of Eluned's hand, turning and straightening as he did so to a rigid uprightness that looked painful.

"The unfinished ones," he said, breathless yet the words ringing out. "The near hounds. The knife of echoes. The path of cobweb. The shattered dragon. The trials of Albion are set." He was shaking, and made a horrid gulping sound, as if he had swallowed his tongue, and then one of his arms jerked upward to point at Aunt Arianne. "Land's throat. The quartered glance. Heart's blood falls."

Then, like a lamp switched off, all the light went from his eyes and he slumped. The woman with him caught him adeptly by the arms, and despite his considerable size slowed his fall and eased him into a sitting position.

Aunt Arianne's face had gone completely blank, and everyone was staring from the Wise to her, but then she gave a little shrug and produced the faintly amused smile that made it seem like nothing ever touched her.

"Indeed the one thing the day lacked was a doom-laden prophecy. Perhaps you'd care to come in?"

ooOoo

Aunt Arianne sailed through drama as if it was a light headwind, asking Dem Carstairs and the tall blond woman to carry the barely-conscious Wise into the nearest sitting room, and sending the South London Orientation and Expeditionary Force to the kitchen to get themselves something to drink. Melly, perhaps catching signs of strain on Griff's face, helpfully brought the Expedition to an end, and tidied everyone off, leaving only the adult visitors to deal with.

"Tea tray," Eleri said, and kept Griff occupied hunting down the teapot so a fresh brew could be made.

Aunt Arianne must have tidied her own visitors away as well, since by the time Eluned led the way into the long, thin receiving room it held only their aunt, the Wise lying on one of the divans, and his companion sitting beside him, expression rueful.

"...first time it's sent us will-ye nill-ye to London," she was saying. "But once he's taken the oakfire, there's no other path until he's spoken. And if it's a foreseeing for a particular person, he must seek them out."

"You're his coafor?"

"Yes. Thede came to the Order soon after we married, when he discovered his gift, and so recording naturally fell to me. Ah, and I haven't even introduced myself. I'm Nedani Tyse, Keeper of the Banebury Grove. I'd love one, thank you, lad," she added, as Griff held up a cup.

"Are you a dryw as well?" Griff asked as he poured, his chin still tucked and shoulders stiff, clearly wanting to be angry because he'd been frightened. "I thought the Keeper was always a dryw, except for here."

"Sometimes the oakfire takes them strongly," the Keeper said. She looked down at her big husband, and smoothed brown curls back from his forehead. "Then it falls to their coafor to manage the day-to-day needs of the Grove, along with recording all visions. Thede will begin to recover himself, now that he's spoken, but he is never fully in this world any more."

This seemed an awful thing to Eluned. The Keeper of the Tasset Grove, near Caerlleon, had been a sharp, humorous man, showing no sign that the poisonous brew of mistletoe and oak bark used to bring on visions had any permanent impact. His official recorder—his coafor—had been his younger brother, and had loved to tease him about whatever he might have said under the influence of the oakfire, since he couldn't remember his visions at all.

"Is it you who sends the ravens?" Griff was still trying to be angry, but revealed his sympathy by dumping several spoonfuls of sugar into the cup of tea he was preparing.

"Rav—?" Keeper Tyse stopped short, then clicked her tongue. "How senseless. Yes, if you're being plagued by ravens, it's most likely members of the Order. I do apologise."

"The folies kill them," Griff added, clearly pleased by the knowledge.

"I gather this appointment would be hotly contested," Aunt Arianne said.

"Oh yes. Outside White Hill Grove, there is none more desirable, but no need to fash yourself. The vampire Makepeace is beloved of the Horned King, and there is no arguing that, even if he doesn't stir himself over the day-to-day duties. Because Forest House has sat empty there has been a deal of talk, but nothing can come of it." Keeper Tyse accepted the cup Griff offered, and bravely took a sugary sip. "The foreseeing will complicate matters a touch."

Aunt Arianne's response to this massive understatement was forestalled by the dryw, who abruptly tried to sit up. Griff stepped forward, and Eluned decided to distract him with a murmured reminder about tunnels. Judging Aunt Arianne safe to be left, she and Eleri made their pardons, and followed their brother's bee-line for the cellar.

By mutual assent they didn't discuss the dryw's pronouncement, but simply began pushing bricks and tapping wood, regretting the sweeping efficiency of the cleaning party, which had left little in the way of helpful dust to betray vampiric entry-points.

It was at least half an hour later when Aunt Arianne tracked them down, finding them all crammed between two of the wine racks, intently pressing bricks.

"Is that wall particularly interesting for some reason?"

"Shiny spots," Eleri replied, steadily winding the dynamo torch they'd fetched for light.

"And they go click!" Griff added, avidly trying another combination. Nothing could have been better designed to soothe over upsets than the prospect of a genuine hidden door. "This can't be a new tunnel, though. This has been here as long as the house."

"Why would there be a tunnel, new or otherwise?"

Eluned started to explain the rumours of underground passages, then broke off as the entire wall between the two racks swung in. Griff let out a crow of triumph and plunged forward, but Eluned managed to catch hold of his collar.

"Could be traps," Eleri said, winding faster in an attempt to boost the inadequate beam of the torch. "Or vampires."

"There's no-one in there," Aunt Arianne said, with a confidence that spoke of night vision and an awareness of blood. "I rather think you've found the hidden safe."

"Safe? This is a whole room!"

Griff wriggled loose, and no traps stopped his excited progress. Aunt Arianne went to find a better light, and they were both proven right, for it was a safe the size of a room, and was full of treasures. Boxes of jewellery. A little cabinet of delicate ornaments. A drawer containing neat stacks of banknotes. A chest of sovereigns. And whorled, golden evidence of the long connection between Forest House and the Great Forest.

"We could have a dragonfly," Griff said, struggling to lift an amasen horn the size of a pumpkin, far larger than any they'd seen on their visit to the Great Forest. "We could have a dragonfly *each.*"

"They did look rather fun, didn't they?" Aunt Arianne said, with an odd note to her voice, but then she added briskly: "I'll have to do a proper inventory. For now, however, there's a few matters I wish to discuss, and there's an hour or less until sunset—presuming that's relevant."

That meant she wanted to go to Hurlstone to talk: surely the safest place, even though there weren't likely to be any raven eavesdroppers in the cellar. Ignoring protests, Eluned chivvied her reluctant siblings into shutting away the hoard and heading upstairs.

"That all belongs to us, to you, right?" Griff asked. "That's what he said."

"Dem Makepeace owns this house and all its contents," Aunt Arianne said, her attention on the roofs surrounding the grove as she lowered her inevitable veil. "He has given me disposition of it, which is not technically the same thing as it belonging to me. Though I expect it will feel much the same in practice."

Eluned followed her gaze, and then nudged Eleri, for a line of eight ravens had hopped forward to the edge of the roof on the left, where the trees were thinnest, bobbing and watching.

Griff, noticing, made a rude gesture. "Sneaky snitches."

"Folies aren't driving them off?" Eleri asked.

"That spot must give them enough time to get away." Eluned considered hunting for a rock and trying her arm, but Aunt Arianne didn't linger, heading for the gate. "Maybe the Order always spies, and ravens are why it's called Hurlstone."

"Since before London?" Griff shook his head.

The bite mark on Aunt Arianne's hand had healed by the previous evening, but she still called the key without difficulty. Eluned stepped eagerly into the lead as her aunt closed the gate behind them, and they slipped through the shielding trees into a sun-drenched afternoon.

Drinking in drowsy perfection, Eluned gazed around at drystone walls and scatters of flowers against a backdrop of trees. But all her satisfaction dropped immediately away because the broken pillar that should hold an automaton was empty.

"Where—?" Eleri began, then wasted no more words, hunting for any sign of the missing experiment.

"Look for the amasen," Aunt Arianne suggested. "Dem Makepeace said it would stay here on guard. Perhaps it rained, and the amasen put Monsieur Doré somewhere dry."

Wondering if a snake would know anything about rust, Eluned gazed vainly around. They spread out through Hurlstone, even Griff daring the possibility of lurking wildlife, and it was he who called out: "Here!" only a short time later. Eluned hurried between waist-high walls, and spotted him standing with the statue—the vampire in rept.

A block of stone rested in the grass a few feet to one side of the vampire, and the automaton was seated on this, paddle-like hands arranged neatly on the stone either side of its narrow thighs, and its metal-jointed ankles crossed. The wooden head was tilted back, as if it was gazing up at the stone girl.

"Would the amasen pose it like that?" Eluned asked doubtfully, as Aunt Arianne and Eleri came up.

"Think it walked?" Eleri reached for the automaton, but Aunt Arianne touched her arm.

"Let's wait. We can talk here, and see if it reacts to us at all. Any sign of the amasen?"

Griff indicated with his chin the exact opposite side of the square of grass from him, and sunlight on gold led the eye to the horned snake, basking in the sun on the highest point of the surrounding wall.

Aunt Arianne inclined her head formally, and they all awkwardly followed her lead, and then sat down with her in the grass, ending up in a rough circle with the stone vampire and the automaton, as if all six of them were having a meeting.

"That was Lynsey," Aunt Arianne announced. "Leaving as you arrived."

So much had been happening that Eluned had almost forgotten the one solid lead they'd hoped to pursue—the person who had brought the artificial fulgite commission to their parents. She had barely looked at the tall, blond woman.

"Right one?" Eleri asked.

"Impossible to say. She did not react to me—or to sight of you—with any obvious awareness or guilt. But she has a very interesting connection to pursue."

Unhurriedly, Aunt Arianne took them from Lynsey Blair to Lord Fennington, a person Eluned had heard of mainly for hosting dinner parties on the Tamesas during the autumn feastings. But he apparently funded a great deal of scientific research, and so they agreed it was a good idea to pretend to be interested in going to his school.

"Can we take Melly?" Eleri asked, unexpectedly.

"Melly's left school," Eluned said, surprised. "Why would we take her?"

"Because she's left school. I asked Nabah about it. Melly loves words. She writes poetry. But Melly thinks that she has to look after the store for her father, even though Dem Ktai would far rather she did something she loved. Melly says she can write poetry anywhere."

"But that's true."

"I don't need to keep up school to make automatons. You don't need to go to that atelier you keep talking about: you can draw already. But you know that to keep on alone would be like leaving yourself still a sketch. Half the person you could be, a plant that never got enough water. Why should Melly not be everything she could be because the Crown only pays for schooling until you're sixteen?"

"How does taking her to this Tangleways place help? If it's a boarding school, won't it be more expensive than the school she was already going to?"

"So? We can pay her fees. It's not like we can't afford it."

Eleri waved a hand to encompass a distant room crammed with treasures, but Eluned looked instead at their aunt, ominously silent behind her veil. Would being suddenly rich loosen previously tight purse-strings? Or make her worse?

"I suspect you overlook the small matter of pride, Eleri," Aunt Arianne said, voice quiet but at least not sounding annoyed. "I have no objection to you inviting your friends along on a trip to the country, however. I expect you'll all find a visit to Tangleways enjoyable. The original house was inherited by a brother and sister who spent the rest of their lives competing with extravagant extensions and outbuildings. And then the whole thing passed on to a man of a very odd and secretive nature. It sat empty for a long time after his death."

That word brought them all up against the thing that none of them had spoken of, but which had filled their minds ever since they had returned home. It was Griff who asked, in a shy voice very unlike his usual manner.

"Who would be in charge of us? If—if what the dryw said is right?"

Aunt Arianne didn't answer immediately. Then she reached up and took off her hat and veil, wincing only a little in the deepening haze of the late afternoon light. She wasn't smiling.

"Tante Sabet," she said. "Your great-aunt, Sabet d'Lourien. Once things have settled down, I must take you to Lutèce so you can meet her."

"If you're alive," Eleri said, because Eleri of all of them could.

"If I'm alive." Aunt Arianne glanced up at the girl gazing forever at the sky, and her hand lifted briefly, then she dropped it down. "I own, the shadow of death looms less large when you've recently had your throat torn open. Besides, even if that was what he meant, the pronouncements of dryw are not considered inevitabilities, but instead in the nature of warnings and challenges. Did you notice that there were two separate foretellings?"

Griff straightened. "When he pointed?"

"Yes. Nor are either of those foretellings necessarily for a single person, but Keeper Tyse felt quite certain that the visual indication was to make clear that the second was for one or all of us standing inside the house. Possibly still me, of course, but we'd already established that this undertaking had risks. I must teach you three to shoot, once the trunks I'd put into storage arrive."

Without denying the danger, Aunt Arianne made it all seem far less dramatic, and Eluned felt herself relax even though the acknowledgement hadn't changed anything at all.

"The first foretelling is the larger problem," Aunt Arianne added. "The coafor are obliged to report them, you know, though given the audience we had, I wouldn't be surprised if half the borough is already discussing it over evening meal. Talk of the fate of Albion and a shattered dragon is bound to attract attention—not even counting the Unionist *and* the aide of Prince Gustav playing witness. That will make quiet investigation a great deal more difficult. Not, I admit, that we've succeeded in escaping notice so far. You'll find when you go upstairs that someone found a way in and started searching the attic, until the folies chased them off. That one bothers me because I didn't notice them. The attic is on the edge of my ability to sense the living, but I can usually tell when someone's up there."

"You think maybe it was a shabti?"

Aunt Arianne smiled at Griff's eager tone. "I hope not, since that would suggest we're at risk of a visit from those sphinxes as well. But at any rate it seems safest to leave Monsieur Doré here, and to never discuss things we particularly don't want overheard anywhere but Hurlstone. How did your tour of the workshops go?"

"Have what parts can be bought now. And recommendation for a foundry able to cast the others. Used up the money."

Eleri had also bought three vices, and it had been lucky Nabah and Melly had been along to help carry them back. But that surely wasn't what their aunt had meant.

"There was lots of talk of haunted automata," Eluned said. "We didn't have to ask, just listen."

"They were making it up to impress each other," Griff put in.

"Maybe. No-one there had seen any automata activing themselves, anyway." As their own automaton continued to sit unmoving—at least while they were there.

"We'll go further tomorrow," Eleri said. "The best workshops are north of the river, near the airship fields. We can look for the one that makes dragonflies."

But Aunt Arianne was shaking her head.

"No, tomorrow we'll be clothes shopping. Because the day after, we're going to the palace to take afternoon tea with Princess Leodhild. And, I hope, hear the results of Dem Makepeace's investigations in Caerlleon."

THIRTEEN

As Aunt Arianne paid the taxi driver, Eluned carefully straightened her new ankle-length shendy and matching split tunic, immensely aware of the guards standing behind soaring gates, and the crowds of sightseers on the enormous paved area in front of Gwyn Lynn Palace. Only visitors for the palace drove up onto this paved area, but they'd normally have the gates opened for them and drive on through, rather than walk.

Griff, the reason for the eccentricity, was indifferent to their audience, clutching his new sketchbook and spinning in a circle to drink in his surroundings, and then keeping on for several further rotations, delighting in the way his long, pleated shendy flared out into a bell. They were all rather pleased with the new clothes. Mother had been impatient with impractical clothing, so the fine cloth and exact tailoring Aunt Arianne deemed necessary for afternoon tea with a princess became a treat in itself.

It was a pity Aunt Arianne still couldn't quite manage full sunlight, and so looked odd in comparison, though entirely self-possessed as she handed her invitation to the guard standing to the left of the big gates.

"Shall I send for an autocarriage, Dama?" the guard asked, barely glancing at the invitation, and instead marking a list.

"We wished to take our time admiring the bridge," Aunt Arianne said. "If that's permitted."

"Of course, Dama," the guard said, smiling at Griff, who had stopped whirling and was now standing on tip-toe to better view the three finials that crowned the centre of the otherwise rather plain gate. A slender, stylised hare and a coiling dragon bracketed the centre finial, a silvery triskelion, three delicate wings springing from a single central point.

The uniformed woman opened a small side gate, and summoned a page from some hidden recess, instructing the girl to take them to Princess Leodhild. In short order they were striding down the perfectly flat paved drive toward the bridge that had had Griff in a welter of excitement for the last two days. Eluned could not pretend to less eagerness, at least for the splendours of the palace, and because she was going to meet one of the Suleviae. Her. Eluned Tenning.

Wanting to rub a few noses in that fact did not fit with the person Eluned tried to be, and so she only briefly allowed herself to picture Retwold School exploding with disbelief and envy. That helped stifle nerves, and with Griff and Eleri by her side even a princess could not be so very daunting. Eluned only had to remind herself of that with every step.

"Two penny tour, damini?" their guide was asking, surveying Aunt Arianne's heavy veil with bland interest.

"Why not?" Aunt Arianne said.

Caught up in not being daunted, Eluned only listened absently to details of the vast parkland surrounding the lake, and spared less than her usual attention on Griff as he delighted in the Three Dragons Bridge, a rather dull flat arch over the widest part of Gwyn Lynn Lake. More than embarrassment was at stake with this visit. They'd had little choice but to trust Aunt Arianne's vampire, given his control over her, and he had clearly intended to pass on to the Suleviae the things he'd found out. The secrecy of their investigation would be inevitably lost if shared among whoever knew how many royal advisors and friends, and the chance of one of Them hearing about clues and a second automaton and hidden fulgite increased with every confidant. Not that Eluned expected to be attacked at the palace, but just by visiting they drew more attention to themselves.

"Step to this side, please, damini," the page was saying. "Car coming."

It was a tiger, large, sleek and powerful, and Eluned was diverted into wondering if they were now rich enough to buy such an extravagance, and whether that meant they had been poor before. They hadn't owned any sort of autocarriage, back in Caerlleon, but they'd had a house, and people who looked after it, and though there'd always been a separation between necessities and indulgences, because money had been tied up in projects, Eluned could never remember truly feeling conscious of it before.

Losing the house was a major reason for that, but it was more that Aunt Arianne still seemed to expect them to keep track of how much things cost, even after sorting through a safe full of treasures, and unflinchingly buying them vast piles of clothing.

Working to put money and nerves aside, Eluned reminded herself this visit was a privilege, and she had particularly wanted to see the next place on their 'tour', an egg-shaped courtyard surrounded by arched windows and a triumph of carved linework.

This, at least, allowed Eluned to forget other concerns. She'd always been proud that her own grandmother had been among the artists called upon during the construction of Gwyn Lynn Palace, but it was the Running Yard she'd most wanted to see. The walls above and between each and every arch were filled with knotted depictions of the Otherworldly beings the Suleviae, by Sulis' grace, commanded. The three dragons, Nimelleth, Dulethar and Athian, the Night Breezes, and the triskelion. Fabulous. The kind of balance of form and pattern Eluned longed to achieve.

"The two islands are officially called Thurin and Aliden," their guide was saying, "but, of course, everyone calls them the Bean and the Bonnet because of their shapes, like we call this the Egg instead of the Running Yard. There are over seven hundred rooms in the main part of the palace, which fills the Bean completely. The Bonnet, Aliden, is the smaller island, but will look more spacious because the royal residences are widely spaced around gardens. This way, damini."

Patient with their gawping, the page coaxed them past the tiger, waiting with its driver, through an open doorway in the northwest curve of the 'Egg', and into a large, dome-ceilinged room with many exits, the most notable flanked by two very impressive guards wearing both swords and pistols. The walls between were hung with paintings, and the room itself busy with groups of people coming and going.

"The Crossing Gallery," the page said, as Aunt Arianne took her hat and veil off. "The only dry way to reach the residences without a boat—or wings. Let me hold that for you, dama."

Aunt Arianne smiled her thanks, and they paused to study the paintings until Aunt Arianne discovered a mirror set between two enormous landscapes and said: "Is there somewhere I can tidy my hair?"

"Of course, dama—" the page began, but broke off as one of a pair of men heading toward the Egg stopped short.

"Rian?" he said, voice high with surprise. Aunt Arianne turned, and he looked startled, then held up his hands in apology, continuing in heavily accented Prytennian: "Ah, pardon. It is my error..."

Aunt Arianne, after a moment's pause, smiled. "You've changed far more than I, Felix."

Eluned, who prided herself on her Latin, was disappointed to barely be able to make out more than a handful of words in the exchange that followed, though it was easy enough to guess that a large part of it involved: "You look so young!" The man himself only seemed to be in his twenties, his companion a good deal older, and the pair of them almost stereotypically Roman in appearance, with curling dark hair and impressive noses. Like most non-Prytennian men, they weren't wearing a summer shendy at all, only short, sleeveless tunics belted over tight-fitting shirts and trousers, with some rather nice patterns to the cloth.

"But, no, I have learned it with great effort," the man said, switching back to Prytennian. "Diligently, if not well." The older man with him murmured something, and he grimaced. "I must go. But I will call on you, and we will to lunch." He took Aunt Arianne's hands then, adding: "I was sorry, to hear what happened. That was badly done."

"An object lesson," Aunt Arianne said, with her faint, amused smile. "Good afternoon, Felix."

The Roman man kissed her hands, which made Aunt Arianne raise her eyebrows, and then the page was leading them to discreet rooms where they could primp before meeting Princess Leodhild.

"Used to court him?" Eleri asked, as Aunt Arianne slipped a comb out of her daybelt.

"Given he was all of twelve last time we met, no," Aunt Arianne said. "He's a cousin of the Dacian Proconsul, and is apparently in Prytennia with the company assisting the underground railway's construction. Not at all what I thought he'd end up doing."

Eluned watched with interest as their aunt swiftly let down and recoiled her butter-brown hair, settling it back into the heavy knot she liked to wear at the nape of her neck. Eluned's own hair, kept short for convenience's sake, was easily smoothed.

"In charge of digging automata?" Eleri asked, pursuing her own interests.

"Possibly," Aunt Arianne said, as they returned outside to find Griff plumped down on the corridor floor sketching the view into the Gallery. "I'll ask, if I do see him again."

After Griff was persuaded to stand, the brightly interested page led them back into the Crossing Gallery, past the attentive guards, and onto a covered bridge, a short arch of pale stone.

"The Glass Channel," the girl said, as they gazed down the lightly curving corridor formed by two rows of windows, the buildings of both islands deliberately constructed to mirror each other. "During winter the water freezes, and on some days at sunset the whole thing turns pink and red."

A short, well-built man stepped onto the bridge from Aliden Island. "Danel, Her Highness will be waiting for her guests."

Starting, the page fished a watch from inside the waistband of her shendy, and bit her lip. Although they'd arrived well ahead of their afternoon appointment purely so they could linger over their trip through the palace, they had somehow taken a long time seeing very little.

"This way, damini," the man went on, and they followed him obediently down an arched corridor.

The royal residences were technically three separate buildings arranged in a triangle, but the residences of Sulevia Leoth and Sulevia Seolfor were joined together by the rooms that sat along the bank of the Glass Channel. The braided tower belonging to Sulevia Sceadu was more distinctly separate, its square base joined to the others only by covered walkways. Beyond the tower were trees, and ivy-covered walls, and in between the three residences were shrubs and massed flower beds, and a central pavilion that reminded Eluned distinctly of the roofless ruin at Hurlstone. It was in the pavilion that Princess Leodhild waited.

There were no covered walkways to this central point, so the page, Danel, handed Aunt Arianne her hat back. While her Aunt rearranged it, Eluned took several calming breaths. Although she had knelt before Cernunnos himself only a few days ago, that did not make it any less amazing to meet one of the three living avatars of Prytennia's sun goddess. A week ago the idea of an informal chat with the Sulevia of the Song, commander of the triskelion, would have been outright unbelievable, but this had somehow become their life. Gods, vampires, royalty.

And yet, the princess didn't seem like she was waiting for them at all. There was a table set in the middle of the pavilion, and the princess was intently studying wide sheets of paper spread all over it. When the sound of their approach caught her attention she looked up at them quite blankly. But then she smiled.

"I've forgotten my schedule," she said. "Sit down, do, and let me look at you. Benric, send someone to clear away this mess and bring us something nice."

Princess Leodhild's grandfather had been Nubian, and she certainly lived up to the fabled vigour of that people. Eluned had rarely seen anyone more vibrantly alive, even though she was older than Aunt Arianne, with three children of her own. But, of course, she was a living avatar of Sulis herself, one of Three Who Are One.

Dismissing their attempts to bow to her, Princess Leodhild apologised instead for forgetting that Aunt Arianne might have difficulties with the location, and then Griff and Eleri got a look at what was on the table, and any hope of maintaining proper decorum was entirely lost.

"The vampire tunnels!" Griff crowed, and thrust head and shoulders over the table to study the diagram the princess had before her. "They *are* digging south of the river already!"

"Just survey digging," the princess said, thankfully not affronted. "You think vampires are digging tunnels?"

"To get about during the day."

"Not very cost-effective. A well-curtained carriage and a quick dash for the door have been working well enough for millennia. Tunnels would be an extravagance."

Eleri, in the meantime, had drawn out one curling sheet that had been pushed toward the back of the table, and was studying it minutely. It was a flying machine, one quite unlike the lumbering dirigibles that ruled the skies. Eleri, being Eleri, found a pencil on the table and began making alterations.

"Your pardon, highness," Aunt Arianne said. "I fear I overestimated this pair's base level of courtesy."

Her voice was as light as ever, but Griff straightened apologetically and Eleri at least glanced up.

Princess Leodhild waved an indifferent hand. "No matter: I rarely stand on ceremony. And I suspect them to merely be complimenting my character. You feel you have found a flaw in the design, youngling?"

"Only a suggestion." Eleri put the pencil down, and then offered the sheet to the princess, as if being marked on a test.

Glancing down, Princess Leodhild said: "I'll pass it on to Minister Trevelyan. I'm sure she'll appreciate the feedback."

There was no note of sarcasm to the words, and the princess saw them settled on cushioned seats before plying Eleri with questions about the process of adapting their grandfather's old mannequin into an automaton. Griff immediately began to sketch the surrounding buildings, but Eluned hated to even look at the garden. Created by the Queen's Consort, it was said to be an exquisite jewel, but currently shared with much of Prytennia a sadly wind-burned condition.

Peering instead at a small pile of new-looking books on the table, she found fearfully dull titles like *The Principles of Ma'at and Prytennia's Concept of Justice*, and *The Role of Auguries in Roman Decision-Making*. There was one, *Allegiance: Born, Territorial, Bestowed, Taken*, that made her hand itch again, reminding her that Cernunnos now had a claim to her soul, but then a whole line of people arrived, and took the entire table away, replacing it with a fresh one that was rapidly filled with glasses of watermelon juice, and tiny sandwiches, cakes and ices, vivid and sweet and wonderfully cold on a hot summer afternoon.

Princess Leodhild kept them talking, asking questions about their parents, and their studies, and Forest House. She even knew about the visit from the dryw of the Order of the Oak, and what he'd said, though she shrugged off attempts to interpret the Speaking.

"Such a ridiculously vague collection of words. He might as well have recited his grocery list to you. There's sure to be a great deal of fuss, but other than, perhaps, avoiding things with four eyes—or whatever you interpret a quartered glance as—I'd recommend just getting on with life. Put your energy to the task at hand rather than second-guessing the significance of anything so imprecise."

"I fear it's not our attitude that's going to be the problem," Aunt Arianne said.

"Yes. That storm will break today, which makes the timing of this meeting fortuitous, though it's a pity Tanwen is away walking Nimelleth's spine. But Our attitude will be positive, and it will give people something to talk of other than wind. And Egyptians." Princess Leodhild shrugged, setting her curls bouncing. "The scrutiny may be uncomfortable, especially since you have such a romantic background. Do you paint or sculpt yourself?"

Aunt Arianne shook her head. "My parents gave me a great deal of training, but I had neither the talent nor the passion."

During that first busy afternoon at Forest House, Eluned had heard her aunt answer almost the exact same way at least twice, and wondered how she managed to sound so unconcerned. Eluned could readily imagine the crawly little feeling of failure that would come each and every time she had to make the admission. At least Princess Leodhild didn't respond with the flat 'oh' of those earlier questioners.

Griff tucked himself into Eluned's side. Recognising this reaction, she looked about, and spotted the cause in the arms of a tall boy leading three girls from one of the residences.

Although Eluned had only ever seen a few grainy and distant photographs of them in the newspapers, it was impossible not to recognise these newcomers: Princess Leodhild's three children, and Queen Tanwen's younger daughter, Princess Celestine.

"Sorry, mother," the boy said. "I don't think this can wait."

Prince Luc was a rarity: a son of one of the Suleviae, born before Princess Leodhild had ascended. He was thin, had skin, hair and eyes in similar tones of light brown, and was said to be a very quiet person. The animal he carried was far more distinctive: a puppy, white all over except for long, silky red ears.

"Has Arawn been visiting?" Princess Leodhild asked, but she frowned as she joked, for the King of the Dead came to the living world only in times of great need, or to hunt the spirits of the lingering dead. And it would be a remarkable thing, a doom-tiding, to leave one of his hounds, the Cŵn Annwn, behind.

"It was one of the Tuatha Dé Danaan, Mother," said the tallest of the girls. This would be Princess Iona, who had her mother's generous tumble of curls. "Walked in on us from nowhere, and said this was a birthday present for Cele."

"And I would like him back, if you please," said the next-tallest girl, whose hair was very long and straight and dark. "Luc, you had no right to take him."

Eluned had to work very hard not to stare impolitely, for Princess Celestine was reputedly the daughter of a dragon, and thus naturally the most interesting person who could possibly interrupt afternoon tea. The history behind her birth was one of Prytennia's greatest love stories—or grandest hoaxes.

"Named him Falinis, too," Princess Iona said. "Have we done something to upset the Tuatha Dé?"

Princess Leodhild held out her arms, and Prince Luc handed the puppy over. The animal, obviously still very young, tolerated the transfer placidly, and briefly raised his slender head to consider his new custodian.

"A fortnight ago an Alban-bound airship was caught by the windstorms and blown right over Danuin's mist wall," Princess Leodhild said. "This may well be a pointed comment."

"Showing that they can easily reach us, if we repeat the error?" Princess Iona stretched out her hand to allow the puppy to scent the back of her fingers, which he did with a grave dignity. "May I have permission to carry a weapon to lessons?"

"Not in this century," Princess Leodhild said, then added: "Dimity!"

~I-i-EE!~

A whirling pinwheel of blue and white popped into existence, and Eluned cast a brief, delighted glance at Eleri, then drank in this up-close encounter with the most famed of the Suleviae's creatures. The triskelion were completely Otherworldly, lacking mouths, or eyes, or anything but their wings. Their name meant 'three legged', for during pitched battle they had been known to roll along the ground. This one was tiny, its 'voice'—a sound generated by its spinning—high and bright.

"Ask Mi Jiang if he would please come here," Princess Leodhild said.

~I-i-EE!~ the triskelion hummed, and vanished.

"Sorry for crashing in, incidentally, and towering all over the place," Princess Iona said, snagging a marzipan-iced cake as she turned to examine her mother's guests. "Everyone, let's sit down. I'm Iona, but you probably guessed that."

Princess Leodhild tsked. "Execrable child. But this is someone I should introduce you to anyway: Dama Arianne Seaforth, the new Keeper of the Deep Grove."

Princess Iona had bitten off half of her cake, and swallowed it in an unwieldy gulp. "You're Comfrey's accident?"

"Our connection certainly wasn't deliberate," Aunt Arianne said. "These are my nieces, Eluned and Eleri. I'd introduce my nephew, Griff, as well, but he seems to have escaped with most impressive speed."

Horrified, Eluned looked about, but it was true. Griff was gone.

FOURTEEN

"Shy around strangers?" Princess Iona asked.

"I suspect it's the puppy." Aunt Arianne was matter-of-fact.

Straightening indignantly, Princess Celestine said: "How could anyone be afraid of something as tiny as Falinis?"

"Tiny?" Princess Iona selected another sweet treat and gestured with it toward her mother and the docile puppy. "Look at the size of those paws. He's going to be enormous. And that's not even counting his death-hound colouring, and being named for...what was it Luc? High King Lugh's invincible hunting hound? The nephew's got good sense, keeping clear."

"He doesn't like animals," Eluned said, uncomfortably. "He never has, ever since he was a baby."

"Bitten by something?" Princess Iona slowed her cake consumption in order to make a long study of Eluned's right arm.

Princess Leodhild gave her eldest daughter a quelling look, then said: "Toroco!"

A second triskelion, this one red and gold and perhaps a handbreadth larger, popped into being. ~O-o-O!~

"Round up a stray boy-child," Princess Leodhild said. "Match this hair colour."

She nodded at Aunt Arianne, who sat very still as the triskelion—its movements very like a hummingbird—darted toward her, bringing with it a wave of warmth. The triskelion were true creatures of the sun, and the mere presence of the largest could inflict terrible burns. Even the small ones were not something you wanted near your hair.

Then it was gone, trailing its song as it whirled across the gardens, and passing on its way its blue and white fellow leading a tall, thin man who could be none other than the Queen's Consort, Mi Jiang.

His was a famous story. In the earliest days of airship travel, before she became Sulevia Seolfor and Queen, Tanwen Gwyn Lynn had led the crew of the *Palthas* on a grand flight all the way around the world, to prove that it was possible. The *Palthas* had flown close to the Dragon Empire of Yue—a realm like Danuin surrounded by walls to prevent trespass, although Yue used light instead of mist. A flight of young Yue dragons had met and briefly escorted the airship, and one of them had seen then-Princess Tanwen and loved her from that moment.

Eluned had enjoyed several rather fanciful books about Prince Jiang's quest to find out who his love was, the many years it had taken to win his father's permission to follow her, and the astonishment felt by all Prytennia when it had received an embassy from such a fabled and magnificent land, presenting the now-Queen with one of the sons of the Emperor of Yue, as a gift.

Had the Tuatha Dé been deliberately echoing this story, giving Princess Celestine a pup with a famous name and exceedingly unlucky colouring? For, while Queen Tanwen had accepted Mi Jiang as a guest, and eventually taken him as a lover, he had never shown any sign of being a dragon. Some said that his father had forbidden him his true shape as the price for pursuing his heart, but there had long been talk that the 'gift' was instead an elaborate insult, vengeance for an airship flying too close to well-guarded borders. That the Emperor of Yue had sent not his son, but his gardener.

Eluned couldn't guess what the truth was, or even if Queen Tanwen cared either way, for Prince Jiang was an extraordinarily beautiful man: elegant, dark eyed, with a fall of silken blue-black hair that he had passed on to his daughter. And such ineffable presence, as he stepped into the pavilion and inclined his head to Princess Leodhild, that Eluned wished desperately to have never heard such phrases as 'Hoozie Fake', and the other even less nice things said about the Queen's consort.

"A fair afternoon to you," he said, arresting their motion to rise with the tiniest movement of his hand. "How may I assist?"

Princess Leodhild briefly explained, and carefully handed the puppy over. Falinis again raised his head, making Eluned feel as if the puppy had understood every word said, and was politely making eye contact.

"By no means an ordinary animal," Prince Jiang said. "But not on first examination inimical. Instead, this seems to be a true gift, a valuable companion. You wish for him, then, child?"

"Very much, Father." Princess Celestine's response was restrained and measured, all sign of her previous restlessness smoothed away. "There are strings, I am sure, or at least mischief intended. But I will not hold his marking against him." She hesitated, and her careful formality fell away as she exclaimed: "It would *hurt* him."

"Then I have no objection," Prince Jiang said, and smiled at the effervescent delight his daughter attempted to contain, before inclining his head again to Princess Leodhild. "Forgive me, I must return. My staff are enjoying a minor crisis."

With the ceremony that seemed imbued in his every action, Prince Jiang handed Falinis to his daughter and departed. The blue and white triskelion ceased whirling around the ceiling of the pavilion and dropped down to ~I-i-EE?~ at its mistress. It was joined by its red and gold companion, whirling up with an ~O-o-O!~ that by its very tone announced success.

Eluned's relief as she looked around for her brother faltered immediately when she spotted him on the path to the tower belonging to the Sulevia Sceadu, talking animatedly to a striking woman with pale skin and wavy dark hair. It could only be Crown Princess Aerinndís.

Working to hide her dismay, Eluned glanced at Eleri, but her sister hadn't yet noticed the approaching pair. Princess Aerinndís had a forbidding reputation, and was not smiling as she listened to Griff burble on—no doubt telling her all about her own tower, and the unusual gaps left in a structure that looked as if it had been braided rather than built.

Aunt Arianne stood up, and Eluned surreptitiously tugged Eleri to join them in making their bows. Princess Leodhild may have abandoned formality, but Princess Aerinndís did not seem so disposed, studying them expressionlessly before inclining her head a bare fraction in acknowledgement.

"My apologies, Highness," Aunt Arianne said, after Princess Leodhild had made brief introductions. "I was not paying enough attention."

"No matter." Princess Aerinndís' husky voice held a note of indifference. "Our mutual acquaintance has presented himself for a conference."

"Comfrey's here?" Princess Iona was not at all awed by her older cousin's glance. "Can you send him to us when you're finished with him? Tete wants him."

Tete—Princess Tethané—hadn't spoken at all. She was Griff's age, and was considered a not very 'satisfactory' princess. Rumour had it she couldn't talk at all, and had to be carefully controlled, but all Eluned could tell of her beneath the floppy yellow sun hat hanging over her eyes was that her hair was cloudy like Melly's.

"Perhaps you younglings would enjoy a small performance while we see what Comfrey has to say?" Princess Leodhild asked, then added to Griff: "Or would you find that uncomfortable?"

Griff, who had been subdued once again by the near presence of a chancy animal, looked from puppy to the triskelion whirring above, and fascination won over caution. "I'd like that awfully much, thank you."

They were being tidied away, but Eluned was no more minded to object to the distraction than Griff. Though she could not understand Eleri following along without a word as Princess Iona led them toward the Sulevia Leoth's residence, the two triskelion in warm escort, Princess Celestine dancing ahead, hugging her puppy close, and Prince Luc and Princess Tethané bringing up the rear.

"Sorry," Eluned said, stepping uncomfortably into the role of spokesperson as Griff positioned himself by her side to watch for puppy attacks. "We're interrupting you now."

"No, this is perfect," Princess Iona said. "We were due to go to afternoon lessons, and that tutor is so dreary. Your arm looks very complicated. What can you do with it?"

Prince Luc said quietly: "Not a performing animal, Io."

Princess Iona pulled a face at her brother, then said:

"My mouth does run along by itself sometimes, and I say positively awful things. Then Luc points it out to me. Was I being obnoxious?"

"It's all right," Eluned said, glancing worriedly at her sister, since it was rare for Eleri not to intervene during such questions. That was how their family worked: Eluned and Eleri would shield Griff from animals, Eleri and Griff would deflect noxious curiosity, and Griff and Eluned would keep Eleri from killing herself during her inventive streaks, when common sense tended to desert her.

It had to be the plans for that flier: Eleri's imagination had been sparked, and she was lost to anything but possibility. Reluctantly accepting that she was on her own so far as conversation was concerned, Eluned offered a brief demonstration of how she could control her right elbow by lifting her shoulder, and could trigger her hand functions with her left elbow, using switches on the harness beneath her clothing.

"But what happens when you shrug?"

"Embarrassment, usually. I try to only use my left shoulder for that, or I get some odd flailings."

"Is it strong? Can you bend metal? Stop a rampaging horse?"

"The mechanism's too delicate. And it's still attached to the non-mechanical bits of me, which would not stop any horses."

"How did you lose your arm?" Princess Celestine asked, drifting closer. "A birth injury?"

People rarely asked directly. These children of the Suleviae were clearly used to people competing for their attention, willing to tell them anything. Their curiosity at least seemed straightforward, not weighed down by globbish pity, but this was a story that Eluned hated to tell. And yet Eleri was still silent, not even noticing when Eluned threw her an urgent glance. There was nothing for it.

With a firm grip on her glass shield, she began: "There was a kitten."

"One of the folies?" Prince Luc asked unexpectedly.

"The folies?" Eluned turned to stare. "What do you mean?"

"The guardians of the Deep Grove. Foliate cats."

Griff roused to say: "Those are cats? They look like little round bushes."

"That's what the records say."

"Little round bushes with cats inside, it seems," Princess Iona said. "But if Dama Seaforth's family has only recently come to Forest House, it's not likely to be folies. And you tut at me for interrupting people unnecessarily, Luc. So there was a kitten. And then?"

The idea of those clusters of leaves being cats was not enough to distract Eluned from the difficulty of her story, but it did make the shield a little lighter, and so she went on, pacing her breathing.

"We weren't allowed to keep him, but did. We called him Jasper, and we had him for two months without our parents ever realising. But he hated being shut up, and loved exploring, climbing, and one day he climbed through the ventilation window of the main workroom. I saw him go in, but the door was locked and the red flag up, which meant there was a timing test running. I could hear the machine."

"I'm guessing your family are automaton makers?" Princess Iona said.

Eluned could not approach the difference between 'are' and 'were', so ignored the question.

"I knew where the key was, and as I ran for it I could hear the engine stop, and then start up again as I returned. Most automatons run on cams or on sequence cards that control their movements. Sequence cards can be chained together, and the chain made into a loop, so that the automaton will run continuously. In a timing test for a processing automaton, you leave the automaton running without materials, to test whether the sequence stays true.

"The movement had paused when I used the key. I threw the door open, and that frightened Jasper, and of course he ran right into the workings, and I wasn't sure what part of the sequence it was up to, so all I could think to do was run and grab him. And the machine started."

No-one spoke. Eluned was remembering the feeling of fur beneath her fingers. Whenever she thought too much about what it had been like to have two arms of flesh and bone, she could feel Jasper's soft black fur, and see his brilliant blue eyes.

"Only five. Would know now to pull the cards, or the fulgite."

Eluned threw Eleri a look of relief and gratitude, but her sister's gaze was not on her.

They entered a domed playroom—such a delightful construction that Griff forgot puppies altogether and stopped dead in the doorway to drink in an elegant metal framework, and the triangular panels of window alternating with a ceiling painted dark blue and flecked with stars.

"Steel structure?" he said. "This isn't in the original plans."

"Mother had it added," Princess Iona said, continuing on to an island of mats and cushions hiding the centre of a splendid parquetry star. "For Dimmy more than us, I tend to think. Dimmy loves the way her song echoes."

~I-i-EE!~

The blue and white triskelion whirled down to circle around Princess Iona, then shot up to the very highest point of the dome, the volume of its song rising as it did until a high, sweet note pierced Eluned like a needle. She shuddered, then felt a touch on her left hand. Princess Tete, face still obscured, tugged at her fingers, the briefest contact, before following her sister into the centre of the dome.

"It's easier to take if you lie down," Prince Luc said and, with a ready understanding of Griff's competing interests, guided him to the far side of the island from where Princess Celestine had folded herself cross-legged on a cushion with Falinis on her lap.

Eluned, following her sister to the centre of the pile, took the opportunity to murmur: "All right, Eleri?"

It seemed a brief nod would be the only response she was to receive, but then Eleri leaned in and added: "Never met anyone so incredible."

This was such an un-Eleri thing to say that Eluned at first couldn't take it in, and turned the whole of her attention to the problem of formal clothing and proper decorum. Did one simply settle on a particularly wide and squashy cushion and treat royal heirs as new acquaintances? There was nothing to do but try not to look too stiff about it.

But it was impossible to ignore Eleri's words longer. 'Incredible' was not a word Eleri used for people, even the scientists she most admired. Did she mean one of the Suleviae? Or their children?

Princess Iona plumped back on another central cushion, her springing curls tickling Eluned's ear. "Luc, Tete, Cele, you do Toroco. Everyone else can do Dimmy."

Had Eleri meant Iona? That sheer confidence, and full force personality? Or...Eluned turned her head and considered Prince Luc, who was possibly as handsome as the papers said, in his reserved way. He glanced in her direction, and smiled encouragingly, and Eluned looked hastily away, then cursed herself because now he would think *she* liked him. But she supposed he was used to that.

The two triskelion, their song muted, slowed to hover directly above them, sending a faint, warm wind down onto their faces. Then the red and gold, Toroco, sang its name, but drew each syllable out to produce a long ~OOOOOOO-oooooo-OOOOOOO~, and the three designated Gwyn Lynns, a fraction of a note behind, sang along with it.

Eluned's chest throbbed again, and she shot a wide-eyed glance at her sister, but Eleri's head was turned away. Toward Princess Celestine.

Celestine? Eluned couldn't understand it. Fine-boned, and a little taller than Eluned and Eleri, Celestine she had her father's long fall of straight, black hair, and exceptionally nice, clear skin. And...she had seemed to like her new pet? Attractive, yes, and with a fascinating parentage, but 'incredible'?

Deciding she was misunderstanding something, Eluned turned her attention back to the dome above as Dimity blurred in a series of sidewise darts before settling above them again to sing its name. It was impossible to match the high, ethereal notes, but Eluned at least managed to keep her pitch true, and she took a deep breath after, wondering if she could truly feel the triskelion's reaction. Everyone spoke of the joy of the Solstice Singing, but she'd had no idea it would be so intense.

Then the two triskelion sang at the same time, spiralling together along with the notes of their names, and they all sang back, even Eleri and Princess Tethané, who had a sweet, true voice, deep for such a small girl.

It was easier after that, to set aside the confusion of Eleri, and the memory of soft fur, and the discomfort of being thrust on prestigious strangers to entertain. The triskelion made all the difference. They could do nothing but spin, and speed or slow their song, but their delight was a second sun. Creatures of Sulis, sky-born, wind-hearted, completely different from her own human existence, present thanks to the tie of full allegiance between Sulis and the Suleviae.

Her hand itched.

FIFTEEN

Prytennia's Crown Princess had a reputation for being unsociable, and her official photographic portrait certainly seemed to show a stern and uncompromising young woman. After a less than successful State visit the Dauphin had even taken to calling her 'La poupée d'acier': the Steel Doll.

That piece of mockery in no way suited Aerinndís Gwyn Lynn on a warm summer afternoon, wearing the lightest of Continental frocks and with her waist-length hair unbound. While not so deliciously tall as Lynsey Blair, she still had several inches on Rian, and seemingly endless legs. Her mouth—wide and generous, but with an upward crimp in her lower lip—might give her an air of being permanently unimpressed, but automaton-like she most certainly was not.

Rian stole appreciative glances, but during the short walk to the princess' tower she set aside formidable distraction and refocused on goals. There were immense advantages in the Suleviae becoming involved in the investigation, particularly Princess Aerinndís. As the Sulevia Sceadu, the Crown Princess commanded 'the Night Breezes': a very mild name for one of Prytennia's main defences—and sources of information-gathering.

Hoping Griff had not been too inconsiderate in his explorations, Rian followed the princess to her tower's central stair, and was not surprised to be led downwards. She knew his heartbeat now, the vampire whose blood she shared. There was a certain resonance as well, not entirely pleasant. Part of herself, sitting before her.

Or, in Makepeace's case, lying sprawled on an oval table, reading a newspaper.

He was dressed as he had been when she'd first seen him, in a casual wrapped shendy and a worn shirt lacking its laces. The formal clothing of the other day must have been on Cernunnos' account. Perhaps Makepeace—with a millennia supporting Suleviae rule behind him—offered the Gwyn Lynns the same disdain he spread so liberally elsewhere.

Princess Leodhild and Princess Aerinndís, with barely a pause, gripped one side of the table and tilted it, sending the ancient puppet master and assassin sliding. Makepeace made no effort to arrest his fall, landing on two chairs, which clattered hard to the polished wooden floor.

The vampire folded his paper as he lay in the tangle. "You'll damage the furniture."

"No matter. You can cover the repairs." Princess Leodhild settled herself at one end of the now-righted table, opposite Princess Aerinndís. "Or you could keep your feet—and the rest of you—off the table, Comfrey."

He responded by reaching up and placing the paper where they could see it. An early evening edition, only a portion of the headline visible, but more than enough.

"Make the effort to send word, Wednesday, should any other events of interest occur in your presence. A minor declaration of war, perhaps, or trivial invasion."

Rian, adjusting her thoughts to the unexpected family atmosphere, sat down on her vampire's opposite.

"You neglected to furnish me with an address."

"I'm always contactable through the palace."

"Is the common post not read? Shall I invent a code?"

He shot her an irritated glance as he levered himself to his feet and recovered the chairs. "This latest excursion of yours is hardly secret." But he waved the discussion away. "Any other developments?"

Rian described the visit of Lynsey Blair, the Alban woman's connection to Lord Fennington, and the proposed trip to Tangleways.

"Folly *does* fund research into fulgite alternatives," Princess Leodhild remarked. "His company led the development of those roof-mounted turbines, you know, and the conversion of existing water- and windmills to fulquus generation. Whether he'd need to outsource is another question. Are you proposing to question him directly about this secret commission?"

"That depends on his reaction to Aedric and Eiliff's names." She glanced at Makepeace, who had propped his head on one fist. "As you say, the one who commissioned those automatons had small reason to steal them. We had a second visitor to Forest House—searching through the attic where Eleri has been setting up her workroom. So far as I can tell, this one came in through the street-side attic windows, and it took longer for the folies to notice. I don't think that bull creature could manage that."

"Mm." It was difficult to tell if his boredom was feigned. "What did you expect 'Felix' would end up doing?"

Rian stared. She'd said that when alone with Eleri and Eluned, with only Griff and the talkative young page nearby, and not within earshot. "How did you—?"

Princess Aerinndís' husky voice cut through her confusion. "He can make you not notice him. The Amon-Re line can control minds." Hands neatly folded on the table, the Crown Princess looked merely disinterested when Makepeace turned an expression of genuine annoyance on her. "Pouting from someone so ancient is ever entertaining, Comfrey, but it wastes time. Accident or not, you've bound yourself an apprentice. Use her effectively, for in this matter I have no patience left for games."

She had very dark blue eyes. It took increasing effort not to fall into them.

Makepeace sighed as if greatly put-upon, but then lifted a shoulder. "Wednesday recognised the one calling himself Gaius Silvanus, come with the head of Ficus Lapis to show the progress of the tunnelling. In this fashion for taking the old Republic names, that one is exceptionally common, almost a cliché, and thus infinitely suspicious attached even to the junior assistant of a very reputable engineering firm. So who is this 'Felix'?"

Putting aside the rather large revelation concerning the Amon-Re line's abilities, Rian said: "He's from the Tarinus branch of the Silvanii. Gaius Silvanus Tarinus. Felix is simply a family pet name."

Makepeace clicked his tongue. "Now I know the expectations."

"What relation to Darius Silvanus Tarinus?" Princess Aerinndís asked.

"Grandson," Rian said. "Favourite grandson. The omens around his birth were particularly good, and when I knew him he was being groomed to be the family's bright hope, was in Dacia to observe a successful Proconsul's handling of his duties. Though that was ten years ago, and as I said I would not have expected to find him outside the territories of the Republic. Not digging tunnels, at any rate."

"Perhaps he likes trains," Princess Leodhild said. "A lot of people do."

The good humour of her words was belied by narrowed eyes and the glance she offered her niece, who responded only with: "I'll look into it."

Rian hoped she hadn't brought unnecessary trouble down on Felix's head. After all, it was possible he had fallen out of favour, or simply refused his family's plans for him and pursued a career outside of politics. But his grandfather had served multiple times as one of the New Republic's Consuls and it truly was odd for Felix to be working in London.

Still, while Rome would certainly care deeply about functioning artificial fulgite, Felix had no obvious connection to Aedric, so Rian set him aside and returned to her core concern.

"Did you find anything suspect in Caerlleon?"

Makepeace, still propped on one fist, shifted his gaze back to her. "The local Constabulary think you sadly obsessed, looking for conspiracies in an obvious accident."

That was no revelation. "Yes. They liked to hold up Eluned as proof of Eiliff and Aedric's lack of care. I've done my best to prevent Eluned from realising that. What of Aedric's apprentice?"

"The boy was right." Makepeace, clearly aware of how she stiffened at his words, waited a double beat before continuing. "A friend of this Willa's asked her to buy what she could—told her he planned to start his own workshop, and didn't want his current employer to realise. That same friend fronted the auction, unusually well-funded, and made any number of purchases. Primarily of containers of smaller objects. And then he died."

"At the auction?" Princess Leodhild asked.

"The evening after he took delivery, though he wasn't found until several days later. Fell and broke his neck, very clumsy. His purchases were still there, though, and his family had them on-sold in due course. But there would have been plenty of time to search through them."

"A literal dead end, then?"

"Not quite. The man had his friends. He managed to not gossip about his purchases, but he was known to associate with the local grey trade. The thriving market there is stolen fulgite, of course, but if that's the reason for his involvement, how did they know these two pieces of fulgite existed in the first place? And why weren't you and those brats of yours attacked before Sheerside?"

"Did Willa know about the fulgite?" Rian asked.

"No. Only about the commission of an automaton, and she seems to have taken that at face value."

"That's all I knew as well, before Sheerside," Rian said. "The children had managed to keep it strictly secret, and Aedric and Eiliff had certainly taken pains to obscure the true nature of their commission. If they succeeded, the most likely source of information would be whoever commissioned them."

"And when a hasty search gave them only one of the fulgite pieces..." Makepeace lifted his head from its prop, frowning. "Ma'at vampires are far from the only truth diviners among the god-touched. If someone of that sort had questioned you when you didn't know about the fulgite, that would explain the progression, and the determination to get hold of the household contents."

If that was correct, then Rian had talked to one of the thieves—the most probable people behind Aedric and Eiliff's deaths. But she had spoken to dozens while sorting out the estate, none of whom stood out as particularly unusual.

Saying this, she added: "And then something happened to make them decide I had it after all. It's possible Dama Hackett mentioned a strangely-behaved automaton, but since no-one stole Monsieur Doré while I was unconscious, that seems unlikely. Which leaves the sudden interest of a sphinx. If those sphinxes have an interest in the artificial fulgite, perhaps whoever stole the other piece has encountered them already."

She turned to Princess Leodhild, careful to keep her tone entirely unassuming. "Did you have any fulgite with you, Your Highness?"

Princess Leodhild looked unexpectedly amused. "I did not. But that creature was not interested in me at all. Only the room I was in."

Princess Aerinndís studied her aunt, then said: "I recall hearing that Prince Gustav assisted in fighting off the attack."

"Roared about distractingly, at least. Though that axe of his is something of the Aesir's, and might well have done some damage if he'd been silly enough to actually engage the creature." She chuckled. "Too clever for his own good, that one, with his pretty little wing painted on his wrist. Lovely shoulders, though."

'A man with a painted wing' was someone who saved money while not caring about the cost to others. Rian had encountered a couple on her own account, and treated them with due contempt, for the Dose was far cheaper than the equivalent the Thoth-den had developed for women. Prince Gustav's motives were unlikely to be penny-pinching, despite Prytennia's laws and centuries of Suleviae rule making clear the futility of staking claim to the Trifold throne by means of a blood tie.

Her reminiscent smile fading, Princess Leodhild continued: "There was an interesting lamp in his room. A small thing in a leather holder, not much larger than a travelling clock. It cast patterns on the ceiling. The cabinet it stood on was crushed, and I'm not certain what happened to the lamp. Once we knew about this fulgite issue, I amused myself asking Msrah whether he happened to own such a thing. Which he does not."

"No reason to suspect it's powered by artificial fulgite," Makepeace said.

"It can be a working assumption," Princess Leodhild said, shrugging magnificently. "We need to get on, try to draw some conclusions. Let us say the sphinxes are connected to the windstorms—based on their appearance during a prolonged storm, and Egypt's sudden interest in helping us—and that they are hunting certain pieces of fulgite. And here is a thought: that theft of the fulgite shipment at the beginning of the year—that happened before the first of the windstorms, did it not?"

"Well before," Makepeace said.

"When did this latest spate of haunted automaton stories break out?"

"Those never really go away, but again...since the theft."

"Excellent. So the shipment contained special fulgite— artificial or haunted—and these sphinxes want it particularly. They certainly seem able to find it, if our understanding of the events at Sheerside are correct, which suggests some connection. Perhaps it's the Egyptians who have developed a process for creating artificial fulgite. A god-touched method would explain the success."

The princess glanced at Makepeace, who didn't respond, so she continued.

"But even if that was so, it does not explain the determination to retrieve fulgite if they can produce it. There must be something more, a reason why the Huntresses have descended on us in such force."

"It was news of the sphinxes that brought them," Makepeace said. "Not fulgite."

"Sphinxes from Hatshepsu's tomb, hunting fulgite, and in turn sought by Egypt." The princess pursed her lips. "Could Hatshepsu herself have Answered? Done something to her tomb guardians that allows them to produce fulgite?"

"What, lay it like eggs?"

Princess Leodhild made a choking noise, then threw her head back and laughed. Makepeace grimaced, but Princess Aerinndís smiled.

Rian looked away, and found Makepeace was watching her, but thankfully he didn't comment, simply saying: "I hope you're wrong, Hildy."

"So am I," Princess Leodhild said, sobering. "If this is artificial fulgite, and it is produced not by chemical process, but by some god-touched gift, and whatever produces it is *here...*"

"Then we will no doubt receive many more deputations offering to help with windstorms," Princess Aerinndís said, unmoved by visions of disaster. "This theory is almost entirely guesswork."

"Oh yes, held together by string and paste," Princess Leodhild agreed. "Still, the timing makes me fairly certain that there is a link between the storms and those sphinxes, and the sphinxes and the fulgite. The rest, well, we shall see. What about this climbing bull of yours, Comfrey? Linked to the sphinxes?"

"It didn't resemble anything I've seen out of Egypt. At a guess, that belongs to the thieves."

"A better description than 'a clawed bull' would help me in searching for it," Princess Aerinndís said.

"How many clawed bulls could there be in London?"

"Do you have paper and a pencil?" Rian asked. "I saw enough to give you an idea of it."

Directed to the table behind her, Rian produce a clean sketch, and slid it across to the Crown Princess.

"And yet, not an hour ago, you told me you hadn't the talent for art," Princess Leodhild said.

"I was thoroughly trained. This is simply a skill for me, not a calling."

"The winds can play with that then," Makepeace said, tilting his head to glance at the picture. "And send it off to Bermondsley to see whether she can identify it among the known god-touched—it's rare there's something I don't recognise. I'll continue on after the thieves. Hildy, you could, perhaps, tolerate more of Gustav in order to see where leading questions take you. And Wednesday will pursue Folly."

There was a hint of mockery in that last, which Rian ignored, her own attention on the Crown Princess' hands as she lifted the sketch.

"What of the second piece of fulgite?" Princess Aerinndís asked. "Do you not want to send it for analysis?"

"The original experiment—the idea that this particular fulgite will produce an automaton capable of functioning without command—is worth pursuing." Makepeace folded his arms, and dropped his head down to rest on them, adding: "The thing is moving, isn't it?"

"Not while we've been there," Rian said. "But it was no longer in the place we left it. The amasen wouldn't have shifted it?"

"Lila has been tasked with guarding and reporting, no more."

Blinking at the discovery of a name, Rian said: "You can speak to them?"

"Cernunnos can."

"Then that's settled for now," Princess Leodhild said, briskly. "Thank you for coming in, Dama Seaforth, and do send word if anyone else pronounces you saviour of Prytennia. Don't forget that Tete wants you, Comfrey."

Makepeace heaved another sigh, but levered himself out of his chair obediently. Rian quickly followed suit, making the briefest of bows before trailing her vampire out. She couldn't resist stealing one last glance back at the Crown Princess, languidly rising, and then put the woman out of her thoughts.

Ignoring Makepeace's derisive expression she said: "You really were at Forest House all along? Griff will be disappointed—he's very attached to the idea of a secret entrance to the house."

Her vampire didn't respond immediately, climbing the spiral stair. But he paused in the shade of the tower's portico entrance and turned a measuring look on her. Rian was aware of her own heartbeat quickening, but ignored the memory of teeth, not allowing physical fear to keep her from meeting his gaze.

"No," he said, eventually. "Only at the end. I came in through the grove, as I do here."

"Grove? In Gwyn Lynn Palace?"

"Any collection of trees is a grove to Cernunnos." Makepeace followed the edge of the portico around to a walkway heavily draped in vines, and strode on ahead, passing quickly through a section where the wind-burned leaves let through the hazy light of the afternoon sun.

Wondering how many of the design decisions of the palace had been made to accommodate the Wind's Dog, Rian waited until the man had reached a shadier point, then said: "I was thinking that the Suleviae were demonstrating a remarkable trust in my ability to hold my tongue, but of course it's simply that you've made it impossible for me to speak out of turn."

"You were the one looking to put a collar around your throat."

"The children weren't." The standard mesmeric abilities of vampires did not allow for nuanced commands, but she'd felt him lay an order to hold their tongues upon them. A control of minds, perception—what would that permit?

"Are you an open secret? Had I just not heard the gossip?"

He ignored her, leading the way into the Sulevia Leoth's section of the royal residences, to an uncomfortably warm room thrumming with song. The children sprawled on cushions, and shifted as the two triskelion descended to whirl around Makepeace's head.

"Go roast someone else," he said, waving a hand as if shooing flies. "Tete, I hope you've something worthwhile to show me."

The youngest of the Gwyn Lynn family jumped to her feet and took the dangling cuff of Makepeace's sleeve in both her hands.

"She has a whole sequence done," Princess Iona said, levering herself up on one elbow while the rest of the children clambered upright. "Tete makes lumiscope strips," she added, her gaze now on Rian. "She won't show them to us until Comfrey has sneered at them."

The youngest princess was pulling Makepeace urgently toward one of the room's three exits, but Griff had set himself up as a roadblock.

"Why don't you talk old-fashioned?"

Makepeace sidestepped. "Why would I?"

"Because people talked differently back when you were growing up?"

"People talk differently in Lutèce as well, but I see no reason to speak French to you." He glanced at Rian. "I'll send one of the midges to see you out."

"I'll do that," Prince Luc said.

"So obliging, Luc," Princess Iona murmured from her cushions. "What are you up to?"

"Indulging my curiosity," her brother said. "You never look properly."

"What's that supposed to mean?" The princess began to sit up, but then lay back as if the effort was too great. "Ah, I'll get it out of you later. Lovely to meet you all. Thanks for the excuse to skip lessons."

Rian was pleased with her charges for responding with reasonable aplomb, particularly as one Gwyn Lynn was disappearing out the room, a second half-asleep, and the third's attention almost entirely on the animal in her lap. The last quietly indicated an exit.

The twins seemed particularly subdued, but Griff's spirits bounded as soon they were out of sight of the puppy, and he peered eagerly in every direction, keen to view as much of the palace as possible.

"I intended to ask our escort if we could visit the Stone Garden," Rian said to the young prince, "but I suspect that's where you're taking us."

"Then I was right," Prince Luc said, looking pleased. "It took me an age to work out why your nephew seemed so familiar."

"Me? What do you mean?"

Attention divided, Griff almost walked into the page who had been their initial guide, who had clearly been lurking ready to escort them back. She skipped nimbly aside, and at a word from the prince fell into step behind them.

"You look a great deal like your father when he was your age," Rian explained.

"What's that got to do with anything?" Griff studied the prince suspiciously. "You never met my father, did you?"

"In a way, I grew up with him," Prince Luc said. "You'll see in a minute, we're nearly there."

They had reached the Crossing Gallery, and headed right, collecting numerous interested glances and a discreet escort of the guard who had been stationed at the entrance to the royal residences. The Stone Garden was only a short walk beyond the Gallery: a conservatory looking out over the western reach of Lake Gwyn Lynn, its glass and restrained plantings carefully designed to complement a work that had taken so many years of Charlotte Seaforth's life.

"*The Processional*," Eluned said, brightening. "I was hoping to see it."

"One of the highlights of the palace," Prince Luc said, and added to Griff: "Can you see what I meant now?"

The look Griff offered him was deeply suspicious, and the boy walked toward the centre of the room as if expecting some trick or trap. Rian watched his face anticipating the moment of recognition, but the unreality of the day combined with fragments of her own childhood and made it difficult to overlook that this was the first opportunity Rian herself had had to see her mother's masterwork in full. She had become someone who counted, who received invitations, and could go to a palace as a guest not a servant, using the front entrance, even indulged with tours of its treasures. And this abrupt increase in her own value had so little to do with her determined effort to climb out of a well, but mere circumstance.

The Processional was not a single piece, but a circle of statues. The Sulevia Leoth, the Sulevia Sceadu, and the Sulevia Seolfor, each leading the creatures they, by Sulis' grace, commanded. Every piece brought Rian's mother back so strongly. Her cutting sarcasm when they discovered she'd been given the wrong measurements, and had had to rework her design. A technical discussion over the difficulty of depicting the triskelion. Laughter, warm as honey, at the vanity of a model she'd used for the entourage. One of the rare arguments between her parents, over nothing Rian had been able to guess, and her father's immense contrition when a wild gesture had sent one of the stone hares crashing to the studio floor.

There had been long absences as well, when her mother had been working on the depictions of the Suleviae of the time—Queen Mennia, her sister Princess Nyroe, and Princess Ashwen. Whenever his wife was away, Rian's father would rattle about the studio, starting new projects and then abandoning them half-done, frequently disappearing off to London and leaving Aedric and Rian to the care of neighbours, his latest student, and once even with a confused visitor. Each time her mother's return had been spring after winter.

Griff had made his discovery. "Is this really Father?"

Rian nodded, and gathered together her composure to join the children crowded around the train of the Sulevia Leoth. Three dragons, miniatures of Nimelleth, Dulethar and Athian, each escorted by a child of twelve, one hand resting lightly on neck, or flank, or crested spine. This represented how the Sulevia Leoth could use people as vessels for the dragon's fire, for it was an extreme rarity for the dragons themselves to rise from beneath the land. Aedric had modelled for the third of these pairs, fingers barely brushing Athian's flank. The marble dragon looked back at him, to be met with a smile of solemn reassurance.

That was very much Aedric: serious, steady, and sure. Rian swallowed the cold anger swelling in her chest, mindful of Griff, Eluned and Eleri's loss made newly raw. She had wanted them to see *The Processional*, but there had been no way to avoid the hurt that would inevitably accompany the sight of this past Aedric.

Catching the fraught atmosphere, Prince Luc looked from face to face, then said: "Were any of the figures modelled by you, Dama Seaforth?"

"Ah, there should be..."

Rian turned to the stone Sulevia Sceadu, Queen Mennia, with a long-limbed and attenuated menagerie in her wake. Among the hounds and hares, the owls and mice, were two larger pieces: the sacred three-tailed mare that led the Night Breezes, and a long-necked stag, both with children on their backs. The mare carried a graceful girl of ten, who gazed with frank interest across at the triskelion. On the back of the stag a child of five sprawled, fast asleep.

"Mother had me pose on an old saddle, every day for what felt like months. Aedric read to me, in hopes of keeping me still. I would always fall asleep—and then be up half the night, racketing around the house and garden."

"It's like you've always belonged," Eluned said.

For one startled moment, Rian thought the girl was referring to the Sulevia Sceadu, to her past self's presence in a train now belonging to Princess Aerinndís. But she caught the direction of the girl's gaze. The stag.

The world revolved, rearranging itself around the idea that the past few weeks had not been a series of unrelated incidents, but instead a predetermined course, a path laid out toward creating an Amon-Re vampire in Cernunnos' service. Producing not an apprentice for Makepeace-Heriath, but a successor.

And one of the steps along that path had been Aedric's death.

SIXTEEN

A blank page was an invitation, an opportunity waiting to be taken. It should not sit in mute accusation. Eluned gripped her pencil, willing herself to at least start, to put down a single line. Before her was the perfect subject, a tangle of briar roses, all serrated leaves and thorns, shapes she loved to work with, and not touched in any way by withering heat.

One line.

Hopeless. Eluned's fingers tightened, and then she snatched up the sketchbook and hurled it into the tangle in a wild flutter of paper. Chest heaving, she gripped a handful of grass and threw it after the sketchbook, and then flinched as her right arm flailed in response to incautious movement. Instinctively she locked its movement, then let all her breath out in a rush and flopped heavily back onto the grass.

It didn't make sense, none at all. No-one need see the result. It could be as bad as she liked, clumsy, even a stick figure. Scribble. Anything.

What was wrong with her? Why had the thing most central to her become a cliff she could not climb?

A slender, gold-crowned head lifted against the background of blue and leaves. The amasen's warm scales brushed her arm as it rose higher to look down at her.

"Sorry," Eluned said. "Did I startle you?"

A flicker of vivid tongue.

"Is your name really Lila?"

The faint dip of the head could mean anything. Eluned wondered if Lila was a girl's name among amasen, and whether being female was the reason Lila's horns were a short, backward-jutting curve, or if that was because it—she—was young and small, and eventually she'd have the heavy, curling ram horns of the larger amasen.

"I try not to get angry around other people," Eluned said, her gaze returning to the hazy blue above. "I make them nervous."

She remembered being more temperamental, before Jasper. And utterly furious in the first months after. Because she'd failed him, and because of all the things she suddenly couldn't do. She'd given up on long hair, and clothing with difficult buttons, and had had to learn how to draw left-handed, to discover work-arounds for things that were *easy* with two hands. It had been so frustrating that for a while it had seemed she was always boiling over.

Then she'd noticed how worried it made people. As if having half an arm made tantrums against the rules. And, when she was a little older, with the first, clumsy, mechanical hand, there were times people would even flinch.

"I taught myself not to shout at the world," she told the amasen, or the sky. "I think maybe I need to yell a little more."

She consoled herself by gently stroking Lila's head before collecting her sketchbook and returning to Forest House.

Dawn had come and gone while she'd fought a blank page, but it was still early. There'd be at least an hour before they were due to leave for Tangleways.

Last week, Eluned had been aching with impatience to get to this school and see if Lord Fennington knew anything worth asking. Now she dreaded the trip, because before they'd visited the palace, Eleri had invited Nabah and Melly, and then had...done nothing.

"Oh, Eluned, perfect."

As Eluned wiped her feet on the mat inside the main hall, a mass of pink and white approached from the kitchen, ginger curls visible above a riot of lilliums.

"Be a pet and take these up to your aunt, will you? Let her know breakfast will be ready in twenty."

With enough of a pause to allow Eluned to tuck her sketchbook under her arm, the woman passed over the heavy vase, checked that it wasn't in danger of immediately plummeting, and whisked away.

Dama Seleny had been Aunt Arianne's response to the deputation of the Wise. They'd arrived the morning after the visit to the palace, and had for the most part been ponderously polite while telling Aunt Arianne all the things she should and shouldn't do. Eluned suspected there would have been more not-quite-shouting if not for the foreseeing, and the bite marks the Wise clearly could see, though even Eluned's had healed oddly quickly. Once they'd left, Aunt Arianne had gone to visit Dama Chelwith, and the next day a gangly woman with freckles on her freckles had come to stay.

Dama Seleny's official role was 'Grove Administrator', with a budget for management of the house and the press of visitors wanting to access the grove. Most of the work would be done by day staff, leaving Dama Seleny free to attend classes at Rutherford University, but she took care of early visitors and making breakfast, and was particularly good at stonewalling those with questions about the foreseeing. A simple flower delivery must make a nice change.

Blinking in the cloud of scent from the lilliums, Eluned spotted an envelope tucked beside a fern frond. An extravagant admirer: the arrangement would be impressive even in a normal year, let alone at the end of a summer of scorching windstorms. Speculating idly, she climbed up one flight of stairs and headed along the short corridor of bedrooms that now belonged to herself, Eleri and Aunt Arianne: chosen because their walls were less faded and carpet newer than the other bedrooms.

Tapping with her foot on the door at the end of the corridor, Eluned waited for the faint response, and managed to hook the handle with her elbow, passing on Dama Seleny's message as she entered. The half-light of the room was a mark of Aunt Arianne's progress toward tolerating the sun. So long as she stayed out of the direct rays, she'd stopped wincing.

"Put it on the sill," Aunt Arianne said, glancing at Eluned's burden in the mirror of the dresser.

There was room beside Aunt Arianne's growing collection of invitation cards, and Eluned gladly lowered the heavy vase, then admired the way the sun picked out veins in the fleshy petals. Greatly daring, she pulled out the envelope, then paused, frowning.

"What are you doing?"

"Working on making myself look a little older, in the hopes of discouraging propositions from people I consider to be children. I don't think I've been very successful, do you?"

"Well, you definitely look like you're trying to look older," Eluned said diplomatically, handing over the envelope and turning away to tweak at the arrangement of the flowers.

"Have you been in Hurlstone? How's Monsieur Doré?"

"In a different spot, but again there was absolutely no sign of a shift while I was there. Shouldn't we try more to communicate with it?"

"The pattern of movement suggests a desire *not* to communicate," Aunt Arianne said. "Out of distrust, or perhaps simply a need to adjust to what must be a very odd state of being." She put down her letter and began wiping clean her face. "Will you check if Griff and Eleri are up?"

Eluned hesitated, shifting her weight from one foot to another. Perhaps the day ahead wouldn't be nearly so awkward as she anticipated, and there was no need to speak. But just because she hadn't created the school situation didn't mean she could ignore it, so she made herself say: "We...would it be so bad to pay someone's fees?"

Light brown eyes met hers in the mirror. "It's left to you to follow through on whatever plan Eleri had for Melly Ktai? Does your sister often decide to arrange someone's life for them, and then lose interest halfway through?"

What to say to that? Angry as she was, Eluned couldn't let Aunt Arianne misunderstand.

"Eleri sees things that are broken and she can't help but to fix them. Automatons, crockery, people. Sometimes she barely realises she's doing it. She...she hasn't talked to you about this at all?"

"The only thing your sister has said to me the last few days was to demand to be present when the Suleviae come to Forest House."

Though this was said as calmly as the rest, Eluned's heart sank. Instead of her usual effortless arrangements, Eleri had put Aunt Arianne's back up, and then spent all her time in the attic drawing. Even the visits to automaton workshops had been put on hold, and all because of a princess!

"I'm sorry," she said, and added helplessly: "Eleri's not usually like this. She's taken leave of her senses."

Aunt Arianne began applying light touches of colour to her face. "Don't be too hard on her," she said, to Eluned's surprise. "She's adjusting to a new experience."

"Adjusting? She thinks she's going to marry Princess Celestine!"

"So I gathered. Not technically an impossible goal, since the princess could choose to not offer herself to Sulis when the next succession is on us, and thus would not be subject to the Suleviae's ban on marriage. Though I expect Eleri would be perfectly happy to be Princess Celestine's lover."

Eluned boggled. When Eleri had returned from the palace talking and thinking of nothing but Princess Celestine, it had seemed self-evident that the whole idea was madness.

"The princess didn't even speak to her. I'm not sure she more than glanced at her!"

"Very taken up with her new puppy."

"The whole thing doesn't make sense," Eluned said. "Eleri can't know what Princess Celestine is like, can't really like her properly. Love at first sight is a silly idea."

"Silly is not going to change how your sister is feeling right now. Call it passionate attraction, if that makes it easier to understand." Aunt Arianne picked up her brush and began arranging her hair. "After a few days or weeks she'll have more attention to spare."

Eleri would get over it. Of course. It was obvious, inevitable. "She'll see that princesses don't mix with ordinary people like us."

That won an amused glance. "One thing you three are not is ordinary. Though I imagine Eleri is well aware there's a vast gulf separating her from Princess Celestine. It's difficult to romance someone you have no opportunity to meet."

"She lives in a different world."

"Your grandmother used to say that genius transcends all social boundaries, but then, your grandmother was...transcendent. Still, Eleri is a remarkable girl, and she at least has a possibility of meeting Princess Celestine again, at the Moonfire Feast. It's highly likely that most of the Gwyn Lynns will attend the Treaty's renewal, so she can try to forward the acquaintance then."

"Shouldn't you discourage her? She's going to end up hurt!"

"Probably," Aunt Arianne agreed. "But I expect she will enjoy herself along the way."

When Eluned drew an outraged breath, Aunt Arianne put down her brush and turned to face her, a hint of sternness succeeding in making her look more like an adult.

"Yes, Eleri almost certainly will be hurt. Princess Celestine will have power, wealth and beauty, and despite being rather young is no doubt already courted by many who are far better positioned to win her affection. Should Eleri concede defeat? When you meet someone who fills you up until there's no room for anything else, trying to put all those feelings away is harder than even the most hopeless pursuit. Unlikely as her chances are, there's no reason not to support your sister in her feelings. Love requires a certain bravery, but it's one of life's great gifts when it's not making you miserable."

Eluned squeezed her hand into a fist. She had never been angrier at her aunt, and her voice shook when she said: "You think this is funny, don't you?"

Aunt Arianne's eyebrows lifted, then she smiled sympathetically. "I think it ironic. Though I must say, Eleri took your sudden passion in much better part than you are receiving hers."

"*Me?* I haven't lost my sense over anyone."

"You fell in love with Hurlstone, didn't you? Something that led you to give your allegiance to Cernunnos, a thing likely to have far greater consequences than Eleri's heart-twisting. Cernunnos is both hunter and prey, and his dual nature is something we will both face, for the choice we each made."

"I—" Eluned's hand had stopped constantly itching, but she knew that gods did not bestow their blessings lightly. And it was true: Eleri had made no fuss at all when Eluned had decided she wanted Hurlstone.

"To address your earlier concern," Aunt Arianne continued, "Dem Ktai runs a very successful store, and is perfectly capable of sending his daughter to school. From what I can gather, Melly has made a pragmatic choice not to pursue an education she considers unnecessary to her plans for expanding their business. Possibly she will come to regret that, but there is certainly no drama attached to her joining our trip to Tangleways. We will not be taunting her with a future out of her reach."

"Oh." Relief cut the tightly-wound wires that had troubled Eluned for days. "I'm glad."

With a nod at the sketchbook Eluned still carried under her arm, Aunt Arianne added: "Speaking of futures, it was the Morris Atelier you wanted to enter, yes? With ambition that high, you should be working seriously on your portfolio even though it's a few years away."

This was the last subject Eluned wanted to discuss, so she said hastily: "Is it that Roman you knew when he was twelve that you consider a child?"

"Felix?" Aunt Arianne glanced at the lilliums crowding the windowsill. "Perhaps, though I suspect he'd have wasted no time dispelling the notion if he'd had the chance. A moot point. Felix's family have a great deal of ambition centred on him, and have hauled on the reins once again. He'll be halfway to Rome by now."

Wondering if Aunt Arianne was disappointed, Eluned recalled that she'd been told to make sure Eleri and Griff were awake, and took the excuse to escape.

Eleri was at least in her bed, and not at a desk. Curled into a ball beneath a light sheet, she looked worn and thin, and though none of them had been at their best since the beginning of summer, there were new shadows beneath her eyes that even sleep hadn't erased.

Biting her lip over the poorly concealed exasperation she'd displayed the past few days, Eluned touched her sister's shoulder, and murmured: "Breakfast's nearly ready," waiting only until she was sure Eleri had woken properly before slipping out.

Griff, after failing to find any hidden bedrooms, had settled on the opposite side of the great hall, in a room with an entire wall of drawers and cupboards. It was meant to be a linen press, and there was barely enough space for him to fit a narrow bed and still open the doors, but Aunt Arianne had shrugged and let him have it. They did, as she said, have other places to put the sheets.

Since Griff was not inclined to be tidy, a tiny room full of shelves still required wading through all his latest projects to get to the bed. Eluned picked up his newest passion—drawing the routes of the train lines over the maps he'd coaxed out of Aunt Arianne—and put them out of the way, then tackled the task of getting him up. He was sleeping in his usual manner, sprawled almost on the floor, and required far more than a touch to shift, but Eluned's spirits were rising, and so she kept at him until he stirred, and then let herself enjoy a fine breakfast, and greeted Melly and Nabah's arrival with an unalloyed cheer that only increased when a long-bodied tiger purred softly up to the curb behind them.

"All ready to go then?" asked a bright-eyed girl underneath a very proper chauffer's hat. It took Eluned a moment to recognise the dragonfly girl, Sun Li Sen, who'd fetched them an umbrella.

"Mama Lu has a small transport empire," Aunt Arianne said, in response to Eluned's unspoken question. "And yes, all ready. Might Griff ride up front? It may help his travel sickness."

"'Course," said Li Sen, and opened the front passenger door, adding to Griff: "Let me know if you want me to pull up."

Eluned settled onto the right of the back seat, with Aunt Arianne between her and Eleri, and Melly and Nabah opposite, both formally thanking Aunt Arianne for the invitation. Melly had pulled her hair into two short, fat braids, the ends threaded with silver and puffed out into little balls, and Eluned admired the way they bobbed whenever she excitedly turned her head.

True to Aunt Arianne's assessment, there was no shadow on the tall girl's face, only pleasure at a rare treat.

"Which do you like more?" Griff asked their driver, bouncing on the front seat. "The tiger or the dragonfly?"

"Dragonfly's a fun challenge. The tiger goes fast." Li Sen swung them sedately around a corner, heading west past the Great Barrows. "But it's a new thing coming out of Nathaner's that I like best—a courser—basically two wheels in a line with an engine between them. It's got the tiger's speed, and going around *corners*—!" She sighed happily.

"Driven something not released yet?" Eleri asked, proving that she was, after all, listening.

"Grandama has a controlling interest in Nathaner's," Li Sen said. "I get to do test-driving sometimes."

"Do you worry about having your fulgite stolen?" Griff asked.

"It's a risk," Li Sen said, and fished a pistol out of a pocket in the driver's door. "Getting enough to keep the business going's as much a problem as stopping it from being taken. Nathaner's is looking at motopetrol engines. Smelly and noisy, but a nice surge of speed."

At this point conversation died away as they joined a larger road heading west out of the city, and Li Sen demonstrated that tigers could indeed go fast. Not enough to outrun the morning windstorm, but it was a fortunately weak one, buffeting but never threatening the tiger's swift racing.

For a time they simply gaped out the windows, but they had a nearly two hour journey ahead of them, so Nabah was soon asking Aunt Arianne about the places she'd travelled. This was a formidable list: Aunt Arianne didn't seem to have stayed more than a year in any one place.

"Did allegiance not concern you?" Nabah asked intently. "If you had died in these lands, you could have been trapped in an unlife, or a punishment Otherworld."

"That's why so many travellers attempt a bond of allegiance with Epona, whose Otherworld can be reached almost anywhere—though given that in Epona's Otherworld you get to be a horse, you do need to genuinely like the things to want that future. Some do as

I did and thoroughly research a new country's laws, then obey them strictly. So long as the land has a strong territorial allegiance, most gods will accept a traveller who has respected their edicts even if they were not born there—they want observant souls in their Otherworlds, after all. There are places I would never visit, but most because of how I stood under secular laws, not the requirements of the Answered."

"But even then, if your soul didn't go to Annwn you would have no chance to meet..."

Melly, turning to peer at a roofless house, elbowed Nabah in the ribs. This brought a moment's annoyance, then Eluned could practically see the forthright Nabah remember why the Tennings were with Aunt Arianne in the first place.

"Wasn't it dangerous, though?" Nabah asked instead. "Being a Prytennian woman travelling alone?"

Melly and Eluned exchanged helpless winces, for that was a question even Eleri would think twice about asking when you considered some of the stories about other lands and their ideas about Prytennian women. Aunt Arianne was wearing only a light veil today, but being able to make out her features didn't help with guessing her feelings.

Sounding as unconcerned as ever, she said: "I usually travelled in the company of friends or relatives, which does make matters easier, wherever and whoever you are. There were occasions where the stories told about Prytennians drew some uncomfortable attention, but nothing more. Still, don't think of Prytennia as some blessed haven of safety in an unjust world—the nearest I've ever come to being attacked was in my parents' own house."

"What happened?" Eluned asked, startled into the kind of prying she'd usually back away from.

"One of your grandmother's students, very drunk, decided I liked him far more than my own opinion on the topic." Aunt Arianne shrugged. "I kicked him somewhere memorable and spent the night in my treehouse."

"What did Grandama Seaforth do to him?"

"I never told her. The next day he behaved as if he couldn't remember the night before, and I couldn't decide whether he was lying. But that was around the time your grandmother's illness started to really impact her, and soon she had no energy for students."

In the silence that followed this, Griff, from the front seat, said: "Can we have a treehouse?"

This was such an entirely self-centred thing to say even for Griff that Eluned drew breath to snap at him, but Aunt Arianne simply said: "I gather it's not me, but Cernunnos that you'd need to ask that." And then she laughed, a spontaneous sound lifting above her usual calm. "Oh, though I would enjoy the reaction of the next deputation of the Wise. Don't tempt me. Plus we must remember that the trees are full of folies, and they don't seem to love company."

They all speculated on whether the folies really could be cats wearing bushes as a disguise, and then Melly began to ask about France, and whether Aunt Arianne had ever met any of the winged god-touched of the Cour d'Lune. Eluned sat back and listened, and tried to work out how old Aunt Arianne would have been when Grandama Seaforth died.

SEVENTEEN

With a name like Tangleways, and so much talk of strange feuds, Eluned was disappointed when Li Sen turned down an orderly driveway bracketed by regimented and freshly clipped rows of cypress. The building ahead looked no more interesting: three stories of windows arranged in a flat horseshoe around a gravelled courtyard.

"Boring," Griff said, as Li Sen drew them around a plain central obelisk and stopped neatly behind a horse-drawn carriage.

"Looks new," Melly said, following Eleri out the door. "Perhaps they knocked the original building down."

"That would be a rather dull approach," Aunt Arianne said. "Let's hope the promised refreshments can make up for it."

She paused to speak briefly to Li Sen, while Eluned stole admiring glances at the occupants of the carriage, now crowding the wide entry-way. Three sisters, very handsome, with wonderful manes of bronze hair.

"...don't care whether it's convenient or not," one was saying, in a carrying whisper. "Any school run by Folly Fennington's bound to be a madhouse."

"...half the fun," another replied.

"Just because *you* think school is for swinging from the chandeliers," the first said bitterly, while the third cast an apologetic, amused glance at their accidental audience, and followed her family indoors.

"This trip will be worth it to see whether Lord Fennington's half as strange as they say," Melly murmured. "Or are we all gullible for believing he never wears the same shendy twice, and has an automaton for brushing his teeth?"

"And a whole mechanical menagerie," Griff said, striding ahead up the broad, flat stairs. Animal automatons rarely bothered him, unless they were covered with fur. Then he stopped short.

Eluned quickened her pace, but Griff's reverential sigh told her there was no crisis.

"Oh, they built in front of the old house," Melly said, glancing around at orderly stairways and halls leading off to either side, and then through a matching set of double doors to a semi-enclosed garden where a festive marquee and a clock tower partially blocked the view of a house where logic and symmetry had long been abandoned.

"Two front doors," Eleri murmured. "Moat."

"Sunken garden," Eluned corrected, catching glimpses of the tips of what looked like a collector's bounty reaching up around the two separate bridges into the main house.

There must once have been a simple square building, large but unexceptional. Eluned could see a patch of bricks of a slightly different red where the original front door would have stood, before being replaced by the tall, skinny green door and the fat, nearly rounded blue door. Impossible to guess what came next: the tower on the right or the crenellations on the left. The bulbous bay windows or the opposing series of portholes. The statues or the ironwork filigree. And then the extensions, entire wings of completely contrasting design bulging to either side. Beyond them, smaller buildings.

"Follies," Melly said, grinning widely. "Appropriate."

"There's tunnels," Griff said, in an urgent whisper, pointing to the arch of a brick drain out of the garden moat, and then he was off, circling the house.

Eluned wanted very much to join him in exploration, but she could not forget what they were there for, and looked around for the real reason for their visit. Both the green and blue door were firmly closed, and there was no movement behind the many windows in either the new or old buildings.

"Follies and folies," Melly said, half under her breath. "Fools, follies, folies."

"But no Fennington," Nabah said. "There's hardly anyone here. Are we early?"

Eluned looked about for Aunt Arianne, who had detoured toward the shade of the marquee. Yesterday she had instructed them to look around for anything unusual while she approached Lord Fennington—though Eluned had no intention of missing out on his answers—but the whole trip would be wasted if the man wasn't even there.

Eleri and Nabah started after Griff, and Eluned hesitated between following and checking the marquee. They shouldn't let their guard down. Even if Lord Fennington did turn out to be the person who had commissioned the stolen automaton, that didn't guarantee that he hadn't found a reason to hide any discoveries Mother had made. They needed to be careful.

"Is your sister feeling ill?" Melly asked. "She seems very quiet today."

"Ah..." How to answer that? "I guess she's been thinking a lot about her future." Would Eleri *want* the whole neighbourhood to know her feelings for Princess Celestine? "Mother and Father were both brilliant in their fields, and for Eleri no school is going to be able to replace them. This place, or the one in Lamhythe, will be a total waste of her time without at least a very good science teacher, let alone a practical mechanics workshop."

"Oh." Expression lightening, Melly led them off toward the corner where Griff had disappeared. "I'm not much for the sciences, so I couldn't say how good the teachers are at Tollesey. Nabah would probably know. Though, all other things being equal, I'd choose this place over Tollesey—for the sheer entertainment value, to say nothing of the connections. Lord Fennington would be enormously useful."

"For poetry?" Eluned asked, startled.

"For the business empire I will one day command," Melly said, with a quick, amused smile. "Though for poetry too, since Folly Fennington's mad keen on Prytennian literature, and I'd love to get among his collection of folios and first editions. I'll have to get my hands on the prospectus and see if they've bothered to put the prices, so I can work out whether I could swing the fees."

"What kind of business empire are you going to run?" Eluned asked, fascinated. She could not have been more wrong about Melly's reaction to this trip.

"I call it 'Finders Keepers'. People were always coming into the store and asking for discontinued products, or things that aren't sold locally. My Da and I had a lot of fun tracking remainders down—you just need to know the right people to ask—and it's turned into a nice sideline. I've lots of plans for expansion, for mail order and advertisements, and one thing I particularly want is to break into the kind of clientele who could afford to send their kids here. Not," she added, glancing back toward the marquee, "that this Tangleways looks like it's going to end up with much in the way of students."

"I guess a reputation for inspired silliness isn't the best basis for setting yourself up as a teacher."

"I'd feel sorry for him, but I expect all that money will console him."

They rounded the corner of the sprawling house and found stables to their right, a pair of long heads tossing restively. Knowing Griff would never head that way, Eluned moved in the opposite direction, toward a smaller building like a pepper pot. There were three more of different shapes behind it.

"This place is like a little village," Melly said. "What did they want all this for?"

"Lots of guests?" Eluned looked around, and spotted Griff leading the others toward a white pavilion full of people. Headless people.

"Oh, clothes mannequins," Melly said, sounding as relieved as Eluned felt. There were only two real people: one very tall and a bit fleshy, and the other lithe and lightly muscular.

The taller one had noticed them approaching, and turned, beaming. "Halloo!" he said. "Welcome, welcome, welcome! What perfect timing. I need a second opinion, and a third and fourth as well!"

"Folly Fennington in the flesh," Melly murmured, and hurried to catch Griff up.

Eluned took a moment to steady herself before following. Here he was, this man, finally standing right in front of them. He might be a murderer. He might simply have commissioned an automaton. Or he might have had nothing to do with them at all. Now was their chance to find out.

Lord Fennington had a mournful face, floppy brown hair, and a booming sort of voice, and he rounded out his words as if playing with the way they sounded. "Come, come, come," he said, beckoning them toward the pavilion and holding out an anxious hand toward the display he'd apparently been working on. School uniforms. There were a dozen mannequins, all dressed in dark blue and creamy-beige.

"Now tell me bluntly, no holding back. Should it be the double line of red, or the single?"

Eluned didn't see any red at first, then spotted a pencil line around the cuff of one of the jackets. And the four-panel summer shendy had a plummy double line making a border around the two side panels.

"There's hardly any difference," Griff said, as Griff would. "But I like the double more."

"One vote for the double!" Lord Fennington said. "Can we gain a consensus? Any champions for the opposing view?"

"Two is better," Nabah agreed.

"One," Eleri said immediately.

"One," Melly said.

"A tie! But one last vote to settle the matter."

Since he sounded so serious, Eluned took a moment to study the collection of uniforms, personally doubting most people would even notice the difference. Then she fished in the small pouch she had laced to her new day-belt, and found one of the coins Aunt Arianne had distributed earlier that week as an allowance.

A simple toss and catch, and then she said: "Two."

Lord Fennington, fortunately, found this funny, his long face lighting as he laughed. "Yes, yes, the judgment of Sucellos! Two it shall be."

"Lakshmi's smile," Nabah added, looking pleased.

"And how nice that the Daughters are taking an interest in Tangleways!" Lord Fennington added approvingly to Nabah, before saying to his companion, an excessively handsome blond man, "Matthiel, take these appalling one-line variations away."

"My Lord," said the man, then picked up two of the mannequins with effortless grace, and walked off.

"Have you been on the tour?" Lord Fennington asked then. "You mustn't miss it. Hedley's been with the estate for decades, and has endless tales of Lord Webley's experiments and inventions."

"Inventions?" Eleri said. "Engineer? Or scientist?"

"Both, in a manner of speaking. He called himself a deiographer and was devoted, you might well say, to the Science of Gods. What sparks them to Answer? Is there some unifying purpose or meaning? Can devices be constructed to quantify their energies and boundaries? A brilliant man, though, of course, more than a little mad." He gave them a small, shy smile. "Speaking as an authority on the subject, quite potty."

"Eccentric," Griff corrected, before Eluned could decide if it would be rude to laugh. "If you have money, you get to be eccentric, which sounds a lot more fun." Then he held out his hand with the grave formality that he sometimes produced to get his way, and said: "My name is Griff Tenning. These are my sisters Eleri and Eluned Tenning."

Eluned held her breath, searching the man's face for any hint of recognition, but all he did was shake Griff's hand with matching formality and say:

"Dyfed Fennington. And do only two of your companions have names?"

"Melly Ktai," Griff said slowly, a little too obviously still searching for some hint of reaction. Then he shrugged, adding: "Nabah hasn't told us her last name."

"Satkunan," Nabah said. "Do you mean to say there are machines here designed to—to *measure* gods?"

"Indeed! Or there were. Unfortunately the Mini-T carted most of it off years ago, and handing over anything interesting left behind was part of the conditions of sale. Not," he added, with a conspiratorial gleam, "that we didn't give everything a good and thorough dusting before shipping it off. And you can see the housing of some of the larger pieces during the tour, since it's not as if they could pack up the clock tower."

"My Lord, the podium is ready," said the man called Matthiel, returning with a sheaf of papers.

"Already? Where, where is the day going?" Lord Fennington took the papers and fanned his face with them. "My young friends, I must rush. Do, do enjoy yourselves."

He was striding off as he spoke, and there was no more time for leading questions. They'd lost their chance, at least for now.

Eluned turned to the man called Matthiel: "Can we help you with the other mannequins?"

"Thank you, but there's no need," the man said. "Don't miss My Lord's speech, damini."

Exchanging a glance with Eleri, Eluned decided that it would be best to wait for another opportunity before they tried the blunt approach. "We won't," she said, as neutrally as she could manage.

"What's a Mini-T?" Griff asked, as the man lifted another two mannequins and departed.

"Ministry of Science and Technology," Eleri said. "In charge of airships, the Patent Office, things. Let's go find the Aunt."

This proved less easy to do than to say. When they reached the central garden, they found it packed with people, apparently back from touring the school facilities. It gave some measure of how large Tangleways must be, that there'd been so many people about, completely unseen.

It took half Lord Fennington's speech just to spot Aunt Arianne, and by the time they'd worked their way nearly to her the speech was over and everyone was streaming about chasing refreshments, lining up for other tours, talking to the teachers, or gossiping.

"Too many hats," Melly said, standing on tip-toe as she tried to spot where Aunt Arianne had gone.

"Give it up," Eleri said.

"Shall we try one of the tours?" Nabah suggested, and that's what they did, and then stopped for refreshments before splitting up—ostensibly to hunt individually, but more so Eleri, Griff and Eluned would have a better chance of button-holing Lord Fennington again.

Tired of crowds, Eluned abandoned the chase altogether, and found stone stairs down into the sunken garden moat. There in cool quiet she found moss, lacy ferns, and a treasury of saxifrages clinging to rocks and tucked in hollows.

Memory of that morning soured her appreciation. What was wrong with her? It was silly and senseless not to have brought her sketchbook on a trip like this. But she loathed constantly trying and failing and not understanding what was wrong.

Hating that this was tying her in knots when she was supposed to be concentrating on finding Mother and Father's killer, Eluned followed the high arch of the drainage channel out of the garden, trying to decide whether Lord Fennington had really not recognised their names, or was a very good actor. And what did they do if he simply denied everything?

The drainage channel ended in an ornate grate: interlinked hands, with oxalis growing up through it. Eluned crossed this and found a slope of green down to a river—a tributary of the Tamesas, according to Griff. To her left was a path and she followed it as it curved through a small patch of trees to, inevitably, another folly: a circle of columns with a domed roof.

There was a woman sitting alone on the steps, and Eluned started to turn away, then recognised the hair colour and reversed direction.

"You're not wearing your hat," she said, as Aunt Arianne turned her head at her approach.

"A disguise of sorts. A great many people want to discuss foreseeings, but all they know of me is that I'm recently bound and wearing a veil."

The pavilion was shaded by trees, but it was still the first time since she'd been bound that Aunt Arianne had been outside during the day without a veil, and Eluned suspected that the curious crowd must have been particularly trying.

"What do you tell them?" Eluned asked, sitting down on the circular stair beside her aunt. There were no proper seats, the floor of the folly being taken up by a beautiful, if sadly cracked mosaic depicting constellations in a night sky.

"I tell them as much as I know, which is nothing at all, at least where the Dragon of the North is concerned."

"Do you think it might really happen? That you'll find Albion's fourth dragon?"

"I think I'm not going to waste my time on guessing games. Better to simply prepare as best we can for whatever tests are thrown our way."

"But Cernunnos accepted you as Keeper. Why do that and then test you?"

Aunt Arianne tipped back her head, studying the inside of the pavilion's dome. More stars, brilliant against a wash of dark blue. She looked tired.

"Oakfire speaking comes from the forest, not Cernunnos," she said. "The Horned King is one of the Great Forest's many gods, one aspect of something vast. There's very little of this world that was not forest at some point. Even deserts have ancient forests beneath them. Perhaps only the oceans are outside its bounds. Can't you feel it? All around us is forest."

Eluned started to point out that there was a stand of trees only a few feet away. But a cool breeze whisked her face, bringing a hint of loam. And was Aunt Arianne looking up at the inside of the dome, or at sky through sheltering branches?

"The trees are always with us," Aunt Arianne said. "We asked to be part of it, and we must prove ourselves worthy."

"You keep saying 'we'," Eluned said, almost under her breath, though it was not as if she could forget Lila's bite, or the key that would come when she called for it.

"Keeper Tyse cannot say with complete certainty who those foreseeings were intended for. She recorded me officially because my arrival triggered the speaking, but given that you received the same blessing from Cernunnos, it seemed to her a high probability that you and I are both the subject of these challenges. Pretending that you are not involved is not going to prevent you from being drawn in."

"I don't know anything about the Dragon of the North either," Eluned said.

"No. But if that 'shopping list' was in chronological order, dragons will be the last of our problems. What, to you, most strikes you as an 'unfinished one'?"

Since Aunt Arianne was being so serious, Eluned cast her mind about for something that seemed unfinished to her. It could be anything, although the phrasing had made it seem like a person, and people usually weren't...

Stiffening, Eluned stared at her aunt's profile. "The independent automatons. Eleri doesn't consider them finished, because she hasn't verified reliable movement. They are—" She choked, head spinning.

"I spent some energy on the question of cause and effect, Aunt Arianne said, serene as ever. "Were we accepted by Cernunnos because we had already become embroiled in the first of the challenges? Or were we chosen, and then matters arranged so that we would be willing to give allegiance? Is it possible that what the Swedes would call a 'fate' was laid on us, and that your parents' deaths were part of that fate? I have yet to decide my feelings on this. To be angry at the gods is to scream at the stars. Even if they hear, they will not stop shining."

"Wh-what?" Eluned could not think through what she'd been told. Had *Cernunnos* caused—no, that wasn't what Aunt Arianne had said. Fate. When the Swedish gods laid a fate on someone, the world would rearrange itself to bring that fate about. A wholly different thing to oakfire foretelling.

"Or, of course, the unfinished ones might have nothing to do with automatons. Perhaps we are simply people who were in the right place with the right reasons. I may need to choose to believe that, to be able to not waste myself in anger. I can't be sure which case is true, but I felt you were entitled to know my suspicions."

After that Aunt Arianne didn't say anything at all for a long while, and they sat contemplating a sweep of grass down to a river, and the vast forest that would always surround them.   Only after Eluned's thoughts had progressed through a circle of incredulity did her aunt go on.

"Tomorrow evening I will be visiting this fencing school that Lynsey Blair recommended. In part because I want to investigate her separately from Lord Fennington. But also because I now have a need to learn to better defend myself physically. If the school seems suitable, I want you to attend as well. Unless you prefer Tangleways, of course. Do you think you'd like it here?"

"It's no good," Eluned said, struggling to shift her thoughts away from fates and gods. "Did you listen to that speech? All that time spent on sports. Horse-riding. And raising animals? At school?"

"Yes, those are reasons Griff and Eleri wouldn't like it here. I asked what you wanted."

"I want to go to the same school as Eleri and Griff," Eluned said firmly. "But otherwise, yes, I think this place would be fun. You were right about Melly, by the way. She likes it here enough she's working out ways to afford it."

Aunt Arianne picked up her hat.   "I expect she'll manage it. She seems very capable. And, Eluned, it never hurts to check rather than fret. Don't ever hesitate to ask me if something is worrying you—or even if you're simply curious. The most I'll do is not answer. Or lie."

Smiling weakly, Eluned wondered whether the possibility of lies was meant to be comforting. Not that lies or truth were going to help with the problem that had been troubling her all summer—or even the new one her aunt had shared.

Instead, Eluned hauled her mind back to the task at hand. "We talked to Lord Fennington already," she said, realising she hadn't even mentioned it. "Griff introduced us, but Lord Fennington didn't seem to recognise our names at all, and with all these people here I'm not sure we're going to have a chance to talk to him again."

"No need to worry there. As I said, a great many people want to discuss foreseeings."

"You've talked to him?"

"Accepted an invitation to view a painting of my father's that he owns, and sample the Towering Folly, a cocktail invented for him. Rather ripe for double entendre, but I gather that's unlikely to be the intention."

The clock in the school's central tower began to toll.

"And there's my cue," Aunt Arianne said, picking up her hat. "Given his ambitions to play principal, he's less than likely to open up in front of prospective pupils. You might find it worthwhile to track down Monsieur Telaque, the drawing instructor, while I'm gone. Alain Telaque is a master of line work, and you'd probably find even a short discussion with him very useful indeed. You're still working primarily with line and floral patterns, yes? It's been a while since Aedric last sent me an example."

"Father sent you my pictures?" Eluned asked, trying not to sound appalled.

"Oh yes. He was very proud of all three of you. If you're nervous about speaking to Monsieur Telaque by yourself, wait until I return and I'll introduce you."

"No, no I'll look for him," Eluned said hastily, cast her mind about for something else to talk about, and asked: "What did he mean, your Roman friend? What was badly done?"

It was a conversational leap, but Aunt Arianne took it with her usual aplomb.

"Oh, when Felix knew me I was in the throes of a serious romance with one of his cousins, the younger son of the Dacian Proconsul." She settled her hat back on her head, lips curving. "At least I thought I was, until his marriage was arranged, and he tried to...tidy me away, so to speak."

"Tidy...?" Eluned didn't know what to say.

"A neat demonstration of what Nabah was trying to ask earlier today. There are many different lands, all with their own gods, and their own laws, and their own definition of right behaviour. Rome has come a long way since the example of Lucretia, but there is a notion of...injury and false promise that I could have used to cause trouble with the very influential friend who had recommended me to the Proconsul. I didn't understand that I posed a threat to arrangements, any more than I had recognised in the first place that in the Republic I'm someone to have affairs with, not the kind of person you marry. At least to people bound up in notions of tradition and respectability."

She shot Eluned a faintly amused glance, then lowered her veil. "Mortifying at the time, of course, but something I look back on as a narrow escape. I hope I can claim to have become a better judge of character."

After confirming arrangements for when they should meet for the return trip, Aunt Arianne left, and Eluned looked out at the shadow of a forest, and wondered if she'd ever had a real conversation with her aunt before. And whether she'd dare to ask her any more questions.

EIGHTEEN

Eluned's tendency to drastically change the subject whenever her drawing came under discussion was a thing Rian would need to revisit. For the moment, her concentration was needed for an uninterrupted progress through a crowd where every third person was keen to strike up a conversation, or at least stop and stare. Becoming a personage of note was truly a double-edged sword.

The advantageous blade was the entirely too handsome young man who appeared to guide her to a maple-panelled elevator in the new school building, whisking her directly to a plush little foyer on the third floor, and then into a most sumptuous example of a principal's office, with a formidable sweep of desk set before a wall of windows overlooking the clock tower and central garden.

The owner of all this wood panelling and fine-cut glass was drooping rather before the view, perhaps because the streaming crowds seemed to be mostly made up of curious locals, with only a small number genuinely interested in having their children attend.

"My lord," murmured Rian's escort, as he accepted her hat.

"Dama Seaforth!" Lord Fennington said, springing from a high-backed revolving chair with a gust of energy. "Oh, how nice of you to come! Let me take you through to the Inner Sanctum, don't mind the capitals. This room is all very well for a fine dose of pomp and awe, but that leaves very little room for comfort."

"An impressive outlook, though," Rian said, rather taken by the tiny pair of pompoms above the hem of his tunic, like a little tail. They were the same colour as the main cloth, and easily overlooked until the man was walking away from you. Her instinct was to distrust purposeful ridiculousness, but in Folly Fennington it felt genuine, a celebration.

Her less than reliable new sense for the emotions of others worked best when she touched a person, but she didn't engineer contact immediately, simply gauging the man as she normally would as he exclaimed over one of her father's farmhand series, and then fussed over settling her into a comfortable chair.

The blond man who seemed to be his personal assistant made a timely arrival with a silver trolley laden with bottles, and stood by to hand over tongs and glasses at critical moments while his lord prepared their Towering Follies.

"I was terribly complimented, of course, when Lady Prentegast named this for me, though always, always there lurks at the back of the mind a little bit of writhing embarrassment. Is it pretentious to serve a drink named after yourself? And what if people don't like the taste? It's a little sweet for some."

He turned, holding out a more than generous glass of splendid sunset gradient, adding: "Gin, a dry white wine, grenadine, maraschino liqueur, and one single caper to finish it off. Do drink up, and tell me what you think of my little school."

"I think it's not very little," Rian said dryly, glad she'd managed to find an opportunity to eat during his speech. "And that it would be an adventure to attend. I do, however, have a nephew with a positive horror of even the smallest animal, and a niece who considers organised sport an interruption to her studies. How would they fit in at Tangleways?"

"Niblings!" Lord Fennington beamed. "I have four nephews myself. A delight, all of them, though still at the dandling stage. As to yours, there must, of course, be a certain flexibility to our programs. The idea is to guide our students to find their best, not crush them against their limits.

"A lad who cannot handle an animal can still learn about them, and assist in tasks that do not require direct contact. A lass who finds sports a bore might have her interest sparked by exploring the history, or even the physics involved. Or perhaps just be exposed to a sufficient variety of games to find one she likes. The point is to develop systems and methodologies, to not leave children stranded as they too often are, even in these modern times, with a hapless village teacher of no qualifications reading lists out of random books."

Taking the bit between his teeth, Fennington spoke passionately and at length, while Rian obligingly sipped her very strong cocktail and wondered if she should pretend to be tipsy.

"But I mustn't maunder on," he said, once most of her drink had been safely swallowed, though to be fair he'd tossed off all of his own, and was working on a second. "Nor, never fear, will I pester you with silly questions about foreseeings. I'm sure you've had your fill of them! But, as has no doubt been transparently, simply transparently clear, I did want to have a little gossip. Do forgive my blatant lubrication."

"Time for the caper?" Rian asked.

"Ha! Yes! The pickle, the sting, the little kernel of sour that cuts through all the sugar. Dear Prentegast was being too, too pointed with her recipe."

"I'm not likely to forget your business ventures are almost invariably profitable, Lord Fennington, whatever your enthusiasms."

"Call me Folly, do. I can tell we're going to be friends."

"My friends call me Rian," she replied, surprising herself because she had been keeping a certain mental distance with the subjects of her investigations. But she did like Folly Fennington.

"Then I shall be honoured to do so," he said. "Rian, I want to ask you about Comfrey Makepeace."

Unexpected. "Not my favourite topic," Rian said. She was not entirely certain of the limits Makepeace had placed on her, and wondered idly if she would be choked off mid-sentence if she tried to tell what she had been forbidden.

"Quite understandable, my dear. Do, do squash me thoroughly if I rouse painful memories. I will deserve it entirely, I assure you."

"What do *you* know about Makepeace?" she asked. "I hadn't even heard of him before I encountered him at Sheerside."

"Exactly! *I* hadn't heard of him. Do you know what an achievement that is? I am a snoop, a busybody, a chinwag, an inveterate pryer, and a natterer of monumental proportions. Now, if he were, perhaps, an obscure little vampire, recently blooded, or never stirring from some dreary backwater... But instead it is apparent the man is the Suleviae's personal agent, on terms of complete intimacy with the royal family, and has been since the early days of the Gwyn Lynns' ascendency, being one of Prytennia's more senior vampires. In addition! In addition he is the Keeper of the Deep Grove, the most important of the groves in the whole of the country, which, as I understand it, means this vampire must give his allegiance to Cernunnos! Yet until his most unfortunate attack on you, Rian, I'd never even heard his name."

"I suppose he can be those things, and not be notorious. Especially since he delegates the Keeper role. And it's to his advantage to not be well-known if he investigates on behalf of the Suleviae."

Fennington tossed off the last of his second glass. "And yet, nor is he unknown. Quite half the people I spoke to—among those who make it their business to know things—were fully aware of the 'Wind's Lapdog', as they call him." He smiled at Rian's helpless snort. "Yes, it's a marvellous name. Brings to mind the Heriath of the Melanian rule, without the teeth. Surely a marvellous little titbit to share, yet no-one does. Those who know simply don't talk about the man, as if he was completely uninteresting."

The Amon-Re line can control minds. To the extent that dozens, even hundreds, unconsciously chose not to discuss Makepeace?

"You're talking about him," Rian pointed out.

"I am! It's not as if people don't answer questions when asked. Young Lynsey Blair explained how you came to encounter him, and I found him entirely unexceptional to talk to. And yet I am fascinated! He is like the word on the tip of one's tongue, out of reach and ever so tantalising.

"To talk to?" Rian blinked, then decided it wasn't worth anger, that she should have expected it. "You've met him then?"

"Oh, yes, a few days ago, quite as if he'd heard I'd been asking about him. We chatted about the Sheerside attack, and the Huntresses, but he managed to tell me nothing at all."

"The main thing I know about him is that he dislikes blood service. And seems determined to annoy me." Makepeace had evidently found nothing to pursue after vetting Fennington, but Rian decided to press on anyway. "To be fair, he did put me forward for the Keeper's role once he'd made it impossible for me to serve as Lord Msrah's Bound. Forest House will give the children the stability they've lacked since Eiliff and Aedric's deaths."

"Then I hope that Tangleways will aid in that goal," Lord Fennington said, with not the slightest hint that the names meant anything to him.

"I saw that you had an excellent workshop," Rian continued doggedly. "Eleri's the only one who has followed her parents into automaton work, but she's certainly inherited the Tenning flair."

"If ever there was a school suited to a budding—why, Matthiel. Are you ill?"

Rian turned, and hid a tiny sigh, for on the face of Fennington's handsome assistant was all the recognition that his lord had lacked.

"Do you—forgive me Dama Seaforth," the man said. "But do you mean to say that Eiliff Tenning is dead?"

"She and Aedric died toward the end of spring," Rian said, keeping her voice neutral while she strained to gauge his feelings. "In an odd accident, after the theft of an automaton." She allowed a trace of suspicion to leak through. "Did you know Eiliff?"

"What is this, Matthiel?" Lord Fennington asked.

"The—the self-determination experiment, my lord. Eiliff Tenning was the independent commissioned." The golden young man stared at Rian. "I—I am sorry, did you say an automaton was stolen?"

Lord Fennington puffed out his cheeks, cheer fading into bewilderment, and then his skin mottled red briefly before he shook his head. "I am at a loss. Rian, could you please explain what it is that has happened?"

She told them an edited version of the truth, leaving out Monsieur Doré, and any suggestion that she had been investigating anything.

"The children insist that the house had been searched, and an automaton was missing from the workshop, but I've not been able to find any trace of it, or who it was intended for. This was you, then, Folly?"

"So it seems," Lord Fennington said. "Matthiel, why have I not heard of this theft until now?"

"The arrangement was for Dama Tenning to report at the beginning of autumn, unless a breakthrough was made." The man blinked rapidly, though Rian realised this was due not to fear of his master, but simple distress. "You believe the accident was staged, Dama Seaforth?"

"The children were convinced of it," Rian said. "I could find no proof, though I did try to push the authorities into looking deeper. I don't understand—Fennington Industries runs several workshops. Why would you need to commission Eiliff and Aedric at all? What was the need for secrecy?"

"For that investigation? Every need." Lord Fennington rose and placed a hand on his assistant's shoulder. "Sit," he said. "No arguments, please." He waited until the man obeyed, and then poured him a generous shot of brandy.

Offering Rian one before he sat back down, he tugged at his lower lip briefly, then said:

"Haunted automatons. There have always been stories, guesses as to what could cause such movement. Angry spirits who have escaped Arawn, or lesser godlings finding strange new homes or...oh, any of a dozen explanations. They make a fine tale, but there is a fear that underlies them. Automatons are tools that should only ever dance to their master's tune. An automaton that acts on its own—that could replace people—well, fear of that's what the automaton riots were about. Any research that moves to create such a thing must be done on terms of utmost secrecy."

"You—you think that the automaton was stolen by anti-technologists?"

"Upon my soul, I have no idea. But that movement is why, when some particularly odd fulgite fell into my hands, I had Matthiel send most of it to a skilled independent. There is no way to keep such a thing secret in a workshop."

"Particularly odd?" Rian said.

"Round! And practically unbreakable! I hit one with a hammer, and didn't even chip it. I bought them from Jilly Eyleson, who races, you know. Ridiculous engines, and a need for more than the fingernail-sized shards that is all you seem to be able to get of fulgite these days. She rather lost her enthusiasm when her latest toy kept taking off without her, finally touring half Tollesby Falt with her youngest in the passenger seat, and no driver. Ended in a mill race, and the lad left with a broken arm. Between that and all the attempted thefts, she's gone back to horses, with a sideline of one of the new motopetrol things.

"Fulgite is becoming unsustainable," he continued. "Fennington Industries lost a dozen pieces in a most curious accident last month, and we switched to wiring the workshops rather than try to replace it. Why, Jilly was telling me that even her own source was trying to buy back the pieces she sold me."

"I suppose it's possible that a large piece of fulgite itself may have been the target," Rian said. "Simply for its value. But, no. Why take the automaton, if that was the case? It's so strange, though, since even Aedric's apprentice had no idea there was anything unusual about the commission."

"If the arrangements I made were kept, then I should have been the only person who knew that the Tennings had that fulgite," said Matthiel.

"How did you find Eiliff in the first place?" Rian asked.

"We had a list of exceptional independents prepared when looking for teachers for the school," Lord Fennington said. "A useful smokescreen."

Matthiel said. "Actually, my lord, Dama Tenning came on personal recommendation from Dama Blair."

"Young Lynsey? Well, we won't find the source of the leak there. A most close-mouthed child. Still, I will ask her if she mentioned it." Lord Fennington held out his hands to Rian and gripped hers warmly. "I hate, I simply hate the thought that my commission brought this upon your family, but I'd be a fool to ignore the possibility. If there is anything you need, please, please do not hesitate to tell me."

He wasn't telling her the whole truth, but there was no outright lie behind the gust of sincerity that washed over her. Rian thought rapidly, balancing her decision to pretend there had been no direct investigation with a need for further details, then said:

"Did you say someone tried to buy the fulgite back?"

NINETEEN

The fencing school recommended by Lynsey Blair proved to be a nest of United Albion sympathisers. This did not surprise Rian in the least, and she danced around their avid interest in dragons while learning all she could about their former Alban instructor.

This was little enough. Lynsey was twenty-two, and had been born in Craigneith. She had taken a first in mathematics from Argynion, but had followed her interest into practical combat, and made it a career. Her family had suffered a slide in fortune, thanks to some complication of an entailed property, but were otherwise unremarkable.

Since casual gossip did not produce any revelations, Rian abandoned this particular rabbit to concentrate on lessons. Her instructor, Dem Tilit—a short, scarred man originally from Wabanaki—outlined the stages of her training, then taught her how to grip a wooden practice sword, and began on foot placement and movement.

"Do not concern yourself too much with the weapon, just yet," he said, as she attempted to keep her knees slightly bent and her feet facing in different directions. "Until this is second nature to you, your drill will be entirely stance and movement. No, keep your back straight. And forward. Retreat. Yes. Practice that for the next week, at least an hour each day."

With thigh muscles screaming after even a short lesson, Rian did not regard this command with any enthusiasm, but thanked her teacher and took her time in the changing room, thinking over protective clothing and practice rooms. The school would rent her equipment, such as the wooden practice weapon she was taking home today, but obtaining her own would be necessary. Strange not to have to budget for the cost, let alone the time involved.

"Arianne!"

"Lyle." Rian thought he looked particularly well that evening, dressed more casually than usual, but very handsome. "Come to watch me sweat?"

"Should I admit to it?" he asked. "My excuse is making good on my invitation to dinner. I know the area thanks to Lynsey, and there's an excellent place down the street that's used to the students and their weapons."

"That sounds ideal," Rian said, hefting her cloth-wrapped stick-with-a-hilt, and followed him down the stairs from the fencing studio. "You seem to be spending more time in Prytennia than Alba at the moment."

"Or my mornings in one and evenings in the other," he agreed. "Alba initially escaped most of the scouring, but as it's grown worse, Prince Gustav's become less inclined to leave Prytennia to solve this herself. Not least because if he should happen to ride in heroically and fix things, there's every chance the vote to extend the Protectorate will pass. I am, incidentally, under orders to cultivate you. I expect you understand why."

"Shattered dragon, etcetera etcetera," Rian said. "I am very bored with being asked."

"Playing witness to that foreseeing won me no end of approval, however. It was very obliging timing." He led her to an unprepossessing door that opened on to a gust of spicy scents, and a busy interior, worn but clean.

"Do you find all the conflicting loyalties difficult to manage?" Rian asked, as she glanced over the menu tacked by the door. "Alba first, and Gustav second, and with a sister who is a Unionist? Doesn't that make the prince suspicious?"

"Gustav trusts me to be Alban," Lyle said, with a satiric tilt to his brows. "He has other aides for matters where it's necessary to be Swedish. Lynsey...well, Gustav

admires Lynsey very much and she wisely avoids him.
Probably the best thing about her deciding to work for
Folly is it'll keep her safely out of Gustav's path."

Rian considered this while Lyle ordered and then led
them to a table. Gustav would make a political marriage
eventually, and—from what she'd seen of the man—
probably keep several mistresses. She doubted Lynsey
had the temperament for that: both the Swedish Empire
and Alba allowed women to own property and seek careers
and education, but they had the same confusing divide
between 'proper' and 'improper' women that Rian had
struggled to adjust to when she'd first started travelling.
It was little wonder so many of the United Albion League
happened to be female—particularly since Alba's
inheritance laws favoured sons over daughters.

"And where do you stand on union?" she asked.

"My ideal would be for one of Alba's own gods to
Answer," he said. "But I'm resigned to it not happening.
We barely know their names, after so many centuries of
the Duodecim, the Cour d'Lune, the Aesir and the Green
Aesir. There is so little of the true Alba remaining: our
days are Swedish, our months Roman and our years
Egyptian."

"So are Prytennia's," Rian pointed out.

"But you at least have Sulis. For all the gods whose
conquerors have trampled Alba's fields, not one could
establish territorial allegiance. We thought it a triumph
once, proof that we had our own Otherworld, that there
was a place where Albans truly belonged. Now all I want
is certainty."

"And you think Sweden will bring that?"

"They managed it with Greenland, and Highfall. It's
one of the biggest advantages of the Protectorates—the
Swedes are able to systematically bring about territorial
allegiance with the Aesir through the simple *choice* of the
people, and so I'm willing to encourage Alba to make that
choice. Anything to end this eternal disadvantage to

Alban souls, this uphill struggle to gain an Otherworld, or face unlife. To which point, I'm happy enough for a united Albion if you—or anyone—should happen to find the Dragon of the North, since Sulis and Arawn's territory is tied together. But enough of the Union—I'm sure you've had your fill of the subject. What did you think of Folly's collection of follies?"

"I liked it. But I'm afraid the children have ruled Tangleways out on account of animals and exercise. It's such an unusual array of classes—I would never have thought of teaching animal care in an academically-focused school."

Lyle laughed. "Folly met some precocious brat who didn't know where milk came from. That's what started him off on the whole thing. It's unfortunate: his heart's in the right place, and he's found some excellent teachers, but it's looking like the whole thing will flop badly."

"And then Lynsey will be back in Gustav's path?"

"Well, she'll be disappointed." His face grew solemn. "And is already dismayed, having learned who it is your family have recently lost. She looked up to Eiliff Tenning, and feels responsible for suggesting her for Folly's commission."

"How did Lynsey know Eiliff?" Rian asked, pleased not to have had to raise the subject herself.

"Through the Mini-T Scholars program—which actively recruits at Alban universities, and causes no end of tension in doing so. Fortunately Folly knows Lynsey well enough to be certain she hasn't gone around babbling about his secret projects to all and sundry."

"Did she tell you?"

"Well, yes." He grimaced. "At least, she mentioned that she'd been able to send a plum commission Eiliff Tenning's way. But I didn't know the details, and certainly haven't mentioned it to anyone. Even so, Lynsey's second-guessing herself, convinced she somehow caused this, so I've strongly hinted to Evelyn that he should go tour Folly's latest extravagance. That's sure to take her mind off blaming herself."

"Because?"

"Oh, Lyn's been in love with Evie since the first time I dragged her down to Sheerside. I pretend not to know. He certainly has never realised—thinks of her as my pig-tailed little sister. It would be unfair to tell him, don't you feel?"

"But you're telling me?"

Lyle's expression turned mischievous. "What's a little light sabotage between friends?" he asked, then leaned back as a server approached with a steaming platter.

Because she wouldn't indulge in an affair with Evelyn if she thought it would hurt Lynsey? Rian decided to take this leap of logic as a compliment, and settled back to enjoy a good meal with an accomplished flirt. The food was an eclectic mix—beginning with a Stomrurian grain dish, then a meat-and-potatoes staple, with a sorbet for afters—but it was all nicely done, though the wine a little heavy for her tastes. She didn't push particularly hard for information relating to Eiliff, and only learned that Lynsey would provide a little mathematical tutoring at Tangleways, along with swordcraft.

"Let me find you a taxicab," Lyle said, as they emerged back on the street.

"No need—that omnibus runs right into Lamhythe. Thank you again Lyle."

She kissed him lightly on the cheek—for they were cheekbones worthy of such a salute—and trotted to catch a passing omnibus. It was a new double-decker model, and yet steam-powered, and as she climbed up to the open top level to enjoy the evening breeze, she reflected on her involvement in matters that might solve the shortage of fulgite, and change how buses were made.

And then she thought about catching an omnibus, even though she could afford a taxicab easily. Habit dies hard.   Still, the view was better, especially now that shadows held no mysteries for her.

And what now for her ponderously slow investigation? It had only taken most of summer, but at last the question of Lynsey was solved. Yet the answer brought her so little. Two weak suspects in Folly Fennington and his Matthiel. She was fairly certain Fennington had held back something about the third piece of unusual fulgite he'd retained—possibly an investigation into whether it had been artificially created—but her unreliable new sense had found a distinct lack of murderous guilt in any of the four who admitted to knowing about Eiliff's commission. If not them, then perhaps an eavesdropper?

The one thing she had gained, as tactfully as she could manage, was the name of the less-than-reputable person who had sold and then tried to buy back several pieces of unusual fulgite. She'd taken a certain pleasure in adding that to the brief report she'd sent on to the palace, and hoped very much that it was something that Makepeace had not already learned, when he'd questioned Folly Fennington before she had the chance.

Undecided on her next step, Rian allowed her thoughts to drift to flirtation. She did not mind that the pursuit had openly become part of Evelyn and Lyle's playful rivalry. No-one was pretending they had fallen in love. But was Lyle right in thinking that long-standing feelings on Lynsey's part would make Rian less inclined to trifle there? And what would it be like to bed anyone when contact would inconsistently tell her exactly what they were feeling? Exciting, or awkward?

A greater complication were her 'niblings', and whether the idea of aunts with lovers would put further strain on them. Particularly with Eleri, who would be raw to all instances of romance.

There was unmissable irony in an aunt and niece meeting the Queen's two daughters and having entirely opposite reactions to overwhelming attraction. Eleri saw

Celestine and was convinced she had found the one person she would ever want to marry. Rian's pulse might quicken whenever she let herself think of Aerinndís Gwyn Lynn, but Rian also knew that she had a type—incisive, highly competent, and with a hint not so much of disdain as of being supremely hard to impress. This combination invariably hooked her deeply, and she had learned to recognise when she was being pulled off balance, and avoid the cause.

That was not a response she had considered wise to suggest to Eleri, and she hoped she'd chosen the correct attitude: to not quite dismiss the possibility that the girl might find some future with Princess Celestine, and to do what little she could to support plans for courtship. It seemed unhappy timing, though, for such a goal-oriented creature as Eleri to face another challenge that could not be reliably solved by a precisely-drawn schematic and a stint in the workshop.

Leaving the bus for the short walk back to Forest House, Rian set aside travails of the heart and tried to decide her next step. If the thieves suspected she had the last piece of artificial fulgite, could she use that to bait them? Or should she attempt again to communicate with the 'haunt' that seemed to drive the converted mannequin's movements? She'd chosen, at least, not to mention its existence to Lord Fennington, even though it appeared he was the true owner of both fulgite and finely-crafted commission.

"Llllland of Whores, Land of Euuu-nuchs!"

Two women and a man, arms linked, were making unsteady progress down the street toward her, bellowing Prytennia's unofficial national song. It must be later than she'd realised. Well-versed in the vagaries of drunks, Rian started to move further to the side of the street, but then stopped and stood still, concentrating.

"Lleeeeggss are wide, brrrreasts are bare!

"They'll wring you dry and hang you oooout to air!"

The three passed her by, weaving faintly and not glancing once in her direction. Which proved nothing at all, of course, especially since to them this would be a very dark and unlit section of street.

Shaking her head, Rian wondered if Makepeace would ever stop resenting her long enough to give her some idea what to expect. He was not someone who would respond well to polite requests.

A cool breeze whisking around her legs, Rian turned back toward Forest House, and then froze. Directly in front of her, running silently in place, was a long-eared, long-legged, and insubstantial black hare.

One of the Night Breezes of the Sulevia Sceadu.

TWENTY

No-one could see the wind, but the Night Breezes were more than currents of air. The hare's ears lengthened as it raced relentlessly in place, streaming dozens of feet behind it before abruptly snapping back. Rian could see its nose twitching, and the eyes, black on black but clearly directed at her. A living creature, but with no river of blood driving it.

Hares were a thing that she associated strongly with her mother, a part of the *Processional* work that had appeared often in her parents' house. And here was what those many statues had represented, bounding past her. She turned, only to discover, inches away, the antlers of a black stag hurtling toward her face. There was no chance to even take a step back before a roar of wind blasted over her, snatched her from the ground, and carried her away.

Clutching her cloth-wrapped stick, Rian found herself on the stag's back, the sensation very different from riding a horse, since there was no gait to adapt to, and she could both feel its back beneath her, and the wind supporting her like a hand. Exhilarating! Also terrifying, as she rapidly rose to a fatal height, though it did not feel possible to slip from the stag's back and fall. The city spread out blue and silver beneath her, with hot notes of gold for the street lights and still-waking windows.

"That's one way to sweep me off my feet," Rian gasped, then laughed at her own leaping heart, for there was no chance the Crown Princess had romantic intentions. Reviving her common sense, Rian instead simply admired the beauty of the moment. One to treasure, no matter the circumstances.

When her semi-tangible mount slowed and circled a figure high in the sky, Rian had herself in much as order as was possible given a stag made of wind had carried her off to meet a princess riding a legendary three-tailed mare high above London.

"The stars seem larger up here," Rian said as she came into earshot, which was not businesslike at all, but true.

Aerinndís Gwyn Lynn was wearing a reinforced vest of leather, a long split tunic, and close-fitting trousers. With her hair braided and clubbed, and both a sword and a pistol at her hip, there was no doubt that she was dressed for duty. But all Rian saw was the Crown Princess' beautifully slender throat and the clean line of her jaw as she tilted back her head to consider the vast sweep of stars.

The three-tailed mare tossed her head as Rian's stag crowded close. The winds seemed able to intersect without causing more than eddies, and Rian found herself within inches of someone she had thought to avoid, easily able to hear that husky voice without straining.

"I doubt there is a measurable difference, Dama Seaforth," the Crown Princess said, the dry note in her voice perhaps for Rian's mesmerised stare. "We are only two hundred feet closer." Her gaze dropped to the cloth bundle Rian was holding, and tiny wind-mice swirled about Rian's hands, lifting it away. "What is this?"

"A practical response," Rian said, watching as the cloth unwrapped itself, exposing the crude weapon.

Princess Aerinndís was a noted swordswoman—simple good sense for the Suleviae Sceadu, who did not have access to godly defences during the day. She took the practice sword by its hilt and cut the air, a short, sharp stroke that made even a length of light wood seem deadly. But then she wrapped and returned the weapon without comment.

"And how can I assist you today, Your Highness?" Rian asked, resigned to the fact that her heart would spend this conversation playing pit-pat and thunder.

"Look," the Crown Princess said, nodding to the roofs beneath.

They'd moved, and were now above Forest House, distinct for the enclosed trees and the clear circle of stone. Rian saw nothing to cause remark in the blue-tinged scene, and she was too far away to sense the rivers of blood that were living creatures. The Sulevia Sceadu was known to be able to see in the dark, but it was difficult to guess what had caught her attention.

Movement spared Rian from admitting defeat: a lithe grey cat trotting along the spine of one of the warehouse roofs to sit beside a larger feline already waiting in the lee of a chimney. They were barely visible from the height, but even the cat was unusual given the general lack of anything but ravens willing to come anywhere near Forest House. That the larger watcher was a distinctive sand-and-white feline with black tufted ears gave Rian her answer.

"The Huntresses."

"The foreseeing or your involvement with the sphinx is likely to have drawn them. Look for signs of controlled animals during the day."

It seemed the Crown Princess was only pointing this out in passing, for the stag and mare were moving again, with a small escort of hares and hounds. Knowing the increased acuity of her own hearing, Rian hoped the children were minding her warning not to talk of true secrets outside Hurlstone, and then gave herself to the pleasure of this unique view of the city, and the privilege of witnessing the Night Breezes.

In the late evening the main roads were not yet quiet, and many of the entertainment houses were hot points of noise and brilliance, but along less central streets most windows had blacked their eyes. They were heading east, and as they passed along the river some of the dark hounds in the Sulevia Sceadu's escort raced down to gambol around the turbines of the wind towers, so that they whirred and hummed. Many of the towers, though, were foreshortened stubs, and even the great Wind Clock lacked its blades. Every night the Crown Princess would have this view of the toll of the summer's scouring, of the threadbare canopies of trees, the withered gardens, and the patched roofs of houses.

For Rian there was another roof, green and boundless and now always with her. An ever-present reminder that she not only belonged to the forest, but was being tested by it.

They descended into the docklands, half London crossed in a bare minute, and were deposited light as goose down on the flat roof of some form of factory. Makepeace lay on his back at their feet, hands behind his head, apparently occupied in gazing at the stars.

He turned his head a fraction. "You may be unbearably smug, Wednesday, but not for more than five minutes."

"I'll save it for later," Rian said, looking around the factory roof for some reason why they were there. "You found this fulgite dealer?"

"Him, his superior, and now, hopefully, the head of the group responsible for the loss of the fulgite shipment earlier this year. You happened on a link between the resellers, who are kept carefully ignorant, and the core of this operation."

"Surely worthy of at least ten minutes' smugness," Princess Aerinndís murmured.

"It's a tightly-run organisation," Makepeace said, thumbing his nose at Aerinndís Gwyn Lynn, Sulevia Sceadu and Crown Princess. "Those making sales outside the core group received fulgite from a masked figure known to them as 'Wrack'. The description of this Wrack varies wildly—clearly a half-dozen different people all wearing a mask of the same pattern. More annoyingly, after initial contact the exchanges are conducted via package drops, and they seem to have an instinct for when one of their dealers has been discovered. Delway's lot have spent all summer watching packages that are never picked up, and I can't claim better luck since I was called in, which suggests someone god-touched is involved."

"Delway's lot?" Rian had never heard the name.

"Police Special Force," he said, customary irritability resurfacing. "No sign that they've been compromised, but I'm not risking them tonight. The dealer I've traced arranged a meeting at midnight at the warehouse across the street. I've been looking forward to talking to the real Wrack for some time."

The trip past the Wind Clock meant Rian knew there was a half-hour to go. She glanced about and then sat on the edge of an inner dividing wall.

"What of the cat plague?" Makepeace asked the Crown Princess.

"Forest House, the palace, Alba Place, Ficus Lapis' office, and the main digging site under the Tamesas."

"Now that last..." Makepeace sat up, puzzled. "Ficus Lapis naturally uses fulgite to power their diggers, and so could have some of this special batch. The firm's machines are in demand and they've assisted underground construction in a dozen different countries, with no hint of complaint beyond the usual price-gouging, but I don't know of a reason for the Huntresses to connect them to sphinxes. Is it because it's traditional to suspect Romans of being up to no good?"

Princess Aerinndís seated herself neatly opposite Rian, looking no less completely in control for being perched on a railing. A lone transparent owl circled her in a wide loop, and her expression was thoughtful. "The winds have found no variation from the planned tunnels. There's a sealed area in their centre of operations, but those are so common as to be unremarkable. Here, there is a safe, but otherwise the place is open."

Of the Suleviae, the Sulevia Sceadu was most feared, for there were few places the Night Breezes could not reach to carry back whispers. Or to do as they did now, abandoning furred and feathered forms to create the miniature outline of a room occupied by two people. One writing, the other drinking. Shadows without colour, the page empty of script beneath the moving pen, for this was a representation of the surfaces touched by the wind.

"Can I see the man writing in more detail?" Rian asked.

The image changed, so that only the desk remained, with its faintly-smiling writer intent on the black page. He was very thin, with a curling mop of hair.

"I think I've met him," she said, slowly. "Reddish hair, and talks very rapidly. One of the auction house people? Yes, he came to run over the details of the auction with me. So." She stopped, for it was confirmation.

"Ready for your revenge, Wednesday? Will you hit them with your little stick?"

Rian stared at Makepeace, then down at the wrapped sword she'd forgotten she was holding. "I don't particularly care what happens to him. What's necessary is proving that Aedric and Eiliff did not die from their own incompetence, so their legacy is their achievements, not an ignominious death. That's what will make the difference for their children." She paused. "No, that's not entirely true. Killed, jailed, brought to justice somehow, but the most important thing is still proof."

"That's the aim—" Makepeace began, then stopped as Princess Aerinndís held up a hand.

"...and get out," the wind whispered. A woman's voice, diction slurred. "We've got back as much as anyone could hope to. I don't care what they're offering for the rest."

"You'll care when your cut runs out, Min." Like his face, the man's voice was familiar. "If we can get our hands on the last of the big pieces, the bonus will see us swimming easy until you've drowned yourself in that rotgut."

"No bonus is worth the risk. The plan was get it, sell it, fade. We were idiots to ever agree to try and get it back."

The wind's image changed to show the room again, tiny figures to match the voices as the man blotted his writing and stood.

"You won't get far calling Dane an idiot."

"Dane's half the problem! She's changed, Penry. Something's been off with her all summer. And this thing with the masks has spiralled into an obsession. Ever since that Alban came along, she's lost all sense."

Makepeace raised his eyebrows at that, glancing at Rian.

"Got twice the money for the same haul, that's what we've done," the man said briskly, stooping with a key to unlock what must be the safe. "You need to stay out of your cups, Min. You've washed away your stomach."

"I'll be wash-eaagh!"

A third player had bounded onto the darkling stage. Massive shoulders, heavy head, an enormous clawed paw batting the woman from her chair. The bull-bear.

"*What in—?*" the man began, but Rian did not see his fate, for Princess Aerinndís had reacted immediately, the three-tailed mare and two stags snatching the eavesdroppers from their roof and hurtling them over the street and through the doors of a warehouse two buildings down, the heavy wood shattering like glass as they blasted past.

Stacks of crates blocked their view across the cavernous interior to an office tucked into the corner. As the three Night Breezes rode close to the ceiling, Rian saw the panes of the office's windows were shattered, the exposed interior painted with orange and gold. Fire.

Set on her feet outside the remains of the internal door, Rian looked hastily for the bull-bear as a flurry of dark hares darted through the blaze, causing it to roar higher as they snatched objects—and two bodies—out into the main part of the warehouse. Meanwhile, wind hounds leapt in every direction, vanishing out to the street.

"Nothing else in the building but a few rats," Makepeace said, as he stomped on one of the books rescued from the blaze. "No sign of how it got in or out, let alone where it went to."

"It went nowhere," the Crown Princess said. "It neither came nor left; it simply was."

The winds returned, heavy with moisture, and tossed a sizeable portion of the Tamesas over everything, leaving acrid smoke with a fishy undernote. Princess Aerinndís dropped to one knee beside one of the two bodies, and Rian saw to her horror that the person was still alive. A woman wearing knee-length trousers and a sleeveless tunic striped with red and white where the cloth had been shredded in parallel lines, the exposed flesh so deeply gouged that she looked like she had fallen under a plough.

"...hurts," the woman said, clutching at the hand offered to her.

Eyes wide, she was breathing in little gasps, the noise harsh and desperate, and Rian found that her own hand was at her throat, remembering the effort, the pain, and the sinking certainty that nothing could be done.

Makepeace knelt on the woman's other side, shaking his head as he did so. He made no attempt to try to feed her his ka and blood. Even a Thoth-den would hesitate to try to save such a badly mangled woman: the risk of creating a ghul was too great.

Then he said: "*Attend me.*"

That was too much, and Rian turned away, forcing her thoughts to a more useful response. The fire had been thoroughly doused, leaving the office a damp mess, but there were sections barely touched. Lifting a still-lit fulgite lamp onto a box, Rian found a tumbled ledger and a stump of pencil, and made quick work of two portraits.

The woman was talking, a thready but unemotional whisper. She didn't react to Rian's approach with the lamp, brow smooth as she gazed steadily at Makepeace's face.

Makepeace glanced at the ledger Rian held out to him, then took it and held it up for the injured woman to see.

"Do you know these people?"

Calmly, the woman looked at the pages, then said: "The Alban. Has Dane—"

And then she closed her eyes and died. Of course.

TWENTY-ONE

The Crown Princess lowered the dead woman's hand so that it rested over the terrible wound, and then gently closed the woman's dimmed eyes. Her own hand was covered in blood, and she used it to draw on the still forehead three circles around a central dot to represent the first island of Annwn.

"May you find your path," she said formally.

"And may we find Dane," Makepeace said. "Whoever she might be. Perhaps we can ask your Alban," he added to Rian.

Rian drew a long, calming breath, taking sudden violence and death and setting them in a place that would not interfere with larger goals. "I can't even guess which of them she recognised. I thought I might even be eliminating them, showing her those portraits."

"I admit that I'd dismissed that pair as suspects, particularly the brother, since I'd questioned him under trance." He frowned down at the ledger. "Guileless and guiltless and yet, apparently not."

Princess Aerinndís stood. "God-touched resistance?"

"The most likely reason, though that would make Lyle Blair an extraordinary actor—one whose emotions match the falsehood he's telling. We now seem to be overwhelmed with god-touched possibilities: the possible truth-diviner, whatever that beast is, and someone who may perhaps be able to resist my abilities." He began picking up the various objects the winds had pulled from the fire and examining them.

A water-logged hare gusted in to swirl around Princess Aerinndís' hands, and Rian pulled loose the voluminous wrapping from her sword to offer up as a towel. Then she surveyed the mess. Would there be proof among all this that could remove the tarnish from Aedric and Eiliff's reputation? It seemed clear that the aim had been to destroy evidence, and it was particularly unfortunate that the safe had been open.

"Where did the fire come from?" she asked, puzzled. "They were using fulgite lamps."

"Where did our bull-bear come from?" Makepeace replied. "Some fire-breathing, teleporting animal whose existence no-one has ever reported?" He picked up a wad of scorched, sodden black cloth and held it up to display the design: a vertical and horizontal line meeting in the centre, like the hands of a timepiece at three o'clock. A sinuous eye filled the section within the two lines. "Nothing to do with the Aesir, I think—I can spot their thumbprints—but we can't overlook Gustav's possible involvement. And he might become even more of a headache if we haul off one of his aides for interrogation."

Princess Aerinndís retrieved the ledger, and used it to write a short note, which she then tore out. A transparent bird—perhaps a nightjar—whisked the sheet away.

"Do you propose anything further tonight?" she asked.

"I won't waste my time sitting around here," he said. "Delway's lot can sift and door-knock and give us a better picture of what's survived this. I'll find out what the Blairs have been up to."

"Lyle was having dinner with me," Rian offered. "It can't be more than an hour since I was with him, over at Westing Gate. Lynsey is theoretically at Tangleways." She briefly summarised the conversation she'd had with Lyle.

Makepeace eyed her narrowly, then said: "Him dancing attendance makes sense if he thinks you have that fulgite. Perhaps we can use it—or you—as bait."

Princess Aerinndís carefully tore the two portraits out of the ledger, and handed the volume back to Makepeace.

"We will leave mention of Albans out of official discussions, to minimise the chance of warning our target.

Tomorrow evening Commander Delway and Professor Bermondsley can present their reports on their respective investigations, and we will decide a plan of action. I will return Dama Seaforth."

"Highness," Makepeace said, with a nod of acknowledgement, surprising Rian since he'd called Princess Leodhild "Hildy", and the otherwise formal Crown Princess treated him with a familial lack of ceremony.

Rian was now almost used to being whisked from her feet by a wind with antlers, and at least the pace was less unnerving as they slipped out of the warehouse and rose above London's rooftops. Events had moved as rapidly as the Night Breezes—after such achingly slow progress she had at last had confirmation that the fulgite thieves had been interested in the house at Caerlleon. The proof would come.

A gibbous moon had crested the horizon, thinning the blue tones of Rian's night vision and picking out the glistening capstone of the nearest pyramid. The major pyramids were the only structures rising above the ever-present shadow forest, and they reminded Rian forcibly that Egypt was part of this hunt, and that spies more formidable than ravens were waiting back at Forest House. But, oh, it was hard to be serious beneath this grand sweep of sky, above a forest that existed beyond the world, with curl-tailed hounds lolloping at her side, and Aerinndís Gwyn Lynn directly ahead. She rode with the gods.

And they were already descending, the trip just long enough to make Rian ache for more. Half-expecting to be deposited precisely where she'd been collected, she managed to hide any reaction when they swept directly over the roof of Forest House and stopped in front of an innocuous chimney. Two pairs of golden eyes blinked from the shadows, but the caracal and cat did not stir.

More wind hounds began to gather: long-legged, narrow of body, heads elegant, ears streaming back, and feathery tails low. They were sisters to Arawn's hounds, and they could strip fields, flatten towns, and easily tear even vampires apart. The damage wrought by the summer's scouring wind was nothing to the force the Night Breezes could muster, and here they massed, dozens, hundreds, until the whole of the grove was covered by a swelling wave building and yet not crashing upon the shore the warehouse roof.

Although most of their power was being held in check, the Night Breezes still produced a gale that tore at the leaves of the grove and made the tiling rattle. The two small felines that were the focus of the intensifying blast hunkered down, eyes slitted to nothing, only the chimney behind them keeping them in place.

And then the massed winds were gone, a hammer-blow dissipating before it landed, and there was only the stag and the three-tailed mare, cantering slowly in place.

"Goals may be obtained more quickly through co-operation," Aerinndís Gwyn Lynn observed, in passable Egyptian.

The cat and the caracal stood—with a hint of trembling muscles—then turned and walked unhurriedly away. Utter disdain, as represented by slowly switching tails, and twin nether eyes.

Below, the grove had filled with folies, but their numbers began to decrease. Forest House, thankfully, remained quiet. Rian glanced at Princess Aerinndís' face, expecting affronted hauteur. The Crown Princess was undoubtedly angry: the confrontation had been an expression of the Sulevia Sceadu's opinion of a foreign power offering help while prosecuting its own agenda. But the princess was smiling through her annoyance, her response more grim amusement than rage.

"Very likely they are under Command," Princess Aerinndís observed, as the wind whisked them to the attic windows. Tiny mice worked on latches, and dark hares gently gusted the casement open.

Rian ducked her head as they wafted inside, and found herself intensely glad that Makepeace was not there to know her feelings, to look at her and see her excitement. What did it say about Rian that she was so enormously aroused by the *display*, by the sheer power of the Sulevia Sceadu? Rian did not know whether to be entertained by herself, or embarrassed.

"I do not see what it is that makes you less than an artist."

Wrenching her thoughts back to less exciting paths, Rian saw that the Crown Princess was still holding the sketches of Lyle and Lynsey Blair. The question at least was a familiar one, and she used it to pull herself together, to shrug lightly, as she had so many times before.

"I could bore you with a long monologue on the nature of art, but the short answer is that I grew up thinking that I was an artist, and spent many years diligently training my skills, because it never occurred to me to be anything else. When I eventually realised that the whole of my motivation revolved around my parents, and none of it for the work, I gave it up."

"You do not miss it?"

"Not particularly. It's not as if I swore never to pick up a brush again—I help one of my cousins painting theatre backdrops whenever I visit Lutèce. I'll draw something if I particularly want to remember what it looked like. But I don't..." She paused, pushing aside an impulse to explain properly. "I treat it as a craft. A semantic quibble, perhaps."

Princess Aerinndís had crossed to the workbenches, which fortuitously were no longer strewn with studies of her young sister. Instead it seemed that Eleri had at last started work on Eluned's replacement arm. She had shaped the forearm from a length of dark wood, and all the small joints of the fingers had been laid out, leaving a gap for the back of the hand.

"Did you consider your brother an artist?"

"Oh, yes. I hope we recover this missing automaton. His work was always beautiful."

"And the girl who is making this? Is she an artist?"

Rian was becoming amused. "Eleri's drive seems to lean to the science behind the process, but yes, I would call her one. The work I've seen of hers is very stripped back, but there's a certain spare elegance that she strives for. Does it offend your sense of what is correct, Highness, that I choose not to name myself an artist?"

"It concerns me that the new Keeper of the Deep Grove may be so fractured within herself that she will fail in her duty."

This was a large leap into the unexpected. "My duty being considerably more than opening a gate every twenty-five years?"

"The service of the Keeper is Cernunnos' contribution to the Treaty of the Oak," Princess Aerinndís said. "You are the second to hold the position since the Trifold Age began. Comfrey is dragging his feet in acknowledging that because you represent the beginning of his end, but avoiding change will not alter the fact that Prytennia's defences now involve you. The foreseeing was an immediate acknowledgement, as much as we have attempted to downplay it. Having taken on this duty, you must do everything you can to prepare for it."

Rian frowned at her, bemused. "By facing my own failings?" she guessed.

"There are attacks a sword cannot defend against." The Crown Princess had found herself a chair, her habitually upright posture giving her the manner of a strict teacher waiting to hear a student's excuses.

Since Aerinndís Gwyn Lynn was all of twenty-three, Rian was not entirely certain she cared for the image. But this, for all she'd been run into the choice with no preparation, was part of what she'd agreed to by giving her allegiance to Cernunnos, and so she set herself on the nearest trunk and approached the question seriously.

"I can't say I've ever thought of myself as fractured," she said. "Resilient, yes. Not broken. I don't consider my relationship to art to be some unhealed wound, but a reflection of the environment in which I was raised."

"Child of famous parents?"

"A house where art was venerated. Not that that was necessarily a bad thing, and my parents were very supportive of me doing whatever I wanted. Naturally, what I wanted was to be like them, to do the things that they valued. It did not come so easily to me as it did to Aedric, but technique is something that hard work can address, and so I worked very hard indeed. I made considerable progress, and my parents were proud of me."

"And then?"

"That's where we get to the discussion on what is art. My parents' house overflowed with guests, students, patrons and petitioners. These last, I soon learned, were pitiful creatures who produced 'daubs', or were derivative, or had nothing to say. They would come wanting to be taken on as students.

"My father was quite open in his scorn. To him there was nothing worse than the deluded, the pretenders. My mother would allow anyone to show her their work, and would offer constructive advice. And my father would give her a questioning look after she left them, and she would give the tiniest shake of her head.

"I was a little too young for such dismissal, of course. I'm not certain if anything would have been different if she hadn't died when I was fourteen. Perhaps she would have found some way to direct my energies elsewhere. As it was, she died and I fumbled about trying to understand the family finances—I fortunately have always found numbers easy to get along with—and then I threw myself back into the next important step in living up to her legacy: developing my own style."

"The difference between derivative and worthy?" The Crown Princess was listening with solemn attention, a single owl drifting in a tight circle above her.

"You don't advance anything copying other people, and if you're not trying to reach, to transfigure, to say something, to realise a goal beyond an image...then all you are doing is producing daubs." Rian shook her head. "Which is in itself a rather limited view of art, but it is what I was drowning in.

"My father had not coped well with Mother's death, and his anxiety about me leaked through, though he tried very hard to be encouraging. Some of his visitors were less careful, and I worked myself to the bone to prove them wrong, to make the breakthrough I kept telling myself was inevitable. And then my brother came home from university with Eiliff Tenning."

How nervous and proud Aedric had been! And her father had revived for a while, become more like his old self.

"Eiliff gave me a great gift. She was quite a brilliant person, you know. Prytennia really suffered a loss with her death. I admired her immensely, and she tried to have a conversation with me about something other than art."

Rian blushed. She felt the heat rise up, as scorching as it had been that day.

"I attended a village school. And back then the law only required attendance until you were twelve. Even when I was there, I did nothing but draw, and the teachers encouraged this because I was Charlotte Seaforth's daughter, and of course I would earn my living through art. I could barely read."

"What was the gift?"

"Incredulity. Eiliff, who was a rather blunt person, tried very hard not to gape at me in disbelief. She valued art—and had a good eye for it—but she also venerated knowledge, and believed in...*contributing*, in working toward the betterment of the world. She thought me selfish for spending my time painting when I was not producing something of worth, and she did not hide that she believed I should redirect my time toward being what father termed a 'devotional'—someone who, lacking the capacity themselves, centred themselves around the valuable work of others. I didn't care for that idea at all, but the strength of her reaction forced me to look at myself from the view of someone other than my parents. And I kept looking long after her visit. All that time trying to reach without copying, trying to express something ineffable, and the problem was I had nothing to say. I had no passion for the work, let alone its subjects, and no goal beyond my parents. I stopped trying to make myself into an artist to give myself a chance to be me."

"This must have been years ago. Do you still have nothing to say?"

"That's...I don't look at it that way," Rian said. "I've never felt the decision to stop as a loss. Only a relief."

The Crown Princess stood, leaving Rian feeling like she'd faced a test, and perhaps not passed.

"Can anyone excise a portion of themselves and call themself whole?" the princess asked. "I will trust to your judgment, Dama Seaforth. Comfrey will bring you to the meeting tomorrow."

The sacred mare moved so quickly, whisking the Crown Princess out of the window before Rian could even stand up. Rian crossed and looked out over the now-quiet grove, and then sat on the sill, feeling drained.

A great deal crammed into a few hours. She had watched someone die, and she had discovered that she had misjudged one of the Blairs. She had flown above London, then been asked if she was whole.

Wouldn't you know it, if you were broken inside? Rian had certainly reached adulthood mired in her own ignorance, mortified by how little she knew, but she had methodically worked to catch herself up, climbed out of the well, and enjoyed herself a great deal once she'd reached the surface. What was wrong about who she was?

Her mistake had been taking the question seriously enough to even try to answer. Dredging up her childhood never left her feeling even-keeled. Now she'd waste her time wondering what it was Princess Aerinndís had seen in her to make her ask. Stupid to not stick to the short answer.

It was a romantic impulse, this wish to be properly understood. The last person she'd told all that to was Carelius, and he'd given her a sharp lesson in status in return. But at least she could not delude herself into thinking that Aerinndís Gwyn Lynn would ever consider marrying her: the Suleviae's ban on marriage took that out of the question altogether.

What a distraction. Rian needed to put herself in order, to set aside ideas that would lead her places fierce and full of jagged edges. She would leave it to Eleri to pursue princesses, and return her attention to murder. They were so close now.

Rian looked out over the grove into the boundless forest, and refused to think of flying.

TWENTY-TWO

Aunt Arianne had left a note that she wasn't to be woken for breakfast: an irritating development because Eleri wanted money from her before they set out on their next round of workshop visits. The morning improved when Griff found a wooden sword in the attic. Even Eleri joined in for dashing fights against a broomstick, but that soon palled, for they were impatient to get on.

"No money left in the safe," Eleri said, restively swinging the sword while Griff went for drinks. "Amasen horns are gone too. Doesn't trust us."

"She probably sent it to the bank," Eluned said. "Would you have taken some?"

"Why not? Said she'd give it to us. Not really the Aunt's anyway. Or half yours."

"I don't think I had to give nearly as much allegiance. I only see the forest when I'm with her."

"Still wasting our time. Stayed out late drinking. Only cares about herself."

This was entirely unreasonable, but Eluned knew Eleri in this temper wasn't going to listen to argument. What they needed was a distraction.

Griff, pounding up the stairs, happily provided.

"Elli, Ned, the things from the old house have been delivered!" he shouted, grabbing a crowbar and racing out again.

"Don't call me Elli," Eleri snapped, though she lost no time chasing down after him, eager to retrieve what little they'd been allowed to keep from their parents' workshop.

The main hall of Forest House was far too large for a dozen crates and trunks to make much impact, but it was still a formidable pile up close. Griff was already working on the first crate with the help of one of the new day staff, an easily-flustered man called Jack.

"There's my big trunk," Eluned said, not sure she was ready to be reunited with her old sketchbooks.

"The one on top of it should have the design folders," Eleri added, relieved.

Griff produced a tremendous cracking and splintering noise, and hopped backward as the side of the upright crate he'd been working on fell toward him.

"Try not to scratch up the floor," Eluned said, then frowned, counting. "Why are there so many crates?"

"This isn't ours!" Griff said, tugging a large framed painting out of the crate. "Is it?"

It was a landscape, a heat-drenched grassland dotted with gazelle, and a lone flat-topped tree drawing the focus of the scene.

"It's a Ngoyo." Eluned slid another painting out, and found a lush-curved woman done in quick brushstrokes of deep purple and black. "This is a Salzine."

Eluned forgot the floor in the flurry that followed, until the great hall was strewn with paintings, along with a mixture of things that clearly belonged to Aunt Arianne— pistols and neatly bundled letters and a very silly hat, all red and purple plumes.

"She had these all along."

Griff, who had been dancing about in the hat, stopped short, then said: "I think I'll go wake Aunt."

He put down the hat and scurried up the stairs, and Jack followed his lead, picking up one of the empty crates and carrying it off toward the cellar.

"She had these all along," Eleri repeated, voice throbbing. "We could have kept the fine tools. The workshop. The *house.*"

"But why should Aunt Arianne have to sell her things, so we could keep ours? And besides, we had that fulgite all along."

It did seem a pity that Aunt Arianne could not have sold just one of the small fortune of paintings, but Eluned was careful not to say that—not that anything would make much difference to Eleri now that seething anger had overtaken her. She began listing all the things she had particularly wanted from their parents' workshop, stalking through the strewn artwork.

"*This* is what we're having a drama about?"

Aunt Arianne, barefoot in her nightgown, looked like she'd had no sleep at all. She definitely didn't seem at all inclined to calm Eleri down, and Griff glanced from her to Eleri, then took a skittish leap off the stairs to stand beside Eluned. He could be so fearless about some things, but Eluned could see he was going to work himself into a sick-fever if she didn't do something soon.

"You're not even able to understand what you did!" Eleri was only just not shouting. "You took away all their things! How could you be so selfish as to have all this, and yet still make it so *awful!*"

"Those are copies," Aunt Arianne said, the words very crisp and clear. "Done by students of your grandparents."

Eleri drew breath, then swallowed it as she processed what had been said. Aunt Arianne stalked the last few steps down into the hall, looking among the scattered contents of the packing crates, and picked out a leather case. From it she took a bundle of cloth and unwrapped an exquisite bronze, two hands in height, of a hare poised to take flight, ears high and eyes alert.

"This, however, is one of the few bronzes your grandmother ever did, and worth more than your parents' entire estate. It's the only thing of my mother's that I possess. So tell me, Eleri, should I have sold it so you could keep a collection of tools intact?"

"She didn't mean it," Eluned said hastily.

"Eluned, there's no need for you to play peacemaker. Your sister is perfectly capable of facing the consequences of her own temper." But Aunt Arianne's expression was no longer so tight, and she sighed. "Why don't you and Griff go put together a picnic basket, and we'll have morning tea in Hurlstone?"

That meant she had investigation things to talk about, but though thankful for the excuse to escape, Eluned shot a worried glance at Eleri, not certain she wanted to be left. Eleri's jaw was set. Not a good sign, but she gave no hint of wanting Eluned to stay.

"Do you think I could have the picture of Rome?" Griff asked, hurrying Eluned to the kitchen to avoid any further explosion. "Who was that by?"

"Was that the ink in Huaxia Classical style? I'm not sure—maybe Han Ying? I loved the bronze."

"Mm." Griff was not likely to be impressed by anything about a bronze hare but its value. "Could we take the custard tarts, Ned?"

Eluned hesitated, since the tarts were clearly marked 'dessert', but then nodded defiantly. "We could use a treat."

They planned a lavish morning tea: thick slabs of bread layered with cold corned beef, cheese and pickle, and they could use precious oranges and lemons to make fresh juice.

Griff drifted away during the bread-slicing, then hissed: "Eleri's *crying*."

Eluned was at the kitchen door in an instant, but the argument was obviously over. Aunt Arianne was sitting on the far stairs, and Eleri had her head in their aunt's *lap*, and she really was crying, really sobbing, as she practically never did. Eluned stared, then hooked her fingers into Griff's collar and hauled him back to the table, and when Jack poked his nose cautiously up from the cellar she roped him in to juice oranges, and gave him a doorstop of a sandwich in return. Then, when Eluned checked that it was safe, they all went out and moved empty crates into the cellar, and the paintings and trunks into the dining room. They finished before Eleri and Aunt

Arianne came back downstairs, both thankfully looking more like their normal selves, in a drawn sort of way.

"No, Tante Sabet was using them in guest rooms," Aunt Arianne was saying. "But it seems she's decided that now I have a permanent address, she has an excuse to redecorate." She smiled down at Eluned and Griff. "If we go by airship, do you think you could cope with a trip to Lutèce, Griff? It really is past time you three met some more of your family, and we could easily fit in a trip to celebrate Eleri and Eluned's birthday before the school term starts."

"Really an airship?"

"Truly an airship."

Griff danced briefly on the spot—a sign that he was still quite anxious—then said: "We could try. I want to see the Towers of the Moon."

"They're certainly worth seeing. What do you two say? Birthday in Lutèce?"

"Yes," Eleri said, definitely. "So long as we can visit the museums."

Collecting the picnic basket, they strolled out toward the grove, discussing the technicalities of travel, and the fact that they would be entering an area of different territorial allegiance, and all that entailed. Strange that yelling at Aunt Arianne had somehow brought about a relaxation, a feeling of family that Eluned hadn't found with her before.

As usual Aunt Arianne studied the roofs as they walked toward the gate, though there was only a single raven today, which could very well really be a raven, and not people spying. But once the gate to the Great Forest had closed behind them she said calmly: "The Huntresses are keeping watch on the house as well. Personally at night, and probably controlled cats by day."

"What?" Griff clutched at Eluned's arm, looking over his shoulder as if expecting an attack. "Why?"

"My best theory is they're watching for another sphinx attack."

They walked through the tumbled walls of the town before London, to what had become 'their' spot: at the feet of a vampire turned to stone, overseen by a ram-horned snake of Cernunnos and watching in turn an automaton perched stubbornly motionless on a waist-high wall. It should not feel at all familiar, should be scarcely believable: to sit on the fringe of the Great Forest, to glance up at a castle shrouded in cloud, and across at a shining white tower, while remembering Dem Makepeace warning them about 'passing gods'.

And then Eluned forgot even the wonders of Hurlstone as Aunt Arianne caught them up on all the things that had happened the previous night. They let her talk without interrupting because it was hard to believe they'd finally found what they were looking for.

"Then it's over?" Griff asked. "The police will find out the rest?"

"I very much hope they will find the proof we were looking for," Aunt Arianne said. "And there is a strong chance that one of those who died last night was directly responsible. But untangling this gang of thieves does little to solve the problem of Monsieur Doré, and of sphinxes, and whoever it was who asked for the stolen fulgite to be bought back. And Albans." She frowned.

"I want to continue investigating workshops," Eleri said firmly.

"Then be more than ordinarily careful. I suspect we are currently in more danger than previous, not less."

"We better get on if we're going to go today."

Eleri stood, stepped toward the path back, then turned and walked over to the converted mannequin. And it dropped off its perch into the tall flowers on the far side of the wall.

"Did it fall off?" Griff asked, springing up to peer into the floral mass.

"No, it moved." Eleri hitched herself up on the wall, then dropped down among the flowers. "And it's...can you see where it went, Griff?"

Aunt Arianne calmly repacked the picnic basket and Lila watched with regal indifference as Griff, Eleri and Eluned hunted among cosmos and cowbells for an automaton that really was not small enough to hide so easily.

"You've got pollen all over your face, Griff," Eluned said, trying not to giggle.

"Least I'm not wearing a spider in my hair," Griff retorted, then hastily checked his own head. He was less bothered by insects than furred and feathered animals, but that didn't mean he was willing to give them rides.

"What do we do, Aunt Arianne?" Eluned asked, swiping semi-accurately at her hair with her wooden hand. "How are we going to catch it?"

"I suspect the first step would be to stop trying," Aunt Arianne said, hoisting the picnic basket. "The more interesting question, don't you think, is why you suddenly need to?"

"You mean why did it finally move?" Griff asked.

"What were you planning to do, Eleri?" Aunt Arianne asked.

"Check whether any moisture had gotten to the mechanism." Eleri's nose was orange, and she stood indifferent to purple petals tickling her chin, her brows drawn together. "Can it possibly—how can it possibly have known? It doesn't have any ears or eyes, and even if it did, I've picked it up more than once since we put it here. It's never reacted before."

"Not until you decided to open it up. Which of course makes the reaction entirely to be expected—what would you do if someone proposed to remove your lungs, just to check them over?"

"You—are you saying it read her mind?" Eluned scanned the area again, unsure whether to be nervous.

"I have no idea. But whatever is controlling Monsieur Doré clearly finds us strange and threatening." Aunt Arianne set the basket on the wall, and looked at the gold-crowned amasen draped on a broken pillar. "Lila less so, I think. But we are effectively keeping...a kind of person prisoner here. I find myself decidedly uncomfortable with the question of what to do next."

"We should put a pencil and paper out, in case it wants to write us a message," Griff said.

Aunt Arianne glanced at him, then smiled. "I think I'll do that. And you three, if you're intending to be taken at all seriously at these workshops, better go wash up."

Twenty-Three

The trip to the sprawl of workshops, factories and occasional farms that made up London's west had not been productive: no new haunted automaton stories, and even fewer bored craftsmen willing to take interested children on a tour of the facilities. They were all too busy, or outright suspicious. Nathaner's, which they'd particularly wanted to look over, had barely spared them two words. The only bright point was a smaller workshop called Gretcher's, where they were given a cool drink while Eleri haggled her way down to almost all the money she carried in exchange for an extensive fine tool set.

"You drive a hard bargain, young dama," the workshop foreman said. "I'm making you a gift here, but it's better than them gathering dust, I confess."

"I'm glad you can spare them," Eleri said, buckling shut the last of the packs.

"We don't have anyone who does the miniature work any more," the man said sadly. "True automatons have become a luxury. It's all ugly little boxes on wheels these days, with no thought to artistry."

"Not everywhere," Eleri said, with all the determination of the future she had mapped out for herself.

They waved the man goodbye and shouldered their packs. "Enough for the day," Eluned said firmly.

"Let's take a taxi back," Griff said.

"Don't have the money," Eleri told him.

"Aunt could pay when we got there."

"Mightn't be home."

"You did keep enough for the bus, right?" Eluned asked.

Eleri only had a few coins left, and they counted them doubtfully, then decided they would take a bus as far as they could go, and hope that wouldn't leave too much walking at the end.

"What will we do tomorrow, then?" Griff asked, as they trailed back toward the nearest main road.

"See if the Aunt's right about that automaton," Eleri said.

"You think it's really a person?" Eluned asked. "How are we—?"

Griff, a few steps ahead, stopped abruptly and Eluned had to sidestep to avoid smacking into him.

"Look," he said.

Eluned studied the scene ahead, trying to work out what had caught his interest. Two growlers were drawn up in front of one of the buildings, and various boxes were being briskly loaded. There didn't seem to be anything unusual about that.

"Roof."

Following Eleri's direction, Eluned spotted two cats on the roof opposite the growlers. They were entirely ordinary-looking cats: a fat ginger and a moth-eaten tabby, but their unwavering stares did remind Eluned of a row of ravens. Though cats often looked like that.

"You think they're being controlled? They're probably just cats."

"Except, see the name by the doors?" Griff said.

Ficus Lapis. The company that had been contracted to provide digging automatons and engineers to the Prytennian Underground Rail Project.

"Tiny sign," Eleri said. "Low key."

"They look like they're moving out." Griff was bouncing on his heels now, excited, but he remembered to keep his voice low as he added: "They're making a run for it! I bet they're the ones who wanted to buy back the fulgite. They probably sold it accidentally in the first place."

This almost made sense. Eluned exchanged a glance with Eleri, remembering Aunt Arianne's warnings about danger.

"Ask about the parts we're looking for," Eleri said. "Keep our eyes open. Leave."

Eluned weighed their choices. They couldn't try to follow the growlers—not with less money than bus fare. They could find the nearest policeman and make a very likely ineffectual fuss. They could assume that Prytennia's investigators knew perfectly well what was going on—or that the cats on the roof really were controlled by the Huntresses—and leave keeping an eye on the growlers to professionals rather than exposing themselves to danger. Not that a glance in the door should be all that dangerous.

The sheer, frustrated desire to *do* something finally decided her. It was time they contributed, instead of putting all the risk on Aunt Arianne.

"Let's go."

There were a few casual glances as they marched confidently up to the wide-open entrance to Ficus Lapis' workshop, but no particular interest or suggestion of threat. No-one tried to stop them as they slipped past the growlers, and a single look confirmed that the place was indeed being emptied out. Eleri homed in on a weathered little man who was watching proceedings, and began as usual by indicating Eluned's arm, and asking about fine machine tools, and the availability of parts.

They'd been lucky in their choice. Although the man's Prytennian was only functional, he was very interested in Eluned's arm, and particularly in Eleri's plans for a replacement, and Eluned and Griff had plenty of opportunity to make full use of eyes and ears as the discussion became deeply technical.

Most of the things being taken out looked to be exactly what you'd expect for a workshop that dealt with industrial automatons. Tools. Massive gears. Tubs of grease. But every so often out would be wheeled a middle-sized crate, very stoutly made and so heavy that four men together were needed to lift it into the growler.

They were being quite open about it though, treating the boxes as heavy, but making no attempt to hide them. Eluned squinted through the trees, then slowly recognised what she was doing.

The trees had been there all along, even if she had only just noticed them. The Great Forest, always with her, but suddenly pressing down. Why? What had changed?

Eluned barely had time for the stone sinking realisation that Griff had pulled another of his vanishing acts when he was hauled into view by a sternly handsome woman who had his ear in one hand and a cane in the other. She walked with difficulty, each step obviously painful, but that did not slow her as she called for the attention of the men loading the truck.

Reaching Griff a few beats before the men did, Eluned and Eleri stood firm, though there were now a half-dozen people looming over them and nothing felt safe at all. The woman said something angrily, but it was in a language Eluned didn't recognise, and the woman didn't even seem interested in listening to what Eleri was trying to say to her, but instead was addressing an older man coming out of a different room, his progress halting.

He said something back to her in the same language, point clear whatever the words, and Eluned flinched at the heavy hand that grabbed her left arm. She muttered: "Go low and run," to Griff, preparing to hit out with her right arm in the hopes that surprise could win them free.

"Enough, enough!" said a new voice, and the crowd around Eluned parted to allow a man through. It was Aunt Arianne's friend Felix, who had obviously not left the country at all.

"What a display," he said, in very clearly enunciated Latin. "Practically brawling in the streets. What will our clients think of Ficus Lapis, to have this uproar over a curious child?"

The woman said something back to him, again quite incomprehensibly, as Felix rested one hand on Griff's head, and the other on Eluned's back—a gesture that she did not know whether to regard as support.

"But there is nothing to see, no secrets to fall across," Felix replied, still in Latin. "You yourself told me that not an hour ago. Why must we then have dramas, and risk bringing Ficus Lapis' name into disrepute?" He was now addressing the man who seemed to be in charge.

The older man dropped his chin, and Felix seemed to take this as agreement, steering Griff, Eleri and Eluned through the crowd and toward the street. No-one moved to stop them, or argue, but Eluned did not let her breath out until they were past the growlers, and nothing stood between them and safety.

"Thank you," Griff said, voice high with relief.

"There is nothing to thank for," Felix said, his heavily-accented Prytennian difficult to understand because he spoke so low. "That place you live. It has the protections of two gods, yes? Go to it. Go quickly. Go for your lives."

He gave them the tiniest of pushes, and turned away. Wasting no time, Eluned grabbed Griff by the arm and practically hauled him down the street, Eleri close behind. Eluned knew it wasn't over. The forest was still with her, looming and dark. She hadn't understood what it meant before, but she did now: Cernunnos was the dual-nature god, hunter and hunted. The danger was getting worse.

"We need a taxi," she muttered. "Look for a taxi."

"Ned, they're not coming after us," Griff said.

"Doesn't matter. We have to get out of here."

"There." Eleri began waving her arms over her head, and when Eluned saw what she'd spotted, she followed suit and thankfully the distant figure of a girl balanced above a central wheel dipped, and then came rapidly toward them.

"Lost?" Li Sen asked, the three stabilising wheels of the dragonfly spreading into a rest position as she purred into a stop in front of them.

"Trouble," Eleri said briskly. "Need to get home before we're killed."

Li Sen stared, then said: "Follow me," and wasted no time sending her dragonfly in a skittering circle and accelerating back the way she'd come. They had to race at top speed to keep pace, but that suited Eluned, who was drowning in trees, branches whipping her face, overwhelmed by the sense of a hunt rising. Her share of the tools Eleri had purchased bounced and jolted with every pounding step, and her breath soon came ragged in her throat, but the forest faded a little in the process, making her hope.

Their dragonfly guide led them straight to Nathaner's Workshop, and this time there was no chance of being turned away at the door, as they barrelled right in after Li Sen, past stern workmen in the process of stripping down an engine and up to a clearer space near the back of the building.

"Emergency," Li Sen told the woman who came over in response to their arrival. "What cars are free?"

"Only number two," the woman said, wiping her hands on a rag. "'Emergency' is no excuse for rudeness, Li Sen."

"I'm sorry, mother," Li Sen said, glancing back as Griff sat down in a gasping heap. "Please may I take number two? I think this is important."

"God-touched something sent to kill us," Eleri managed, between panting. "Need to get to circle at our house."

"I don't think we have time to get to Forest House," Eluned added. "It's already coming. I can feel it." She could hear it. Something crashing distantly through the undergrowth, sending up flights of birds.

"Need nearest strong circle or grove then," Eleri said, pragmatically. "More than strong—strongest circle nearby."

"The airfield's Burning Circle." Li Sen's mother studied the three of them, then said decisively: "Take the coursers. Li Zhi, help her."

"Yes, mother!" said a boy a year or two younger than Eluned, lending Li Sen a hand dismounting before dashing off with her to the far side of the workshop.

"Why are you so sure, Ned?" Griff asked, sitting down on the stained floor.

"It's the bond with Cernunnos," Eluned said briefly, not equal to explaining all that she was seeing and hearing. "We really need to go. Now."

But Li Sen and Li Zhi were already returning, each pushing what looked like a very heavy velocipede that supported a long padded seat instead of a small saddle.

"Two with Li Zhi," Li Sen said, peremptorily. "One with me."

She threw a leg over the seat and balanced there waiting. Eluned didn't hesitate, hopping on behind Li Sen.

"Put your feet on the rests, and don't take them off," Li Sen ordered. "Hold me around my waist." She pressed a button and the courser buzzed into life. The sound was deeper than Eluned had expected, not as heavy as a growler, but definitely a full-grown cat compared to a dragonfly's kitten purr. They started moving immediately.

She remembered to call back "Thank you, dama!" to Li Sen's mother, and then yelped as the brisk turn out of the workshop stepped up to *fast*.

Even with the forest looming around her, delight came to steal Eluned's thoughts. Wind streamed through her hair, and the uneven surface of the road flashed past: a foot carelessly dropping from the rest would definitely be a thing to regret. But, as had been pointed out, the *corners*.

"Burning Circle's not public access, but don't worry about that," Li Sen said, voice whipping past Eluned's ears. "We know how to get past the gate. Hope your aunt doesn't mind paying a few fines!"

The forest loomed thick and dark, and they raced through a narrow corridor of towering trunks. Eluned could see stars above the trees, and heard a thudding, far too close.

"I think we need to go faster."

Li Sen started to glance back, then concentrated on avoiding a hummingbird.

"A lot of fines then," she said, and called out to her brother: "Open her up, Li Zhi!"

The boy, already grinning madly, shouted back: "Yesssss!" and then fast became heart-stopping.

They shot, one after another, down a narrow lane where the hedge bent over the road. A dog barked, and a man shouted as they emerged in front of his cart, sending his horse jolting in its traces. An orderly line of children on a day trip from a nearby school broke ranks and chased after them, and the bleating of horns rose on every side.

Still, it was not fast enough. In the forest, hot breath touched the back of Eluned's neck. In the city of London, the people who called angrily after the two speeding coursers flinched as something slid by, a thing not yet with them but brushing too close for ordinary comfort. Death slipping through the streets like a shark.

Li Sen felt it too. Eluned could tell by the way the joy went out of her movements, and her shoulders tensed. On the other bike, all three riders were hunched low, Li Zhi's sharp chin almost touching the handlebars. And yet, they were nearly there. Eluned could see the bulky form of one of the great transcontinental airships lifting over the roofs ahead. The coursers slewed around one of the corners, and there was the airfield's main entrance, blocked by a sturdy looking boom gate.

"Tuck in," Li Sen said, accelerating toward the gate.

Eluned thought for one horrified minute that she was going to try to go directly through the solid-looking wooden pole, but the gate was designed to keep out larger vehicles, and Li Sen aimed for the gap to one side, and the man who was angrily trying to wave them off. He looked stubborn enough to face down a pair of speeding coursers, but then he stared past them and his expression changed before he hastily retreated into a little guard hut. Eluned did not look back. She could hear a sound, almost like the ocean.

"Lots and lots of fines," Li Sen muttered, as a claxon started blaring from the guard hut.

They tore past large buildings and out onto a road running along the edge of the vast flat grassy field. Ahead a crowd of people milled about, preparing to board a smaller airship, and the two coursers dodged out onto the grass rather than risk hitting them, although this made progress slower and much more bouncy. The shouts and screams behind them at least sounded more like shock and fright rather than anyone being attacked.

Zipping around the tethered airships, they roared out alongside a well-known building: the compression dome. Shaped like a top that had been cut vertically in half and laid on its side, it was where the Sulevia Leoth commanded the triskelion to bring trilesium from Sulis' realm: the gas that kept Prytennia's airship fleet aloft. The Burning Circle stood at the far end, so-called because of its strong association with the triskelion—and the resulting sere and yellow grass around it, withered by heat.

It was also one of the largest circles, dozens of feet across, and each of the stones the height of two or even three people together. This at least meant there was no difficulty in roaring right in, barely slowing down until the last moment, so that they skidded to a stop near the centre, in a cloud of dust and powdered grass.

Safe.

TWENTY-FOUR

The thing that wanted to kill them crashed against the Burning Circle like a green-grey wave meeting a breakwater. Hands of mist groped and snatched, but withered as soon as they crossed the bounds, and briefly the hunter flickered away to nothing, but then surged and swept onward, a formless intangibility reaching, grasping, until it completely surrounded the whole of the wide circle of stone. There was a noise, words that Eluned could not distinguish, constant as rain.

"Something under the ground?" Li Zhi panted, as out of breath as if he'd been running.

"If we'd been on foot..." Griff slipped off the courser, took two steps toward the edge of the circle, then retreated back to the exact centre.

People were streaming out of and around the compression dome, but wisely stopped at a distance as the green-grey tide waxed higher. It was as if the thing's failure to gain its prize was causing it to swell and double in force with every passing moment.

"Who in the Fifteen Hells and Thousand Heavens did you annoy?" Li Sen asked.

"Romans," Griff said. "Or...I didn't really understand what they were saying."

"I think it was their accent, or a dialect," Eluned said, and let out a sobbing little laugh because what did that matter right now? "Pray," she suggested, as one of the triskelion-inscribed stones tilted, and another began to sink. "Pray!"

Sulis rarely answered prayers directly. She worked her will through the Trifold, and the most supplicants could hope for was a nudge to their fortunes in the areas that were Sulis' particular domain. As Eluned tilted her face to the sun and fumbled for words, she wondered if she should be calling on Cernunnos instead. But the airfield was singularly clear of trees, and all hint of the Great Forest had left her. Surely Sulis would find this affront to one of her circles an act worthy of response.

"Dimity!" Griff gasped, finding his own form of prayer. "Please come help! Dimity. I-i-EE!"

Eleri joined in. "I-i-EE! Dimity, for Sulis' honour! I-i-EE!"

Two of the standing stones rose several feet, and then heeled over. Another was only half its former height. The grasping hands were reaching further into formerly safe territory, but were not yet able to entirely breach the circle. The incomprehensible words grew in volume, though Eluned still could not make out what was being said.

"Stay back from us and they might ignore you," Eluned said hurriedly to Li Sen and Li Zhi, then joined Eleri and Griff in calling out the name of a faceless pinwheel that had so loved to hear its name that Eluned could still remember the reflected joy.

"But what are you trying to do?" Li Sen asked, making no move to gain any distance—though there was precious little area outside the centre that was now not threatened by snatching hands.

"It's solstice singing," Li Zhi said, adding his own voice. "I-i-EE!"

"I-i-EE!" they all sang, as one of the great flat stones was dragged completely under. They clung to each other and sang louder, voices rising above the constant whispering as both coursers started to sink.

~I-i-EE?~

The blue and white triskelion burst into existence, whirling in a narrow circle in what little clear space remained between children and snatching mist. The hands recoiled, but then simply dropped lower to the ground, reaching for ankles.

~I-i-EE!~ Dimity spun faster, and was joined in a wave of heat by red and gold with a trill of ~O-o-O!~, and a yellow and green ~O-e-oo-a!~.

And then, far far above them, one of the greater triskelion emerged, its wings deep black, their reach so vast that the airship that had recently taken off was visible below it, buffeted by the downdraft.

~A-a-a-A-a-a-A-a-a-A-a-a-A-a-a-A-a-a!~ it sang, washing half of London with heat.

And then it vanished again, leaving only a tumult among the clouds, but all three of the smaller triskelion remained, and had turned from horizontal to vertical to drive along the ground, cutting through the grasping mist and setting the withered grass alight.

"I think it worked!" Li Zhi said, coughing. "The noise has stopped."

The smoke made it difficult to be entirely certain, but Eluned thought he was right. The standing stones were no longer shifting, and no hint of reaching fingers remained.

"Help me with the coursers," Li Sen said urgently, and they hastily came together to haul the rear wheel of one out of the dirt, and then push both vehicles out of the remains of the circle.

~I-i-EE?~

"Thank you, Dimity!" Eluned called, as the three triskelion rose rapidly into the air. "Thank you, Toroco, and, uh—"

"Lorenoola," said a woman, mildly informative. They turned to discover the leading edge of the crowd had reached them, a number armed with buckets and blankets, and at their head was a small woman dressed neatly in overalls, who tossed water briskly onto the smoking grass.

"With the triskelion so frequently called here, we are well drilled with grass fires," she said, looking with interest at the two coursers. "Are those out of Nathaner's? I heard they were doing new things with motorised velocipedes."

"Yes, dama," said Li Sen, pride competing with reaction to the near escape. "These are the prototypes, but we'll be going into production with the coursers soon."

"That wheel looks damaged. Bring them into Workshop Two and we'll see what we can do with it before the police arrive." She cocked her head at the scene behind them, and added: "Along with a representative of the palace, I expect. And the Sun Keepers. And, of course, airfield security."

Eluned turned because these last were just arriving, stopping to stare at the wreck that had been the Burning Circle, one of the most famous in Prytennia. At least half the stones had fallen, and two were shattered. One was missing altogether while the top quarter of another poked out of the ground like an emerging tooth. Beyond, the airship buffeted by the greater triskelion was hastily landing. Above, the clouds had twisted into a gyrating swirl, and the remaining smoke from the grass streamed every-which-way in the suddenly pounding wind.

"Send the palace representative in to me when they arrive, Joshua," the short woman said to a man beating out lingering flames with a blanket. "Come along you five."

Eluned hung back a moment. "Please, dem, could you tell the police to go to the Ficus Lapis workshop? We think that's who sent that...whatever, and they looked like they were leaving."

"Over on Fitchley?" said the man, and glanced at the woman, who nodded.

"Good thought," the woman said. "I'm Trevelyan, by the way."

Lady Aranxta Trevelyan, the Minister for Science and Technology. Eluned could almost see Eleri prick up her ears at this news, for Lady Trevelyan was on Eleri's very short list of people she might consider working for, before starting her own workshop. The Minister had a formidable reputation as a physicist, but also a passion for aeronautical mechanics, and her workshops were at the forefront of development in Prytennia. Eluned was glad for her calm authority, and the way that she blithely led them away from all the people who wanted to exclaim at and interrogate and perhaps yell at them, even if it was clear that she was doing so to ask questions herself. Most fortunately she started by taking them to her book-choked office, sitting them down, and pouring tea into them until they all—and Griff particularly—stopped looking quite so peaky.

And she had even known mother a little, and was made thoroughly indignant by the possibility that she had been murdered—for they ended up telling her what Aunt Arianne called 'All The Truth But The Dangerous Bits', where they left out the artificial fulgite and the adapted mannequin, and presented themselves as convinced there were strange going-ons afoot, but were most certainly not in active pursuit of them.

"What then, young man, did you see in your wanderings through Ficus Lapis?" Minister Trevelyan asked, when they had, via many tangents and asides, explained how their quest for cheap tools and fine automaton components had led them to the Roman workshop. "What was this secret that a reputable firm was so very keen to hide that it has left all of London pointing at the sky?"

"Chicken wire," Griff said.

"Seriously?" Li Zhi, who had been following the story with avid interest, couldn't hide his disbelief. "They sent something god-touched after you, brought down the Burning Circle, annoyed Sulis enough that she sent a greater—that was Ah-ah, you know—a greater triskelion that hasn't shown itself since the end of the French Occupation. Over *chicken wire*?"

"I think maybe whatever they were hiding had been cleared out by then." Griff was clearly enjoying their reaction. "It was one of those rooms with the really thick, well-fitted doors, and no windows—you know, designed so the Night Breezes can't get in. They'd been carrying crates out, but when I looked there were only some empty tables, and a few rolls of chicken wire in a corner. A stack of newspaper, and nothing else. Then the lady with the sore feet grabbed me."

"Indeed." Lady Trevelyan ran a hand absently through her short-cropped dark hair. "I suppose they were worried you had seen something they had missed. And, of course, if this man Felix hadn't warned you, you would have been walking along unsuspecting."

"Waiting for a bus," Eleri said, with a glance at Eluned that agreed not to mention god-bound certainties.

"In that area, there's a good chance that no-one would even have noticed three children vanishing. Pulled underground with barely a chance to cry out." Lady Trevelyan tsked. "They sent a large power to do something small. And now will pay a vast price for their over-caution."

At this point the 'representative' of the palace arrived in the form of Princess Leodhild, along with Aunt Arianne— fetched by Li Sen and Li Zhi's mother—and everything had to be explained all over again, while Eleri drew pictures of the people they had seen.

"Not without precedent," Princess Leodhild said, after Eluned had rambled back to the same conclusion. "Triskelion have very occasionally responded without the direction of the Sulevia Leoth—usually when something has drawn the attention of Sulis herself. Not that it's impossible that Dimity heard her own name called, but for Ah-Ah to appear....Sulis is very angry indeed."

There was a wry twist to her mouth, perhaps because the last time Sulis had been stirred to anger had been during the Three Sisters' War, the unprecedented dispute over Prytennia's throne that had ended very abruptly with Sulis killing all three Suleviae, leaving Prytennia exposed to an invasion from France.

"Still, we seem to be making progress at last, and I thank you younglings for that, though share your aunt's winces. I shall go see what our Romans have left behind, and will speak to you later, Dama Seaforth. You wanted, incidentally Aranxta, to get your hands on the person who 'drew all over' your flier plans. Here she is, most convenient."

With an amused nod at Eleri, Princess Leodhild left.

"Oh indeed?" Lady Trevelyan studied a suddenly scarlet Eleri. "Quite a breach in etiquette, you know."

"I—I beg your pardon, Lady Trevelyan," Eleri said.

"The proper procedure, setting aside the error of examining unpublished plans in the first place, would be to open correspondence with the designer. At which point a response might have let you know that we had considered that option, and discarded it—for reasons that can be touched on when you are not recovering from distracting excitements. At a later date, perhaps you would enjoy a tour of the workshops here."

"Very much, thank you."

Leaving Li Sen and Li Zhi to discuss the coursers, they climbed thankfully into the tiger brought by the pair's mother. This lady's name was Lu Lan Ying, and she was Mama Lu's middle daughter, and had taken up a managing role in Nathaner's Workshop nearly ten years ago. She didn't feel it would be a big problem that the coursers were currently being examined with great interest by people at the Ministry workshop, since Nathaner's was already geared up to produce them. The whole drama of the day might even prove to be a useful advertisement, since the whole of London would most certainly be talking about dramatic dashes for safety before the day was out.

Sitting in the seat behind Aunt Arianne and Dama Lu, Eluned was impressed at how naturally Aunt Arianne could ask all these questions without sounding like she was rudely prying at all, and then manage to insist on a generous payment despite Dama Lu's polite demurrals. Eluned knew she would never be able to make that conversation anything but graceless, just as sometimes only her eternally heavy glass shield allowed her to keep her composure, while Aunt Arianne floated through awkwardness so effortlessly.

Most particularly, Aunt Arianne so rarely let slip what she was really thinking and feeling. It wasn't until they were inside that Eluned was even sure she wasn't angry, when Aunt Arianne, resting the back of her hand on Griff's forehead, said:

"I think your punishment will be a few days in bed."

"I'm not tired," he said immediately.

"Well, that will make it feel more like a punishment then," Aunt Arianne said, looking amused. "Do we need to stop by Hurlstone before you drag your feet reluctantly upstairs?"

Griff pulled a face, but then dug in his pocket and produced a ball of chicken wire, which he silently held out to Aunt Arianne. Eyebrows lifting, she took it from him, examined the shape, and then picked it apart to reveal a crumpled but precisely moulded hand.

TWENTY-FIVE

A walk through the fringes of the Great Forest helped Rian enormously in regaining her centre. It had been an altogether difficult day, beginning with a shameful near-argument with a grieving child, and then a parade of visitors interrupting her attempts to catch up on sleep.

Dama Lu's arrival, and the tense journey to the airfield, had left her berating herself for the decisions she'd made moderating the children's desire for an active role in this hunt. She had thought visiting workshops a relatively safe pursuit, and could not have been more wrong.

Felix had spared her the worst, a favour she would remember, whatever his involvement in this tangle. She allowed herself to accept good fortune and move on, just as it was best to simply recognise that she had misjudged Lyle and Lynsey Blair, rather than castigate herself for starting to like them.

Two things, however, were not so easily settled, and Rian had to resort to a long bath after dinner to tackle the hurdles that had woken her over and over, and then kept her from sleep.

Time should surely make the fear fade. Weeks or months would take the teeth from two words, and return them to being a well-known phrase with no power to make her tremble. Until then, she would simply have to gird herself against memory whenever she was around Makepeace. Nearly dying didn't seem to be something she could shrug off.

The other problem might take even longer to shift, because Rian was suffering from a bad case of 'Why not?'.

Her own words kept coming back to haunt her. *When you meet someone who fills you up until there's no room for anything else, trying to put all those feelings away is harder than even the most hopeless pursuit.* Rian's level-headed dismissal of the idea of a romance with Aerinndís Gwyn Lynn had not held up well against a moonlit flight with her, let alone that conversation in the attic.

She had sat in the dark and exposed her throat: opened up her cupboard of vulnerabilities, and invited comprehension. She had wanted a response that had nothing to do with duty, or protecting Prytennia. She had, she could not deny, wanted the Crown Princess to truly see her.

The question was what to do now, when every spare thought drifted to analysis of the Crown Princess' response, to trying to discover a hidden reason for those questions. Had Princess Aerinndís, very serious about her duty to the country, truly detected some great fault in the latest tool given to her service? Or had her interest been for Rian herself? Or was it both?

It did not seem possible to think in terms of light flirtation. Everything felt desperate and world-shaking, as if Rian had been catapulted back to her earliest fumbling romances, where to be the first to admit to longing was an act of boundless courage—or weakness, a baring of the stomach to the wolves of mockery and scorn.

Uncertainty and second-guessing were not good for maintaining the calm centre Rian relied upon. But that brought her back to the 'Why not?'. If she was going to suffer either way, why not take the more active path? Unlike her last attempt at something serious, there was little chance she would have to hastily leave the country so that the 'accidents' would stop.

Stupid thought. She was not fool enough to try to pursue Aerinndís Gwyn Lynn. There would be a great deal of fantasising, a period of interminable aching, but it would pass, and the calm centre that kept her going would return.

Still, when Rian left her bath she dressed herself with care. Practical clothing, a touch of colour to the lips, and a lot of time brushing and arranging her hair. She doubted she looked any different from usual, but she was acknowledging a change to her frame of mind.

Since past evidence suggested that Makepeace did not have to wait for sunset so long as the grove was in shadow, Rian could not be certain when she would be 'collected'. She busied herself checking on the children—Griff's light fever at least did not seem to be climbing—and then reviewing the neat household account Dama Seleny had prepared. And then she contemplated, once again, the mysterious hand Griff had brought out of Ficus Lapis' workshop.

The craftsmanship was very good. The fine-gauge mesh had been precisely cut, and then each severed link neatly joined so that the seams were barely visible. Rian had done her best to return it to its pre-crushed state, and thought it was intended to be a woman's hand. When Makepeace finally made his entrance, as the last hints of sunset were fading from the windows, she held it out to him and said:

"I cannot think of a single reasonable explanation for this."

A small victory to confuse such an ancient monster. He took the hand, started to say something, then frowned and looked at it more closely. "Chicken wire."

"I have no idea whether they knew Griff picked it up. He says it was on the floor inside the door."

"Your brats need to learn to draw a line between precocity and stupidity."

"I hope to keep them alive long enough to teach them that distinction. Have the authors of today's lesson been found?"

"In part. We'll save the dissection for the meeting."

He strode off, then waited impatiently on the stair when Rian detoured to let Eluned and Eleri know she was leaving. She was finding it easier to manage his presence, though that perhaps was due to the distractions involved in trailing him through a close night in the Great Forest. Amasen were not the only things coiling among the branches.

Rian paid attention to the path, wondering if she could make the trip alone. This part of the Great Forest was Cernunnos' domain, and in theory she would have his protection, but she suspected it was not so simple, especially since she had seen no path at all when she passed in this direction earlier in the day, and certainly no gate less than five minutes' walk away. It was made of iron, and far less ornate than the grand work at Forest House, but presented the same basic image: two amasen holding a lock in their mouths. It opened into a tight cluster of trees wedged between a wrought iron fence and a faded green door.

The gate into the Great Forest vanished altogether when Makepeace closed it. He fished a more ordinary key out of a pocket and unlocked the door, leading her into a long corridor distinguished by several tea trolleys, a broom, and a reel of cable.

"Where is this?" she asked, peering through the trunks of the forest always with her.

"The MoP."

The Museum of Prytennia. Not where Rian had expected. "How far can you go, doing that?"

He ignored her. But perhaps after a thousand years she too would take some time to warm to the 'beginning of her end'. Rian had certainly not yet accustomed herself to the idea of a life measured in centuries.

It mattered a great deal how long she had before Makepeace went to stone. There had been so few Amon-Re vampires that she had little basis for comparison. Makepeace—Heriath—was said to pre-date the Trifold Age, which meant he had lived at least eleven centuries. But Hatshepsu had ruled for seventeen before she entered rept, and her daughter had vanished almost immediately after.

He led her to a lift, barely giving her time to enter before tugging the grill shut and hauling on the control lever to send them downward. Sub-basement Two, kept warm and dry, and filled with racks and drawers, and one useful cupboard that swung like a door. Rian would be amused to discover that the sprawling museum in the heart of the oldest part of London functioned as a secret base, but she was caught up in anticipation.

Makepeace glanced back at her, no doubt in response to the sudden leaping of her pulse, but forbore to comment. After a millennia, she supposed he found the distractions of attraction exceptionally boring. Vampirism removed the drive for sex, and the stoneblood tended to avoid romance with mayfly mortals.

Despite herself, Rian was enjoying newfound passion. That she could cross the Great Forest, and follow a vampire through a locked museum into a hidden room, brought expressly to discuss the conspiracy she had spent months attempting to unravel, and yet see one and only one occupant: back ramrod straight, mouth in its habitual downturn, heavy hair braided into a coronet. And for that mere sight to set her blood singing, as if the moon and all the stars had been given to her as a gift.

Foolishness of the grandest order, but Rian allowed herself a moment to savour it, then put away longing, as much as was possible, and looked past transparent ropey roots to inspect the rest of the scene. A very secure second door, some incidental cabinets, and a long, scarred table with two princesses and three strangers sitting around it.

"Chicken wire," Makepeace said, tossing the sculptured hand on top of the neat pile of papers in the table's centre.

Princess Leodhild laughed. "Very dramatic, Comfrey. So the young lad found a little more than he admitted, Dama Seaforth?"

"Picked up within the door of the sealed room, Your Highness," Rian said, following Makepeace's lead in taking a seat. "He thinks he was unseen."

The Sulevia Leoth leaned forward to collect the hand, held it up so Princess Aerinndís could glance it over, and then passed it to the woman at her right.

"Fascinating," the woman said, lifting the pair of pince-nez she had hanging around her neck and using them as a lens. She was a large-framed woman, muscular, and very stylishly dressed.

"Welcome to the Night Council, Dama Seaforth," she said, passing the hand to the angular woman to her right. "I'm Lydia Bermondsley, Curator of the Divinities and God-Touched Collection here at the MoP. This is Commander Delway, of the Special Force. And Finch, the Council Secretary. As we have a lot to get through tonight, shall we start?"

Princess Aerinndís inclined her head, then said: "Your report, Commander Delway?"

"Highness." Commander Delway's features were harsh, angular, and did little to hide a forceful character. She tucked a shining wing of black hair behind one ear and spoke rapidly.

"Latest first: when Fitwald force arrived at Ficus Lapis' headquarters they discovered workers tidying up. Their story is the company found the Fitwald location too remote and have shifted in near the Tamesas tunnel site. They've stuck to that, and kicked no fuss leading the way to the new location. Growlers were there, contents in the process of being unloaded, and they did not resist a thorough search. Nothing of interest."

She gave the hand a disgusted look and added: "No chicken wire. Doubt we'd have been able to trace a thing if we hadn't already had eyes on their tails. Our people followed the growlers, witnessed the offloading of persons and crates when they crossed the river. Also spotted two cats riding on the roof of the second of the growlers.

These boarded the barge onto which the crates had been loaded, but were discovered and tossed overboard. One of my people commandeered a fireboat, and the other arranged an intercept." She clicked her tongue. "The barge was a feint—they crossed the river to waiting vehicles and split up. We've recovered three of the crates, and one driver."

"And?" Princess Leodhild leaned forward. "What was in these crates? Please don't say chicken wire."

"Fulgite." Commander Delway tucked her hair back again, a movement replete with disgust. "*Not* the stolen shipment. More than four times the amount of fulgite that was stolen at the beginning of the year."

"Ha!" Princess Leodhild slapped the table. "You lose, Bermie."

Dama Bermondsley slid a pound out of a purse laced to her belt, and passed it to the princess. "I refuse to believe they're mining it here."

"*And* charging us through the nose for the privilege. You can't fault their audacity."

"It still doesn't make sense—it's not like we haven't looked. A substance only Romans can find?"

"If you have a counter-theory for where all that fulgite has come from that doesn't involve egg-laying sphinxes, I'd be glad to hear it."

"What does the driver say?" Princess Aerinndís asked.

"Little enough." Commander Delway selected a piece of paper from her pile. "Told to take the crates to Folkestone. Deliver them to a ship, the *Pilgar*, and then make his way back to Rome. Claims there's been nothing improper in the company's conduct, though cagey when questioned about people involved in this scene with the Tenning children. Would appreciate your assistance with him, Makepeace."

As usual, Makepeace was propping his head on one fist. He lifted a shoulder, then said: "What was the thing at the airfield, Bermie?"

"Oh, most interesting!" Dama Bermondsley flipped open one of the books. "Not Roman. Hellenic!"

"I thought, technically, those were the same gods," Princess Leodhild said.

"No, not at all—at least not before Rome's Answered, even with the way the Romans went around telling everyone that their local gods were the same as the Romans' but with different names. Look at their attempts to claim Sulis as Minerva—and we all know exactly what *She* thought of that! Rather a lot of Hellenes maintain that the split is along the lines of the Aesir and the Green Aesir—gods that separated before the main wave of Answering, and now are two distinct, almost mirror groups. Not a theory that's popular in Rome, and one liable to put one in a distinctly awkward position if you happen to go around airing..."

"Didn't we have a lot to get through?" Makepeace sighed.

"Ah, yes." Dama Bermondsley coughed. "This particular god is Dolus, according to the Romans. Dolos to the Hellenes. Deceit and trickery. It's extremely rare to see Dolus' powers in such a public display, but there were several recorded incidents of what's known as the 'Sea of Lies' at the very height of the Empire, when the West and East schismed. It's believed to be more usually used as a method of quiet assassination. I was not certain until I heard Your Highness' fuller report, with mention of a woman and a man who had difficulty walking. These, I believe, are our god-touched."

"Were," Commander Delway muttered.

"Yes, chances are they're halfway across the Channel. But that is not a certainty yet and—" Dama Bermondsley glanced restively at the wire hand. "Truly, I don't care to think through some of the possibilities. Those who have given full allegiance to Dolus pay for his blessing with their ability to walk. This is due to the event that gave Dolus his area of duty. Dolus was an apprentice to

Prometheus, and during his master's absence attempted to copy a clay avatar of Veritas that Prometheus had been sculpting. He ran out of clay before he could complete the feet, and when Prometheus fired both statues, Dolus' copy could not walk. The forgery with no feet was named Mendacium, and so are those who give their allegiance to Dolus. Their great skill is forgery, but there will always be a flaw, visible on close inspection."

Everyone at the table was looking at that wire hand now.

"Mining fulgite and forging people?" Princess Aerinndís sounded less than impressed. "While also attempting to buy back stolen fulgite?"

"No verifiable link there," Commander Delway said. She opened a flat box, and set out a row of objects. A fragment of burned paper. A charred mask. A piece of green glass.

"Min Wishon. Penry Hulun. Dane Dayson. Known to the Docklands Force for sale of stolen goods, but not picked up for anything in the past year. Dayson lives alone, adjusts settings for a reputable jewellery firm. She failed to appear some weeks ago. Reported missing, feared dead." Delway touched the piece of glass. "An incendiary, source of the fire. What documents survived establishes a large amount of money exchanging hands, but customer names are abbreviated. The buy-back process appears to have begun in spring on behalf of an 'M'." She glanced at Rian. "An entry two days after the death the Tennings suggests a major sale. No further detail. No sign of any link to Ficus Lapis."

Dama Bermondsley reached for the mask and the charred fragment of paper, and held up the latter to display its shape. A cut-out of an animal, vaguely resembling a bull, or a bear. On the half that had survived the fire, a horizontal line was visible.

"All the usual tests indicate that these two items have been touched by divinity," she said, lifting the mask and comparing the two lines. "It's either something very obscure—even less known than the Mendacii—or it's something new. I'll keep looking, of course, but whatever this Wrack is, I fear I have no guidance on how to counter it."

"It—or this Dane—knew we'd finally found the trail, and cut their losses," Makepeace said. "The warning's likely to have come from the Fennington end, unless they're able to detect the presence of other god-touched. I'll keep looking into that."

"Right." Commander Delway packed the charred remains away. "Sightings of sphinxes. Been around longer than we realised, usually not seen in detail. Several smaller buildings whose destruction had been chalked to particularly bad windstorms linked to stories of flying monsters. One of particular note is an attack on Fennington's Melksham Estate Workshop. They lost an entire upper corner of a building—sounds like they thought it an attack from an industrial rival."

"And yet, presumably whoever wanted this Wrack to buy back the fulgite isn't having trouble holding on to it," Princess Leodhild said. "Either the sphinxes are under its control, or it has some means to prevent detection."

"I'm guessing the latter," Makepeace replied. "Pointless to buy what you can knock down walls and take. Anyone have anything else useful, things we're not spinning wheels on?"

"Pieces of a puzzle," Dama Bermondsley said. "It won't be long before we fit them together."

"One piece from a dozen puzzles is not going to get us a picture worth seeing. I'll catch up with you at Cheap Street, Delway."

This appeared to signal the meeting's end, with Delway, Bermondsley, and the self-effacing secretary, Finch, gathering up notes and making their farewells. Makepeace and the princesses stayed where they were: a secondary meeting was obviously standard procedure, so

Rian also remained seated, and was entirely unsurprised when, after the door had closed, Makepeace shifted so he could look sourly at her.

"Time to stake you out, Wednesday, and see what comes looking for a snack."

TWENTY-SIX

"Should I bleat?" Rian asked. "Do you expect tigers? Or sphinxes?"

"Albans."

Makepeace managed to shift himself to a more upright position as he turned toward Princess Aerinndís and Princess Leodhild.

"I put both these Blairs under Command last night—it seemed worth the risk that they can resist me, given the apparent awareness of the Council's involvement. And two more tiresome examples of blameless lives lived well I have rarely had the misfortune to examine. They've an unfeigned devotion toward Alba, have no acquaintances called Dane, and are particularly pleased to have stumbled across Wednesday here. They've both been instructed to get closer to her."

"Who is instructing Lynsey?" Rian asked, surprised.

"Fennington. That, at least, was worth the time spent. Fennington's a closet Unionist—considerable donations. Seems to be for the sake of business—he's been trying to acquire Alban mining interests, and a united Albion would make that infinitely easier. The brother's technically doing Gustav's bidding, because there is no force in this world that will keep that Swede from poking his nose into things that have nothing to do with him, let alone something that he does have a real stake in. At any rate, I could find no air of guilt about the Blairs, which brings us back to Wednesday."

"They successfully lied to you, Comfrey? Overcame the Command?"

"I don't know, Hildy. If it's a resistance born of allegiance, it's not of a type I've encountered before. All their reactions read to me as genuine, so I want to manufacture a response in semi-controlled circumstances. Given the mounting number of parties involved, and stories already running about entire crates of fulgite, we have little time before this mess spins entirely out of hand."

"You want to bring out Mon- use the converted mannequin?" Rian asked.

"And play pat-a-cake with two sphinxes? No, rumour should be enough. You originally showed no sign of knowing anything about fulgite, but they've had their suspicions, they've searched what they could get to. Easy enough to stage a conversation so they'll believe you're personally carrying about a large, round piece of fulgite. Then see what they do to take it off you."

Rian considered this. "Shall I send the children away?"

Princess Leodhild shook her head. "If I was chasing something small and precious, I would most certainly check to see whether you'd sent it with them. And there are few places safer than Forest House. Most likely you will be lured from the house—by the Blairs or by someone who has been using them as a source of information."

Princess Aerinndís' husky voice forestalled Rian's response.

"This presumes that there is some fundamental need to gain one particular piece of stolen fulgite. Given the sums already exchanged, is this piece worth such risk?"

"Maybe not. In which case we will have wasted vital time following Wednesday about. But it is a particularly large crystal, and the pair given to the Tennings are the only round pieces that have come to light." Makepeace shrugged. "We could focus on the Romans instead, or try to convince Egypt to talk, but...yes, I think a little bleating will bring the best result."

"You suspected this Wrack had a truth-telling ability. Won't it be obvious to them that I'm trying to lure them into a trap?"

"You've gained allegiance since then—there's not many that could truth-tell me." His mouth flattened, perhaps reminded of what the change in Rian represented, but he turned the shift to provocative disdain: "Tiger got your stomach, Wednesday?"

"There is inevitably some risk to you," Princess Leodhild added. "Even with all the protections we can muster, we've already been furnished with a demonstration of how quickly they can strike."

"They apparently want to rob me, not kill me," Rian pointed out. "Besides, resolving this before the children can think of something else to investigate seems the wisest course."

"Then I'll set it in motion after seeing to this Roman driver. After that I'll be at Forest House, though you won't see me. Try not to be lured out during daylight."

"We're heading north to bring Tanwen up to date," Princess Leodhild said. "Do you want Dama Seaforth further tonight?"

Makepeace shook his head, then levered himself to his feet and left by the inner door, while the two Gwyn Lynns gestured Rian toward the shelf-concealed entrance. Princess Leodhild, not able to see in the dark, was assisted by her niece through the unlit museum, and let out her breath explosively as they reached the small garden

"I swear, one day I'm going to kick over some priceless artefact from Prytennia's past and then Bermie will have some fast talking to do." She smiled at Rian. "I'm not technically part of the Night Council, merely dragged in because of all that's going on at the moment. Have your three younglings recovered from their adventures?"

Before Rian could answer they were whisked effortlessly into the air: again the stag for Rian, but two transparent horses for the princesses. Only Aerinndís' had three tails, an observation that made Rian wonder whether the Night Breezes had any continuity of existence, whether particular hares and mice remembered whisking burning papers out of a fire, or fetching water. Did they simply cease to exist during the day, or go to Sulis' realm like the triskelion? Her stag certainly seemed to look about himself as if fully aware, and the lone hound in escort frisked with delight around the three larger winds.

They were travelling slowly, low enough above the old Roman walls of central London that people promenading along the city's most famous walk turned and exclaimed or bowed.

Princess Leodhild, entirely used to sudden transports, was smiling encouragingly as she waited for Rian's response, so Rian pulled together her poise and tried to pretend they were all three out for a ride. She should be able to stop herself from being distracted by the sweeping view. Or Princess Aerinndís, stern and glorious to her left.

"They're well enough, though I think there'll be a few nightmares tonight. The idea of being dragged underground isn't one any of them is liable to shrug off. Griff's my main worry, since his constitution isn't robust, and keeping him in bed requires a certain persistence."

"Getting one of mine out of bed is my challenge!" Princess Leodhild said, chuckling. "This must all be rather new to you, Dama Seaforth."

She meant children, not a slow gallop a foot above the Tamesas, or being catapulted into the inner circle of Prytennia's elite and very royal defences.

"Being a distant aunt was a great deal easier," Rian said, controlling a wry note. "Though I find I regret not knowing them better when I didn't need to try to function as a replacement parent."

"In your view, Dama Seaforth," Princess Aerinndís said, "would Gaius Silvanus Tarinus have intervened on behalf of three children who were not in your care?"

Rian didn't answer immediately, turning to look into the Crown Princess' face. Serious, unsmiling.

"I don't know," Rian said, frowning. "Felix was raised in an atmosphere of enormous expectation, and was forever being shuttled about doing things that must have been tremendously dull for a boy, all in preparation for a stellar future. By the time I knew him he'd become a very indirect person, and rarely shared his thoughts. But still, while I don't think he would go against Rome's interests lightly, killing three children—any three children—wouldn't have been a small thing for the boy I knew."

She paused as they whisked under Three Wings Bridge, for she could not help staring up at it. Could the Crown Princess be deliberately trying to make her gape? She had to know the effect she had on people, even without the Night Breezes.

"He must have been ordered to pretend to have gone back to Rome," she said, struggling to focus. "No wonder, with the papers full of that foreseeing. Ficus Lapis probably started to make arrangements to withdraw as soon as they read about it."

"The Unfinished Ones."

"Yes." Rian stole another glance, and was treated to the clean line of Aerinndís Gwyn Lynn's profile. "If they're important somehow to locating or producing fulgite, then Rome would want to get them to safety as soon as possible. And yet, unless Eluned surviving the attempt on her life counts as passing one of these challenges, they must still be in play, a present danger. Even if there is some vein of fulgite under London that's yet to be exhausted, why would they risk staying?"

Neither princess had an answer. Nor did Princess Leodhild make any attempt to dismiss or downplay what the foreseeing suggested. They returned Rian quietly to the attic at Forest House—not whisking her north to meet the Queen as she'd almost expected—and left her to contemplate being lured from safety by people she'd started to consider friends.

Twenty-Seven

"Evelyn?"

Lord Msrah's usually urbane Bound was fraying around the edges: his tunic creased, the hem of his shendy uneven.

"Arianne, I'm sorry to call so late in the afternoon. I was wondering if you had seen Lyle or Lynsey today?"

Rian looked past Evelyn to the car he had arrived in, blinked twice, then said: "No, I'm afraid not. Isn't Lynsey at Tangleways?"

"She came up for the day. We were to meet for lunch and, well, it's a long story. I'll—"

The passenger of the chauffeured tiger lowered a window, and thrust his leonine head through it.

"It is more no news, then?"

"I'm sorry, Your Highness," Evelyn said, ducking out of Forest House's vestibule. "Yes, they haven't been here."

"Who is that?" Eluned whispered, poking her head around the door. It had been too much to hope that the twins would wait quietly in the kitchen. Rian had felt it too dangerous to *not* tell the girls at least part of what was going on, and so they'd spent the day inspecting everyone she spoke to for signs of perfidy.

"Prince Gustav," Rian murmured as, after a brief exchange, the Swedish prince climbed out of the tiger. Very tall, very golden and, as Princess Leodhild had observed, lovely shoulders.

"Apologies I give, of course," he said, striding forward with snapping energy to grip Rian's hands, bowing over them briefly. "But there is no time for the niceties. My aide, and his most delightful sister, they did not bring to you the map? They did not invite you on the small adventure?"

"I haven't seen or heard from Lyle and Lynsey at all today," Rian said firmly.

"Map of where?" Eleri asked.

Gustav's momentum was broken as he looked from Eleri to Eluned. "The matched set?"

"My nieces, Your Highness," Rian said, trying to guess whether this was the lure, and then pushing the question at least briefly into the background. "Come in, please, both of you."

She herded them firmly to the kitchen, choosing it over the sitting room she usually used for visitors because she wanted the folies as close as possible. The girls had been setting the table, and Rian added two plates, guessing that Evelyn, at least, had not spared time from searching since his friends had failed to appear for lunch.

"Now, Evelyn, take a breath and tell me in order. Why did Lyle want to talk to me?"

"It is this, of course," Prince Gustav said, before Evelyn could speak.

The prince had discovered the collection of newspapers Rian had been studying, headlines all blaring their theories about crates of fulgite, and the destruction of the Burning Circle. Rian's day had primarily involved reading about the consequences of the children's adventures, and being 'not home' to the inevitable flood of reporters and would-be acquaintances wanting more. This had fortunately eased after lunch, so that Dama Seleny had been able to escape to her lessons.

The afternoon papers had brought new entertainments, with many pictures of the entrances to the partially constructed underground train tunnels. Fulgite was worth more than gold, and half London had reacted predictably to the possibility that it was lying about under their feet. The *Courant* featured a highly dramatic image of crowds pressing against hastily-erected barriers bolstered by a double line of police.

"Lyle joined the great fulgite hunt?" Rian asked.

"He investigated this at my instruction," Prince Gustav said, prowling about the end of the table. "He is one of great resource, not of this rabble."

"Lyle obtained a map of the projected rail system," Evelyn put in, "and said he had found an anomaly. He was planning to call on you, to confirm his theory."

"An anomaly?" Rian said. "What was it?"

"There is the problem!" Gustav said, spreading his hands. "He wished to check some detail, and perhaps to consult with you, and now we have no aide, and no direction."

"Try Griff's vampire tunnel map," Eleri said.

That produced a neat little pause.

"Need to wake him for dinner anyway."

"Try to keep him from running on the stairs," Rian said, and explained 'vampire tunnels' as the girl departed.

By the time Eleri returned with her brother, Rian had succeeded in coaxing the two men into sitting down, and had sent Eluned out with something for the waiting driver to eat.

Unsurprisingly, Griff arrived in a glow of excited gratification, and a voluminous flutter of paper. He unceremoniously pushed aside plates to spread out his annotated maps of London, with their different coloured lines cutting beneath the printed images of London's landmarks and houses.

"What did Lyle say exactly?" Rian asked.

"He sent me this," Evelyn said, producing a crumpled telegram.

ROUTES CANT BE COINCIDENCE STOP COULD USE YOUR EYES BRING OWN CHISEL MEET DUCIERS MIDDAY STOP LYNSEY AND I LOOKING FORWARD RUB YOUR NOSE IN FULGITE STOP LYLE

Rian eyed Griff's maps doubtfully. "Did Ficus Lapis choose the routes of the lines? I thought their role was coordinating the drilling and maintaining the machines."

"They performed the geologic survey, and advised on the best locations. No final say, but they certainly had a major impact."

"And the idea is they knew of a seam of fulgite beneath London, and made sure the tunnels went as close to it as possible? That would mean we're looking for anything odd to suggest they were trying to get as near as possible to a particular point."

They all stared intently at the printed arrangement of streets, palaces, gardens, museums and groves. The coloured lines of the expected rail lines cut sharply beneath it all, sometimes curving, sometimes straight. Only a small amount in the centre was coloured blue to indicate that it had been completed.

It was Griff, of course, who jabbed a finger triumphantly on a line south of the river, saying: "Why does this curve so early? It would make more sense if it crossed through Southwark near Bridge Hospital. And this one up here—why not follow closer to the river?"

Eleri leaned forward and placed fingers on the far side of curves, covering up some particularly notable landmarks.

"London's two largest pyramids," Eluned said.

"Ha! I have it!" Gustav thumped the table in triumph, and the plates all leapt. "They mine *under* the pyramids. They are devices for focusing the power, are they not? Their form divine, to the point that even the god-touched of those not of Egypt find benefit. There is nothing surprising to learn the crystals of power would form in such environment."

"But if you dig too much under a pyramid you might destabilise it!" Griff said, horrified. "Ours aren't nearly as big as Egypt's older ones, but they still need solid foundations."

Rian sat down, working to hide how much she needed to. "There would be a need, an absolute need, for secrecy. They couldn't risk word leaking."

Her eyes were on Eluned and Eleri as she spoke, as they made the same connections she did, between forged people and pyramids, and stared at each other and then at her, and then firmly closed their mouths.

"Where was it you said you were going to meet for lunch, Evelyn?" Rian asked, wishing very much to know whether Makepeace really had spent the day lurking unseen and on guard, praying that he was listening now.

"Ducier's. It's—ah, I see!" He pointed to a spot directly between the Black Pyramid and the line of completed tunnel. "Right here."

"You've probably visited the Black Pyramid before."

"Of course. It's the most convenient for my Lord when he is in London."

"I know there are conducted tours, but I don't know the process for vampires. Does Lord Msrah reserve a time to use it?"

"Exactly. Though being Shu, he would have priority, able to override other bookings if there was some need. He would of course have to give way to the Nomarch of the East, but Lady Adiol usually uses the Green Pyramid. You think—what—that Lyle wanted to look within the Black Pyramid for signs of damage?" Evelyn's face was a picture. "He told me to bring a chisel," he added.

Not knowing of that wire hand, would they make the same connections Rian had? And could Griff be prevented from announcing the possibility if he realised it?

Mindful of the hearing range of vampires, and of cats, Rian said briskly: "Perhaps he wanted to check whether anyone from Ficus Lapis had visited? Or —" She gestured toward the pile of newspaper. "I don't think he could have planned to go into the tunnels, not when the entrances are all guarded and there is, I'm sure, some kind of official search. But this possibility at least gives us a starting place. Please, eat something, rest a moment, while I get ready. Griff, Eleri, do you think you could find a small hammer and chisel? No running, please, Griff. I don't want you sick for another week."

Eluned came with her to her room, and poked her head unceremoniously out of the window, looking to see what was on the roofs. "How do we know any of this is true?" she asked. "They could be making it up."

"Or either Lyle or Lynsey could be using them in rather dramatic style," Rian agreed, finding her sturdiest travel belt and checking over her smaller pistol before slipping it into the main pouch. "But then, I am *supposed* to be lured."

"There's at least an hour until sunset."

"I know that." She considered the girl, and thought that she was bearing up well enough, though none of the three had simply shrugged off the Burning Circle. "I'd push to delay them more, but I don't think Evelyn or Gustav will wait. And I cannot bring myself to ignore the possibility that for all our suspicions the Blairs have innocently walked into some very real danger. Until I return, do not leave this house for anyone other than Makepeace or the Suleviae. I don't care if your Great Uncle Tobermory shows up to whisk you to my death-bed."

"Aunt Arianne..."

Halfway out the door, Rian glanced back. Eluned murmured "Never mind," but no matter how anxious she was to get on, Rian had to go briefly grip the girl's hand.

"It would be odd for me to claim to have faith in Dem Makepeace, but be assured I think him very dangerous, and more than capable of overcoming so small an obstacle as an hour's sunlight. If not, well, I am a good shot."

If only they had not already encountered so many things to which bullets meant no more than flies. But she did not mention that.

TWENTY-EIGHT

Prince Gustav's excellent driver, a compact, dark-haired man, brought them all too quickly over the river to the Black Pyramid. It was really more a dark grey, with a gold-covered capstone, and sides made sheer by a polished granite casing. While less than quarter of the height of the Great Khufu Pyramid, it still rose imposingly above London and of course, unlike those earliest pyramids designed solely to uplift a single ruler's soul, the Black Pyramid of London incorporated into its structure a grand entrance involving two statues of Ma'at, each with one wing held across the portico, and the other forward. The last of the day's tour groups was flooding out beneath this, meandering down the stairs, chattering and arguing.

"Find somewhere for the car and come back, Ishi," Prince Gustav said to his driver, then turned to study the pyramid, golden brows knitted.

Lyle had warned them not to underestimate the bluff Swedish prince, and during the drive Rian had found herself agreeing with that judgment. Recovering his aide was certainly a goal, but he clearly understood the impact of a connection between fulgite and Egyptian pyramids, even if that connection was simply crystals forming in the stone beneath instead of the possibility Rian feared. The world would shift around this truth.

"The administration building is over here," Evelyn said. "I'll check to see whether Lyle's made any booking, or if they remember talking to him."

Long shadows stretched across the road, but sunlight still gleamed bright on the southern face of the pyramid and set alight a capstone untarnished by any pigeon's leaving, since the divine forces channelled through it would kill anything except the bennu bird that Amon-Re at times used to survey the lands under his dominion.

"You are bound to the vampire Makepeace, Dama Seaforth?" Prince Gustav said. "Yet serve Cernunnos?"

"That's correct, Your Highness."

"And you will unite Albion for the Trifold, perhaps?"

"I have no idea," Rian said, well aware that Gustav would be very unlikely to regret something thoroughly fatal happening to her. Already the news of the foreseeing had thrown predictions about the next vote on the Protectorate into disarray.

"The mixing of allegiances, that is a dangerous thing. Tied to too many gods, the soul becomes a scrap to be fought over."

"I'm certainly not looking to expand my collection," Rian said, all too aware of the trees now ever with her.

"And sometimes a pivot," the man murmured, apparently to himself as he considered her. Like all Swedish royalty, Gustav would have undergone a trial at sixteen to gain formal allegiance to one of the Aesir, and would be subject to demands which would not necessarily align with his king's.

The gun and the chisel in her belt-pouch were a not at all comforting weight, but Rian put aside the difficulties of allegiance to more immediate concerns.

"Did Lyle tell you anything of his plans today?"

"Yes, yes. He was to lunch with his friend, and bring me his sister for the evening meal, though I do not doubt that some obstacle would promote itself." He smiled, but ran a hand over his close-cut beard worriedly. "He has met a bad thing, there is no doubt. The Lyle, he is a very scrupulous boy. When he does what he can for his Alba, he will tell me 'these things, they serve my interests', as if I do not know that! He does not like the vampires, though, and yet he has gone into a place of theirs. No small reason could drive him. Look, the friend has news."

Evelyn was returning, trailed by a bird-framed elderly woman with a powder-pink complexion.

"He has been here," Evelyn said, without preamble. "He made a booking in Lord Msrah's name for two this afternoon."

"I thought it an unusual time for the Nomarch to attend," said the woman, pale eyes curious but friendly.

"This is Dama Wishart, the Black Pyramid's Day Custodian," Evelyn said, well-trained manners kicking in. "Dama Wishart, Dama Seaforth, and His Highness Prince Gustav."

As soon as the polite murmur of responses had passed, Evelyn went on. "There were also two missing...the tour groups are counted in and out, and before lunch one group came up two short."

"The attendants checked, of course," Dama Wishart said. "It's a frequent problem with the tours, and we're quite experienced at making a thorough sweep. We concluded that they'd simply left early—some get quite overwhelmed, you know, by the sensation of being within one of the larger pyramids."

"There's no description of the two absentees, but the timing surely can't be coincidence." Evelyn moved restively on the spot. "But what now? Where do we go from here?"

"Inside," Rian said, adding to Dama Wishart: "Even if it's been checked already, it can't hurt to look again. Unless it's in use?"

"There's time enough for a thorough tour, if you think that it will help in any way," Dama Wishart said, clearly more than happy to see what developed.

"Then we go," Prince Gustav said, and started toward the stair, gesturing for his returning driver to follow.

Past Ma'at's wings, a painted entry hall offered them three choices. Briskly, Dama Wishart led them directly ahead along an upward sloping corridor to the central chamber, where the celestial forces would be concentrated: a large and carefully undecorated room with a single monumental chair facing the open doors. In the forest, the space was almost clear of trees, but for one massive trunk rising from floor and through ceiling, exactly where the throne-like chair was set.

For Rian, even entering the pyramid had required steeling herself to manage simple matters like walking in a straight line, and not sitting down in a corner to gasp. The central chamber brought a faint stagger to her step, and she had to stop and breathe deeply. Dama Wishart's bright curiosity burned as a small sun beside her, while Evelyn's confusion and fear gathered in a grey fog ahead. Even Prince Gustav, striding buoyantly around the room, became less opaque to her, sparking with determination, excitement, and an undernote of concern. The god-touched resistance of his connection to the Aesir was not proof against her new senses in this place where Amon-Re, above all others, held sway.

Fortunately, they did not spend more than a minute in the central room, eliminating it for sake of form before returning to the entry hall and making a quick circuit of the tight ring of offering rooms located at the level of the top of the stair. Then they went down to the crypts.

The weight of the structure would not support large open spaces, but as vampirism had spread through Egypt, and the pyramids had ceased to focus on a single exalted tomb, a design involving a honeycomb of crypts had been perfected. The corridors were narrow and dimly lit, but Dama Wishart had drafted one of the attendants, and a couple of powerful torches, which played across walls painted with images of the lives of vampires gone to rept, their names recorded in a mixture of Egyptian cartouches and Prytennian writing.

"It's been decades since there's been a new internment at the Black Pyramid, of course," Dama Wishart said cheerfully, as the attendant and Prince Gustav's driver blocked two vital junctions, and she directed them through the method of ensuring no-one was lingering around the many corners. "Completely full, and Green near capacity. But the design is quite efficient, with the weight-bearing blocks each surrounded by a set of tombs—rather like bookshelves, really. They're sealed and inscripted after the internment. The only variation are the Nomarches' tombs, right at the centre. While Shu vampires don't have quite the primacy here as they do in Egypt, they're also rarer, longer-lived, and the most powerful outside the Amon-Re." Dama Wishart smiled. "So they rate a larger shelf."

Tenement housing for ba. Vampires, could, of course, have their rept forms maintained anywhere, but Rian quite understood why they would want to share in the uplifting effect of large and expensive pyramids. Here their transformed souls had a far greater chance of gaining the strength for the grandest of ambitions, becoming a ruling star rather than simply another soul in the Field of Rushes under the dominion of Osiris. Besides, the Egyptian Otherworld was difficult to reach, and required high standards of virtue to enter.

The torch dazzled Rian's night-efficient eyes, but she did not need to see to know there was no-one in the area they were searching: there were no unexpected rivers of blood lurking around a corner. Gustav had progressed far in his guesswork, and was clearly looking for intrusion rather than missing Albans, gaze constantly straying to any hint of damaged masonry. Rian saw no sign of more than wear, but she had not expected to.

"There we go," Dama Wishart said, sounding disappointed as the last of the search quadrants proved as empty as the first. "No-one here, not even a forgotten coat or umbrella. I am sorry not to have been able to help more."

"What then next?" Prince Gustav asked, still eyeing the stonework.

"There must be someone we can speak to about accessing the rail tunnels."

Evelyn's voice was hoarse, reminding Rian that he had already lost one old friend, a bare few weeks ago. Delia Hackett's life had changed on the same night as Rian's, but in a markedly different way, and Rian could only hope that Dama Hackett's soul had successfully reached the shores of Annwn, and that some disporting had been achieved, though the islands were not known for their sun-kissed beaches.

But there were other lives changing now, and Rian was suddenly, urgently convinced that the Blairs were not currently occupied in setting up an opportunity to rob her.

"Evelyn, as part of being Bound, you're aware of living people, yes? You can sense those nearest you?"

"Yes, of course," Evelyn said, distractedly.

"Then don't you...Evelyn, I'm sure there's someone *beneath* us."

The tall man stared at her, and then at the flagged stones of the floor.

"You think the thing from the Burning Circle dragged them down?" asked the helpful attendant, with ghoulish interest.

"So *faint*," Evelyn muttered, took several long strides down the corridor, paused, and then moved again. "Here. Directly below here." He dropped to his knees, running his fingers around the edge of the flag. "Only a short way down. Ten feet perhaps."

"But there's nothing permitted beneath the pyramids," Dama Wishart said, blankly. "Not even drains."

"What was he planning to *do*?" Evelyn muttered, attempting to dig his fingernails into the tiny cracks between the close-fitted flags.

Rian handed him her chisel, but Prince Gustav stepped to the fore. He was holding an axe that had certainly not been in any belt-pouch, with a haft nearly six foot in length, and long, tapering double blades. A thing of the Aesir's, according to Princess Leodhild.

"Stand away," the prince said brusquely, and gripped the axe in both hands, the position ceremonial, with the haft down and the blades before his face.

He struck the centre of the flag sharply, a single blow that rang like the Tintarel Bells, and the heavy stone square split neatly in two. Evelyn bent to pry up one edge of the flag, and Rian and Gustav's driver were quick to help him, especially when it became clear that there was an open space beneath, a shaft, with neatly-cut handholds up one side.

At the bottom lay Lynsey Blair.

Twenty-Nine

"Go get a Thoth-den and the police," Rian told the attendant tersely, as Evelyn lowered himself down the shaft. "Run."

"Lyns?" Evelyn, voice tight with distress, lifted the Alban woman carefully. "She's so cold."

"Then hand her up, man!" Prince Gustav said.

Rian climbed swiftly down to join Evelyn, glancing from a wadded bloodstained cloth to the trail of dark red smears decorating the floor of a downward sloping tunnel leading from the shaft. The blood was tacky, crusted. Lynsey had crawled to this point, then collapsed.

"I'll prop, you lift," she told Evelyn, and wasted no time in doing just that, with Gustav and his driver hauling from above.

Climbing back up, Rian said: "Stabbed, I think. I can tell that her heart's still beating, but it's very weak."

"Where is the nearest Thoth-den?" Evelyn asked Dama Wishart, managing to stand cradling the tall Alban woman in his arms. "We can't wait here."

"I'll show you," Dama Wishart said. "Not far, thankfully—we are at a pyramid, after all."

"Good, good," Prince Gustav said. "Go without delay, as will I. The sound it will have carried, the rats they will run. But they do not escape."

Taking the torch from Dama Wishart, he leapt into the hidden tunnel, his driver quickly dropping down after him.

Evelyn wavered, but Rian took his shoulders and turned him toward the exit.

"I'll look for Lyle," she said. "Go."

How would Lyle feel, knowing that only vampiric intervention was likely to save Lynsey? Climbing back into the shaft, Rian decided she would not ask him if she found him.

Gustav and his driver had already disappeared around a curve, two rivers rapidly gaining distance. Rian shook her head, wondering what diplomatic consequences there would be for Prytennia if one of Sweden's princes, and Alba's current Lord Protector, met a messy end in London.

Had she become someone who protected Prytennia's interests? It was an odd thought, as strange as the idea of living a thousand years in the service of Cernunnos and the Trifold. But to do that she needed to survive now, and so did not race immediately after the Swedes, taking the time to ready her pistol and strain her senses, feeling for other rivers ahead. Nothing seemed to be in range.

The tunnel was neatly cut but narrow, close enough to brush elbows on either side, though she did not need to bow her head, and could manage a brisk pace without making a great deal of noise. Height and her Makepeace-given senses allowed her to gain on Gustav, so that she was within sight of him when he stopped, outlined by a dim glow.

A reverent curse drifted back to her, and the two men spoke softly before moving forward at a much more cautious pace. They had not progressed more than a few feet by the time Rian reached the entrance of a long chamber lit by several fulgite lamps.

Work tables, camp beds, and corpses. It was a slaughter house, reeking.

Rian recognised the head of a man lying on the ground to her right. He had been with Felix, coming from a meeting with Princess Leodhild. His body was several feet away, meaty chunks. She looked hastily around for Felix and Lyle, not spotting them immediately, counting five bodies, three men and two women, all torn apart.

Prince Gustav had found a sixth, the one that mattered above all others. Gleaming in dull purple tones, it was spread in countless crystalline fragments on one of the tables amidst a collection of the tools used to break it down. But enough was intact to be damning: a forearm, part of a foot, an entire hand.

"So it is true!" Gustav said, picking his way toward the table. "I guessed but did not believe, because the stone of rept does not at all resemble the crystal of fulgite. But I see the way of it. Look here, this is used."

He had found a machine, resembling a tall drum or barrel, which opened up to reveal a scarred interior and a partially shattered fulgite person.

"So, it is fulquus itself they use," Prince Gustav said. "Not a special thing that Rome alone controls." He threw Rian a vastly entertained glance. "The cat, the pigeons, yes?"

No understatement. Egypt's Otherworld was not easily reached, and even those who did not strive to become stars relied upon a well-preserved body to house their ba while it gathered strength to make the journey to the Field of Rushes. To destroy the body of an Egyptian was, potentially, to leave their ba homeless, without any choice but to attempt that journey immediately. Unlike Prytennia, where efforts were made as soon as possible to sever the tie between body and soul by breaking the body down, or the Nordic lands where the soul was sent on by means of fire, there was nothing more dreadful to the Egyptian than to interfere with the preserved bodies of the dead.

And over the past few decades, half the world had started powering their lamps with them.

Even looking beyond Egypt's reaction, if the world now knew how to make fulgite, what would happen? None of the experiments in replicating fulgite's ability to store and release fulquus had come anywhere close to creating a battery of similar capacity. None of the alternatives, old or new, could begin to compare to fulgite's efficiency.

"I begin to see why the Nesweth sent the Huntresses," Rian said, and Gustav ceased to be amused.

"No, it is impossible," he said. "They could not have known, and could hold no hope to hide this now." He looked around, then recovered his cheer. "Rome, it is about to enjoy a war, I think."

"None of these are Dem Blair, my prince," said the driver, Ishi.

"That is good. Let us find the Lyle."

"There were several exits, one of them blocked by a heavy, close-fitting door, and two others that proved to lead to partially filled shafts—not, in Rian's estimation, beneath the Black Pyramid, but perhaps one of the smaller pyramids used by the Thoth-den. They soon returned to examine the heavy door.

"They ran, and sealed it behind," Prince Gustav said. "Do the vampire parts of you feel them near, Keeper of Albion?"

Rian had been trying to gauge that very thing, hoping to select a direction, and finding it not an easy process. "There's no-one close," she said.

"Then we make noise again," he said, and did so, this time shattering the stone door into flying fragments.

Beyond, the tunnel divided, and Gustav chose left without preamble. Rian paused to check her pocket watch. Makepeace would surely be on the move by now, perhaps even able to enter the south-facing pyramid.

"Someone alive ahead," she said, catching Prince Gustav up. "And others, further away."

"Good, good. But not so good."

They were in a straight section, and Ishi's torch had picked out another door, and the uneven lines of a rock fall scattered around a man's body. Lyle.

"The rats have teeth," Prince Gustav said, as they moved quickly to uncover the fallen Alban. Beyond the door was a clanging, mechanical digging noise.

"Heartbeat is strong," Rian said, then winced as the Swedish prince employed some rough-and-ready methods to encourage Lyle to consciousness.

"...Highness?"

"Today I am the aide, yes?" Gustav said, with a note of genuine relief. "You make the bad show, Lyle. It is a poor warrior that adventures without weapons."

"Lynsey had—Lynsey!" Lyle attempted to bolt upright, and reeled.

"She's alive," Rian said quickly. "Evelyn's taking care of her."

Further discussion was forestalled by additional banging, as if a horse was trying to kick down a stable door.

"Is it that they run?" Prince Gustav wondered.

"What happened, Lyle?" Rian asked. "How did you end up here?"

Lyle was holding his head, investigating lumps, and spoke haltingly.

"There was something I guessed...but you must know it, if you've been through that first room. I wanted to check the tombs...the tombs for any sign of damage, so we took a tour, and dropped off the back. We found one that looked freshly painted...didn't make sense. Then a piece of the paving lifted up. Did they know the timing of the...? We hid, and watched as they worked on the freshly-painted tomb, making the inscription look older. Then..."

He trailed off, face creased with confusion, and then flinched as another round of banging came from beyond the door.

"Why did we follow them? We must have followed. We were—I remember standing outside that room's entrance, watching them. They were making preparations to seal

tunnels, to fully erase any sign that they had ever been—
ever been... Did someone come up behind us?"

He stopped, bewildered.

"Enough for you this day, my Alban," Prince Gustav
said. "There are no bones broken, yes? The Keeper, she
will lend you a shoulder."

"There's at least eight people in there," Rian said, since
the prince was clearly contemplating going through the
door. "And...I'm not sure it's them making that noise. We
can't be sure it's the Huntresses that killed those people."

"It is the stomach of milk that would not find out!"
Gustav said cheerfully, and bent to help Lyle up, and out
of the way.

"Your Highness," Lyle said, clearly horrified. "The
risk..."

But axe haft was already meeting door, and Rian
decided she would really rather not see what the thing
would do to people.

"Let's get you out of here, Lyle."

"Do you know what the Swedes will do to Alba if he
gets himself killed?" Lyle staggered toward Gustav.

Rian rather thought Sweden would exact a blood price
and send a new Lord Protector, but forbore to comment,
moving to join the Alban man as he followed Gustav
through the door.

Beyond was a siege.

A makeshift barrier, a jumbled combination of mining
spoil and metal plates, sectioned off part of the room. In
the very corner an upward ramp had been cut into the
wall, and two men using noisy machines were breaking
into a wall of stone blocks exposed near the ceiling, while
most of the remaining Romans struggled to ward off a
now-familiar hulking creature.

The bull-bear was smeared with dirt and covered in
gashes. From the condition of the rest of the room, it
looked as if the creature, like Lyle, had been brought down

by a rock fall, though one that had involved collapsing an entire tunnel. Perhaps the Romans had believed themselves safe from it, and turned their attention to opening an escape route until it had dug its way free.

Gustav, of course, bounded directly for the thing, and it turned to throw itself at him. The Swedish prince met the bull-bear's attack with competence, if not ease, while his driver drew a gun of his own, and circled so that he had a clear shot if it became necessary.

The Romans' response to sudden assistance was to redouble their efforts to break through the wall above. As they moved, Rian stiffened, spotting two people she had missed at first glance because they were kneeling on the floor. A middle-aged woman and an older man, hands pressed together, lips moving in silent chant. Strangers to her, but familiar thanks to Eleri's precise sketchwork. The Mendacii.

Obvious what they were doing. The most logical response to a god-touched creature like the bull-bear was a god-touched counter. And the thing that had chased the children had been monstrously powerful.

Rian shot the man first. She had a good angle on him, and the bullet struck him in the temple, but the woman flinched away as he fell, and Rian's second bullet pinged off the far wall.

And she had acted too late. The whispers came from every corner, words not quite strong enough to be audible, skittering around the cramped room. Rian's spine crawled, and she moved to try for a clearer line of sight, but the Romans were using their barrier to block her now, and she had to dash quickly for an overturned table when two produced guns, and fired back.

Lyle gasped, and she thought that he'd been hit, but it was worse. Greenish-grey hands had reached up from the uneven floor, and were pulling him down. Before Rian even understood what was happening, he had vanished to his knees.

"Ishi!" Prince Gustav shouted imperatively, landing a creditable blow on the bull-bear.

Gustav's driver had already acted, joining Rian's attempt to bring down the shooters, or the remaining Mendacium. Rian took the chance and grabbed Lyle's hand, then dragged the fallen table to him, as if it was a life buoy that might keep him afloat. He had sunk to his waist, and Rian struggled to hold him without coming into contact with the reaching spectral hands. Her efforts seemed to make no difference.

"Arianne, I..." Lyle's eyes were wide, his panic and horror beating at her.

But then that blast of emotion calmed, his features firmed, and, gaze fixed on her...he pulled her toward him.

THIRTY

Rian gasped, and flung herself away, a chill finger brushing her arm. A more natural hand caught her ankle, and Lyle's smile was quietly pleased as he vanished underneath a clutching grey-green tide, pulling Rian behind him.

She kicked, and caught at the shielding table, but the power of the thing was beyond human strength. The hands were icy, and it felt like they were dragging her into ancient, wet mud, the kind that sent a knife of chill straight to the bone.

Twisting, she tried to spot the remaining Mendacium. No sign, so she snapped off two shots at one of the Romans she could see, grazing his shoulder. But no, she had to conserve her bullets. Somehow choke the horror down, and work for a chance, and that was not a thing that was easy to do when bitter hands clutched at her thighs. How many bullets did she have left? And why, why had Lyle—?

Rian pushed that question away. Why did not matter at this moment. Only a woman, over there behind the barrier. A woman who had called death, and whom Rian must answer with death. The Mendacium had been kneeling, and that one man was in the way, and that at least was an easy shot, and Rian took it.

There. The proudly handsome face, in profile, barely visible through a gap in the barrier. How many bullets left? One? Or was it none? Again, that was not a thing to think about, not yet, because cold hands had Rian's waist, and her grip on the table was making little difference, and this was as difficult a shot as Rian had ever tried, after years of training diligently because a Prytennian woman travelling took care to be prepared.

A red flower bloomed.

Rian's hand shook so much at this success that she dropped her pistol. Taking great gasping breaths she hauled at the table. It seemed in her desperation that perhaps the grip of the hands had loosened, but the Sea of Lies had not fallen with the ones who had called it, and she scrabbled with no care for dignity at unhelpful wood, until she noticed that her efforts were observed by a black hare, running silently in place.

Rian could have wept at the sight of it, a conflation of her sole memento of her mother and someone who had begun to dominate her thoughts, but most of all a sudden and real hope for survival.

The Night Breezes swirled around her, a vortex of mouse and hare and hound dragging her upward. But the Sea of Lies did not release its grip, and Rian cried out in pain.

An arm across her back, solid and human, brought a sudden end to the wrenching tug-of-war. The grasping, spectral hands vanished, driven from existence by a stronger power, and Rian was lifted to the withers of the three-tailed mare. The Crown Princess was dressed very much for combat, and made a formidable armful, but that and royal protocol did not keep Rian from abandoning resolution and embracing her with the whole of her heart.

"Thank you," she said, in a choked fragment of a voice.

Aerinndís, Sulevia Sceadu, let out her breath. For a moment, one single moment, she touched Rian's shoulder. But then she straightened, and that movement brought Rian to her senses, and she allowed her arms drop, gathering what little remained of her self-composure.

The fight had been summarily concluded, the few surviving Romans helpless in a whirl of transparent hounds, though from the crashing noise out in the corridor it seemed the bull-bear had run, and was being hotly pursued.

Prince Gustav, a little clawed about the edges, strode over as the three-tailed mare dissipated.

"The Lyle?" he said, but he'd already seen, and raised his axe to the ceiling in grave salute. "This, no-one deserves."

Rian, remembering a hand around her ankle, looked down and away, and spotted Makepeace striding into the room. He had been thoroughly clawed, his shirt tattered, and the flesh beneath furrowed.

"Lost the thing," he said to Princess Aerinndís. "And the winds seem to have trouble keeping hold of it."

"There was not, this time, an immediate vanishment," the Crown Princess said, watching dispassionately as Makepeace's exposed wounds began to stitch themselves together. "They still have it in sight."

"You know of this animal?" Prince Gustav asked, brightly interested. "Not a thing of Rome or of Prytennia."

Makepeace started to speak, then stopped, grimaced, and said: "And now an excess of cats."

The noise that came close on the heels of this statement was rough, grating, and very loud. The roar of a lioness. The power and fury caught up in that sound would surely echo across the world. Prince Gustav, looking appreciative, headed toward it, Ishi at his heels.

"Comfrey, Dama Seaforth is out of her depth," Princess Aerinndís said. "Return her to Forest House, and then find me."

"Highness," Makepeace said, then added: "Don't dawdle Wednesday."

He followed the two royals toward the roaring, giving no indication that he'd noticed the flush so hot it left Rian dizzy. True enough, perhaps, given she was surrounded by those with considerably more power, but Rian had thought her conduct creditable enough in the situation. She had needed rescue, true, but...

Or had Princess Aerinndís' order been meant as a rebuke for an unwanted embrace? Rian examined that thought, then lifted her chin and walked after Makepeace with all the poise she could muster. Whatever else, this was certainly not the moment to wallow.

A single hand of the Huntresses crowded among the bodies and damning evidence of the first room, three of them in lion form and still roaring, the other two likely the Pakhet and Bastet members of the hand, small women whose current silence did nothing to distract from their fury.

The noise was considerable, threat palpable, and yet Aerinndís Gwyn Lynn spoke with no more or less than her usual grave formality, while Prince Gustav looked on with all the appreciation of someone who would gain from these events, at only the small cost of one aide. Makepeace walked through without pause, and brushed past the handful of police and pyramid staff that had ventured so far as the room entrance before wisely deciding to wait.

People moved aside without looking at Makepeace—or Rian—or even asking questions. They did seem to be marginally aware of him, enough to get out of his way, but reacted without any interest. Given Makepeace's still-healing injuries, this was quite an achievement. The power to control minds: not only the minds of vampires, but any who did not have sufficient god-touched resistance to prevent it.

A crowd had gathered out in the deepening dusk. The Huntresses, particularly the Sekhmet vampires, could not storm through London's heart without comment. Here, Rian did see occasional reactions to the advent of a man in a shredded shirt with nearly-closed rents in his skin, but even the people who looked frowned and blinked as if they had only caught a fleeting glimpse of the unreal, and then went back to gazing avidly at the pyramid's entrance.

Makepeace was moving toward one of the squares of trees that could be found all over London, but once they were past the crowd Rian spoke up.

"I'm going to go check on Lynsey. You don't have to escort me back—I'll take a taxi."

"Interesting thought," Makepeace said, not breaking pace. "But this night has only started, and you are still bright and shiny bait, even if someone else was the one to be eaten. That tedious creature—Wrack or Wrack's servant—was there, where you were intended to go. Her Highness will track it wherever it runs, unless it somehow vanishes again, and we will hunt as soon as Her Highness can diplomatically shovel this Roman mess into Hildy's lap. Wrack must know the Sulevia Sceadu's abilities, know the only way to escape will be to avoid her until dawn, or flee over the border. If the fulgite really is so important to it, it's barely possible it may make one last attempt. The best place for you is Forest House."

"Did you guess? What fulgite was?"

He didn't answer immediately. It was not until they were walking toward the centre of the pocket-sized parkland that he said: "Most ba would have moved on long ago. None of the fulgite I've ever handled felt like more than rock to me, bar that piece your brats have been hauling about. Something so small could not possibly house a ba, and they usually would never waste their energy trying to communicate with this world even when intact—it would be enormously difficult, and greatly impact their ability to reach the Field of Rushes. When I touched that piece, I guessed that there was a living creature involved in the production, but hadn't taken the next step. I wonder if whoever is buying back the stolen fulgite is specifically seeking that where the ba still has some connection to the shattered form."

Rian waited until he had taken her into the Great Forest, then told him, as unemotionally as she could manage, all that had happened before he and Princess Aerinndís had arrived.

"Double-souled?" Makepeace mused. "Or is this Wrack one of the Hungry Dead, eating a living host from within? Surely I would have felt that?"

"The woman called Min said Dane had changed since meeting the Alban," Rian pointed out.

"True. Not likely to be one of the Hungry Dead, then. They use up their host before hopping to another. Unless it's multiple..." He shook his head. "Either way, the hunt's up. We'll see what we have when we bring the bull-bear down."

Since she had rarely felt less happy in herself, Rian was struggling to see her own best course. But there was something logical and obvious, and the fact that she very much didn't want to do it should make no difference. Especially when whatever had driven Lyle had apparently attempted to kill her out of pure spite.

"You weren't strong enough to hold it before," she said.

"That's one of the reasons we've involved Hildy. It's a rare creature that is resistant to both the Night Breezes and the triskelion."

"I thought she was going to be dealing with a lap full of Huntresses." Rian took a slow breath, then made herself say: "You're injured and my blood and ka, by all accounts, will make you stronger."

He shot her an annoyed glance. "Oh, very noble, Wednesday. Yes, I so want a meal of the terror and revulsion radiating off you right now. Marvellous thought."

"Isn't that what vampiric trance is for?"

"I can do all sorts of entertaining things with you, Wednesday, but I can't keep you in trance and eat you. No vampire can keep their Bound in feeding trance."

She hadn't realised that. She really wished it wasn't so.

"Then we can be mutually revolted. It's still by far the best sense."

"Spare me."

Rian started to point out that the sphinxes were still an unknown factor, and the Huntresses apparently entirely disinterested in diplomacy, but stopped herself. At the moment, arguing Makepeace into doing something she would really rather he didn't was beyond her. She had seen someone she'd liked die, and almost been murdered by him, and then forgotten her place in relation to Prytennia's Crown Princess and been swiftly made to remember it. That was surely the meaning behind that 'out of her depth'. Rian could hardly claim to be surprised: the usual result of any blazing pyre of attraction was a failure to spark even a flicker in response.

But she'd thought—just for a moment she'd absolutely believed that Aerinndís' response had been positive. And that had crashed through common sense, left Rian off-balance and reeling, as stung by the Crown Princess' subsequent dismissal as if she'd been slapped in the face. Walking in a straight line felt like an achievement.

Ridiculous over-reaction. Looking seventeen had evidently erased the twenty-odd years of growing up she'd done since then.

When they reached Hurlstone, Rian hesitated, searching the blue shadows. "What do we do about the automaton?" she said. "It's grown increasingly responsive, and now we know what's haunting it."

Makepeace clicked his tongue, but shook his head, continuing on to the gate. "We'll hand it over to the Huntresses tomorrow," he said. "You're right that they're not in a diplomatic mood. Don't be irritatingly right too often, Wednesday. It will make you intolerable."

It wasn't until he came through the gate with her that she was sure that this meant he'd conceded a larger point. It took sheer force of will to stop her hand from creeping up to her throat, and intense concentration to regain enough control of herself to greet two tense girls alert for any development.

"However did you manage to get Griff back to bed?" she asked, guessing from their exchanged glances that she had failed to produce a reassuring appearance. Though Makepeace, even with his wounds erased, rather announced that.

"He's starting to feel better," Eluned said briefly. "It always makes him sleep a lot. What happened?"

Rian explained in the briefest of terms, still circumspect in case of interested listeners lurking on roofs. The whole world would know the largest of secrets, all too soon, but she still didn't quite dare to let her guard down.

"I held it in my *hand*," Eluned said, even so. "Someone's *eye*."

That was very likely, and not what Rian wanted to discuss at that moment.

"Would you two find Dem Makepeace a new shirt, please?" she said. "And wait in the kitchen?"

The only way Rian could face what came next was to get it done as quickly as possible, so she turned and walked briskly across Forest House's large central hall to the receiving room, seating herself at one end of a faded chaise lounge. When Makepeace came through the door, she met his eyes and coolly held out her wrist.

"This will only reinforce the link," he said, shutting the door.

"It was fading?"

"Marginally. But what will happen with you is that the weaker my command over you, the more likely your colony will rouse and finish bringing you across."

Rian's resolution was failing her over and over today. Although she managed to keep her wrist held out, she had to turn her face away as Makepeace reached the lounge and sat down. He at least was not interested in drawing anything out, taking hold of her hand immediately. The touch brought Evelyn's tour through 'antiseptic, watered-down domestication' to the surface of Rian's thoughts.

He will lick your wrist, which will numb the physical sensation somewhat, but not enough for your skin to not know it has been pierced.

The muscles of her arm and shoulder knotted at the prospect, but she did not flinch away at the brief, moist contact. And of course Evelyn had been describing the experience as a Shu, not an Amon-Re Bound, and so had no reason to mention the sharp intrusion of her vampire's emotions with that touch. Reluctance, irritation, pity. Hunger.

The numbing did seem to distance her to the entry of teeth, but Rian was keenly aware of the following moment, of Makepeace's mouth sealed to her wrist.

It's not the drawing of blood, but the ka that is the challenge to face.

Rian's breath hissed between her teeth.

First because it hurts—it always hurts...

A vice had clamped around her chest, and her lungs felt as if they were being squeezed.

It is a sweet pain.

It was sex.

There was no other word for it. An entirely physical response, jarring in the moment, startling a gasp out of her. Makepeace hesitated—she could feel his surprise as a clear note like a bell—then drank again, leaving her shuddering and twisting, crashing onto summits of physical pleasure without any of the climb.

He dropped her hand, shifted so fast that memories of that first night at Sheerside barely had a chance to rise before he was straddling her lap, teeth in her throat, and the result was back-spasming pleasure, and a fierce hunger, as much Makepeace's as her own, the Amon-Re ability to sense emotion taking the very real gratification a vampire experiences when feeding, and adding the physical sensation it produces in the Bound, magnifying it back and forth between them. It was confusing, shattering, engulfing thought and leaving only the urge to continue. One of her arms was wrapped around his back, another gripped his hair, and she twisted so that she was biting him, drinking as he drank, hot blood burning her mouth.

They stopped. Rian felt the effort of will Makepeace mustered to achieve this, a sledgehammer decision that moved him back a necessary inch, and broke the loop that made her want to drink from him. She coughed, shuddered, and fought an urge to spit as Makepeace's blood, smeared around her mouth, slowly crept across her lips, found soft tissue, and sank.

"Too much of that and nothing will stop you crossing over, Wednesday," he said, sitting back as soon as she loosed her grip on his hair.

In aftermath, beyond simple emotion, they looked at each other, dishevelled, breathing deeply, exposed. She could feel his heart racing, almost as quickly as her own, an ancient monster energised.

Then Makepeace bit his own thumb and held it against her mouth, and she felt the flow of his ka, reinforcing the bond between them and bringing to the fore a combination of dismay and satiation that echoed Rian's own response.

"Your sensitivity to light will spike again," he said, climbing to his feet and walking without further delay from the room.

Of all the people she'd met since she'd returned to Prytennia, Makepeace was the last she'd expected to tumble with—which is what it most definitely felt like she'd done, even though all clothing had remained on. An embarrassing development, something she might cringe from when she was no longer so trammelled. She was not a person who needed a meeting of hearts to bed someone, but usually her dominant emotion wasn't annoyance, or fear.

Rian had no certainty as to how long that had taken, but the light-headed exhaustion, the dragging confusion of thought, suggested that he had drunk very deeply of both blood and ka, and she was fortunate indeed that he'd found the wherewithal to stop.

It had at least briefly distracted her from earlier events. Possibly she now felt even worse, but that would pass. The one lesson she had no trouble remembering: in time she would recover, stop feeling so mortified, find her calm centre and move on.

She always had.

THIRTY-ONE

Aunt Arianne looked very small and crumpled, sitting with her knees drawn up under her chin. Though her eyes were open, she didn't seem to notice Eluned and Eleri's arrival until they put their hastily-assembled tea tray on the low table in the centre of the room. Then she unfolded, and said, "Thank you," and then her face went tight and blank, like she regretted saying that and was trying to hide it.

"What happened to your hands?" Eleri asked, bluntly.

The way Aunt Arianne looked down at her collection of broken nails and scrapes made it clear she hadn't even noticed.

"Oh," she said, voice croaky with exhaustion. "That Sea of Lies thing. Nearly pulled me down—I was trying to drag myself out." She lifted her head. "But I killed both Mendacii. I find I am inordinately proud of my shooting today."

Aunt Arianne hadn't told them that she'd been caught by the same thing that had killed Dem Blair. Eluned was willing to bet she'd have never even mentioned it, if they hadn't asked about her hands. But even Aunt Arianne couldn't be lightly amused tonight: she'd never sounded less able to breeze through all difficulties.

"He bit you, didn't he?" Eluned said, putting a cup of tea almost sweet enough to please Griff in her aunt's hands, and then sitting down and slipping her left arm around her waist to steady her upright.

Even though the day had been quite warm, Aunt Arianne's skin was cold, and she seemed boneless and limp, only managing to drink a little tea before resting it on her lap. Eluned considered Forest House's excess of stairs, then mouthed "Blanket" to Eleri.

"I don't think I would have liked doing anything even resembling that with Lord Msrah," Aunt Arianne said, distractedly. "Raw. Yes, raw. It would not have suited."

Eluned freed her hand so she could rest it against Aunt Arianne's forehead, but this was clammy, not hot. Still, the action seemed to bring her aunt a little way back to herself, and she offered Eluned an amused smile.

"It's the loss of ka," she said, and sipped her tea. "Not quite like being drunk, but I am rather disconnected."

"Did he—did you decide to serve as his Bound after all?"

"No." Aunt Arianne paused, then repeated more definitely. "No, that was an exigencies of battle thing, not a career decision. And something of a foretaste..." She looked absently at her cup, then up at Eluned. "Speaking of careers, Eluned, why is it that you change the subject whenever I try talk to you about your atelier application? Is it because you won't be able to go to school with Eleri any more?"

Ambushed. "It's nothing. I don't."

"I did receive a lot of artistic training, you know, even if I don't...but if not me, I know a great many people— indeed, I believe I've met Nathalie Morris. Would you like me to arrange for you to talk to her?"

"*No!*" The idea of admitting to a National Artist that she couldn't even... "It's nothing."

Aunt Arianne didn't push, just sipped her tea again. It was only Eluned's imagination that she slumped. She'd only been asking because she was a dutiful aunt.

But how true was that? One thing Eluned had come to understand was that Aunt Arianne was both nothing like the shallow care-for-nothing mother had thought her, nor the detached sophisticate Eluned had struggled to accept.

Eluned should have seen as soon as she noticed that every second person Aunt Arianne met remarked on her parents, and Aunt Arianne had to tell them she didn't have the talent to follow in their footsteps. That light, vaguely amused tone made it into nothing, a small thing, so they wouldn't ask again. A glass shield of pride, so expertly wielded it looked weightless.

But it felt like Aunt Arianne's shield had become so much a part of her that she couldn't put it down. This might be the first time Eluned had seen her without it, and only because it had shattered under multiple blows. To add another, even a tiny one, seemed impossibly cruel.

"I can't draw," she admitted, barely loud enough to be heard.

Eluned expected some kind of protestation, some insistence that that couldn't be true, when the house in Caerlleon had been dotted with framed examples of her work. Instead, Aunt Arianne drank the last of her tea, then said: "You'll never be able to show Aedric anything again."

"What?"

"He was your teacher, yes? The one whose opinion mattered. Nothing you do from now on, no matter how good or bad, can ever make him proud of you."

Eluned felt short of breath. It was true, true.

"But, then, what can I do?" Her throat hurt from the words.

"Stop. If the only reason you have is Aedric's approval, you should find a better way to spend your time."

Eluned stiffened. She knew she shouldn't have asked Aunt Arianne.

"And there," Aunt Arianne said, with a smile in her voice. "Now you can prove me wrong. But I meant what I said. Be someone who doesn't draw. Don't even try, until something comes along that makes it impossible to not draw, which makes it not even a choice. Then it won't matter who is proud, or not, because that isn't the point, is it?"

"I..."

"You'll find a way, Eluned," Aunt Arianne said, and dropped her head to rest on Eluned's shoulder.

Her weary certainty was oddly warming, and Eluned sat quietly until Eleri returned, and they tucked their drowsing aunt under the blanket.

"What next?" Eleri asked, as they left Aunt Arianne a covered plate and took the teapot back to the kitchen. "Sit up? Bed?"

"I don't think Dem Makepeace is likely to come back tonight," Eluned said. "I don't think I can sleep yet, though."

"Going—"

The window rattled. Not from wind, but as if something had tried to tear it open from the outside. Eluned managed, barely, not to drop the teapot, and stared into the blackness of the grove, and at the shape barely visible in the soft gaslight, standing on the sill.

"Cat. Folie?"

"Must be," Eluned said, staring at the small head, the slender legs. "*That's* what chased off that thing on the wall?"

The folie clawed at the window again, and the whole casement shook, the glass in extreme danger of breaking. Tiny as it was, the folie was clearly capable of doing serious damage if they didn't let it in.

Eluned opened the window next to it, to avoid knocking it from the sill, then stepped hastily back as the folie leapt onto the long countertop. It was less than half the size of a normal cat, the top of its head and back brown gradating through shades of orange to a white belly. Narrow black stripes were visible on its face and front legs. And there were tiny leaves and flowers growing out of its fur.

"Leaves lift up to hide it?" Eleri wondered.

"Maybe they retract? Unfurl?" Eluned could not work out how the scattering of leaves, mostly toward the lower back and tail, could possibly hide the whole cat. "What's it doing?"

The folie had walked toward the window, and then back toward them, and back to the window again, where it looked impatiently over its shoulder.

"Follow it. Obvious."

"To do what?" Eluned asked, then realised there was only one way to find that out. "Find the torch. I'll write a note for Dama Seleny."

As Eleri hunted quickly for the hand-wound torch, Eluned ran through all the thousands of things she should or shouldn't say, and opted for the simple truth.

Following folie. Don't wait up. E&E

ooOoo

"Need a better torch."

"I don't think it's going to wait."

In fact, Eluned had already lost sight of the folie, but it was a simple assumption to head directly for the gate, and rediscover a tiny, tail-switching nub of impatience. The leaves in its tail made a rattling noise as they moved.

"Hurlstone at night?" Eleri said, doubtfully, then added: "Automaton?"

"Maybe?" Eluned wasted no time as the folie, having apparently achieved its goal, leaped away, scaling the nearest tree in two effortless bounds. She reached for and grasped the key she had been granted, fit it into the gate, and turned.

Warm breeze swept through the grove, bringing heady floral scents, and a puff of wind-blown seeds. And one amasen.

"Lila?"

The pale horned snake slid around Eluned's ankle, and then transferred to her arm when Eluned bent down to her. The violet tongue flickered. As much as a snake could look urgent and distressed, Lila managed it, but she was even less able to express herself than the folie.

"Check the automaton?" Eleri suggested, winding hard on the torch to build up a better glow.

Chasing that automaton—whether it was controlled by the ba of an Egyptian or something else—about in the dark did not strike Eluned as an easy proposition.

"Surely we can work out some way to communicate," she muttered. "Nodding—if she understands us at all, we can manage that. Lila, can you bob your head once for yes and twice for no?"

The amasen's gold-crowned head bobbed immediately.

"There. So is there something wrong with the automaton?"

One bob.

"Do you want us to go into Hurlstone to get it?"

Two bobs.

"Not in Hurlstone any more?" Eleri asked.

One bob.

"What? Did it go into the forest?"

Two bobs.

"Came through gate when vampire left?" Eleri guessed.

One bob, which sent them staring around the grove, until Lila's increasing movement drew them back to questions.

"Is it still here, Lila?" Eluned asked.

Two bobs, and then the amasen partly uncoiled and stretched out her head, pointing back in through the gate into the Deep Forest.

"It's not here, but you want us to go...do you want us to go through the Deep Forest?" Eluned asked slowly. "Like Dem Makepeace does?"

One bob.

"Stray gods," Eleri commented.

"And at night."

"Should look around here—can't have gotten far."

Lila's repeated bobbing made it clear she thought this a bad idea. Eluned and Eleri glanced at each other. Eluned's heart was racing at the very thought: Hurlstone itself was in theory a minor risk, but the Deep Forest was vast, and dangerous, and even escorted by one of the amasen, their safety could not possibly be guaranteed.

"Let's do it," she said.

"Bringing a proper light, then."

Eleri sprinted back inside, returning with one of the few fulgite lamps they had. A recent purchase by Aunt Arianne, it was a tall, slender bronze of Sulis herself, holding a glass sun above her head. Powered by a piece of vampire.

"I'm not sure of the symbolism there," Eluned said.

"What?"

"Never mind. You'll point the direction we have to go, Lila?"

The amasen nodded, then stretched toward the lamp, and when Eleri held it closer to her, transferred to twine about the bronze figure. Then Eluned pulled the gates shut behind them.

The scent of flowers was even stronger, a heady pungency that suggested a night-blooming species. There were birds calling. At least, that's what Eluned thought they were, because the sound seemed to come from above. They seemed very high, so she tried to ignore them, and concentrate on closer problems as Eleri upended the lamp so that the sun was pointing to the ground, and Lila's head was silhouetted above it, pointing toward the small stream that cut through the ruined town.

"Stars are enormous."

They did seem closer, but perhaps they dazzled so because everything except the area directly around them was utterly black, with not a single amasen statue relieving the dark.

"Let's hurry," Eluned said. "Look at Lila and the ground, and go."

"Can't see anything else anyway," Eleri muttered, but did as suggested, walking quickly with all her attention on her feet, and the occasional changes of direction of the slender wedge-shaped head, with its two glinting horns.

Eluned had toured the boundaries of Hurlstone more than once, and she was sure the path they found beside the stream hadn't been there before. It wasn't particularly wide, an animal track, but did make progress a little quicker through the thick grass, though it was only marginally helpful when they left the open space of Hurlstone, and gnarled roots crossed and criss-crossed the way, more than ready to trip the unwary.

Almost as soon as they stepped under the trees, the scent of flowers dropped away, and a sharp smell of sap took its place. Insects chirred, lead singers in a forest chorus that fascinated and threatened at the same time. Owl, leaves, unidentifiable rustle, fox.

Lila's head pointed confidently forward, and Eluned breathed loam and pine, and tried to guess at what swooped so loudly above, and then swallowed a gasp when the tree ahead to the left shuddered, as whatever it was landed, in a massive cracking of twigs and clash of leaves.

They stopped, Eluned holding on to Eleri's shoulder, wary about continuing forward, uncertain what the dipping of Lila's head was meant to convey. And then the whatever it was hopped from the first tree to the one immediately above them, a branch crashing to the ground in the process.

Eluned pulled Eleri down, and barely in time, as a head dipped through the canopy, and jaws snapped in a sharp clack.

"Leave the lamp," Eluned whispered. "Crawl!"

They wasted no time, Lila sliding free to lead the way, racing on bruising knees along the path. Crawling was one of the things that a mechanical arm complicated for

Eluned, because she could not feel what was below her on the right, or adjust for the uneven surface. She tucked the arm against her chest instead, unable to stop herself from falling behind Eleri, concentrating simply on going as fast and quietly as she could manage.

A second heavy flier landed in the tree above, and twigs and leaves rained down, and she sped frantically, ignoring rocks bruising her left palm, and something scratching her hip. She strained her eyes to keep sight of Eleri, and almost rammed her, sitting with her back to a heavy iron gate.

No room for hesitation. Eluned rose to her knees, calling the circular key and thrusting it into place. A turn and they were through, banging the gate shut behind them and then falling when it vanished altogether, leaving them in a windbreak of trees, staring across a paddock at the long, half-cylinder buildings of the airfield.

THIRTY-TWO

"Nearly dawn," Eleri said.

The thin line of light on the horizon made this undeniable, although it had been well before midnight when they'd left.

"Hopefully the same night," Eluned said, licking a cut on her palm.

Lila twined up Eluned's right arm, and her head swung to point directly toward the end of the line of buildings, where the Burning Circle had once stood.

"Don't see how automaton could reach here in one night. Not likely could catch taxi."

"At this stage, I wouldn't be surprised if the thing *drove* one here," Eluned said. "So, now what?"

"Over fence? Out of field, anyway."

They trudged, mostly avoiding cowpats, found a convenient stile, then crossed the road. The fence around the vast airfield would not be nearly so easy. A ditch, six feet of chain-link, plus two lines of barbed wire.

"Your next arm, going to build at least a knife in," Eleri said, considering the fence unenthusiastically.

"Wire snips might be more helpful right now. We're really going to have to keep some of the tools on the ground floor—running up to the attic for all the useful things takes too much time."

Lila bobbed impatiently, then changed the direction she was pointing, sending them walking along the fence away from the distant guard gate, and near to the corner of the boundary. The ditch was full of bushes at this end, and when Lila pointed them into it, they found that it featured quite a bit of water at the bottom. But it also had a carefully cut hole in the fence on the far side, the wire pulled back into place but easily moved.

"How did you know, Lila?" Eluned asked, impressed. "There's no way you could have seen that."

Lila, of course, could do no more than bob her head, and then point once again toward the cluster of buildings at this end of the airfield: the compression dome and Workshop Two.

"There'll be some kind of guard patrol for sure," Eluned said, as they walked rapidly. "And people getting ready for the early airship flights, before the morning windstorm starts up."

"Try to look like we belong, then," Eleri said. "Say we're looking for Lady Trevelyan. Could even look for Lady Trevelyan, ask for help."

"Let's hurry," Eluned said, breaking into a trot as Lila's head bobbed and wavered impatiently.

As they neared the ruined circle, Lila changed direction, sending them past the fallen stones out onto the airfield. This section of the vast, flat space was reserved for the smaller airships and offered more cover, but meant they couldn't tell if there was anyone ahead.

"It must be on one of the ships," Eluned said. "Come on!"

They picked up their pace, the pre-dawn haze allowing them to shift from trot to jog to an all-out run toward the back of the rows. Then Lila's graceful head swung left, and they spotted a small form in the half-light. A cat—no, too large—a caracal, and on its back the automaton.

It sped past them, and they raced in its wake, quickly spotting that it was heading for one particular airship, where a woman was busily releasing tethers, even though the running lights were not lit.

Most of the smaller airships were dynastats, and prepared for flight by achieving 'equilibrium', which meant they carried just enough trilesium to offset the weight of ship, cargo and passengers, and relied on forward momentum and adjustable wings to achieve lift and descent. The woman's airship had obviously not been balanced for its cargo, and so tilted drastically as the ropes were released, and then shot directly upward as the last one loosened, the woman only barely making her leap for the gondola door. The wings weren't even extended.

The caracal leapt, but could not possibly reach the gondola. Instead, as it dropped back toward the grass, the automaton snatched at the trailing tether rope, and was hauled into the pink-touched sky.

Two girls and one caracal came to a panting halt, but then the caracal was gone, and a tall woman in a halter-top shift stood in its place. Her red-brown skin was beaded with sweat, and while she spoke she opened and closed her hands several times, as if they hurt her.

"I'm sorry, dama," Eluned said, between pants. "I don't understand Egyptian."

The woman pointed at the airship as it extended its wings, then to the nearest airship on the ground, and then at Eluned and Eleri.

"Locking seals on airship engines," Eleri said. "People kept stealing them."

"Let's try Workshop Two," Eluned said. "Someone there might remember us, and have a seal key."

The Huntress at least understood that they wanted to help, and followed without protest as they sprinted back toward the Burning Circle. The workshop on the far side of the compression dome was encouragingly well-lit, and the entrance wide open, but no-one answered their calls.

"Ransack office?" Eleri said, not very eagerly. She was not going to be quick to forget the rap on the knuckles she'd received during their last visit.

"Maybe someone already has." Eluned pointed a neat sign that said: *In case of emergency, pull handle.* The handle, and part of the wall behind it, had been ripped away.

The Egyptian woman strode abruptly off to the right, in among bays of tools and parts. She returned carrying Lady Trevelyan.

"Is she—?" Eluned began, horrified, but though there was a large welt on Lady Trevelyan's temple, she was definitely breathing, and responded sluggishly when set down on a worktable.

The Huntress flicked the top of the semi-conscious woman's ear, so hard it left a vivid red mark, and Lady Trevelyan flinched, and sat up.

"Eidola?" she said, then stared from the Huntress to Eluned and Eleri. "You two again?"

"What happened?" Eluned asked.

"Eidola—one of my supplies crew. I confronted her about the fulgite she'd been sourcing, and she...is that an amasen?"

The Huntress spoke: a quick, commanding statement, and the Minister looked doubly dismayed.

"No time for explanations, need to chase airship," Eleri said. "Do you have one?"

The Minister touched her hand to her throat, searching, and they saw a line of red where a chain had been pulled away.

The Huntress spoke again, and at least Lady Trevelyan looked able to understand the clipped, urgent words, and replied briefly in the same language before switching to Prytennian.

"I fear that it may well be my airship you want to chase." She looked at them doubtfully, then seemed to come to some resolution. "Use the swallow."

The swallow, whose plans Eleri had 'scribbled all over', was in the very centre of the workshop, hooked to the floor. They had to hold it very firmly after untethering it, though the assistance of the Huntress meant there was no chance of it escaping them to drift to the ceiling. It resembled a tandem velocipede with a winged canopy and an engine to drive a rear propeller.

"Hollow frame filled with trilesium," Eleri said. "Not enough for equilibrium with riders and cargo, but off-sets most of the weight." She glanced at Lady Trevelyan. "Central panniers can be used as extra trilesium cells?"

"No time for that. You two are light enough." Lady Trevelyan looked at the Huntress' lithe and muscular form and added something diffidently in Egyptian.

The Huntress gestured for Eluned and Eleri to climb onto the narrow saddles, and waited until the swallow's wheels had touched the ground before releasing her hold on it. Then she flipped open the top of one of the panniers, resumed her caracal form, and looked thoroughly ridiculous trying to squeeze herself into the container. Still, she managed it, tufted ears poking above the rim.

"You'll need a counterbalance," Lady Trevelyan said, and pulled a large rock from the path border to place in the other pannier. "Good. I will send support after you as soon as I can find anyone to send."

They started off simply by peddling, Eluned keeping them in a straight line until their bumpy progress became a smooth glide a few feet above the ground.

"Keep peddling, Ned," Eleri said, and experimented with the wing controls, briefly gaining and then losing height. "Steering's up to you. Try it out before I turn the engine on."

This proved a fortunate recommendation, as Eluned immediately oversteered them into a flat spiral. But the natural buoyancy of the swallow's frame meant the move was merely nerve-wracking, not deadly, and she could use careful touches to correct, grateful that the morning was very still. Then Eleri brought the engine to humming life, and they surged forward and up.

A warm blanket of night lay over most of the landscape, but the glow on the horizon was now touched with hints of gold, and the sky was paling above, enough that she could search the near distance for the airship. Then searched in the opposite direction when guided by Lila.

"What do we do if it's faster than us?" she asked, as she gingerly swung the swallow into pursuit. The stolen airship was already a long way ahead.

"Go to France, by the looks."

But they were gaining. Not as quickly as Eluned would like but steadily, so that the question became what would they do when they caught up. The automaton clearly no longer clung to the end of the rope, but there was no way to tell if it had managed to get into the gondola, or had fallen.

"Steer directly over it, Ned," Eleri said, adjusting their height. "And..." She paused, then added: "Do it quick."

It was only when the necessary adjustments had been made, and Eleri was preparing to cut the engine, that Eluned realised where the need for haste had come from. There was a rising wind. A familiar breath of heat, tickling at their heels. The morning windstorm, come hours too soon.

"Peddle to keep pace once we come overhead," Eleri said, as their surging forward drive fell to a less relentless glide.

A violent wriggle nearly upset Eluned's attempt, as the caracal surged out of the pannier and dropped without hesitation onto the ballonet of the airship. The swallow immediately began to bear to the right, and Eluned could not work out what she needed to do to break out of the spiral.

"Can you reach the counterbalance, Eleri?" she asked, trying to steer and still keep an eye on the gold and black caracal. Had it slid right off the top?

"Ned."

Eleri's attempts to fish the stone out of the pannier were doing odd things to their flight path, but after she succeeded in tossing it to the trees below, she pointed toward the increasingly bright horizon. Something was following them.

"It can't be the Night Breezes." Eleri squinted into the light, then turned her attention back to their target as the semi-rigid ballonet dimpled, and the airship began to rapidly descend.

THIRTY-THREE

Landing proved to be a great deal more difficult than taking off, mainly because of drystone walls and sheep. And a hedge of blackberries, which did interesting things to the swallow's wings, and Eluned's legs, and made her glad for the hand that did not feel when she used it to hook the anchor chain to the strongest-looking branches.

"So unprepared," she said, hopping out of the thicket. "We didn't even bring the wooden sword."

"Could wait here. Leave it to the Huntress."

"We could," Eluned said, picking up the sturdiest stick she could see, and starting in the direction Lila was pointing. "But the sun's well on the way to being up."

Down on the ground, the Huntress would have more protection from the brightening dawn, and it was not as if she would turn to stone immediately, but Eluned was taking no chances. Whoever had stolen that airship surely knew something about the fulgite thefts. Eluned had a few important things to ask them.

They had not managed to land within immediate sight of the downed airship, but at least they could now see easily, and their hurried walk only involved startling the sheep and scrambling over the fences. Soon, they spotted pieces of the ballonet, strewn over the top of a grove of trees.

A high-pitched snarl made them quicken their pace, but they stopped dead at the rumbling growl that followed. Eluned had heard that sound before.

"Still want to go?" Eleri asked.

A thief was one thing, that hulking shape they'd seen on the grove wall another altogether.

Before Eluned could reply, a gunshot cracked above the sound of combat. Eluned and Eleri exchanged a glance, then moved forward, much more slowly.

The gondola had touched down not quite upright, a sapling crushed beneath it. The nose was facing Eluned, and the windows had shattered, but she could only see the door at a sharp angle. She had a much better view of the caracal, and a creature with a heavy snub head, weighted by wide, horizontal horns. Its shoulders bulged with muscle and its feet were great clawed plates. The thing Aunt Arianne called the bull-bear.

It clearly outmatched the much smaller caracal, even with the healing, speed and strength given to the Huntresses. It was only when a second shot rang out, scoring the caracal down one flank, that Eluned realised that part of the reason the Huntress was struggling was because she was using the bull-bear's bulk to shield herself from the shots from the gondola.

At this angle, Eluned couldn't see whoever was shooting, and sorted rapidly through their sparse options. A frontal approach through the clearing was out of the question: even if they did not draw the attention of the bull-bear, the shooter would easily see them and have a chance to fire before they reached the door.

Besides, no matter what they did about the person firing, there was not a thing they could do about the bull-bear. Intervening would get them killed as well.

"Stay here," Eluned hissed to Eleri, and slipped away from the clearing to lessen the risk of being spotted as she circled to come up behind the gondola.

A glittering glass reef clung to the rim of the windows, telling Eluned that her initial plan of crossing the gondola to ambush the shooter wasn't viable. She could see the person, though: a woman with light brown hair slipping from a loose braid, and with one sleeve of her tunic soaked with blood.

What now? If she couldn't easily get close, could she distract the woman and then run? Or...

"Rocks." Eleri had not stayed put, and now bent and collected a chunk of stone of the same grey as the walls they'd crossed.

Another shot added frantic speed to their efforts to gather enough ammunition, but it was difficult to gauge the progress of the battle over a rising roar that reduced even the bull-bear's growl to an inconsequential undernote. The windstorm, giving the trees voice, thrashing branching, whipping the shreds of the ballonet's skin into a flapping frenzy.

"On three," Eluned said, cradling her armful of chunky stone.

Her first rock went wide, bouncing off the side of the doorway. Eleri's hit a hanging piece of glass, sending glittering fragments spraying dangerously. But the stone still struck the woman's back, and she turned in time to receive a second barrage in the face.

Eluned had never done that before. Never thrown a rock or a punch, and seen blood, a visible hurt, as a result of her actions. She could blind this woman, this stranger, could scar her, even kill her. And all of Eluned backed away from that, from the permanency. From someone, somewhere, feeling about this woman the way Eluned had about Mother and Father, sent on prematurely to Annwn, and perhaps out of reach forever.

Bright anger lent her the will to throw another stone, to aim it, to put all her strength behind it. To perhaps not even cringe when it struck with a hollow watermelon noise, and the woman dropped.

"Good shot," Eleri said. "Don't think that will work on that bear thing."

"If we distract it enough, the Huntress might be able to hold out until the pursuit arrives," Eluned said. "Hurry— the brighter it gets, the more she'll slow—ah!"

A shard of window had been blown loose by the increasing gale, slashing across her chin. She lifted her hand, and brought it away red, but then Eleri pushed her forcefully down, and they both covered their heads as all the remaining glass became horizontal hail.

"Not sure we could even get its attention over this," Eleri said, lifting her head cautiously.

The entire gondola was rocking with the force of the gale, and when they crawled to the fore to peer into the clearing, twigs, leaves and grit pelted them. It was by far the worst windstorm Eluned had ever experienced.

"Any airships sent after us won't be able to fly in this," she said, and studied the sky, searching not for rescue, but something less welcome. And there they were, coming not from the direction of the wind, but flying into the gale. Lion-bodied, with the faces of women, and wings of blue and black.

They were larger than Eluned had expected. One of *those* had fit into Aunt Arianne's room at Sheerside House?

There was no question of battle after the sphinxes dropped down. One simply landed on the bull-bear, with the precise ease of a house-cat trapping an ungainly mouse, holding it still under stony front paws. The roaring gale immediately slackened.

"Really are statues."

"Really are big," Eluned replied. "What now?"

"Not throwing rocks at those. Just watch."

But the caracal, returning to human form, wasted no time turning toward them and beckoning imperatively. Eluned and Eleri were slow to respond, for neither of the sphinxes looked anything but welcoming, their tails lashing and their expressions hostile. Even so...

"How can we help, dama?" Eluned asked, trying not to goggle as a bullet slowly emerged from a wound in the Huntress' shoulder, and fell to the ground. She wondered if the Huntress wanted to drink from them—the Thoth-den blood that had allowed her to survive the loss of her arm should have filtered from her system years ago, meaning the strains wouldn't clash. Though the Thoth-den had said Eluned and Eleri had one of the rarer types of blood, that only vampires with the same type of blood could drink.

That did not seem to be the Huntress's reason, anyway, as she walked briskly into the gondola, stepping over the fallen woman. Eluned had to pause and check that the shooter was alive, though, because if she had killed someone, she wanted to know as soon as possible. Finding steady breathing, she prudently picked up the woman's gun, then surveyed the interior of the airship.

In three rough sections, with the pilot's fittings and side-benches at the front, heavy storage in the centre, and a privacy cupboard and the engine housing to the rear, the entire gondola was strewn with leaves, lurking fragments of glass, and an unexpected wash of water. This was coming from one of three barrels in the central storage area, which had escaped stowage to fall on its side. The Huntress lifted it upright and finished the job of breaking open the lid, releasing a final gush of water. What remained was familiar purple crystals.

Three barrels, three fortunes in fulgite. And one crate that made Eleri and Eluned gasp when the Huntress lifted away its lid to reveal a black and chrome figure curled into a ball.

"Father's automaton!" Eluned could hardly believe it, touching the domed skull.

"Proof." Eleri's voice was low. "Proof."

A much smaller head rose on the far side of the crate, the painted monocle turned in their direction, blank and yet impossibly aware. The Huntress lifted the converted mannequin and placed it with great ceremony in Eleri's hands, then carried the larger automaton outside.

"Do you think it's talking to her?" Eluned whispered as they followed.

"Must have had a reason to bring it to the airfield. Expect she was one of the Huntresses watching Forest House." Eleri regarded the automaton she carried dubiously, and then started as the two massive sphinxes each lowered their fronts to one knee, and bent their stern heads. "Have a bad feeling I know who this is."

"Hatshepsu."

Eluned, who had been hoping very much that Dem Makepeace would arrive, turned at his words, and was even better pleased that he'd brought Princess Leodhild and Princess Aerinndís with him.

"The obvious possibility, once we knew what fulgite was," Princess Leodhild said. "Though I could wish it was not the case. What an appalling mess." She nodded her head formally to Eleri's burden, glanced at Eluned, and then produced a kerchief and pressed it to Eluned's chin. "You two look like you've been dragged through an entire hedgerow backward."

"You two need to be put on a leash," Dem Makepeace added sourly, and handed Eluned a statue of Sulis holding up the sun. "Don't leave things like this about the Great Forest. You'll upset the balance."

"He was worried," Princess Leodhild confided. "Really though, this is quite the result. Will this solve both the Wrack and the windstorm issue?"

The Huntress had seated the large automaton on a fallen tree, and then gone back into the airship for the three barrels of fulgite, which she emptied unceremoniously in a pile at the automaton's feet.

"They were keeping it in barrels of water?" Princess Leodhild said. "Why?" Then, when the two sphinxes— taking turns keeping the bull-bear pinned—paced forward and coughed up some more purple crystals, she stifled a chuckle and added: "Not quite *laying* it, Comfrey."

"The water is a logical extrapolation." Princess Aerinndís was watching the scene dispassionately. "Amon-Re, like Sulis, is aligned with sun and wind. This

Wrack already knew to escape me by going underwater. If they had encountered the sphinxes, they would have searched for methods of concealment."

The automaton seated imperiously in Eleri's arms raised one hand, pointing, and after a moment's hesitation Eleri walked forward and placed it on the larger one's lap. They made a mismatched pair: the rather plain wooden mannequin, worn in places, with metal only visible at its joints, certain features—hands, feet, face—only suggestions. Whereas Father's automaton had been primarily worked in metal: much of it enamelled black, inset with panels of vivid chrome, every joint articulated, down to the tip of every finger and toe. And all of the enamel, every inch, decorated with the cloisonné arabesques that father had favoured in his work.

And yet there was a similarity, for Father had not attempted naturalistic features, but instead used the combination of enamel and chrome to add sharp relief to the planes of the face. The result was remote, but elegant as Father's work always was.

The Huntress spoke, and Princess Leodhild said: "She wants the fulgite taken from the small automaton and placed in the large one, and for the transfer to be as quick as possible."

This was no problem for Eleri, and she did so briskly, though with one involuntary glance at the two sphinxes, which stood abruptly in the middle of the process. Then she stepped hastily back, and they waited.

Eluned immediately became convinced that the transfer had been a mistake. The larger automaton did not react at all, but the two sphinxes did, rattling their odd wings, and shifting their weight restively. When movement came, it was not from the automaton, but the pile of fulgite at its feet. A thousand fragments of vampire, shifting, shuffling, fitting together.

A woman. Quite short, her cheeks broad, lips full. Hairless, covered in countless fractures. And missing one eye. She stood before them for only a moment, and then the body of Maatkare Hatshepsu turned to dust and was swept away on the slackening breeze.

Some fulgite remained. Glittering crystals that Eluned guessed were pieces of other vampires collected by the thieves. It crunched under the feet of the automaton as she stood.

Taking Latin instead of Egyptian in school had definitely been the wrong decision, though the brief exchange between the Huntress and the princesses had a note that suggested it was whatever polite formalities could possibly be appropriate to the occasion of the revival of one of history's most famed rulers, after people had been using her as a battery.

Then all of them—Huntress, princesses, Dem Makepeace, and the automaton controlled by the ruler of the Egyptian Empire—turned toward the two sphinxes, and the creature pinned beneath one paw.

Princess Leodhild said: "Fair warning, dama. If you don't surrender, this delightfully large creature intends to snap your spine."

Completely overmatched, the bull-bear had long since given up attempting to struggle. Her transformation had an air of a shrug about it. Eluned hadn't even realised that it was a person. A sturdy, blond woman, as battered as she and Eleri, and wearing a piece of black material on her head like a cap, cloth dangling down to cover her face to just above the mouth. Two golden lines bracketed the outline of an eye.

The sphinx lifted its paw fastidiously, then paced away as the woman sat up.

"Bow," Dem Makepeace said, and pushed Eluned and Eleri lightly on the shoulder.

Eluned did as she was told, though not quite achieving the depth that he did. The princesses inclined their heads. And Egypt's Pharaoh mounted one of her guardian sphinxes, and flew away.

"Well now," Princess Leodhild said. "I do wonder whether the Nesweth will consider that arrival an improvement on the earlier news of the day? Obliging, at least, for her to leave this one alive." She crossed to consider the woman sitting among the leaves. "Dane Dayson, I presume? Or should I call you Wrack?"

"Wrack?" The response was calm, unconcerned. "Yes. That will serve as well as anything."

"Did you kill our parents?" Eleri said, sharply, before Princess Leodhild could say more. "Tell me."

The woman—or the mask—turned slowly toward her. "Do you ask a boon of knowledge of me?"

"She does not!" Dem Makepeace said sharply. "It's a god," he added to Princess Leodhild.

"No." Wrack again, a quiet correction. "Not such a small thing."

Eluned was not the only one who stared. But before they could ask more, the woman reached up and pulled the cloth off her head, quietly sighed, and passed out.

"Unconscious," Dem Makepeace said, not moving. "I won't give odds on how much she'll know when she wakes. A thief, definitely, but controlled by something vast and unknown."

Did that mean that Mother and Father's murderer wasn't even human? Was something that could never be brought to justice? Eluned struggled with a crushing disappointment, glancing at Eleri and seeing the same reaction. But then she frowned.

"That mask."

Dem Makepeace glanced at her. "What about it?"

"It's a quartered eye."

"Yes it is," he said agreeably. "And a vampire in rept form is arguably an anchor on the soul of a god, and I do wonder what Wrack wanted with it."

He looked up at the now very blue sky, at the leaves outlined with sunlight, and the leading edge of airships come to the rescue, and added: "Done with your adventures?"

Eluned started to respond, but realised the remark had been addressed to Lila, who lifted her head, then slid across to Dem Makepeace when he extended his arm.

"She won't get into trouble will she?"

"For failing in her duty, and then co-opting you two into fixing her mistake? What makes you think that?" He turned away, inclining his head to Princess Aerinndís. "Anything further, Highness?"

"No. I will speak with you tonight."

Dem Makepeace bowed again, then spoke to the exhausted Huntress, and walked into the shadow of the trees with her. Eluned, feeling defeated, sat down on the log by the remaining fulgite, and Eleri joined her, picking up the abandoned mannequin. This was as over as it would be then. Mother and Father were still gone, and nothing had really changed, and Eluned did not feel better at all.

The Crown Princess walked across to them. Trying to remember royal protocols, Eluned started to stand up, but the princess gestured for them to remain seated, and so Eluned reluctantly settled back down. Princess Aerinndís was such a grand and distant person, not nearly so likeable as the comfortable Princess Leodhild, and Eluned struggled to find the energy to deal with formal and proper when all she wanted was to curl up into a ball.

"*The Processional* made the Seaforth name famous throughout Prytennia," Princess Aerinndís observed. "The whole world will know the name Tenning, for the form that Maatkare Hatshepsu will wear as she continues her journey into eternity. I believe she found it a worthy one."

And that did change things, did make it better. Enough to go on with.

"Thank you, Your Highness," Eluned whispered, but the Crown Princess had already turned away.

EPILOGUE

A single tiny leaf, surrounded by an outline of itself, and another, and another: one for every day since Maatkare Hatshepsu had returned to Egypt. It was a drawing exercise Eluned had set herself, and the only thing she would allow herself to work on, until she had completely filled the page. Not long now, and then she would have to decide what she was ready to move on to.

But she was doing it. The cliff had been climbed, and she was marching steadily onward.

"Boring, boring, boring, boring."

Griff tossed prospectus after prospectus back onto the pile. Aunt Arianne had given them until the end of the day to make a final decision on their school, and they were fed up trying to find one that they all found acceptable. Part of the problem was they'd left it so late. There were plenty of close schools, but few that met Eleri's standards for scientific classes, or treated art with any degree of depth. Enrolment at these few involved applying well ahead, or sitting on a waiting list and hoping. None had room for all three Tennings.

Travel by bus across London each morning had been ruled out, and so they had been vetting boarding schools, despite not wanting to be away from Forest House and Hurlstone. No-one was enthused by the shortlist of schools with places available.

"Try this, Ned."

At least the new arm would be done in time for the trip to France. Eleri was still making fine adjustments, but it was already functional. For the third time that morning Eluned shrugged into the jacket that could be worn over or under her clothes, and had been designed to make putting the arm on and taking it off as easy as possible. But the biggest difference was the control design: rather than pre-set functions, Eleri had had the idea of 'mirror movement', and so the jacket came with both a right arm and a wire-threaded left sleeve that extended all the way down to a glove that left only Eluned's fingertips exposed. If she switched mirror-mode on, everything her left arm did, her right arm would copy: precisely, exactly.

"It's marvellous, Elli," Eluned said, after she'd obediently run through the function tests. She hugged her sister, delighting in the way both arms went around Eleri's back and met without any need for concentration at all.

"Don't call me Elli," Eleri said, but didn't break away, and even relaxed against Eluned for a moment. She was still too thin, far worse than her usual state of neglect during a project, but she had begun to improve, and no longer watched the mail for the invitation to the palace that they had had no true justification to expect.

In fact, other than a scrawled note from Dem Makepeace confirming that the verdict on their parents' deaths would be overturned, Forest House had had nothing further to do with palaces or princesses or the fate of Prytennia, except the inevitable flood of reporters and curious strangers mixed in with the grove's normal visitors. The Tennings had taken to staying upstairs, and Aunt Arianne, after making a very brief statement, had occupied herself once again with the avoidance of sunlight, only going out to visit Dama Blair, and Hurlstone.

Eluned did not know what to do about Aunt Arianne, who had had several bad things happen to her all at once, and was slow recovering. She spend most of her time practicing fencing steps, but at least seemed glad to talk to them over breakfast and dinner.

Racing footsteps heralded welcome distraction, and Melly, followed closely by Nabah, burst up the attic stair, waving a newspaper.

"Why didn't you tell me? Why didn't you tell me?"

"Tell you what?" Griff asked, abandoning prospectuses.

The newspapers had definitely been interesting the last few weeks, full of fulgite's true nature and Rome's perfidy, and the sudden dilemma these revelations presented. War had not yet been declared, but was considered an inevitability, while the question of whether Egypt would demand all fulgite returned to it had not yet been answered. The highlight for Eluned had most definitely been a picture of Egypt's Pharaoh, re-ascending her throne. The automaton built by Eiliff and Aedric Tenning, on the front page of every newspaper in the world.

But the afternoon edition Melly was waving had a picture of Aunt Arianne, and a familiar massive whorl which the black and white of newsprint somehow managed to convey was gold. The headline read: "A GIFT OF THE FOREST".

"So that's what Aunt did with the amasen horns," Griff said, after snagging the newspaper from Melly.

Eluned peered over his shoulder, and read that Arianne Seaforth, Keeper of the Deep Grove, had donated one of the largest amasen horns ever seen to the Museum of Prytennia, and arranged for a dozen smaller horns to be auctioned. The proceeds would be used to establish "The Lamhythe Scholarship", a fund administered by the Lamhythe Warden. Five students each year would receive a contribution toward their tuition.

"Think you'll get it?" Eleri asked, shooing Griff away and reading the story over.

"Given how much Dama Chelwith had been bothering me about leaving school, and how pleased she is about me going to Tangleways, I think the chances are good." Melly bounced excitedly, today's collection of tiny, bell-tipped braids jingling. "This will make so much difference! I'd managed one term's fees, but it required a lot of balancing. Is your aunt in the house? I must go thank her."

"Far end of grove," Eleri said.

"Ah, then I'll wait until a better time. You don't leave until the day after tomorrow, right? Have you picked your school yet?"

"I don't think we ever will," Eluned said. "Maybe we should throw them all in the air and go with whatever lands on top. What about you, Nabah? Still undecided?"

"No." Nabah spoke proudly. "I am going to Karnata, to help establish the first Daughters Hospital in the Empire. Even though it means I will go in my time to a different Otherworld than my sisters who are staying, and there is sure to be adjustments and difficulties, I want to serve Lakshmi in truth, to honour more than Her name." She wrinkled her nose, and added forthrightly: "I felt a coward compared to you and Keeper Seaforth, serving Cernunnos without fear or falter."

"You can only say that 'cause you didn't see the expression on Ned's face when we were running away from that thing made of hands," Griff said, returning to the pile of prospectuses he'd left by the window.

"Doing something despite being afraid's the definition of bravery," Melly said, equably. "Has Keeper Seaforth really been teaching you to shoot?"

"Yes, though we're not allowed to aim at the ravens," Griff said, picking up the prospectuses and holding them above his head. "And she keeps her guns locked away between lessons." He dropped the stack of paper, picked up the one that had landed top-most, then dropped it again. "Boring."

"Let's get the Aunt to pick one," Eleri said.

"Boring," Griff repeated, then added casually: "The Queen's in the back yard."

It was one of the most effective dramatic pronouncements he'd ever achieved, but he barely watched their reaction, craning out the window instead.

"You probably shouldn't call a sacred grove 'the back yard', Griff," Eluned said, peering avidly. There was indeed a tall thin woman with short blond hair in the grove, but she was facing the wrong way, walking down the path with Dama Seleny, and she wasn't exactly wearing a crown or torc. "Are you sure it's the Queen?"

The question was answered when the two women stopped, and Dama Seleny started back to Forest House. If that wasn't the Queen, it was someone who had her profile. And when she reached the currently closed gate, she unlocked it, and went right on through.

"Keeper opening gates every twenty-five years doesn't look all that necessary," Eleri said.

"I guess it's symbolic," Eluned replied. "And I guess I'm feeling hungry, and need to go down to the kitchen to get something to eat. Anyone else?"

Griff made it first down the stairs. But it was a close race.

ooOoo

Did aging vampires seek the sun because the pain made them feel alive, or did it keep at bay the ever-swelling host of dead friends and hidden wounds?

Rian was finding her lingering sun sensitivity useful. At the moment her calm centre was beyond her reach, but small hurts like sunlight and aching muscles were wonderfully distracting. Fencing practice in Hurlstone handily combined the two, while giving her hope that the cool balm of the boundless forest would eventually restore her.

Not today, however. She lay at the feet of a vampire older than Makepeace, staring at a vivid blue sky, yet again failing to reconstruct any semblance of internal balance.

Today had brought the news that attempts to excavate Lyle Blair's body had been abandoned. There was no way to be certain if he had even been buried, given that one of the theories claimed the Sea of Lies transported victims to a punishment Otherworld. Since Rome had taken the only possible attitude—to deny any knowledge of fulgite's true source, and lay all blame on the Mendacii—they had not been helpful in establishing the truth. Either way, Lyle was gone, and very likely had been as honest and giving as he'd always appeared, a victim of this Wrack creature.

During her second visit with Lynsey, when it had been clear that the injured woman was not merely grieving, but withdrawn, uncommunicative, Rian had told her just a little of the masked woman Eluned and Eleri had encountered. Rian hadn't been able to explain the whole situation—a ban she had not enjoyed discovering—but she'd been able to say enough to ease the Alban woman's confusion, and Evelyn, though he had only the barest idea of what was going on, was clearly determined to help her through her recovery. They had agreed that the three of them would meet in winter, to dance in the snow. Perhaps by then Rian would be able to tell them more.

So far as Rian could tell, the truth of Wrack's involvement was not going to be released for public consumption. The papers, at least, only mentioned the name as an alias of Dane Dayson. Rian expected she would be told any new details eventually, once her minor exile had run its course.

A double exile, in fact. Makepeace, after their experience in the receiving room, had not come near her, which was in truth the response Rian preferred, though she hoped he would overcome his disinclination before her blood rebelled. And it had not surprised her in the least to be frozen out of the Night Council. It was an easy, non-direct way for Princess Aerinndís to indicate that Rian should not forget her place in future. No doubt, if this foreseeing ran its course, Rian would encounter the Sulevia Sceadu again, and she would be on her best behaviour, and the matter would be forgotten.

All this would pass.

That was the logical, mature response Rian was completely failing to achieve. She had endless nightmares about being dragged underground, followed by very odd dreams about biting. And she thought constantly about the Sulevia Sceadu, analysing every moment of that embrace, marking the fact that the Crown Princess' heart had been racing as fast as her own, gauging the exact intonation of a single exhalation, and measuring the weight of the lightest touch.

All that was stupid in Rian wanted to take that extremely restrained response, add Rian's ability to sense emotions, and declare that, whatever else, Princess Aerinndís had shown herself not unattracted. Rian had been so *sure*. But the Sulevia Sceadu would have a very strong resistence to Rian's minor abilities, and any feelings in that moment were entirely beside the point given what followed.

The only response to clear rejection should be graceful acceptance. Princess Aerinndís had certainly made clear the rejection, and Rian would achieve the acceptance once she'd found her balance again, and would move on from this obsession with someone out of her reach. It was important to concentrate on the positive things. The children had survived, with no more than a cut on Eluned's chin. She'd received a note from Felix, assuring her he had safely returned to Rome. The trip to Lutèce would be a balm, guaranteed to buoy her spirits, especially since she no longer had to count every coin. Rian would be properly grateful for the enormity of these gifts, and put aside foolish self-deception.

An approaching river brought her back to the present. She looked from the stone vampire at her head to the blond woman at her feet, and sat up.

"Your Majesty."

"Dama Seaforth. No, no need to stand. Hurlstone is such a restful place, isn't it?"

Tanwen Gwyn Lynn was a greyhound lean woman, loose-limbed and direct of gaze. She settled on one of the ruined walls, completely at ease.

"I apologise for not calling on you earlier, Dama," the Queen said. "The windstorms made the dragons very restless."

The Sulevia Seolfor's connection to Prytennia's three dragons meant that a sizeable portion of her year had to be given over to 'walking their spines', an act of honour and reassurance that involved long treks over the countryside.

"Hurlstone is a good place to recover from an ordeal," the Queen continued, after Rian had politely assured the Sulevia Seolfor that she had nothing to apologise for. "Despite its ruined state, it is greatly loved by the forest. That warm regard is wonderfully beneficial."

'Warm regard' was a good term for the way Queen Tanwen seemed to view Rian. Rian found herself sitting straighter in response.

"Why is it loved by the forest?" she asked.

"The people who built it were...tree children. Similar to the folies. It was so long ago that even in the Great Forest the town has fallen to ruin. A time before humans." Queen Tanwen lifted her eyes to consider the statue at Rian's back. "It is so old, this world. Ancient, and full of mysteries."

Rian turned and gazed up at the features of a girl preserved in stone, and asked a question she had chosen not to ask Makepeace.

"This is Neferure, isn't it?"

"Of course."

"There are so few of the Amon-Re line that it seemed the only possibility." Daughter of Hatshepsu and the reason for vampirism: her mother had begged Amon-Re to heal Neferure, and he had Answered. "I couldn't understand why she was here."

"After Hatshepsu went to stone, Neferure travelled through a number of Otherworlds, including the Great Forest, seeking guidance for the choice she would soon be making. To journey to the Field of Reeds, or strive for the heavens. She wanted to better understand the nature of godhood, and even whether the Field of Reeds would have been altered by the changes to Kemet—Egypt—made by the Shu line. It was desert when she ascended, you know, not the tapestry of rivers we know today. And before the desert, the whole of that region had been green and fertile. Neferure's travels showed her that her long lifetime was an eye blink compared to the world's. And the gods themselves are young when counted among the stars. And that even stars fade."

The Queen gazed up at the sun, which was not quite the same sun as the one she served.

"I don't know what decision Neferure made before she went to rept. I'm not even certain why she raised Heriath before her end. It seems to have been a boon she granted Cernunnos. His service has benefited Prytennia immeasurably, and you have already proven yourself a worthy successor. I came to welcome you, and give you my thanks."

"Thank you, Your Majesty," Rian said. It was perhaps foolish to feel so complimented, but Rian found herself close to blushing with pleasure. She paused, working to regain some level of perspective, then added: "You're the first person outside Lord Msrah that I've heard call him Heriath."

"In the Great Forest, it is safer to name things as they are. And at times I need to remind myself." The Queen's pale blue eyes crinkled with laughter. "My family, we grow up with an extra member, one who is snappish, and rude, and oh so very tired, and we think him a Ma'at vampire who knows when we lie, so we return his dismissal with confidences, tell him the things we won't tell others, because he behaves as if he has seen everything, and finds us dull. We learn his true name when we ascend, and though we already knew he was old it makes us keenly aware of the long line of Suleviae stretching out into the past, for he has served every one of them."

"You conjure a very effective vision of the years reeling out before me, Your Majesty," Rian said.

The Queen smiled at her. "We all still march through them one at a time." She rose, and held out her hand. "Come, you must introduce me to your nieces and nephew. I owe them my thanks as well."

Conscious of her rather sweat-stained state, Rian allowed herself to be drawn to her feet, and thought Tanwen Gwyn Lynn quietly amused at her embarrassment. Then, on the way out of the grove, the Queen added a titbit of information that made Rian's eyes widen rather, but she managed to suppress further reaction as Queen Tanwen was more ambushed than introduced to various Tennings and other representatives of Lamhythe.

"I liked her," Griff declared, once the impromptu royal visit was over, and Nabah and Melly had excitedly departed to tell their families they had shaken hands with the Queen herself.

"I did too," Rian said, smiling.

"When did you donate those amasen horns, Aunt Arianne?" Eluned asked. "Melly was going to thank you, but we all got distracted."

"Oh, weeks ago. So they've finished shuffling paperwork and announced it, have they? It seemed a better use for the things than clogging up the basement.

And now, before I go up to my bath, tell me which school you've decided on."

"None of them," Griff said flatly. He looked thoughtful, then added: "Could we hire tutors?"

"No," Eleri said firmly. "You pick, Aunt. Then we can't blame each other."

"Just me?" Rian said, highly entertained. "Very well, then it will be Tangleways. Don't pull that face, Griff. Remember there were tunnels. I expect I can prevail on Lord Fennington to exempt you from actually touching animals. And if the sports really are so terribly onerous, Eleri, feel free to develop migraines."

Eluned, who was trying not to look openly delighted, said: "The workshop was very good, after all. And we never did get to look around the house properly."

"Settled then?" Rian asked, and received one pleased nod, and two more reluctant assents. But no real annoyance, or angry rejection. The sense that she had no right to make decisions for them had gone, for they were family, not strangers in a grudging alliance. A blessing as great as Cernunnos', an allegiance with just as much claim on her soul.

"Excellent," she said, trying to stop the curling corners of her mouth giving too much away. "I'll send the forms off right away. I gather I'll need to get them in soon, before the rush."

"What rush?" Eluned asked, while Griff eyed her suspiciously.

"Ah, well. Queen Tanwen mentioned that she and Princess Leodhild are going to send Celestine, Luc, Iona and Tethané to Tangleways. Once news of that gets out, there won't be an open place there for years."

A glow to rival the sun. It kept Rian smiling as she dutifully added forms to envelope and gave it to one very impatient niece, waiting to run it up to the Ktais' before the last post.

But once released to take her bath, Rian acknowledged that her mood had improved well before the question of schools had been raised. And it had not been that interesting but relatively unremarkable conversation with the Queen that had made her feel infinitely better. Instead, a touch that brought warm amusement. The Sulevia Seolfor, equally as powerful as the Sulevia Sceadu, and Rian had for an instant been able to sense her emotions.

And suddenly tomorrow seemed bearable.

Rian soaked for a long time, thinking about being sensible, and moving on, and all the lessons she had learned about who she could be. About the inner calm that had allowed her to continue instead of crumbling. She had thought this a balance achieved through experience, but instead, perhaps, she had only been cutting away hope.

Why else would the merest possibility that she had not been wrong make the world seem new?

After dinner, Rian went to her room, and looked through the trunk Tante Sabet had sent, the one with all the oldest things. There it was, the last gift of her father, who had been so distressed when she had walked away from trying. A ridiculously extravagant leather-bound block of fine, heavy paper. All blank: she'd never touched it.

Methodically, Rian prepared her desk—pencils, inks— and locked her door, because this was a conversation she was having with herself. Then, after several warm-up sketches of hares, she settled down to her first serious work in nearly twenty years. A three-tailed mare, and rider.

Even if it did turn out to be a one-sided passion, Rian was damn well going to do it properly.

In World People

Aedric Tenning	M	Brother of Arianne Seaforth. Married Eilif Tenning. Father of Eleri, Eluned and Griff.
Aerinndís Gwyn Lynn (Princess)	F	Sulevia Sceadu (Sulevia of the Shadow), one of the three aspects of Sulis. Reserved, calm. In France known as the "Steel Doll".
Aranxta Trevelyan	F	Head of Ministry of Science and Technology (Mini-T).
Arianne (Rian) Seaforth	F	Daughter of Charlotte Seaforth and Henri Bordonne.
Astent Gwyn Lynn I	F	Queen who ordered construction of Gwyn Lynn palace. Mother of Mennia and Nyroe.
Brangwen Meldane I (Queen)	F	Queen who first called Sulis and became part of the Suliviae, founding the Meldanian Era.
Celestine Gwyn Lynn (Princess)	F	Sister to Aerinndís. Vivid and brilliant and much-loved by populace. Father is Mi Mijiang.
Charlotte Seaforth	F	Mother of Aedric and Arianne. Sculptress.
Dacius Sabinus	M	Dacian Proconsul.
Danel Haft	F	Page at Gwyn Lynn Palace.
Delia Hackett	F	One of Lord Msrah's bound—the former Wednesday.
Dyfed Fennington (Lord)	M	Wealthy eccentric and industrialist.
Eilif Tenning	F	Mother of Eleri, Eluned and Griff.
Eleri Tenning	F	Twin of Eluned, niece of Arianne Seaforth. Automaton creator.
Eluned Tenning	F	Twin of Eleri, niece of Arianne Seaforth. Painter and pen-and-ink artist.
Elwyswen Fulbright	F	Former delegated Keeper of the Deep Grove.
Evelyn Carstairs	M	Bound to Lord Msrah. Son of Naeemah Carstairs and Magnus Willitson (both also bound to Lord Msrah).
Falwen Chelwith	F	Granddaughter of the Warden of Lamhythe.
Finn Seleny	F	Grove Administrator, Chemistry Student at Rutherford University.
Gaius Silvanus Tarinus (Felix)	M	Cousin of the Dacian Proconsul. Son of Darius Silvanus Tarinus, former Consul of the New Republic.
Griff Tenning	M	Nephew of Arianne Seaforth. Obsessed with buildings and maps.
Gustav (Prince)	M	Swedish prince. Current Lord Protector of Alba.
Hatshepsu/Maatkare Hatshepsu	F	The Pharaoh of Egypt. First known Amon-Re line vampire, along with her daughter Neferure.

She took the throne name Maatkare,

		meaning "Truth in the soul of the sun", when she ascended the throne, and she changed her name from the feminine Hatshepsut to the male Hatshepsu.
Henri Bordonne	M	Father of Aedric and Arianne. Painter. French.
Heriath ("Comfrey Makepeace")	M	The Wind's Dog. Keeper of the Deep Grove. Amon-Re vampire. Irritant.
Iona Gwyn Lynn (Princess)	F	Second child of Leodhild Gwyn Lynn.
Kafele	M	Son of Msrah. Means 'would die for'.
Lanwes Gwyn Lynn I (Queen)	F	Queen who called back Sulis during the French Occupation.
Leodhild Gwyn Lynn (Princess)	F	Sulevia Leoth (Sulevia of the Song), one of the three aspects of Sulis. Full figure, sarcastic, scientist, early forties. Three children.
Luc Gwyn Lynn (Prince)	M	Eldest child of Leodhild Gwyn Lynn.
Lydia Bermondsley	F	Curator of Divinities and God-touched Collection at Museum of Prytennia. Expert Deologist.
Lyle Blair	M	Alban attaché to Prince Gustav.
Lynsey Blair	F	Teacher hired as fencing instructor for upcoming school. Sister to Lyle. Albion Unionist.
Matthiel Shrimton-Wye	M	Lord Fennington's factotum.
Mennia Gwyn Lynn II (Queen)	F	Mother of Tanwen and Leodhild.
Mi Jiang (Prince)	M	A Prince of Yue (sometimes incorrectly referred to as Prince Mi). Father of Celestine and lover of Tanwen. Saw Princess Tanwen (before she became one of the Suleviae) when Prytennia's first round-the-world airship flight passed by Yue's veil, and, years later, had himself presented to her as a gift. After a number of years she accepted him as her lover.
Monsieur Doré	-	A mannequin adapted into an automaton.
Msrah (Lord)	M	Nomarch of Southern Prytennia. His name means 'sixth born'.
Nedani Tyse (Keeper)	F	Keeper of Banebury Grove, coafor for Thede Tyse.
Neferure	F	Daughter of Hatshepsu and Thutmose II. First 'sub-Pharoah'. Amon-Re line vampire.
Ngoyo	F	A Zanzaran painter.
Patmahset	M	Nesweth of Egypt, and an Amon-Re vampire.
Raya	M	Title of ruler of the Karnata Empire.
Redick Chelwith	M	Grandson of Warden of Lamhythe.
Reswen Chelwith	F	Warden of Lamhythe.
Tanwen Gwyn Lynn II (Queen)	F	Queen of Prytennia. Sulevia Seolfor (Sulevia of the Silver Light). Strict, brave, inspirational. Name means white fire.
Tethané (Tete) Gwyn Lynn (Princess)	F	Youngest child of Leodhild Gwyn Lynn.

| Thede Tyse | M | Dryw of Banebury Grove. Married to Nedani Tyse. |

IN WORLD GEOGRAPHY

Alba	The northern portion of Albion. A Swedish Protectorate, it has no territorial allegiance, meaning that its people must strive for personal allegiance, or risk their souls fading after death.
Aquae Sulis	Location of the Sacred Spring of Sulis and original capital of Prytennia. [In our world known as Bath.]
Argynion	Alban University
Black Pyramid	One of London's three major pyramids.
Cadell Forest	Located in Powys. Arianne's parents had their studio here.
Caerlleon	Home city of the Tennings. Name means "fortress-city of the legions". Walled city. [In our world called Chester.]
Craigneith	A town in southern Alba.
Cymru	A Prytennian city located where Cardiff is sited in our world. Cymru was the name the Cymry (Celts of the area) gave to their land, but as the Trifold 'cult' expanded from Aqua Sulis into the region of the first dragonate, Prytennians began to use Cymru to refer to the city instead of the country.
Dacia Traiana	Roman province where Romania is. Traiana is for the Roman who conquered the pre-existing Dacia.
Danuin	The "Isle of Clouds" to the west of Prytennia. Completely surrounded by mist. Can only be entered with the assistance of a Tuatha Dé guide or by flying over the top of the clouds. Ruled by a High King of Tuatha Dé Danaan. Was completely inaccessible for nearly five hundred years, but started sending out trade boats two hundred years ago. It is rumoured, though denied by the Tuatha Dé, that the wall of mist used to shield the country from invasion has taken on a will of its own.
Deep Grove	One entrance to the Deep Grove is in Lamhythe, London, but the Deep Grove is essentially in the Great Forest, which is everywhere, and yet nowhere.
Deer Run/Outer Crescent	Fenced parkland surrounding Gwyn Lynn Lake.
Demar House	An administrative building in London where births, deaths, marriages and vampires are registered.
Din Eidyn	Capital of Alba. This was formerly situated further south, but when the third Prytennian dragonate roused, the former capital became part of Prytennia.
Djeser-Djeseru	Hatshepsu's template on the western bank of the Nile at Thebes.

Forest House	Located in London, south of the river, and just north of the Great Barrows, Forest House is the entrance to the Deep Grove. It is protected by a ring of warehouses.
Great Barrows	Three almond shaped barrows arranged in the form of a triquetra. The northernmost barrow is Seolfor Barrow. The western is Sceadu Barrow and the eastern is Leoth Barrow. Sulevia Leoth summons the triskelion here to sing each solstice (and also visits a different town or city for a second singing on the same day).
Great Forest	The Great Forest is an Otherworld that covers most of the world, but is shared by many gods.
Green Pyramid	One of London's three major pyramids.
Gwyn Lynn Lake	Surrounds Gwyn Lynn Palace.
Gwyn Lynn Palace	Current residence of the Suleviae.
Huaxia Kingdoms	Huaxia (roughly meaning 'grand and illustrious', and signifying civilised society) was mistakenly thought to be the proper name for the people of Yue. This has spread into use for all people of the area which in our world is Eastern China (and is sometimes incorrectly used to refer to all Asian people). The Huaxia Kingdoms are centred around Yue.
Hurlstone	A name given by humans to the town that stood south of the river where London now sits. Remnants of this town can be found in the Great Forest, at the Deep Grove entrance. The town was not created by humans, but 'children of the forest', now extinct.
Judah	Centred around Jerusalem, this is one of the kingdoms vampires (or any aspect of any power not Yahweh) cannot enter.
Karnata Empire	A Hindu empire covering most of southern India. Capital is Vijaya Nagar.
Kemet	Although Greece and Rome's term for the Two Lands has become widespread, 'Egypt' is known as Kemet by its native people.
Lamhythe	In our world, Lambeth, London.
Lutèce	The city which in our world became Paris. Capital of France, and base of the Cour d'lune.
Parana	South America.
Retwold School	A boarding school south of Caerlleon.
River Tamesas	Means "Dark River". [The Thames.]
Rutherford University	Premier University located in London.
Salinae	Site of a plaza with a famous mosaic of the Wind's Dog. [Our world, known as Middlewich.]
Sheerside House	The Nomal House belonging to the Southern Nomarch.
Sonning	Area west of London. Location of Tangleways School and (Windsor) Forest. [East half of current Berkshire.]
Stomruria	North America. So-named by Norse traders after an early encounter with animikii (Thunderbird)—one of Stomruria's Great Alliance gods.
Tangleways School	Located in Sonning, west of London.
Thebes	Thebes is the capital of Egypt, and is located on both the east and west bank of the Nile. Our area known as the Valley of the Kings is the temple district of Thebes.
Towers of the Moon	Crossing the Seine in Lutèce, there is a tower for each of the Houses of the Cour d'lune. The give Great Towers, and numerous smaller towers, are one of the

architectural wonders of the world, and not possible through human construction.

Wabanaki

A sprawling nation of north-east Stomruria, with allegiance to Gitche Manitou.

White Hill

Site of one of the city's major groves. [In our world located where what would be the Tower of London.]

White Pyramid

One of London's three major pyramids.

Yue

One of the kingdoms of Huaxia. Known as the Veiled Kingdom, it is surrounded by an impassable barrier of pearly light, and is ruled by dragons. They are said to control the rain and rivers not only in Yue, but for much of the region. No-one can cross the barrier, and the people of Yue maintain a city outside their borders for trade.

Zanzar

A kingdom on the eastern coast of Africa (centres around Tanzania).

IN WORLD MYTHOS

Ah-ah

An elder triskelion. All black. [A-a-a-A-a-a-A-a-a-A-a-a-A-a-a-A-a-a]

Akh

The third life of an Egyptian. After life ends in the physical world, the Egyptian soul becomes a ba, dwelling in their preserved body to gather strength (ka) enough to journey onward. When the ba has sufficient ka (or is 'reunited' with their ka) they travel onward as akh.

Allegiance

Allegiance is a link between a god and a human, usually a claim on a human soul in exchange for godly favours.

There are four common types of allegiance: born, territorial, bestowed, taken.

Amasen

Ram-horned snakes sacred to Cernunnos.

Amon-Re

Egyptian god of the Air and the Sun.

Annwn

The Prytennian Otherworld is a series of islands in a vast underground sea. The first of these islands, Annwn, is ruled by Arawn. Prytennian souls seek out wells, pools and rivers to travel here after they've freed themselves from their bodies. It is possible to get lost on the way, but Arawn himself will seek out stragglers.

Answered

When a god responds to a human, they Answer. There are many debates as to whether gods Answered through all of human history, but only sporadically, or if something triggered the waves of Answering that began with the First Wave (the Egyptians, the Yue Dragons, and Bison), the Second Wave (numerous, including Roman Jupiter, the Aesir, Thunderbird) and the Third Wave (the majority of other Answered gods, occurring within a few centuries of the Second Wave).

Arawn	King of Annwn, where Prytennia's newly dead go. Although they may stay in Annwn for many years, most eventually move on to seek other islands of the afterlife.
Arawn's Tears	Water blessed by the priests of Arawn. It becomes a liquid that melts only dead flesh, and leaves clean bones. The liquid is used on crops. The bones are separated and interred in barrows.
Athian	The Dragon of the South.
Ba	The soul of an Egyptian after death takes on the form of a bird with a human face. Ba live within their preserved bodies, and gather strength to either travel on to the Egyptian Otherworld (the Field of Rushes), or attempt to reach the heavens and become a star. When the ba has gathered enough strength (ka), it becomes an akh, and travels onward.
Bestowed allegiance	Bestowed allegiance is a direct link between a god and a human. This can be achieved through certain observances, trials, or increasing affinity (personal links to the god's area of duty). If bestowed allegiance is achieved, then after death that person's soul will belong to that god, and if it is possible to reach it from the location of death, will travel to that god's Otherworld no matter what the territorial allegiance they might be subject to. Particularly favoured humans will be 'god-touched' by a bestowed allegiance, taking on some of the powers and aspects of the god.
Bison	One of the oldest gods who answered. One of Stomruria's Great Alliance gods. [Bison is a god of many names, covering the myriad regions where he has influence. 'Bison' is the name commonly used by non-Stomrurians.
Born allegiance	Born allegiance is usually a result of having a god (or, more usually, a demi-god) as a parent. Examples of born allegiance are the cour d'lune, where a child of a member of the court will develop wings on puberty, and will be unable to remained in the human world during the daytime. Children of the court cannot form allegiances with other gods.
Cernunnos	The horned god of the forest and fertility, of the hunt and the hunted. Attended by ram-horned snakes known as amasen, he can take the form of a stag or a man with antlers. The antlers are hung with the torcs of royalty.
Cour d'lune	The Court of the Moon. France was not so much 'Answered' by one of their gods as invaded by Faerie. The Court can only exist in the human world at night, and so France's government is divided into the Court of the Sun and the Court of the Moon, with the Court of the Moon holding primacy. The Cour d'lune is divided into four major competing Houses, a number of smaller Houses, and one House of Balance. Membership in a House is dependent on the colour of the wings. The attitude of the Cour d'lune toward humans depends very much on which House is currently ascendant.

Cŵn Annwn	The Hounds of Annwn seek out souls in Arawn's territory that have not made their way to Annwn.
Dimity	The littlest triskelion. [I-i-EE]
Dulethar	The Dragon of the East.
Falinis	The white dog with red ears owned by Princess Celestine, given to her as a gift from the Irish King. Named for Fáil Inis, owned by Lugh Lámhfhada of the Tuatha Dé Danann. [A hound invincible in battle, able to catch every wild beast it encountered, and liable to magically change any running water it bathed in into wine.]
Folies	Foliate cats, guardians of the gates to the Deep Grove.
God-touched	A person with strong born or bestowed allegiance that lends them the power of a god.
Ghul	A corpse animated by a vampiric symbiont, but containing no human soul.
Gitche Manitou	Gitche Manitou means "Great Spirit". A god who answered during the Second Wave of Answers in north-east Stomruria.
Ka	More than simply life force, ka is to the Egyptians a stage of the soul. During the Egyptian first life, it is what animates the body, the difference between being alive and being dead. During the second life, the ba must regain ka in order to become an akh and journey onward to the Egyptian Otherworld.
Lila	The littlest amasen.
Lorenoola	A youngish triskelion. Yellow and green. [O-e-oo-a]
Ma'at	Egyptian Goddess of Truth, Justice, Order. Maintainer of existence (while Thoth is protector of existence). Weighs the soul after death.
Night Breezes	Commanded by the Sulevia Sceadu, these are wind taking tangible form. Which are not as gentle as they sound. The most common forms are mice, hares, dogs (resembling saluki), owls, and the sacred three-tailed mare that bears the Sulevia Sceadu. The Night Breezes are also linked to the Wild Hunt, and the Sulevia Sceadu rides with the Hunt on rare occasion.
Nimelleth	The Dragon of the West.
Order of the Oak	Dryw responsible for tending (most) sacred groves of Prytennia. They pay reverence to Cernunnos, but technically give their allegiance to the Great Forest.
Otherworlds	Not all gods command Otherworlds, but all Otherworlds are the domains of gods. There are punishment Otherworlds and reward Otherworlds, and Otherworlds that simply exist and don't seem overly concerned with the souls of humans. An accumulation of souls in their Otherworld increases the strength of the god.
Shu	Egyptian god of Wind.
Sucellos	God of agriculture and luck. Carries a long-handled hammer. Known as the Good Striker, and strikes in the seasons, ending winter and bringing in summer.

Sulis	The ruling Prytennian goddess. Creates three strong god-touched known as the Suleviae. Has aspects of both sun and wind.
	When the Romans originally invaded Albion they took charge of her sacred spring, and declared her to be an aspect of Minerva.
Sulevia Leoth	Sulevia of the Song, one of the god-touched aspects of Sulis. Commands the triskelion.
Sulevia Sceadu	Sulevia of the Shadow, one of the god-touched aspects of Sulis. Commands of the Night Breezes.
Sulevia Seolfor	Sulevia of the Silver Light (reflections of light on water), one of the god-touched aspects of Sulis. Commands the three dragons of Prytennia (who lend their aspect to people chosen by the Sulevia Seolfor).
Suleviae	The term for all three aspects of Sulis.
Taken allegiance	Taken allegiance is godly allegiance taken unwillingly, either by trick or force.
Territorial allegiance	Unless a person has a stronger allegiance, territorial allegiance determines the destination of the souls of the dead. There are an increasingly small number of places in the world without territorial allegiance, and in these places it is believed that the souls are lost, going to no Otherworld. Residents of such places work to gain bestowed allegiance of a god whose Otherworld can be reached from their location.
Thoth	Egyptian god, inventor of all sciences and crafts, protector of existence. Ibis headed (and at times baboon headed).
Thoth-den	Vampires of the thoth strain who practice medicine.
Toroco	A young triskelion. Red and gold. [O-o-O].
Triskelion	Literally 'three legged', but these manifest as three winged. Controlled by the Sulevia Leoth. Can 'separate the air', which in their case means they can do fun stuff like remove oxygen, or produce 'trilesium'. Make a noise a bit like wordless singing—or the whirling of a weighted cord, very fast. They grow to be enormous creatures, but start out as tiny little whizzing things no bigger than a hand.
Tuatha Dé Danann	Peoples of the goddess Danu.

IN WORLD OTHER

Coafor	A companion to a dryw, tasked with officially recording any visions.
Daughters of Lakshmi	A medical clan devoted to Lakshmi. They were given shelter by Prytennia's queen when their practice was banned in their home kingdom, and now offer the major alternative to vampiric healing, running many hospitals.
Deiography	Attempting to measure and define the nature of gods.
Deiology	Catalogue gods and god-touched.
Dragonate	A region under the influence of one of the three dragons of Prytennia.
Dragonfly	A motorised unicycle stabilised by a tripod of wheeled legs.
Dryw	Can be regarded as a priest, but more normally a prophet or future-visionary. . Welsh term for druid or seer.
Exsanguincy	A death caused by a vampire who is in a state of critical hunger—whether due to injury or starvation—where normal control and decision-making is impaired.
Ficus Lapis	Engineering firm based out of Rome.
Fulgite	Crystals manufactured by the Roman Empire that function as super-efficient batteries.
Fulquus	Electricity—taken from the Latin for lightning, fulgur, and horse, equus.
Growler	Truck.
Huaxia	Huaxia (roughly meaning 'grand and illustrious', and signifying civilised society) was mistakenly thought to be the proper name for the people of Yue. This has spread into use for all people of the area which in our world is Eastern China (and is sometimes incorrectly used to refer to all Asian people). Can be distorted into the perjorative "Hoozie".
Hummingbird	Originally a name for early electric taxicabs in London, but here used generally for all smaller electric cars.
Marculism	A movement based on Leah Marculin's theory making a distinction between gods and 'powers', postulating that humanity has yet to encounter a true god, and the beings that have 'answered' humanity have merely taken on aspects of identity found in humanity's beliefs.
Meldanian Era/ Meldanian Rule	Founded by Brangwen Meldan after she called Sulis and called forth the Trifold Age.
Moonfire Feast	The occasion marking the renewal of the Treaty of the Oak.
Nathanar's Workshop	One of the premier electrical vehicle workshops.

Nesweth	From nswt, the Egyptian term for king. While the title of Pharaoh is reserved only for Hatshepsut, in the last few centuries before rept she appointed nesweths to act for her, even before she became stone, and finally succeeding in raising one to the Amon-Re line. Since Hatshepsut entered rept, there has been only one Nesweth, Patmahset, who has ruled in Hatshepsut's stead for the last ten centuries.
Nome	A Normarch's area of weather influence. In Prytennia, these have been combined with the Dragonates, so that there is a Nomarch in each Dragonate.
Proconsul	Governor of a Roman province.
Pyrial	People who eroticise vampires.
Register of Blood	Lists all vampires in Prytennia, classified by line. Maintained at Demar House.
Rept	A vampire could theoretically enter rept as soon as they have become stone-blood, simply by staying out into the sun. The stone of rept is a waxy pale grey, with a soap-like texture. It is very difficult to break.
Senet	Ancient Egyptian game.
Shendy	A corruption of the Egyptian word shendyt, now used generally to refer to certain types of skirts. Panelled shendies are standard school and casual summer clothing for children. Pleated shendys are used for more formal wear, and have both summer and winter forms. Wrap shendys are seen most often in summer, though there are winter versions. Shendies are usually in pale colours for formal wear, and darker for working gear.
Swallow	A two-person dynastat that looks like a tandem bicycle with fixed wings.
Tiger	A large personal electric car, very expensive, and usually powered by a relatively large piece of fulgite.
Treaty of the Oak	The treaty between Sulis and Cernunnos for co-existence in Prytennia. Renewed every twenty-five years at the Deep Grove during what is called the Moonfire Feast.
Trilesium	Gas used by Prytennian airships. This is actually a compound of helium brought from the sun by the triskelion, and altered in the process into something that has greater lift efficiency and yet is easier to contain.
Vampirism	Amon-Re created the first vampires when Hatshepsu begged for him to save the life of her daughter Neferure. Other Egyptian gods soon followed suit, investing each strain of vampirism with a different set of abilities.
Vedas	The common term for those following the Vedic Tradition.

www.ingramcontent.com/pod-product-compliance
Lightning Source LLC
Chambersburg PA
CBHW070909260626
47162CB00007B/2608